HellBound Books

HELLBOUND HIGHWAY
Anthology of Traveling Terror

Curated by Jane Nightshade
and
Ann O'Mara Heyward

A HellBound Books LLC Publication
Copyright © 2025 by HellBound Books Publishing LLC
All Rights Reserved

Cover and art design by Tee Arts
for
HellBound Books Publishing LLC

No part of this book may be reproduced, stored in a retrieval system, or transmitted by any means, electronic, mechanical, photocopying, recording or otherwise without written permission from the author This book is a work of fiction. Names, characters, places and incidents are entirely fictitious or are used fictitiously and any resemblance to actual persons, living or dead, events or locales is purely coincidental.

www.hellboundbookspublishing.com

Table of Contents

Introduction iii
Road Trip Bingo by James H. Longmore 1
Gator by John Wolf.. 26
The Long Row by Ross Baxter.................................... 44
The Next Stop by Harley Carnell 60
Godfather Poker by Jane Nightshade 73
Salvation by David Bartlett....................................... 84
Yellow Car by SJ Townend...................................... 103
Horsemen by Mason Gallaway 120
The Hitchhiker by Damon Nomad 135
Brutal by Eldon Litchfield 146
The Women's Room by Blake Kourik........................ 163
ÓRDEN by Jay T. Levy 179
Closed In by Eliza Hyde 197
Route 58 by Michael Penncavage 207
End of the Road by Andrew Adams 216
What Waits by R.D. Davidson 227
A Cottage on the Interstate by Patrick Wright 236
Not Much Left by D.C. Kugtima 246
Passengers by Meg Belviso 257
Give the Mountain Death by Sean Seebach.............. 271
Comanche Country by Todd Mitternacht 286
The Banished Road by Ricardo D. Rebelo 306
Telaraña by D. Winchester 324
The Last Migration by Ann O'Mara Heyward 342
Watch Me Go by Randall Drum 361
Travel Companions by Nicola Lombardi.................... 373
Killer Road Trip by DW Milton................................ 382
The Last Hitcher by Kevin Hollaway........................ 396
About the Editors 407
Other HellBound Books   411

Introduction

They say travel is broadening. But leaving home comes with justifiable unease. We feel vulnerable out in the world, especially in unfamiliar places. We depend on things going well that we can't control—the car works, the plane doesn't crash, the map app gives us good directions, our cell phones work, the hotel has a room for us, strangers have good intentions. That vulnerability magnifies our emotional responses, too—anyone who's ever seen a meltdown at the airline ticket counter knows exactly what we're talking about.

The journey is a universal story; the very act of embarking on a trip may profoundly change the tripper. Not least because we all fear the unknown. Journeys give us revelations we're not at all prepared for: We are not the people we are at home. Nor are the people we encounter. The world out there doesn't work *at all* the way that we thought it did. As we move into *terra incognito*—unknown territory—our darkest suspicions and fears might not only be confirmed, but exceeded beyond our worst nightmares.

In *Hellbound Highway*, twenty-eight wildly talented authors from around the world (that's fitting, isn't it?) bring you stories of road trips, train trips, plane trips, boat trips, and head trips gone terribly, horribly wrong. Each story is an unforgettable journey into places we fear to tread, with good reason. The stories included in this book amazed and delighted us, while simultaneously scaring the hell out of us. It was not an easy task to decide on the final set of tales here; we received many superb stories that we would have liked to include and simply did not have room for, so we hope there may be a *Hellbound Highway II* in future. We did have some rigorous requirements. Each story had to be fundamentally about a *journey*. Traveling needed to play a significant role in how and why the horror unfolded. We looked for stories that left the characters changed forever by the trip, and the writers who submitted delivered us a dark suitcase full of horrors. Thank you to each and every one of them.

And now, it's time to embark on your own trip on the *Hellbound Highway*. Get yourself packed up and let's go.

Jane Nightshade
Ann O'Mara Heyward

HELLBOUND HIGHWAY

Anthology of Traveling Terror

Road Trip Bingo
by
James H. Longmore

"Tyler's arm is on my side again," Kirsty Slaten whined. She raised her voice because she had in her ear buds; the music loud enough for everyone in the car to hear the tinny *tssch tssch tssch* that was, without a doubt, gradually destroying her eardrums.

"*She* started it." Tyler poked out his tongue at his sister.

"Well, *I'm* finishing it," Luciana played the Mom card. "And I saw that, Tyler. Apologize to your sister this instant!"

"Aww, Mom," her son bleated.

"Do as your mother says," Chuck threw in. He took a hand off of the steering wheel and patted his wife's bare knee. He gave her a supportive smile—*I got your back, Honey.*

Luciana cast a sideways glance at her husband, the contempt barely concealed beneath her half smile.

Chuck's attention returned to the featureless road that seemed never-ending; had it not been for the sporadic road signs and flattened wildlife, it would have been difficult to be sure that any progress had been made on this trip at all.

A glance in the rearview and Chuck saw his kids' surly faces—they both had the air of people attending their own executions rather than a family fun day at the water park—they were so sucking the *fun* part out of the whole thing and at that particular moment in time, Chuck would have preferred to be not taking the ungrateful, sour-faced brats anywhere.

Luciana had insisted on one more family trip before summer ended and the kids returned to school. And who was Chuck to argue with the love of his life, even if personally, he couldn't actually imagine a place more hellish than the water park? The place comprised acres of noisy, hyperactive kids running amok whilst their overheating, frustrated parents followed them around like sun-reddened pack mules. It was a grim place of aching arms laden with towels, swim bags and oversized free-refill drinks cups, of pee-tainted water and bland food, and for Chuck Slaten, the promise of personal horrors.

Firstly, Tyler would nag Chuck's ass off to go on the biggest of the water slides, and then wuss out when they reached the head of the line. Or, even better still, he'd slide down the thing wailing like the devil was on his tail and then throw up in the splash pool at the bottom. Then there was Kirsty, his once precious little princess: with all of her thirteen-year-old logic, she would refuse to do anything more than paddle in the kiddies' splash zone because otherwise she would have to strip down to her bathing suit. The summer had seen Kirsty hit puberty with full force and she was painfully self-conscious about her newly sprouted breasts, which seemed to have developed practically overnight. Of course, Chuck knew full well that the irony was that, next year, his battle would be to get her to remain suitably covered in the presence of the adolescent, priapic boys that the water park seemed to attract in abundance.

Chuck sighed. They were a third of the way through the three-hour trip and Tyler had already tired of his electronic games—something Chuck had never thought possible for a nine-year-old boy—and Kirsty had forgotten to pack the book Luciana had bought her especially for the trip; something sappy about teenaged vampires falling in love, a cynical cash-in on the *tween* market.

Chuck fumed quietly to himself. When *he* was their age, he and his sister had to be content with watching raindrops race down the car windows. They would bet against each other with pennies and sometimes, if the wind was just right, the raindrops would race *up* the windows.

Oh yeah, and they'd fight too.

"I thought you guys were playing Road Trip Bingo," Chuck broke the silence.

It was never a good sign to have gotten to Road Trip Bingo this early on and Chuck wished he'd invested in the in-car DVD system the pretty salesgirl with the mesmerizing cleavage had done her best to talk him into when they'd bought the car. But no, Luciana had insisted he take out the extra warranty instead.

"We are," Tyler said.

"*I* am, you're just cheating." Kirsty curled her lip.

"I *did* see a squished armadillo!" Tyler gave his sister a shove and her head clunked on the window.

"Mom!" Kirsty wailed and gave Tyler a dead arm.

Tyler kicked his sister's shin.

"Tyler kicked me." Kirsty rubbed at her shin. "Prick," she mumbled.

Chuck cast an eye to the vacant third row of seats at the rear of the vehicle. How nice it would be to stick one of the kids there and put an end to their bickering. He had purchased the Tahoe specifically for that extra seating, but Kirsty refused to sit back there because she'd read somewhere that if they got rear-ended, she'd die; and Tyler *couldn't* sit back there because it made him throw up.

Come to think of it, was there anything that *didn't* make that boy throw up?

Chuck fumed some more; he could have had a Mustang.

"Kirsty punched me in the balls!" Tyler's whiny voice broke Chuck's reverie.

"I did not, and it's rude to say balls."

"Stop it, the both of you!" Chuck bellowed. "Just play your game and no punching anyone in the anywheres!" He set his face to stern and gripped the steering wheel until his knuckles turned white, like he was strangling the thing.

"We've almost finished," Tyler offered. His dad's raised voice always scared him. It didn't come out that often, but when it did, Dad meant business. "I only need a Chevy Tahoe to finish the card." He held up his bingo card for Chuck to see all the crossed off pictures of road signs, eating establishments, gas stations, trees, and road-kill. In the Bonus Square—the one that the kids had determined before they'd set off—the boy had written *Chevvy Taho: white*.

"You can't find a white Tahoe?" Chuck said.

"Nope," his son replied, shaking his head for emphasis.

"Really?"

"*Really*, Dad," Kirsty couldn't resist the dig at her stupid brother. She turned up her iPod so everyone in the car could further enjoy the *tssch tssch tssch* that echoed out from her ears.

Chuck bit his tongue—literally—and tasted blood. As much as he loved his kids, there were some days—and this one came pretty damned close to the top of the list—that he could quite gladly drop the pair of them off at the orphanage and flee the country. Kirsty had become unnaturally belligerent of late and Chuck held genuine concerns about Tyler; the boy really didn't seem all that bright and Chuck could only hope that he'd turn out to be good with his hands.

"You're sitting in one," Chuck told his son.

"What?"

"You're struggling to spot a white Tahoe and you're sitting in one."

"*Our* car doesn't count, Dad. Duh!" Kirsty snarled. "*Everybody* knows that rule."

"Okay, I'll give you that one," Chuck was forced to agree. "But we've been on the road for over an hour now and you haven't seen *one single* White Tahoe?"

The kids shook their heads.

Chuck ground his teeth. His orthodontist had warned him against doing so because it was wearing his enamel away and pretty soon he'd be down to bare pulp and raw nerves. Then again, it was easy for his fucking orthodontist to give out that advice because his orthodontist didn't have to live with Tyler and Kirsty, two kids who, in the space of an hour on the Texas road system couldn't spot one of the single most popular SUVs in the entire state.

Kirsty's tuneless singing drifted over to the front of the car. Eyes closed, oblivious to everything around her, she droned her tone-deaf tribute to Gaga's *Government Hooker*.

"Should she be listening to that?" Chuck asked.

"She's thirteen, Chuck, what do you think she's going to listen to?" It was the most Luciana had spoken since they'd left home and Chuck had actually found himself missing her banal gossip about people he knew only through her banal gossip, and crazy friends of hers that he didn't give a rat's dick about.

"You're right, my love," Chuck said. "I guess I'm getting a little out of touch these days." He patted his wife's knee again and felt bristle. Chuck wished his darling wife would shave her legs a little more often; the prickly blonde fuzz that covered them reminded him of gooseberries. Once upon a time, Luciana had shaved her legs to glassy smooth *every* morning, *and* kept her pubic hair trimmed to a neat little triangle that pointed downwards like a guide's arrow. Now she only seemed to shave down there prior to her gynecologist appointments. Funny that.

Chuck glanced across at Luciana's plump legs. They strained the seams of her too-tight, denim shorts and spread out onto the cream leather seat like unrolled dough. Her skin still had the honeyed tone that had so effectively turned his head in high school, although her thighs were now a road map of spider veins and cellulite that somewhat marred the sensual effect.

Chuck's mind wandered back to the lively, vivacious Luciana he'd fallen for all those years ago. She'd been as hot as hell and twice as horny, and while she'd not been quite the head cheerleader type all the other football play-ers had lusted after, Luciana had been the exotic-skinned, doe-eyed smart girl who smoldered beneath her ass-length, jet-black hair. She still had that silken, iridescent hair eighteen years on, albeit cut into a neat bob and kept black with a fair amount of help from a bottle. Yessir, Chuck could conjure with ease a mental picture of Luciana as sexy and enticing as she was back in the day; which meant that in these later years of their dwindling sex life, he at least had that to jerk off to.

"There's one!" Tyler shouted and waved his Bingo card in Kirsty's face. She batted it away and gave him a dirty look. "Bingo!" Tyler shouted in her ear.

Sure enough, a white Tahoe sailed by and then maneu-vered in front of Chuck without using its blinker.

"I should pull him over and let him know his blinker's not working," Chuck rolled out the good ol' Slaten sar-casm.

"Yeah, that would be constructive," Luciana replied and rolled those beautiful browns at her husband.

"It looks like our car." Tyler peered from between the

front seats.

"So do half a million others, Son," Chuck said.

"Yeah, I suppose."

Chuck studied the car in front, pissed that yes, it did look exactly the same as his. Nothing like rubbing his face in the fact that he'd been forced into a lumbering family wagon instead of the red Mustang he'd always wanted.

"Hold on," Chuck mumbled.

"What is it now?" his wife sighed.

"What's our registration?"

"Pardon me?"

"Our registration plate? For *this* car?"

"You don't know it?"

Chuck saw his wife's eyes roll again. Did his existence really irritate her *that* much? "We've only had the car a couple of months, Luciana. And you know I don't memorize numbers all that well," Chuck defended.

"Then how do you expect *me* to know it?" Luciana snapped. "It's not even my car."

No, you get a fucking Corvette to swan around in, bitch.

"You're right, my love, what *was* I thinking?" Chuck gave his wife a weak smile. "Would you mind passing me the insurance card?"

Another loud, theatrical sigh and Luciana dug around in the glove box. She pulled out the insurance card and thrust it into her husband's hand.

Chuck scanned the document. "Well, I'll be—" he stuttered and pushed the card under his wife's nose.

"What is it, Dad?" Tyler leaned forward again.

"He has the same registration as us."

Chuck had heard of this happening before. Occasionally, the vehicle registration computer would screw up and issue the same number twice, often on the same make and model of vehicle. What worried Chuck was the possibility of the criminal types who cloned vehicle identities and used the duplicates for their own nefarious means. There'd been a guy at his previous company who'd had that happen and then started getting speeding citations from places he'd never even been to. As far as Chuck knew, there were still arrest warrants out for the guy in five states.

"What must the odds be of coming across our own duplicate?" Chuck shared his thoughts.

"Perhaps *our* car is the duplicate," Luciana offered, somewhat unhelpfully. "Did you pay to have the background check done?"

"Yes dear, of course I did." It was Chuck's turn to roll his eyes.

"What's UO mean Dad?" Tyler asked. "Is that the model name?"

"Not that I know of, Son, why?"

"Well, that car has an UO sticker on its bumper, just like ours."

Chuck squinted through the exploded insect guts on his windshield at the other Tahoe's rear and saw that indeed, there was a red UO sticker.

Chuck's blood ran cold. Whilst he could rationalize a duplicate registration, even accept the coincidence of running into his vehicle's twin on this particular stretch of desolate Texas road, he struggled with an identical UO sticker.

The little red sticker was ingrained in his mind following the lively argument Luciana had enjoyed with the young girl at the car dealership. The girl had puffed out her not inconsiderable chest and insisted that the UO denoted the University of Ohio, whilst Luciana was adamant that it was the University of Oklahoma, and she should know because she recognized the design and her brother had studied Biology there.

Large Breasted Dealership Gal had lost the argument, and in doing so had learned a valuable lesson in life: don't argue the toss with an early-menopausal Latino woman.

The presence of the sticker made the other Tahoe—from the back at least—a doppelganger of Chuck's.

"Well, I'll be," Chuck grumbled.

"Just let it go, Chuck," Luciana said with thinly disguised impatience. "It's not like *you* use your blinkers every time."

Chuck ignored his wife. His eyes were fixed very firmly on the other Tahoe. He squeezed his foot down on the accelerator to close the gap between the two cars whilst at the same time a weird prickle gnawed at his balls and crawled up into his belly to brew a sick knot in his stomach.

Luciana rolled her eyes once more as Chuck eased into the left lane—using his blinker, lead by example and all that—and pushed ahead to overtake the duplicate car.

The other Tahoe maintained speed, as if its driver *wanted* Chuck to pass.

As he cruised past the car, Chuck looked to his right; the rear windows of the Tahoe were black-tinted and reflected back his own gawking face. Tyler peered through his own dark window, curiosity aroused, whilst Luciana and Kirsty maintained their blatant disinterest.

Parallel now with the front of the copycat car, Chuck squinted sideways again and saw the other driver who was staring straight ahead, hands gripping the steering wheel as if he were strangling it. Next to him, Chuck could see a black-haired woman with a wistful, faraway look on her face, and he thought she looked as if she was wishing herself someplace else.

Chuck saw a rear window roll down a lick and a small boy's face peered from the gloom, followed by that of a small dog. The dog's bright pink tongue lolled from the side of its gaping mouth, the loose skin of its face flapping and distorted in the rattling breeze; it was the weirdest looking dog Chuck had ever seen in his life, yet it did provide some welcome relief.

Identical or not, there was a dog in the other car. The Slaten family did not own a dog, never had. Luciana hated the things.

The boy in the other car stared directly at Chuck and poked out his tongue.

"They look just like us," Tyler said. If they ever got around to making stating the fucking obvious an Olympic sport, then Chuck's boy would be first pick to carry his country's flag.

There is no such thing as coincidence.

Who'd said that? Sherlock Holmes? That smart ass with the buzz-cut from *NCIS*? Whichever, Chuck couldn't escape the creeping feeling that something here was very wrong indeed.

He floored the gas and with the other car safely in the rear-view Chuck gave himself time to reflect; he desperately needed to process what he *thought* he had seen. A glance at his wife's stony face warned Chuck not to vocalize; she would only use anything he said about this as an excuse to further berate him (what exactly *had* happened in their marriage that they had come to that?)

Although he'd denied it at first, as far as Chuck had seen, the people in the matching Tahoe had looked exactly like himself and his family. A trick of the light? Tired eyes or some kind of breakdown? Then there *was* that stupid looking dog, the only difference he had seen between the two vehicles—but the more Chuck's brain processed, the less he was convinced that what he'd seen had actually been a dog at all. There'd been something not right about the pink, flapping skin and oval mouth.

"So, what the fuck was it then?" Chuck said his thinking part out loud by mistake.

Luciana fixed her annoyance of a husband with a

disapproving gaze. "Please watch your language in front of the children, *dear*," she all but snarled the last word.

An insistent *ding* from the dash startled Chuck and his eyes flicked to the little LED gas pump on the display. Chuck glanced at the car following behind at the required safe distance and absently wondered if they needed gas too.

The alternate Tahoe thundered by as he pulled into the services and Chuck let out a long sigh of relief, unaware 'til now that he'd been holding his breath

Chuck pumped gas and stared down the road long after the other vehicle had vanished. His mind was already beginning to doubt what he'd seen and before his seemingly bottomless gas tank was full, Chuck had practically convinced himself that he'd imagined the whole thing.

He paid at the counter inside the gas station and allowed the children the rare opportunity of a free run at the endless racks of candy. Kirsty picked out some zero-calorie gum—watching her figure at thirteen, for Christ's sakes! —whilst Tyler loaded his arms with enough refined sugar to see them all through a nuclear holocaust. Luciana settled for an insanely hot coffee from the serve-it-yourself machine that lurked and gurgled at the rear of the store, adjacent to the restrooms.

Chuck had nothing. He hated to eat and drive and he thought the stewed coffee from those machines had a tendency to taste like scalding-hot piss.

* * *

Back to the long, straight monotony of the open road, and Chuck had all but forgotten the alternate Tahoe. He'd made a note to contact the vehicle registration people on Monday morning, and thoughts of identical people and weird-shit dogs were rapidly being replaced by those of his impending day of water park misery.

There it was again.

Although little more than a white dot on the shimmering road ahead, the alternate Tahoe was quite unmistakable.

Chuck tightened his fingers around the wheel and tried to tell himself that at this distance there was no way of telling if it was even a Tahoe, let alone *the* Tahoe.

Yet he knew.

"Yay! It's those people again!" Tyler's glee at the discovery didn't help Chuck's mood any. This time, Luciana and Kirsty joined Tyler in rubbernecking as Chuck closed in on the duplicate car.

"I don't believe it," Chuck growled. Given the time it had taken to fill up his own tank, and the fact that there were no other gas stations between that one and where he'd caught up with the alternate Tahoe, Chuck realized there was only the one conclusion to draw.

They had been waiting for him to catch up.

Chuck neared the all-too-familiar rear-end of the vehicle with a dry mouth that left his tongue glued to his arid palate.

The other car's right blinker light flickered and the red brake lights flashed. It then drifted to the side of the road, where a crumbling driveway lead up to an abandoned, decaying motel.

Chuck followed.

"What the hell are you doing!?" Luciana demanded with just a soupçon of panic in her voice.

"I think they want me to follow them," Chuck replied, voice calm. "Perhaps they want to sort out this duplicate plate bullshit."

"Oh, for God's sakes," said Luciana with the ubiquitous roll of the eyes. "Sorry kids, it looks like we're going to be late to the park because your Father doesn't know how to let things go." Snide to a fault, was Luciana. "I don't know what you think you're going to do, Chuck." This was the most talkative Luciana had been the whole trip, and where he had missed her voice earlier, Chuck now wished she'd just shut the fuck up. "You know you don't deal well with confrontation. And what if they're homicidal maniacs?"

Chuck ignored his wife and pulled up opposite the stationary vehicle. He killed the engine. Driven by curiosity and the need to placate the eerie feeling in his gut, Chuck simply didn't have the patience for his wife's paranoia. Besides which, since when did murderers drive around in family vehicles with kids and freaky little dogs?

He got out.

The occupants of the alternate Tahoe clambered from their air-conditioned haven and into the blistering Texas heat.

"Well, isn't this awkward?" the man smiled.

"I'll be—" Chuck muttered.

It was like looking in a mirror.

Chuck Slaten stared wide-eyed at what appeared to be his perfect clone; right down to the ashen face and tan Crocs over black socks. Standing beside the Alternate Chuck was a stone-faced, statuesque Alternate Luciana, flanked by Kirsty and Tyler counterparts.

Alternate Tyler held the odd-looking dog in his arms and now that Chuck could see its pink, bloated body he knew for definite it wasn't any kind of dog he'd ever laid eyes on. The animal, the size and shape of an obese tom cat, was totally devoid of fur. It had papery, amphibious skin, six legs, a tail made up of fleshless vertebrae and no head. Instead, the face was sunken into its wrinkled flank, had eight milky eyes that glistened and stared without blinking and an oval mouth that gaped wide like a lunatic's. From the slobbering maw there dangled a fat, oversized tongue that scraped over yellowed teeth as if it were panting.

It looked like an animated, shaved scrotum.

"See, I told you they didn't have a dog," Alternate Luciana chastised Alternate Chuck. She rolled her eyes heavenwards, as if words truly escaped her. "If *someone* had bothered to do their research, we'd not have to have brought that fucking thing with us." She pointed an immaculately manicured fingernail at the pink creature and sneered at Alternate Chuck in a way that made the real Chuck cringe.

"Howdy," Alternate Chuck said, not moving from the spot by his vehicle.

"Howdy," Chuck returned the greeting. Nothing else came out; what the fuck *was* one supposed to say in such circumstances?

"Who are these people, Dad?" Tyler chirped. He'd climbed out of the car without Chuck noticing and stood beside his father.

"Get back in the car, Tyler," Chuck growled and his tone said *no arguments*. Nonetheless, Tyler stayed put and played a staring contest with the kid who looked exactly like him.

Alternate Chuck stepped forward. "They told us we wouldn't bump into you yet." He smiled the warm smile that Chuck reserved for disarming his most objectionable clients.

"Who said?" Chuck struggled to control his racing thoughts. Was this the nervous breakdown the company shrink had warned him had been a long time coming? "And just who the *fuck* are you people?"

Alternate Chuck took a couple more steps, his family following suit. "I'm sorry, where are my manners?" He beamed, his pearly-whites glinting in the harsh sunlight. "I'm Chuck, this here's my good lady wife, Luciana. And this is Tyler and Kirsty." Again, with that disarming smile. "I figured you'd already know that."

"I don't get it," Chuck stammered. "I just don't—"

"What's not to get, Chuck?" Alternate Chuck grinned. "We're you, you're us. It really is as simple as that. We weren't supposed to meet up yet but we did, probably because *somebody* didn't check the paperwork properly." He ruffled Alternate Tyler's hair. "What do I always tell you about minding the paperwork, son?"

"To always do it, otherwise shit happens." The scrotum-dog thing squirmed in the boy's arms, its naked skin already starting to redden under the harsh glare of the Texas sun.

"Precisely." Alternate Chuck nodded.

"Will someone please explain to me what is going on here?" Chuck broke in, his voice an octave and a half higher than usual.

"Like I told you, Chuck; *we* are you," Alternate Chuck said calmly.

"What's going on, Chuck?" Luciana's voice was shrill and grating as she walked around the car to her husband. "It's getting hot in the—" Luciana's face drained of color and a waxy sheen of sweat shimmered across her skin. She grasped her hands to her mouth and made small retching sounds.

"Hi, Luciana," Alternate Luciana called across, as friendly and breezy as an old school friend.

***

"It really is quite simple," Alternate Chuck said as he mopped his brow with the stained handkerchief he carried in his pants pocket. His wife swore it made him look like he had a permanent hard-on, but old habits were old habits, and they died hard.

Chuck mopped *his* brow with *his* stained 'kerchief but the grubby cloth did little to alleviate the damp, sticky feeling.

"It *really* is simple," Alternate Chuck repeated with an exasperated sigh. "*We* are *you guys* from an alternate reality."

"What alternate reality?" Luciana kept her steely eyes fixed on Alternate Luciana.

"The one in which they invented inter-reality travel, of course." Alternate Chuck laughed.

"*This* is what you get for playing safe." Alternate Luciana couldn't resist a dig at her husband. "We could have gone to the reality where they have teleportation and then we wouldn't be stuck with this god forsaken pile of junk." She waved a dismissive hand towards their Tahoe. "Next year, I want time travel, or inter-stellar. This *really* is the last time I let you choose our vacation, Chuck!"

Chuck cringed. Was this how his Luciana treated *him*? Did he really put up with being spoken to with such derision?

"Whatever the reason," Alternate Chuck continued and this time he did a little eye-rolling all of his own, "we decided to vacation here this summer."

"You're on vacation?"

"If you can call it that," Alternate Luciana butted in with a vicious sneer in her voice that made *everyone* cringe.

"And you're us?" Tyler said.

"No, you're us," Alternate Tyler corrected, and Alternate Kirsty slapped his arm.

"What's it like where you guys come from?" Tyler's curiosity cut through the surreal moment.

"It's really not all that much different from here," Alternate Tyler told him, "except there's no Australia and some of the animals are a bit different."

"See. Even the kids think this is lame," Alternate Luciana huffed. She poked Alternate Chuck in the ribs with a vicious finger that made him flinch.

Chuck cracked a wry smile at his alternate's discomfort. It was nice to see that he and the guy who was creeping him out right now shared the same Achilles heel. It really was like looking into some diabolical mirror.

Ever the salesman, Chuck stepped forward, arm outstretched in that universal *let's shake hands and pretend this isn't in the least bit awkward* gesture that men seem compelled to make under even the most awkward of circumstances.

Alternate Chuck took a step back and stared at Chuck's hand as if it were diseased.

"Better not," his voice was firm.

"You don't shake a guy's hand where you're from?" Chuck was offended.

"I can't shake *your* hand. Here."

"I think it's because he's you, Dad," Tyler chipped in. "If you both touch, you'll explode."

Alternate Chuck laughed. "I see your boy's a Trekkie too! I'm afraid that's where kids get most of their science from these days!"

"You're thinking of the matter/anti-matter reaction," Alternate Tyler said. He smiled at Tyler as if they were two best buds at a sci-fi convention and not exact, alternate duplicates. "You put *those* two together and POW!"

Chuck jumped at the loud *POW!* His nerves jangled and were beginning to shred, one by twitching one.

"What's going on Dad?" Kirsty walked around from her side of the car. "And why does *she* look like me?" She stalked up to Alternate Kirsty who returned the stare with those same, accusatory eyes. "Who the fuck are *you* supposed to be?" Kirsty grimaced at her alternate.

"Kirsty!" Chuck reprimanded.

"Yeah, Dad, whatever," his daughter sneered, her mother's contempt towards Chuck already fixed in her repertoire.

Alternate Kirsty grabbed hold of Kirsty's hand and she froze, a half sound stuck in her throat.

In the blinking of an eye Kirsty's T-shirt and shorts had vanished. They were swiftly followed by her one-piece swimsuit which momentarily revealed that her overnight blossoming had been more than enhanced by a generous helping of tissues. Kirsty stood rooted to the spot and within the space of no more than a handful of seconds, her skin had vanished, followed by her flesh, layer by gaudy layer. Next went her internal organs, the white threads of nerves and finally, her bones.

And then there was nothing.

Chuck stumbled in slow-motion towards where his daughter had been standing. "What the hell?!" He stepped towards Alternate Chuck, but stopped himself. "Where's my daughter?"

"What have you done to my baby?!" Luciana wailed, her voice that high, hysterical pitch that never failed to make Chuck's ears hurt.

"Everybody just calm down," Alternate Chuck soothed. He spread his arms out, palms up. *Trust me*, his body language implied.

Chuck knew his own gesture all too well. *You can trust me about as far as you can throw me* is what it meant in Chuck-speak.

"She's okay, I promise." Alternate Chuck grinned.

"If you've hurt her –" Luciana stepped forward. Hesitated.

"She's gone to *our* reality, that's all," Alternate Chuck placated. "She's perfectly fine."

"So *that's* what happens." Alternate Tyler was awestruck. "That is *so* cool!"

"Apparently so." Alternate Chuck nodded. "They really didn't make it all that clear in the brochure."

Chuck's blood pressure bubbled up and his temples throbbed with each thump of his heart. He fought to keep his voice down to somewhere below hysterical and his temper under control. "You need to bring my daughter back," he growled, "now."

"I'm afraid that's quite impossible." Alternate Chuck smiled his – *Chuck's* – warmest smile. "We can't exist in the same reality as our alternate selves, not when there are no *us* back in our reality. It's all because of physics and stuff that, quite frankly, I don't really understand."

"Y-you're replacing us?" Luciana stammered. "Chuck, they're *replacing* us!"

"I guess you could call it that." Alternate Chuck smirked. "There really is nothing to panic about; it happens far more often than you may think. Look at it this way, you guys get to see a different reality too, so it'll be like a vacation for you as well."

"Don't get too excited," Alternate Luciana deadpanned. "It's not all that."

"And, as you can see," Alternate Chuck explained, "there are no explosions, rips in the space-time continuum or any of the other pseudo-scientific mumbo-jumbo you see in the movies." He guffawed at this, as if he'd just cracked the funniest of funnies.

Chuck recognized that laugh, it was the one he held in reserve for when he'd just said something really, really clever.

"We'd rather not," Chuck said. "We want to stay right here, thank you. And we would like Kirsty back."

"Ah, I don't think I've explained myself clearly enough." Alternate Chuck fixed them with his serious face and Chuck wanted to physically assault the guy—*himself!* "Once we've exchanged places with our alternative selves, there's no coming back. You nice people get to live in the reality we came from, and we get to stay here until we're ready to move on." Alternate Chuck smiled.

"So, you had to find us all along?" Chuck asked.

"Part of the package deal," Alternate Chuck told him.

"This is some kind of joke," Luciana interrupted. "All this, you—?"

"It's not *any* kind of joke," Alternate Luciana said. "Unless you count the fact that we came to *this* boring reality instead of somewhere fun." She spat out *this* like it was a bad taste on her tongue.

Chuck's brain ached. His practical mind struggled to comprehend what his other self was telling him – hell, even that didn't make too much sense right now—but he had no option but to believe what his eyes were telling him; that he had just seen his daughter—what? Dissolve? He had to give credence to the fact that she had actually gone to another reality, and if Alternate Chuck was to be believed, the same fate awaited himself, Luciana and Tyler.

There's a part in the human brain that generates hope in even the most hopeless of situations. It's why men walk calmly to the gallows, go merrily off to war, or fight even the most malignant of cancers—there's always the *hope* of salvation. And it was this part of Chuck that accepted all of his counterpart's bullshit, to even consider going willingly to the other reality. He rationalized that the Alternate Slatens would have to go back there eventually. They *were* on vacation, after all.

"We won't be returning to our own reality after this." Alternate Chuck read Chuck's mind. Of course he had, it was *his* mind too! "We signed up for the lifetime's worth of reality-jumping – thought we'd be adventurous." Alternate Chuck grinned. "We came into a few dollars when Mom and Dad died, if you know what I mean?" There was a wicked twinkle in his eye.

Chuck's thoughts switched to his own Mom and Dad who, in *this* reality, were very much alive and kicking; also, they were as poor as church mice. In fact, Chuck had actually had to bail them out of their sticky financial situation on the all too numerous occasions that Dad's sure-fire winning horses failed to live up to their sure-firedness.

And yet, in some parallel reality, Chuck Slaten was loaded. Suddenly, Chuck began to envy his counterpart, and think that perhaps visiting that particular alternative wouldn't be such a bad thing after all.

"Aren't there an infinite number of realities?" Tyler broke the silence.

"In theory, Son," Alternate Chuck replied. "But there's only about two hundred of those actually worth visiting. Don't they teach you *anything* in school here?" A broad *Gotcha* grin. "I mean, who the hell wants to pay to vacation in an alternate universe where the only difference is that some random guy didn't scratch his ass that morning?"

"Even that couldn't be much worse than this place," Alternate Luciana chose her moment wisely for yet another well-aimed dig.

"Thank you, my dear," Alternate Chuck said through gritted teeth. "We all get the message." He shot a glance at Chuck and a look passed between them; a glimmer of camaraderie amongst the downtrodden.

"So, what happens when you guys leave this, er, our, er, here?" Chuck struggled.

"We'll be replaced here by the other Us-es in whatever alternate reality we decide to visit next," Alternate Chuck was quite matter of fact about the whole concept. "They really do teach you nothing about any of this, do they?"

"Not in our curriculum," Chuck replied, inexplicably embarrassed at his own reality's shortcomings. "We don't know of any other realities apart from this one."

"Then you're in for one humdinger of a ride, my

friend!" Alternate Chuck stepped towards Chuck, who before he knew what was happening felt a firm hand grasp his own in a sweaty handshake.

Chuck's muscles froze and a chilly tingle spread through his body. It expanded from his hand, up along his arm and crept through his body like an electrical fungus; prickling mycelia that invaded every corner of him, one cell at a time.

At the same time, Alternate Tyler jumped onto Tyler's back and clung on to him with arms tight around his throat in a sinister piggy-back. As Chuck watched, helpless, his son also began to vanish one layer at a time and as he faded away, Chuck summoned the last wisps of his breath to call out to Luciana. "Get the fuck out of here!" His tightened throat forced the words out as *'et eh fu't 'ere!*

Scrambled diction or no, Luciana got her husband's message loud and clear and darted back to the Tahoe as Alternate Luciana lunged, her expensive fingernails missing her counterpart's hair by a fraction.

The car's engine gunned, tires spun on the disintegrating road and kicked up a cover of thick, red dust on its way out of the abandoned lot. Alternate Luciana turned on her heels, clambered into the alternate Tahoe and raced after Chuck's fleeing wife.

Chuck's clothes felt feather light, a sensation followed by the warmth of the sun's rays on his naked body. An instant after that, his skin felt as if it were liquefying, evaporating into the dry heat. There was no pain, which was a mercy, but the peculiar sensations as layer upon layer of his being were stripped away made Chuck feel quite nauseous. He cast his eyes downwards; saw the glistening pink of his own viscera, the living white/pink bone that shone through the soft tissues.

And then he could see nothing but black as his eyes dissolved away to leave him in the darkness between realities.

Chuck's perception of time had warped beyond comprehension; he'd seen Kirsty vanish completely in a matter of seconds, but the process felt like hours until, finally, Chuck felt his skull disappear and the sun's warmth prickling at his exposed brain. And then, for the briefest of moments, Chuck knew how it felt to exist as nothing more than pure thought.

***

The bizarre lightlessness began to gray around the edges and Chuck had an overwhelming sensation of *passing through*; his conscious mind being the final part of him to complete the bizarre journey. It felt as if his brain had been forced through a chilled, narrow funnel; pushed through with a wet, almost audible *plop*.

Chuck's thoughts went out to his kids and he hoped that they hadn't been totally scared out of their sanity by all of this, although he did think that Tyler would think that all of this had been *totally cool*.

The gray became lighter, gave way to color, which in turn resolved into forms and shapes. Chuck could feel his body again as it grew more *substantial;* he positively delighted in the weight of flesh on his exposed bones.

As Chuck's vision returned, he realized that whatever place he'd been transported to, it looked exactly like the one he'd left, decaying motel and all. He saw black, flying things — presumably buzzards — circling low over something dead and smashed flat on the road. Only, they weren't really buzzards at all; they were shiny, black blobs which flew on broad, leathery wings that were completely featherless. They had fat, clawed feet they held tucked close to their grotesque bodies, and their heads sported faces that were perfectly human.

"Dear God," Chuck murmured, glancing down at the subject of the flying things' attention. It looked like no creature Chuck was familiar with, squashed flat or otherwise. Its blood was a bright, neon green color and was splashed across the dusty road like bizarre urban graffiti. The dead creature itself was around five feet in length and appeared to have at least three heads, none of which had eyes. It also boasted eight legs, one of which was severed and lay mangled on the opposite side of the road and through the congealing blood, Chuck could see that the creature's skin was a coat of short barbs that resembled the writing end of innumerable quills.

It's really not that much different. . .some of the animals are a bit different.

The ground shook and a long, cold shadow fell over the old motel. Chuck twisted his head around so sharply that his neck bones crackled, and he saw the monstrosity that strode up behind him.

The creature was five, six stories high with a squat, blubbery body the same eye-watering green as the roadkill's blood. The monstrous thing's glistening, raw skin was adorned with snaking tributaries of vivid pink veins that pulsed and throbbed as it maneuvered towards Chuck on four thick-set, powerful legs that looked like they had been transplanted from some gigantic insect. Dangling between the creature's legs was a colossal swinging ball sack that hit the decaying roof of the motel and ripped it away from the building.

"Dear God," Chuck whispered again, frozen in sheer terror.

The thing had three tubular, rubbery arms, one on either shoulder, with a third that sprouted from the center of its chest; none of which had what could be called hands, just a sticky pad that reminded Chuck of the end of a chameleon's tongue. Grasped firmly by the center arm, the creature held aloft a writhing, shrieking thing.

Luciana.

It lifted Chuck's wife up to its face, a vast neon moon of a thing that looked as if it had been glued on to the huge, bulbous head as part of some grotesque kindergartener's art project; the head's circumference was lined by a single row of tiny, unblinking eyes that glinted at Luciana with pure malevolence.

Chuck watched in stunned, sickened silence as a hole appeared in the center of the beast's face, and an oozing protuberance slithered out and snaked towards his wife and she screamed long and loud. At the end of the protuberance unfurled a circular, lipless mouth lined with a radula of keenly pointed teeth. As it walked towards Chuck, the creature nonchalantly chewed off Luciana's head and munched on her body as a child would a tasty Popsicle.

The creature peered down at Chuck and the myriad twinkling eyes focused upon him as if he were nothing more than some unusual bug. The thing's ridiculous, Stretch-Armstrong arms reached out for him and Chuck Slaten ran for his life.

Gator
by
John Wolf

The heel of the left tennis shoe was held on by a string of crusty glue and happy thoughts. The wearer was small, with narrow shoulders and a smooth face beneath greasy black hair. She managed to keep it fairly short with the small craft scissors she carried in her ratty pack. Her baggy, nondescript clothes completed the illusion. And so, here on the desolate stretch of highway, Christy became Chris. Hardly the most creative choice, but it was easier keeping names close in case she forgot or got flustered.

So far, she had kept her persona in check. A damned miracle by all accounts, given how long she had been at it. The road was a hungry place, snapping up anybody it could whenever it could. When you slipped up at the wrong honkytonk or camped out in the wrong place, you were just another piece of roadkill.

Despite that grim reality, she knew all the rough miles, sore feet, and swallowed exhaust were better than what lay behind her. At least out here she could change what she was, who she was. Out here she was just Chris the hitchhiker, a nobody roaming from nowhere to no place in particular. The dangers were plain on their face out here too. They didn't wear the face of someone who was supposed to love you. Someone you were supposed to trust.

She slowed every so often, sparing a glance over one bony shoulder, heart momentarily leaping high into her throat with the certainty there would be a familiar, lanky figure gaining ground. Always gaining ground. Then she would turn like she always did, put one sore foot in front of the other like she always did, and stare ahead into the blackness like she always did, content with the emptiness like she always was.

Looking back too often was a foolish move, almost as bad as slipping up on your name. Christy proved this point by glancing back, then immediately tripping over something in the road. The harsh blacktop raced up, eager to smash in her face. Only she put her hands out first, sacrificing her palms to the hungry gods of the dark highway instead. Her jeans were still in decent shape and shielded her knees. Her palms though. . .

It was like someone took a razor to them before splashing on a little gritty gasoline for good measure. Her palms grew warm and sticky with blood while thin tears washed clear valleys down her grimy face. As she sat there on the dusty shoulder, she heard a steady hiss in the night air. She forgot her hands and looked around, visions of rattlers uncoiling about her shoes, needled fangs rising out of the dark to greet her. For just a moment, she even saw them, a dark roiling mass just below the brush.

Christy leapt to her feet and backed up onto the road, bloodied palms out in a weak attempt to ward off any predator lurking amongst the sage and scrub. Another few steps back and the speeding pickup would've run her down. She yipped, sucking down air in a strangled gasp as her life whizzed by in the diesel-stained draft. The genius behind the wheel was running the truck with no lights. The passenger window rolled down and a high, otherwise unintelligible jeer flew past with it.

She couldn't make out a single word of it, but she was able to conjure the universal, single digit response. Just for color she added in, "You redneck piece of shit!"

The road turned crimson as the brake lights flared. The truck screeched to a halt and sat idling in the road. Then the driver gunned the engine, letting the truck roar. Christy bit at her lower lip, mouth curling into a snarl. The cocktail of pain and rage made her almost want a fight. But what were the odds like there? Two or more good old boys against some skinny kid? And what about when they got a closer look and found out the mouthy kid on the side of the road had a little secret to share?

But the idiots in the truck apparently had better places to be out in the desert. Cows to tip and cousins to screw. The truck roared on, leaving Christy alone again with her bleeding hands and nowhere closer to wherever she had to end up.

She dug out a water bottle from her pack and washed her wounds with what was left. She traded the bottle for her phone and tried Google maps. Nothing.

A thin recollection of a truck stop somewhere down the road came to her. It was probably up there somewhere. Something had to be. Hopefully not too far. She told herself this as she put away her empty water bottle.

If only she hadn't tripped. . .

Tripped over what?

She turned on the phone's flashlight and looked.

It lurked beside the shoulder, its long, scaly back so dark it melded with the road. The black, reptile hide clashed with the fine, white whiskers trailing out the sides, resembling a millipede's many legs.

She backed away.

The thing on the road remained still.

She gave it a wide berth, studying the twisted shape by the light of her phone. The diamondback pattern was the tread of an old tire, a dual wheel by the width. The exposed, white threads of the worn inner wall told the short, ugly tale. A blowout discarded in a heap like shed snakeskin. If the truck had come just a few seconds later, Christy knew she'd be lying beside the tire, another broken thing on the road.

The wind kicked up then. The cold gusts scoured her face and sent the blown tire rippling across the blacktop towards her. Christy shrank back and pulled her jacket tighter. She looked up ahead. A red, white, and blue sign stood off to the westbound side. A cartoon Uncle Sam promised her the best fireworks in the country. It was better than nothing. Christy hung her bleeding hands at her side and kept moving.

The fireworks would have to wait, but that was alright. Instead, a truck stop appeared off the highway, an oasis of light in the night. Christy walked in with no trouble. The temporary residents here had all seen worse than a scrawny boy with cut hands and dirty hair. Or likely didn't care. There were schedules to keep and one traveler out here was just like another.

Christy walked by a formation of idling trucks. Inside, truckers slept on while the world carried on outside. Past the semis were a few stray vans. Christy thought it would be nice having enough things to fill a van. She rounded the corner of the main building, heading for the diner, and froze.

The only two vehicles in the front lot of the diner were a gray minivan and a raised truck.

Had the one earlier been this high off the ground? Probably? Where else could the driver have been headed?

She knew it would be better just moving on. Chances were good these were the same dickheads, and if she remembered them they would sure remember a sole hitchhiker out here. But there would be a bathroom. There would be a place to clean her wounds. She kept going.

Christy walked into the diner without a word to or from the waitress. She barely raised her face, half-asleep, and managed to give a weak nod before going back to her phone and chewing gum. A sign above the waitress prompted Christy to:

ASK ABOUT OUR SHOWERS.

She could afford a shower. The last waiting gig back in Laramie paid her on time and it had been steady work. But a bathroom was all she needed. It would have running water, soap, and some privacy. If she was lucky there might be a working lock on the door. She refused to look over at the far booth where three rowdy young men in cowboy hats fell suddenly silent.

The bathroom was well-lit and empty. Four stalls and some urinals flanked one wall with mirrors and sinks on the other. Christy beelined for the furthest stall, only stopping to soak a handful of paper towels in water and locking the door behind her. She set down her pack and did what she could with what she had.

The wet paper towels cleared away the worst parts and there was enough iodine in her small squeeze bottle. As she wrapped a few layers of dry toilet paper beneath a strip of torn t-shirt, the bathroom door creaked open.

The bootheels clicked loudly on the dirty tiled floor. In no time they were at the last stall. The red leather was garish in the fluorescent light, nearly obscene. The wearer said nothing. They only stood there, boots pointed straight at Christy.

She could picture the owner clear as day. She knew the type of truck he drove. If she opened the door, would his two buddies be there backing him up? Would it all come to an end in the toilet stall? Then the boots were gone. The door creaked again. Christy sighed and fell against the wall.

How long could she keep at this? She wasn't sure. Or where she was going. Or what she hoped to do when she got there.

Christy finished cleaning up. She leaned down to check the bathroom for any hidden visitors. When she came back up, she saw the warning scrawled over the white tile beside the stall door: "Look out for Gators." She gave a short, hoarse laugh. It was nice knowing someone else out there was more crazed and aimless than her. Whoever left the warning would have to be. Any idiot could tell this dry stretch of highway had never seen an alligator.

When Christy returned to the diner, the three customers in the far booth had gone. She looked out the windows and the truck was gone too. There were only the tired waitress and the single customer at the counter. Christy bet the customer owned the minivan. The waitress didn't seem the soccer mom type.

The waitress brought a cup of coffee to the booth and left without another word. That was fine with Christy. She didn't plan on staying long if she could help it. Christy lowered her heavy head but kept her eyes open, another survival trick of the road.

"Here, kid." The waitress set down a plate of home fries and eggs and strolled back up to the register.

"I didn't order this," Christy called.

"Yeah, whatever." The waitress said without a look back and flapped her hand in the direction of the customer at the counter.

The minivan driver was older, but not by much. Brown hair stuck out from beneath a pristine Milwaukee Brewers cap. The bright blue windbreaker bore the name of an auto parts store Christy didn't recognize. She bet the yellow polo shirt sticking up over the collar had the same company logo. The driver gave a half-hearted smile and wave before turning back to his paperback and coffee on the countertop.

Despite her circumstances, Christy grimaced. The last thing she wanted was to owe anyone anything. It was never good to get too tied down. She wanted to throw the plate to the side, but she needed to eat.

The coffee was hot, if not good. There wasn't even time for a refill. Christy mopped up the last bit of yolk with the last wedge of greasy potato and settled back into her booth. She let loose a hearty belch and actually laughed, a sound akin to a foreign language in her ears. The driver turned and raised his coffee mug in salute.

Christy supposed it was friendly enough, but the food was gone. Soon as the good cheer had come, it vanished. She set her plate aside and marched up to the counter. The driver, back in his book, jumped as Christy thumped down on the stool next to him.

"Why'd you do that?"

"Do what, man?" The driver spoke in a sharp Wisconsinite accent more honk than human. Up close he still called her "man." That was something at least.

"Why'd you buy me food?"

The driver shrugged. "Looked hungry."

"Why?"

He gestured to the empty diner. "Nobody else was gonna do it." She couldn't argue there. "Been hungry myself, when I was younger. Was I wrong?"

Up close, the driver's eyes were a dishwater gray behind his glasses. Christy kept staring right into them and made ready to run. Good intentions or not, the diner was empty and Christy didn't think the waitress would be riding to her rescue.

"What now?"

The driver set his book down with a sigh. "Huh?"

"How am I paying you back for it? Going to invite me out to your rig? Just 'help a kid out'"?

The driver's face turned from pale to angry red like

some deep-sea squid. "The heck?"

"You don't know me."

"I don't wanna!" The driver's eyes jittered in their sockets and avoided all eye contact with Christy. That was fine. A discerning eye this close might notice a crack in her mask.

The driver stammered, "I-I got a son your age nearly. I would never. I'm driving home to see them. How dare you!"

"Don't owe you nothing."

The driver slurped down the rest of his coffee and hurried off the stool. "Jeez. You do one nice thing." He left his book behind. Some Tom Clancy thing, a submarine on the cover below a simple two-word title.

It felt good to be on the offensive, cornering someone and making them feel small. It even tasted better than her breakfast. That reminded her. She went back to finish her own coffee while it was still hot. She wasn't sure the refills were bottomless, and even if they were she doubted the waitress would notice her coffee needed a warm-up.

Christy almost burst out the door, new energy filling her heart along with the free meal. The backpack hung a little easier on her tired shoulders, her aching feet were a little less heavy. She rounded the corner to the back of the parking lot. Here there was only a single streetlamp illuminating a barren moonscape. Almost barren.

The truck hadn't gone far. It lurked beneath the streetlamp. The three men from earlier all loitered on one side, trading cigarettes and laughing. Like predators tracking a scent, they stopped as Christy came around the corner.

The tallest one waved. "Hey, kid. C'mere!" Another laughed, a guttural, maniacal sound more suited to the African savanna. Christy sprinted back around the diner. With every step, she expected a hand to clap across her mouth and drag her away.

She wasn't surprised to see the driver standing by the van. Neither was she surprised to see the Wisconsin plate or the Packers bumper sticker and stuffed Garfield clinging to the rear windshield. The driver was busy chatting on his cell phone, his back to Christy.

"Yeah, just about done here. Shouldn't be long. Getting back on the road soon."

Christy wasn't sure if she should interrupt him. She shuffled from side-to-side, glancing back towards the rear lot, silently urging the driver to wrap up his call. She only hoped she hadn't torched a bridge she now desperately needed to cross.

"Love you too," the driver said and pocketed his phone. He turned back and groaned. "What now?"

"Um, I'm sorry, okay?"

"Yeah, I think you should be," the driver sniffed.

"I am. I really could use the help."

The driver shook his head and rounded the van. "Sorry, I'm headed home. Got some miles to go." Christy followed him. "Hey, back off now."

"I said I was sorry. Please. I just…" She let her shoulders slump, bent in the knees, let herself get smaller. She held up her hands and hoped the wounds had soaked through a little for added effect. "Got a little roughed up and I'm traveling slow."

The driver grimaced.

"Just need to get to Cheyenne." She let the words hang there in the cold air, watching them sink their hooks into the driver's skin. He sighed and Christy bit her cheeks to keep from smiling.

"What's your name?"

***

It had been a while since Christy accepted a ride from

anyone, and certainly not in a minivan. Here there was room to stretch and set her bag down. The seats were high over the road. From atop her temporary throne, Christy watched the white lines blur together. In the rearview, the truck stop and all its troubles grew smaller. When the last pinpricks of light vanished back under the horizon, she let loose a long breath and settled back into her chair.

The driver's phone rested silently in the coffee cup holder between them. The only sounds were the thrumming wheels on the pavement. The only light from the green glow of the console. Christy's eyelids got heavier. She wasn't sure how long she had slept until the driver piped up.

"Cheyenne, huh?" In the green glow, the driver faded away to almost nothing.

"Yeah." Christy yawned. "Thanks for doing this."

"Not a problem. Like I said, got a daughter near your age."

Cold bloomed in Christy's chest, shocking her back from the murkiness of sleep.

I got a son your age nearly.

If the driver noticed, he didn't let on. "Where you coming from?"

The driver's comment threw her completely off course. She reached for a name, any name from any of the countless towns she'd traveled through. One finally came to her, and she grabbed onto it like a life preserver thrown to a drowning man.

"Lyman. Uncle got me some work in Cheyenne." As soon as the words left her mouth, Christy wanted to haul them back in. It was a baited hook, and sure enough, the driver bit and pulled.

"Oh yeah? What kind of work?"

Christy looked back out her window. The darkness outside was immense. No city lights. No brake lights or headlights of other vehicles coming or going. Only the white lines zipping past.

"Said, 'What kinda work?'"

"Don't know. Said he'd explain it to me when I got there."

"Awful long way to travel on just that."

Somehow the silence became worse, heavy as the darkness beyond. A highway sign mercifully rose up into the headlights' glare. It cautioned travelers to "Click it or ticket," but the secondary message was enough to perk Christy's interests. Spray-painted below the smiling, cartoon seatbelt were the words, "Warning: Gators ahead."

"What's that mean?" Christy asked.

The driver pressed the van on faster. "What's what mean?"

"Gators. The sign back there. At the truck stop too."

The smile was hidden in the dim cab, but it snuck through the driver's voice, sticky and sour. "Oh, sure. You see all kinds of critters out here on the road. Gators are the worst, though. Travel enough, you learn to avoid'em."

Christy recalled the thing in the road, its leathery back and long, ragged tail.

"You see gators all up and down the highway. Blown out tires is all. Call'em 'gators' 'cause of the treads on top of them, see? Look just like a gator's hide. Truckers use the name all the time. Know there used to be an ocean in these parts?" The driver laughed, more to himself than his captive audience. "Probably lotsa gators back then in the dinosaur times. Maybe ours just never left."

The shadow in the driver's seat changed. The hunched shoulders grew broader, the torso taller, the double-chin stuck out sharper and meaner. As it changed, the voice did too. The innocent, Wisconsin honk melted away. In its place came a Wyoming drawl Christy had heard plenty the last few days. Christy wondered how easy it would be to buy a bumper sticker somewhere or swap plates with another car. Just camouflage. She leaned away, but the seatbelt caught her.

Click it or ticket!

"Gators are sneaky. Blending into the blacktop like they do. At night, drivers never know they got bit 'till they hear that gator rollin' up into the guts of their truck. Just tearin' it all to hell."

The horizon up ahead began to glow. Hope grew with it, then was dashed to pieces as Christy watched the same truck stop fly by. The driver had swung around at some point, taking an exit and backtracking when she'd drifted off to dreamland.

Christy's trembling hand found the door handle. Even at this speed, she would try it. She had to. Her other hand hovered over the seatbelt release.

"Where were you really headed, huh?"

Christy took another rough swallow. "Out of here." She pressed the seatbelt release and yanked on the door handle in one clean movement. The handle stayed frozen in place. The driver accelerated. Christy bet the boots stepping down on the pedals were red.

"Childproof locks. They ain't hard to rig up nowadays. Not like when I started, but a man adapts. Yes, ma'am."

The words barely came. "Where are we going?"

"Oh, I got a few spots."

"Let me go."

"No." The driver's flat voice grew faint. "You're here now. You took the ride. Rules of the road. Don't hitchhike, watch for gators." He laughed. "Don't text and drive."

Christy dove for the phone and hugged it to her chest.

The driver shrugged. "Keep it."

Christy punched the power button. The screen remained dark.

"Last rider didn't have a charger on her."

"There wasn't anybody on the other end," Christy said more to herself than to the driver.

"Nah." The dark mouth of the road seemed bottomless. "Just keepin' up appearances." He sighed. "If it helps, you were harder to bait than the others. Most times the free meal is all it takes."

Looking out on the shoulder in despair, Christy remembered the rough black hide of the thing in the center of the road, crouched and ready to strike.

She forced herself to speak. "Saw one once."

"What's that?"

"A gator. Got bit by one a while back." The driver laughed. "But I got away." The road raced under them, the vibration from the wheels coming up through Christy's shoes. She clicked her seatbelt back into place. "Didn't catch me then. Not going to let it catch me now."

She looked out the windshield. When the faded red, white, and blue firework billboard raced past, she brought the dead phone down hard onto the driver's nearest hand.

A hearty crunch erupted from impact. The driver yelped and yanked at Christy's jacket with his other hand. The seatbelt kept her inside the seat. Christy dashed the phone across the driver's nose. Scarlet drops decorated the windshield

A familiar, humped shape rose up out of the road. The black hide spotted with white threads, mouth a gnarled tangle of shredded rubber and wire ready to bite. Christy jammed the wheel hard to the left, letting the driver's side of the van meet the gator in the road dead center. She thought she saw the shredded mess in the road writhe in anticipation, the mouth stretching open wide for a new meal.

***

Christy came to, lying on her side. The wounds on her hands seemed comical compared to the ringing in her head or the stabbing pain in her side. But it brought her back to earth. She looked around the wrecked van. The windshield was a mess of spiderwebbed glass encircling a ragged, red smear above the bent steering wheel. While her own seatbelt remained locked onto the seat, the driver's had been torn apart. Christy sighed in relief, but the pain in her side cut it short.

The metal wall let out a long *screeeeech*. Just turning her head was enough to send black dots swarming across Christy's vision like flies over roadkill. The screech called again, this time further away back around the upturned cab. The sound circled the wreck. In no time it would be at the passenger side window.

It was the driver, she had no doubt. Probably dragging himself along, knife ready to cut and rend. Coming around to see if his new plaything still had any life in her. Christy found the seatbelt release, pushed it, and crumpled onto the roof. She gritted her teeth, kicked her aching feet, and squirmed towards the shattered windshield.

Outside, the desert air was still clean and sharp as a knife but tinged with the acrid scent of gasoline. Something else lingered in the air: heavy, oily, the smell of charred black top sizzling beneath the desert sun.

The front wheels still spun in the aftermath of the wreck. Each slow turn around the twisted axle produced the long, agonized wail of twisting metal. She couldn't understand how it still turned. She crept closer to inspect the damage, wondering what could have left those three perfectly aligned scratch marks on the underbelly of the van.

A clammy hand seized Christy by the back of the neck, driving her headfirst into the van's side. She spun around and wasn't surprised to see the bloodied face of the driver before her. She recognized him even with the long scalp wound painting half his face. This was the *real* driver now. Not a corn-fed Packers fan, not the good ol' cowboy in a van, but a snarling animal. That was alright. Christy thought it best they be on clear terms in these final moments.

"The hell you think you're going?" he growled. If he had been planning on a knife or gun to do his vile business, that time had passed. Now his sweaty hands would do the trick. They pressed down into Christy's narrow neck. She kicked his ankles. He simply pushed harder and lifted her off the ground. As the pressure grew, the searing pain in Christy's broken palms faded away. So did the ache in her feet, the calluses on her shoulders no longer throbbed, and all the other troubles of a hard life disappeared. Somewhere in that murky place, Christy felt perverse satisfaction. At least she wouldn't have to keep going. At least she knew the other dark figure from her past would never catch up. She had won that race at least.

Bullshit.

For once Christy was grateful life on the road left little time for any kind of proper hygiene. Her ragged nails gouged the skin from the driver's arm. He howled, his grip faltering long enough for Christy to catch a breath. Over her ragged coughs, the screech came again.

Headlights washed the road in sickly yellow light. The driver released his prey and turned to face the oncoming vehicle. Christy collapsed into a coughing heap at his feet, promising herself that the instant she got her wind back she'd grab a handful of the creep's balls and yank.

The screech tore into the night sky, the headlights grew brighter. The driver held up one hand to shield his eyes. The wide, dark shape behind the oncoming headlights reminded Christy of a lowrider. But it crawled too slowly along the road, the headlights were far too close. The screeching morphed into a throaty rumble equal parts machine and flesh.

The headlights blinked out, but the sound continued to grow. It vibrated through the road. Christy covered her ears, but it did no good. The rumble became a roar and reverberated deep into her bones.

"What?" The driver gasped.

The dark shape lunged, a living shadow split nearly in two. Crunching metal and glass shattered the night. The driver's scream was louder. He was yanked clean off his feet and flung to the ground. Something heavy thwacked into the wrecked van, spinning it like a top and knocking Christy down with it.

She lay eye-level with the driver. In desperation he reached out and clung to Christy's arm. Another shriek of twisting metal erupted behind him. The lights flooded back over the road, sending weird, twisting shadows over desert rock and scrub. The heavy form reared up with the lights, searching. The driver looked back over his trembling shoulder. He turned back, eyes wide with terror.

He crawled forward, calling out, "Oh God! Jesus Christ, please!"

Christy wondered just how many other travelers like her had made that very same plea. The rumble answered and the driver was dragged back towards it. Fingernails fruitlessly dug into the blacktop and were quickly torn loose. They scattered across the road and mingled with broken glass. Another snap, another scream.

The crunch of bone and meat brought Christy to her feet. She leaned against the upturned van. The strange headlights framed the dying man, and Christy looked on with the grim curiosity compelling any traveler to slow down and gawk at a car crash. What she saw seemed like a bad special effect in one of those cheapo sci-fi flicks, or one hell of a magic trick. The driver was sinking into the road like it was black quicksand, vanishing inch by horrific inch into utter darkness. But no, there was something else.

Behind the lights was a broad back studded with a diamond pattern. The back was immense, nearly the entire width of the lane. Fine, white hairs stuck out in crazed, nonsensical patches where the black hide had grown thin. On either side of the barrel body, radiator hoses bunched together to form squat legs. Foul, tar-stained breath rippled around a long, wide mouth glittering with broken glass fangs. A true gator, made from the road and of the road. The apex predator of the highways.

This tar and gravel and rubber monstrosity slithered over the road, became part of the road, and then broke away again like a whale breaching the ocean's surface. The radiator hoses bunched and strained as the gator secured its prey. The mouth opened, and an engine rumbled deep within the gator's chest. It grew louder with anticipation, a V8 heart going a hundred miles an hour. It swung its broad head back and scooped the driver deeper into its gullet. The man was nearly all gone now. Something wet burst inside the gator's throat as the teeth crunched down.

Christy couldn't be sure, there wasn't much left of him to do anything, but she thought the driver begged one last time. Whether for assistance, a quick death, or something else, she didn't give a shit. She only raised her hand in the universal, single digit response.

The gator's mouth snapped shut a final time. The engine purred, satisfied. A pale hand flopped to the blacktop like a dead fish, its ragged wrist cauterized with hot tar. The thumb poked up in grisly reflex, hitching a ride that would never come.

Christy's thin shadow stretched in the pale, yellow glow of the gator's headlights. Metal creaked as the creature raised itself from the road. It crawled forward, snout raised, tracking her scent. Christy shrank back, made herself smaller than she ever had.

The stink of burning tar was almost unbearable now. Christy choked and coughed. When she struggled for another breath, hot air burnt her nostrils. She closed her eyes, but the yellow glow penetrated her lids. She collapsed back against the van, screaming in primal fear. The gator roared in response, shaking her from the inside out with its sound. Then the lights were gone. The sounds faded. The beast's burning breath vanished from the cold night air.

Christy stood up, her body shaking with disbelief. She rummaged through the van for anything useful. When she came across an envelope of polaroids beneath the driver's seat, she looked away. She scavenged what she could scavenge, then got moving.

When headlights split the night, she did not stick out her thumb or look out with hope for a ride. With every step she expected the gator to breach the blacktop and snap its jaws over her ankles. But what else could she do? The road was, indeed, a hungry place. She had looked into its true face, stared down its tar-lined gullet, but she had survived. For how long, she couldn't be sure. She only knew she had to keep moving, hoping her exit would come long before she found out.

The Long Row
by
Ross Baxter

Day 1

Beth didn't think about the physical exertion of rowing for the first ten miles, despite the fast pace at which they propelled their tiny craft, the *Derry Girl*. Hundreds of boats filled New York harbor and the route to Staten Island, the horns, claxons and loud cheers spurring them on to pull hard on the oars on the first leg of their long eastbound journey. The annual transatlantic rowing race still captured the imagination of many. Thousands turned up to watch the send-off. Helicopters circled overhead, news crews aboard filming the forty small boats as they pulled away, adding to the general excitement of the event.

Beyond the Statute of Liberty, the flotilla of well-wishers started to thin, and the helicopters turned back to land. With the tide and the Hudson's current in their favor, two hours later they passed under Verrazano Narrows Bridge connecting Brooklyn and Staten Island, and the remaining tooting boats of supporters headed home. By midday, the United States coastline slowly receded behind them, and the splash of their oars in the choppy sea became the only sound.

"I want to take a final picture," said Beth. "Can we pause a minute?"

"If you must," sighed Kate irritably from behind her, "But we are actually in a race, you know."

As both rowers sat in tandem, facing backwards, Beth could not see Kate's face, but she knew without looking it would be sour. They had been paired together less than a week earlier, when Beth's rowing partner discovered she was pregnant, and Kate's rowing partner developed a mystery illness. Given their investment, the sponsors drafted in two replacement rowers to take over Kate's boat, and Kate joined Beth in the *Derry Girl*. The relationship between the two started quite tensely, and in the previous week had not improved at all. Beth found Kate bad-tempered and overbearing, quite the opposite to herself. But, with very little choice in the matter, Beth had to make the best of it. Privately though, the prospect of being alone with the surly Kate for almost two months, as they rowed the tiny boat over three thousand miles of ocean toward the British Isles, felt far from ideal.

Day 2

Beth awoke when Kate shook her roughly.

"It's your shift on the oars now," said Kate.

Beth looked at her watch. "It's only four o'clock. I'm not due to row until five?"

"That's not what we agreed," countered Kate. "We agreed you would row from four until eight."

"Five until nine," replied Beth. "I wrote it in the log. And I only stopped rowing three hours ago."

"We agreed four o'clock, and the one until four shift is the hardest anyway," muttered Kate, already out of her life jacket and coat and easing herself onto her narrow cot.

Now awake, Beth decided not to argue less than twenty-four hours into the marathon race. Instead, she emerged from her sleeping bag, quickly dressed, and grabbed a protein bar from the tiny galley. Squeezing through the narrow door, she emerged out onto the rowing deck of the *Derry Girl* in almost total darkness. To the west, a faint strip of light on the horizon showed the light pollution emitted by New York, and ahead to the east an even fainter strip heralded the far-off dawn. To starboard, the lights of settlements on Long Island twinkled in the distance, with the rhythmic rotating beam of Fire Island Lighthouse flashing every six seconds.

Despite the unwelcome early start to her shift, she felt good. A calm sea and warm westerly wind helped, but being in peak physical condition after training for many years gave her the self-confidence to know she could do this. Taking an oar in each gloved hand, she swung the blades powerfully forward and then deep into the dark ocean, pulling strongly in the darkness towards faraway Britain and the finish line.

Day 5

"We're gaining on them! Row faster!" Kate urged loudly.

Beth turned to look ahead. The white boat ahead bobbed on the small waves around four hundred yards away, seemingly with oars retracted. "They're not rowing."

"Good, we'll pass them quicker," said Kate. "Come on, we need to row faster!"

Beth sat back down and fell in with the rhythm of her partner's rowing. She was a professional, she reflected, at the top of her abilities, and she had no doubt at all about completing this race. But her faith in Kate lessened every day. Although they were similar in age and physical strength, something about her impromptu partner both worried and riled her. Certainly, Kate's personality grated, but she knew that all professional athletes needed a particular disposition and temperament to get them through the long and grueling hours of training, plus a degree of selfishness, to make them winners. Unfortunately for Beth, in Kate this seemed to manifest itself as extreme self-centeredness and humorless arrogance, with a generous pinch of sullen dourness.

"Row!" Kate hissed. "We nearly have them."

"Ahoy, *Derry Girl*!" called a cheery voice from off the starboard quarter. "Good morning!"

Beth lifted her oars clear of the water and turned to look. Two men sat casually in a race boat, drifting maybe twenty yards away, idly drinking tea. She recognized them immediately; Dan Moy and Tony McAllister, British rowing gold medal Olympians and hot favorites to win the race.

"Morning," Beth shouted back. "Everything OK?"

"Perfect," smiled Moy, the experienced older rower, who had graced many a magazine cover over his thirty-year career. He saluted her cheerily with a steaming mug. "Just having a tea break. Us Brits have to stop regularly for a brew, else we simply can't row! Do you want one?"

"No, we have to keep going," cut in Kate quickly, her voice unnecessarily severe.

Beth turned on her seat, lowering her voice. "Really? You turn down a cup of tea with two of rowing's royalty? We can't beat these two. We may as well spend a pleasant five minutes with them!"

"Are you sure we can't tempt you?" cried the younger McAllister, the tanned pin-up boy of the rowing world. "We have a couple of spare mugs, especially for occasions like this. Dan might even share his chocolate biscuits!"

"No thanks," yelled Kate, pulling hard on her oars.

Beth shook her head, debating with herself whether to push back against her rowing partner. She shrugged, giving the two rowers a resigned smile. "Hopefully we'll take you up on your kind offer once we reach London?"

"You're on!" Moy shouted back. "See you on the other side of the pond!"

She stuck her oars back into the sea and started pulling, angry and disappointed.

Day 8

"It's your shift," Kate grumbled, shaking her awake.

"Fine," Beth yawned drowsily.

"And when did you last shower?" Kate said accusingly. "It stinks in here."

Beth's drowsiness instantly dissipated. "Last night. I shower every night outside on the thwart."

"Well, something stinks in here."

Beth sat up, her short-cropped blond hair touching the low ceiling of the cramped cabin. "It's your clothes that stink. When I shower, I also wash my underwear and shirts. I don't think you've changed yours since we left New York."

"How dare you!" Kate hissed.

"How dare you!" Beth responded. "Take a look at yourself, before you start accusing me!"

"You're making this journey a nightmare for me," countered Kate. "I cannot wait to get to London and tell them what a horrible person you are. Putting up with you for forty days is going to be the hardest thing I've ever had to endure!"

Beth climbed out of the narrow bunk and dressed in her rowing gear in angry silence, not wanting to waste any more words. She squeezed past Kate out onto the deck, slamming the door behind her. The light and colorful logos of the sponsors plastered across all the outer surfaces of the small boat were in deep contrast to her dark thoughts. She looked longingly at the gay images of the pink gin bottle, the logo of Windsor Gin Distillery, the main race sponsors, and felt that she desperately needed a very large glass.

Day 10

Beth increasingly struggled to keep her depression at bay. With only a quarter of the route covered so far, the thought of another thirty days or so with her hateful rowing partner was proving hard to come to terms with. Only the daily call home on the satellite phone gave her any comfort, sparse though it was. Rules of the race strictly limited the use of the device to just ten minutes per day, per boat. Her five minutes of happiness every one thousand, four hundred and forty minutes served as a stout psychological prop, and the only thing she looked forward to apart from completing the race. All two thousand, one hundred nautical miles remaining.

With her solo rowing shift ending, she entered the cabin to use the satellite phone for her daily call with her partner. She saw Kate sprawled out idly listening to music through her headphones, the tinny sounds still filling the small space. The phone cradle stood empty.

"Where's the Inmarsat phone, Kate?" Beth asked.

Kate reluctantly removed her headphones. "It got dropped over the side. A wave hit the boat, and it fell into the sea."

"You dropped it overboard!"

"No, a wave knocked it over while I was using it, on my shift last night," Kate answered.

"And you didn't think to tell me?"

"You were asleep," she shrugged.

"You always wake me up for any petty issue you have,

but you don't wake me about the phone!"

"Don't worry, Beth, we still have IPERB if we get into an emergency," said Kate irritably.

"The Emergency Position Indicating Radio Beacon is just a distress signal. We can't talk on it, or communicate with anyone!" Beth cried.

Kate shrugged.

Beth rounded on her. "What, not even an apology?"

"The wave knocked it out of my hand. It is not my fault, and I've nothing to apologize for. Shit happens."

Beth closed her eyes, wanting to scream.

Day 14

Two hours into her four-hour solo shift Beth felt strong, and pleased with her pace. Her watch gave her all the bio-analytics she needed, showing that despite the emotional miserycaused by her rowing partner, at least her physical performance remained near peak. Using the GPS data, showing their average speed to be almost three knots, she calculated that they could finish the race in a strong position, likely in the top ten of the forty boats taking part. A crossing time of thirty-nine days would be an excellent achievement and a success for the sponsors.

Most importantly, it meant she only had another twenty-five days to endure the hateful Kate.

Day 15

There were just ten minutes remaining of their four-hour morning dual row. The two rowers exchanged very few words during dual shifts, which suited Beth perfectly, although Kate would always berate her if she felt their progress ever slowed.

Beth saw a dot on the blue horizon. With relatively

choppy seas and a large swell, the dot disappeared every time the boat slid down the trough of a wave, and reappeared when they crested. At first, she thought it could be a small aircraft, but as the minutes passed and it did not get any larger, she dismissed that idea. She wondered if it could be a bird, even though it seemedunlikely. They were a thousand miles from the nearest land. An albatross could cover such a distance, she thought, although she also knew they only flew in the southern hemisphere and the Pacific. Grateful for the break in monotony, she continued to watch the small dot as it slowly got closer. It *was* a bird, she decided.

"Kate, there's a bird following us," she announced.

"There are no birds out here," said Kate dismissively.

"Look over there," Beth nodded in the direction with her head, "twenty degrees off our port quarter."

Kate did not answer.

"Do you see it?" Beth asked.

"Yes," came the flat reply from behind her. "It's a damned seagull."

"I think it's an arctic tern. I can see the black head and the white and grey body," said Beth, excitedly.

"A damned seagull then," muttered Kate.

"Terns aren't gulls," retorted Beth. "Arctic terns are beautiful. They fly thousands of miles over the oceans."

Kate remained silent.

Beth continued to watch the tern with growing excitement as it flew closer and closer to their small boat. It skimmed over the rolling waves, gliding for the most part, its red bill a flash of welcome color against the dark blues of the sea and the blue of the sky.

"I think it's going to land on the boat," cried Beth excitedly. "It must be desperate for a place to rest."

"It had better not," warned Kate darkly. "I hate seagulls."

"It's not a seagull."

"It's a filthy seagull," Kate hissed. "It's not landing on my boat."

"Why not?" Beth shot back sharply. "It'll be nice to have a distraction after fifteen of the dullest days of my life. And the *Derry Girl* is not your boat, it's our boat."

The tern banked left and steered to land ungracefully on the stern, a few feet in front of Beth, where it flopped down.

"Get it off!" Kate screamed from behind her. "Get it off my boat!"

"Calm down, for God's sake!" Beth called. "What the hell is the matter with you? The bird looks exhausted; it's just stopped for a rest."

Kate grabbed Beth's right shoulder, struggling to get past her in the narrow boat to the bird. Beth turned to push her back down on the front seat. Kate immediately rose again, brandishing her oar.

"GET OFF MY BOAT!" Kate screamed at the exhausted bird.

Beth tried to grab the oar but missed, the aluminum shaft catching her painfully on her right ear. Kate swung the oar again as Beth reeled, bringing the sharp carbon fiber blade down onto the back of the bird. Pushing past the stunned Beth, Kate smashed the oar down again and again on the prone tern, the sharp blade cutting deep through the now bloody feathers.

"Stop!" Beth yelled, grabbing the blood stained oar and twisting it away from the frenzied Kate.

Kate laughed, looking down at the bloody mess of the seabird. "That'll teach it!"

Beth stared in horror at the tern, its body cleaved in half by the sharp blade of the oar, one broken grey wing still vainly twitching even in death.

"You're a monster!" Beth cried in shock and disgust.

"Whatever," Kate spat, a sickly smile on her face as she stomped back to the cabin.

Day 19

Normally, they spent very little time together in the tiny, cramped cabin on the boat. The rowing shift patterns were optimized by algorithms; either one or both of them were always rowing. Shifts allowed for eight hours' sleep spread through twenty-four, but only when the other rowed. This allowed the cabin size to be reduced to a bare minimum. The system worked well, unless a storm made it unsafe to be out on the rowing deck.

Without the satellite phone, they had no warning of localized storms, and the one that now raged outside had struck quickly. Beth and Kate lay braced in their tiny bunks as the fierce wind battered the tiny boat and the heavy waves flung it around and broke violently over it. Although neither usually suffered from seasickness, the heavy, erratic churning of the ocean meant both of them were nauseated, despite preventive pills.

"This is all your fault," muttered Kate through gritted teeth, breaking a three-hour silence that started when they both abandoned the rowing deck as the storm hit them.

Beth looked across the narrow space between them. "What is?"

"This storm. If you'd have rowed harder, it would be behind us."

The statistics from Beth's watch showed a different story. The boat made slightly more headway when Beth rowed than when Kate did. Beth had never mentioned this, partly because it made no difference, and partly because she knew that Kate's own watch must be giving her similar statistics. She said nothing, tiredly closing her eyes as another wave slammed hard into their tiny vessel.

"I should have entered the race on my own," Kate continued.

Beth refused to answer the ridiculous comment, especially given that Windsor Gin Transatlantic Race only sponsored crews of two.

"I sometimes wish you'd get washed overboard," said Kate. "That I go to start my shift on the rowing deck and find you gone. Lost at sea. I would be so happy."

Beth clenched her fists so hard that she almost drew blood. She was not going to respond to Kate, no matter what. As early as day two on this hellish journey, she had thought that Kate needed some sort of psychiatric help, and since then her belief had hardened into conviction. The extent and depth of Kate's personality issues had become increasingly apparent over the journey, and begun to worry Beth. She was now seriously concerned for both their safety. Without the satellite phone, there was little she could do except row, and hope that Kate could keep it together until they reached England in twenty-two or so days.

Never had she wanted a race to end so much.

Day 20

Twelve hours after the storm first hit the boat, the winds suddenly died and the colossal rolling waves gradually receded. In the early light, the two emerged shakily from the cramped and stinking cabin to survey the damage. At first glance, *Derry Girl* seemed to have escaped lightly, with only the aluminum guardrails at the front bent inwards, and one of the rubber deck mats ripped off and lost. Then Beth noticed the missing AIS transceiver aerial. Her heart sank; without the whip aerial the Automatic Identification System would be unable to transmit their location, making other ships aware of their position. Aside from the safety concerns, loss of the aerial also meant the race organizers would have no way to track the *Derry Girl*.

"The AIS aerial has gone," said Beth flatly.

Kate stared at the broken stub on the forecastle. "Why didn't you take it down, you were last on deck?"

Beth shook her head, resigned. Of course, Kate would blame her. "The aerial is fixed to the boat. It's not designed to be taken down."

"I think the storm would disagree with you on that!" Kate fumed.

"It's not designed to be taken down," repeated Beth. "Those were bloody serious waves last night, in case you didn't notice."

"You should have taken it down!" Kate shrieked, jabbing her right index finger hard into Beth's chest. "Are you deliberately trying to sabotage us?"

Beth took a step back, out of finger jabbing range.

"Well, are you?" Kate demanded. "You've been sabotaging us from the start!"

"Kate, we are only halfway to England. We have half of the North Atlantic Ocean left to row, and I suggest you ram that pointing finger of yours all the way up your unwashed ass and see if you can use *that* for an antenna," Beth spat.

Day 26

"Get back out here!" Kate screamed from the deck outside.

Beth, tired from her four-hour shift, turned around from her bunk and squeezed back out through the small cabin door. "What now?"

Kate faced her, red with rage. "There's blood on your seat!"

Beth moved forward, looking to where Kate's finger angrily pointed. On the left-hand side of the white fiberglass thwart, a smear of dark blood showed in the failing dusk light.

"Yes, there is," she replied calmly.

"It's disgusting!" Kate cried. "Why the hell didn't you clean it up?"

Beth looked again at the small smear of blood, no more than two inches long and half an inch wide. "I must have missed it. I cleaned up the rest, but it was going dark."

"It's disgusting," repeated Kate.

"Disgusting?" Beth said, even now still surprised by Kate's idiosyncrasies. "How?"

"Menstrual blood is disgusting!" Kate hissed.

Beth looked at her, bewildered. If she were less tired, she might have laughed. "For one, it's not menstrual blood. Even if it was, I can't understand why you would think it's disgusting. We're both women, and periods are a natural part of being a woman. Why is that disgusting?"

"It's just disgusting!"

Beth sighed deeply, having no energy left to continue arguing. Instead, she held out her hands to show Kate the dark scabs, dried blood and deep scarring around the stubby remains of her ruined fingernails. "This is where the blood is from."

Kate glanced at Beth's hands indifferently and shrugged, saying nothing.

"I've become so anxious and stressed over the past two weeks that I'm biting my nails. I can't seem to stop, and my fingers are a bloody mess. I'm getting worse, and I'm not sure how long I can continue like this."

Kate pushed past her towards the cabin. "Just tell me when you've cleaned up the mess you left, and I'll come back out to row."

Day 31

Beth stopped rowing halfway through her solo evening shift. Her nails were gone; she couldn't bite them to relieve her anxiety anymore. All her waking thoughts now centered solely on getting away from the living hell that the *Derry Girl* had become. Not on her loving partner, waiting for her, not her family and friends, not her successful rowing career, just the twenty-two feet of the boat, and the demon with which she shared it.

She shuffled over to the starboard side and looked over the water, which for once wascalm and almost still. Her reflection stared back; haggard, gaunt, and unfamiliar. She hardly recognized herself. When Alzheimer's disease claimed her grandfather, his decline had been slow and steady, taking years before the person she knew and loved became absent. Her own mental decline, in contrast, had taken just thirty-one days. Just a month, to put her in the bleakest place she had ever been. Whether or not she could hold it together for another fortnight before reachingEngland, she had no idea.

Something in the water caught her attention. A few feet from the boat, a dead fish floated. A cod, large and bloated, its once sleek scales ruined by decay, a green-tinged hole in its flank spilling dark stinking guts. The sickly stench of decomposition wafted up, obliterating the usual fresh smell of the sea. A single milky dead eye, soft and flaccid with putrefaction, stared up at her.

Try as she might, she found herself unable to break the stare. Something dark seemed to be reaching out to her from the depths, penetrating her mind through the stare of death. She let the corrupt tendrils creep in, flowing into her consciousness.

Sometime later, the presence withdrew, returning to the depths as the fetid fish slowly sank beneath the surface. She slid back to the center of the seat and began rowing; her mind filled with purpose and clarity on what she needed to do.

Day 37

"Ahoy there!"

Beth looked up, pausing her rowing.

"Ahoy *Derry Girl*!"

She recognized the voice and British accent immediately and turned to see the boat of Dan Moy and Tony McAllister approaching from starboard. Pulling in her oars, she stood shakily.

"We hoped to catch you up after you passed us a month ago!" shouted Moy from the forecastle. "Do you fancy that cup of tea now?"

Beth remained silent, watching them wearily as they pulled alongside.

"I say," said McAllister, "are you alright?"

"Not really," she replied. "My rowing partner must have fallen overboard last night. I've been rowing around for the last three hours but there's no sign of her."

"My God!" cried Moy. "Have you sent the emergency signal?"

"The satellite phone got dropped overboard in the second week, and a storm tore off the IPERB aerial."

"Did she have her life jacket on?" asked McAllister.

"No. Nor her protective rowing gear either."

"Damn," said Moy. "I'm so sorry."

"Look, come on board with us, it's no good being alone waiting for rescue to come and pick you up. I'll put the kettle on for some tea," McAllister said, grabbing the side of the *Derry Girl* so she could board.

Beth nodded her thanks. As she rose from the rowing seat, she noticed a small bloody glob of Kate's brains on the thwart. She must have missed it whilst cleaning earlier. She casually flicked it overboard, then crossed over to the

British boat.

The Next Stop
by
Harley Carnell

"We'll get off at the next stop," one of the women opposite me said.

"The next stop," the other agreed.

It was early, although it would be late soon. The last dregs of sunlight were trickling away from the sky. I had been surprised to get a seat when I got on the train, so much so that I had to quickly check that I was on the right one. Although I had purposely stayed later at work to avoid the rush hour, there were always a few people left over, a rush hour remnant.

I checked my phone, to see if I had the right time. Had the clocks maybe gone forward without me knowing? My head was so gone recently that it was not beyond the realms of possibility.

But no. Right time, right train.

Looking out of the window confirmed it. The same smudge of scenery seeping against the glass. The factories, the sad houses crammed together, and the smoke spewing into the air.

This, I had to incant to myself, as always, is why you are on this train. This is why you are taking this two-hour journey; to escape what's outside the window. I thought of the time, in around thirty minutes, when the hills and trees would at last blossom into view.

I looked down at my phone again—dead, and would not be revived with a tap. I was sure that I'd had enough battery when leaving work, but perhaps I'd misread the percentage bar.

With nothing else to do, I decided to eavesdrop. The woman on the left said to the woman on the right:

"Did you get it in the end?"

The woman on the right responded:

"Oh, no! I tried to, but I couldn't. Isn't that always the way?"

"Yes, always the way!"

I groaned internally. An hour and a half with no phone and not even a good conversation to listen to.

As we approached the next station, the first woman said:

"Are we getting off here?"

The second one thought about it for some time and then shook her head.

"The next one," she said.

When we pulled into the station, which was the last in the city, I noticed that there was nobody on the platform. This was *very* strange. Even late in the night—so late it was early in the morning—you would expect to see at least a few people. I had once worked an early shift, coming into the city on the 4:30 a.m. train, which had been packed even then.

I checked my phone again, to see if the station had been closed or there had been an accident (sometimes people died on the tracks), before remembering the phone had died. It was funny, not only how reliant we were on our phones, but how instinctual and unthinking this reliance was.

For a second, I thought I saw a flicker of motion at the

corner of my eye, in the carriage next to ours. When I looked more closely, there was nothing there. It was obviously some sort of a trick of the light. The other carriage was empty.

"How's your head?" the woman on the right asked the woman on the left.

"Oh, it's still bad," she said, rubbing her forehead and laughing.

"You still feel cloudy?"

"As a storm!" she said, and they both laughed.

That was funny. Because my own head was feeling a little funny, too. Had been for some time. My thinking was not always clear, or linear. In my more naïve, doe-eyed days, I'd even tried to book a doctor's appointment for it, but you couldn't book doctor's appointments now.

Perhaps I could tell this woman about my head. Maybe it would give us something to talk about. Then again, I didn't want to be trapped in conversation with them, or for them to feel that they were with me.

"Here it is," said the woman on the right.

"Are we getting off here?"

"No, the next stop."

This stopped me. Frowning, I turned around and saw that we were indeed pulling into a station. Although I was usually buried in my phone or a book, and did not know the precise intricacies of every stop, I knew that the first one out of the city was at least fifteen minutes away.

When I looked out of the window, aside from seeing another empty platform, I also saw a sign for a station that was neither on my route nor one whose name I even recognized.

I was on the wrong train.

I was about to get up, but the doors had shut and I would have to wait for the next stop. God knew when that would be. Once you left the city, where you became accustomed to stops with staccato frequency, you could go as long as half an hour, forty-five minutes, between stops.

I felt like I could cry when I wondered what time I might get home now.

I was about to ask the two women if they could tell me where we were, when I heard a noise behind me.

Behind me was the toilet. I had been vaguely aware of it being occupied since I'd boarded the train. I had not thought much of it. Train toilets were not so much used as toilets, as they were private carriages for ticketless youths, hiding from the conductor. I just assumed that some kid was in there on his phone waiting until his stop came.

Yet apparently, the person in there was ill. They sounded like they were vomiting, or at least frantically trying to clear something from their throat.

The two women opposite me laughed. The one on the left said something that caused them both to howl with laughter.

"Oh yes," the woman on the right said. "It wasn't right for weeks after that." Then, slowly, her smile seeped away. "That was twenty years ago."

The woman on the left's face was equally drained.

"Twenty years." She shook her head. "And it only happened yesterday."

"Excuse me," I called out. They turned to me.

"Hi, I'm really sorry to bother you."

"Not at all," said the woman on the left. "We're getting off at the next stop."

"Yes," said the woman on the right. "That's us."

"And what is the next stop, if you don't mind me asking?"

The two women stared at me blankly.

"Sorry," I said. "It's just, my phone—my phone's gone, it's died. I'm on the wrong train."

"How did you do that?" the woman on the left asked.

"I don't know," I said. "I mean, I thought I was on the right one, when I first got on. I must have made a mistake. My head, it's not been right recently, you know. I must've read the board wrong. What train is this?"

The two women didn't answer.

"Where's it going?"

I thought that I was going to get another set of blank looks, but the woman on the right responded:

"It's going where it always goes."

"And where it's always gone," the woman on the left clarified.

"And where is that?" I asked, struggling to restrain my frustration. When I got no answer, I asked: "Could I just borrow one of your phones, please? Just so I can see how I'm going to get back home."

The women clutched their bags close to them.

Above us, a pre-recorded announcement said:

"Please be aware that pickpockets operate in this area. Be sure to keep all your belongings and all you hold dear close to you. Thank you!"

"We're getting off at the next stop," the woman on the left said; the woman on the right nodded. Then, they burrowed back into their conversation as if I wasn't there.

I sat in silence, waiting for the next announcement. Maybe it would tell me where we were. It was only at this point that I realized how dark it had gotten. It was not quite pitch black yet, and I could still make out some of the scenery, but visibility was disappearing fast. And what visibility I had left was, or had to be, illusory. There were shapes in the dark that couldn't have been correct. It was almost as though buildings were upside down, and trees (or things that moved like trees) were in the sky. Lights flickered in one place and then were seen in another a few seconds later. Then I saw a congregation of shadows that seemed to be prostrating up to the sky.

I needed something to eat. I was trembling from low blood sugar, and that must have been responsible for transmogrifying whatever I had seen outside into this nonsense. My head was shuddering. When I reached into my bag, I screamed. There had been slight movement and then, suddenly, a creature that looked like a rat scuttled away faster than I could follow it with my eyes. Then, it poured itself like water under the train door and was gone, out into the night.

Shaking, I opened my bag. Then, I swore to myself.

The bar of chocolate I'd bought was completely destroyed. Other than tattered remnants of the wrapper, it had completely disappeared. The rat had gotten to it. I then had another thought. Swearing again, I ripped open the front compartment of my bag. Instead of the stack of purchase orders and invoices I needed to work on tomorrow morning, I was met with confetti.

Or, rather, shreds. Because it looked more like the intricate, chaotic jaggedness of the industrial shredder we used at work for highly sensitive documents. Looking at the paper as it seeped like sand through my fingers, I shuddered to think at the kind of teeth that could have done this.

"That's why you never leave anything on the floor," Right said to me. I looked up at her.

"There's things out there," Left continued. "Things you can't even imagine."

Right nodded.

"And they get in, you know. You won't always see them, but believe me when I tell you that they get in."

"Well, what are they?" I asked.

Both women laughed.

"Oh," said Left. "You don't want to know that, not if you don't already."

Right nodded.

"It's much better for you, if you're on here, that you

don't know what goes on out there."

"But where are we? Is this one of those old lines? I've heard about them. They go through old places, where people don't live. You get things that live in cellars and places, abandoned buildings. Rats that grow as big as dogs. Animals that breed with each other and create strange new ones. Is that it? Do they come out to the trains to get food?"

The two women gave each other a look and then shook their heads.

"This is our stop," Left said.

I turned around and saw that we were pulling into a train station. It was lit by a solitary light that shuddered on and off. Even when it was fully on, it only gave scant illumination of what seemed to me less like a train station and more like a solitary bus stand in the middle of an abandoned factory's grounds.

"No," said Right. "We're getting off at the next stop."

"Yes!" said Left, laughing. "Of course. The next stop. Just like always."

I, however, *was* getting off at this stop. If nothing else, I would be able to ask one of the staff on the platform to tell me where I was. Maybe I'd have to bankrupt myself getting a cab back home, or spend a night in a questionable train station hotel, but at least I wouldn't be on the train any longer.

As I was getting off, one of the women called out something to me. Perhaps they were trying to get me to reconsider. I ignored them.

When the train stopped, I opened the doors and stepped outside. My impression from inside the train was confirmed. There was a small patch of concrete where the train station's sign was implanted. Other than that, there was nothing. I couldn't see so much as a light in the distance or hear the faint groan of a faraway bus.

Then, suddenly, I was overcome with a feeling. I

struggled to describe it to myself, even as I was drowning in it. Not so much a sense of fear but one of overwhelming, all-encompassing dread. A sense of misery and hopelessness. It was the sort of feeling I imagined you might have after all your hopes and dreams were swept out from under you at once, as opposed to the slow erosion that tended to happen. The sensation was so intense I was almost doubled over with it. I wanted to fall to the platform and weep. My nerves shuddered like a spiderweb in the wind.

Then, I looked back at the train. I jumped, when I saw the two women at the window. At first, I thought that they were screaming at me. Then, I saw that they were pointing to something behind me, warning me about it, and beckoning me to get back on the train. Without thinking, I rushed back to the train. The doors began closing, and I had to all but leap through the narrowing gap. As I slid through, I felt something grab for me, although I wasn't sure if it was something from outside, or my coat getting caught on the door. The train began to speed away, and I heard a loud thump against the door behind me. It had been something outside, then.

"You got lucky there," Left said to me.

"Much better to be in here, where everything makes sense," Right averred.

"Are we going to get off at the next stop?" Left asked.

"The next stop," Right agreed.

I was panting, both from fear and the exertion of running back into the train. Then, I realized, the noise I was hearing wasn't me panting. Rather, it was the person in the toilet, who was not panting but crying. He was saying something which at first I couldn't make out, but then realized was repeated utterances of 'Oh, God! Oh, God!" interspersed with hacking tears.

"Is he okay?" I asked the women.

"Him?" said Left, gesturing to the toilet. "I wouldn't

have thought so, no."

"Oh yes, I think we can safely say that nothing is ever going to be all right with him ever again," said Right, solemnly.

I was about to ask her what she meant and how they knew this guy, when I saw another shadow out of the corner of my eye. When I turned to face it, I saw that it wasn't a shadow, but a man, walking through the other carriage. Judging by his uniform, he was a conductor of some sort. Even if that uniform was incredibly shabby, looking like it had been stolen from a factory fire.

The conductor was moving from seat to seat in the empty carriage adjacent to ours. He appeared to be asking the non-existent people for tickets, and carrying a manually-cranked ticket dispenser that I did not think existed anymore outside of retro TV dramas.

Suddenly, the conductor turned in my direction. He mouthed something that looked a lot like a swear word and then began walking towards me. I might have been more concerned, especially as I didn't have the correct ticket, but at least I would be able to ask him what was happening. Although I would have to wait for the next stop, as, contrary to what I assumed were fairly set-in-stone safety rules (one of which warned of death for such excursions), the conductor ripped open the door of the other carriage and then climbed across into ours. He began pacing towards me. I was about to say something when he walked straight past me, and reached into his pocket for what I saw was a fob or electronic key of some sort. Using it, he unlocked the toilet door and then ripped it open.

"Oh, yeah?" the conductor said. "Oh, yeah?"

From inside the cubicle, I heard a loud shriek.

"Going to take you to see the driver," the conductor said.

"No. God no! Please!"

Then, there was another shriek. The conductor exited the toilet with a man who appeared to be in his forties. The conductor was pulling the man by his hair (although the conductor had such a tight clutch on him that it was more like his scalp), as he dragged him through the train. I turned to the women; both were looking down, purposely avoiding eye contact. I would like to say that I intervened; that I shouted something; that I at least made a pretense at helping. But I did nothing.

Not only was I not quite sure what was happening, the conductor was huge and was grinning as he dragged the man, looking like he was having the time of his life. He also reeked of alcohol and some sort of strong coppery concoction. It may have been shameful and cowardly of me, but in my defense, I couldn't see any other outcome from my heroics apart from my lying on the floor in a pool of my own blood and teeth.

The conductor opened the door to the other carriage and dragged the screaming man along with him. As he was pulled through the train, his shouts for help gradually dimmed to complete silence. I turned to the women.

"What happened?" I said. "We have to get out of here."

"Oh, there's no getting out of here," said Left.

"You shouldn't have got on," said Right.

"But I didn't get on!" I said, almost petulantly. "At least, not deliberately. I didn't realize…I thought that…"

"It doesn't matter what you meant to do, or what your intentions were." said Right. "You did what you did, and now you're here."

"No," I said. "No, I want to get off. I'll get off at the next stop."

The two women smiled at each other. At first, I thought that they were doing so mockingly, but then I realized that it was a sympathetic look. They felt sorry for me.

Under normal circumstances, I would not have liked to be pitied. Now, I was too shaken to think of anything other than fear.

"That time has long passed," said Left. "Once you're on here, you're on here, I'm afraid."

"Besides," said Right, "look outside."

I was about to protest, saying that there would be nothing but darkness, but then I saw the sea. Now, it was my turn to smile. It was obviously some kind of optical illusion. Or, perhaps, given the late hour and the stress of everything that had happened, and given my head, it was an outright delusion.

Because what I saw in front of me was a sea of cascading waves. A sea that was frothing and chomping at itself. A sea whose waves flung themselves as high as skyscrapers, tearing at the sky above and clawing at clouds.

I heard screams from this sea. I realized that this was the wind howling against it, as if the two were fighting each other in some great elemental battle. I remembered a poem I had read once—"When the Oceans Come to Me in My Dreams"—although I did not remember who it was by, or where I had read it, or if it even existed.

As I looked closer into the sea, I saw what at first I thought were lights, perhaps stars reflecting, but then realized there was a teeming highway of unseemly sea creatures. They were not like anything I had ever seen. Fish with a constellation of eyes sprayed across their faces. Things that would have caused a shark to shudder, with teeth so crammed into their mouths they were spilling out and poking through the skin. There was something that resembled a jellyfish, only it was nearly the size of an elephant and through its transparent skin I could see thousands of little creatures swarming and screaming. A giant, spiderlike crab thrashed through the sea like a combine harvester. And from the sea, I saw a large plume of smoke, as though it was boiling, or steaming.

I quickly checked the tops of the windows, to make sure that they were definitely closed. They were, although I had an irrational fear that a particularly large wave might come crashing towards us and open them, washing in whatever horrors were outside.

At first, I thought I saw thousands of little fish bobbing in and out of the water, like atoms popping in and out of existence. When I looked closer, I saw that they were bubbles. It then occurred to me how hot it was. Both the women had removed their coats, and one of them was taking off her jumper too. I was sweating, and imagined that my white work shirt was now see-through with sweat.

"Do you see now why you can't leave?" Left asked me.

"But I want to," I said. "I don't want to be here."

"It's all the same either way," she responded. What she said made no sense, but I understood completely what she meant.

Suddenly, my ears began to ring and then they popped. I turned outside and saw that we were in a tunnel.

I wasn't sure if it was because of this, or simply because we were no longer next to the steaming sea, but I was freezing. My cooling sweat did not help, either. I began scrubbing at my arms with my hands, desperate to get warm. My teeth chattered. I shivered. Then, as my temperature plummeted even further, I felt as if I had been punched in the stomach. I bent forward and groaned.

Around me, the lights in the train began to dim. It was so dark that I could barely see my hands. Above me, there was a muffled announcement over the speakers. I couldn't hear what was said, although it sounded like it had come from a voice rusted with screaming.

One of the women said something to me. I could not see which one it was, as they were both fully slithered into sleeping bags and seeped into the dark.

"Sorry?" I said.

"Next stop's not until the morning," one of them said.

"We're getting off then," said the other.

I was about to ask what she meant when I felt a hand on my shoulder. I screamed, and felt like doing so again when I saw that it was the conductor leering down at me. I was grateful that his breath stank of alcohol, as I did not want to have to encounter the rot it was clearly struggling to mask. I remembered my time in the hospital – the losing battle the industrial-strength cleaners fought against the decay and death.

"Have you got your ticket, sir?"

"Oh, no, look. Let me explain. I got on at—"

"That's what I thought. Let's go see the driver, my friend."

"No, look, you need to listen, I—"

Before I could say anything else, he stood me up and grabbed me so hard by the shoulder I could not breathe.

"Yes, my friend," said the conductor, chuckling. "We'll go and see our driver, and we'll have a lovely old chat."

As I was dragged through the carriage, I heard the tunnel roaring, and the women screaming, as the conductor began to laugh and whistle.

Godfather Poker
by
Jane Nightshade

An elderly man lost control of his bowels some-where outside of Lodi. He was seated on the aisle, near the back of the Greyhound, but the smell per-meated the whole bus, even up near the desirable left-hand front window seat that Ethan had managed to secure.

Most passengers groaned, waving their fingers like a folding fan or pinching their noses. Those with window seats slid the small, slat-like glass down as far as it could go. Blasts of heat rushed through the openings; it was early summer in the Central Valley of Northern California, and the temperature was in the triple digits.

"Lawdy!" cried a booming woman's voice. "I need a man to come help this gentleman to the toilet! I need some-one to get him into some clean pants! Is anybody gonna help me?"

Ethan stared back down the aisle that separated the two sides of the bus. A hefty black woman attired in a pris-tine, butter-yellow pantsuit and matching yellow fedora-style hat was standing up and gesticulating at the seat across the aisle from hers.

She caught his eye. "I can't do it myself, young man! I'm a Christian lady!" she pleaded. "Tell the driver and get him to stop for a clean-up," said a man, turning around to face her.

"Are you crazy? It's Greyhound. They don't stop for nothin' 'less you're dyin'. And even then, it's a crapshoot if they'll stop," squawked a methy-looking white girl in her twenties.

No one stepped forward to help. Ethan sighed. His head hurt, and he was still in a brain fog, trying to recover from that insane bender he'd had the night before, partying and playing cards with Johnny Featherweight and other guys from their dorm to celebrate the end of the term.

He recalled that Johnny gave him some really bad shit he'd never taken before—ayahuasca—because he couldn't remember anything after taking what Johnny offered.

Now, however, he felt like he had to act, no matter how bad he felt. It was either help the man himself or feel guilty about it for the rest of the trip—the full eight hours to Los Angeles.

Plus, the bus now smelled bad. Really bad.

Ethan stood up and walked back toward the elderly man and the woman in yellow. The whole passenger list seemed to let out a collective sigh of relief as they watched him go. The old man was sitting in his soiled pants, crying so softly that it was barely audible. He looked up at Ethan pitifully and mumbled, "I'm a retired investor, living on a pension."

Ethan thought that sounded weirdly familiar, and then he realized it was a quote from *The Godfather, Part II.* He smiled wryly and thought, *the old man is totally bonkers.*

Aloud he said, in a halting tone, his head still totally betraying his reason, "I'm going to get you to the toilet, sir, so that you can get cleaned up. Do you have some other pants somewhere?"

The old man stopped crying long enough to point to the overhead cabinet across the aisle, where the woman in yellow stood. She moved aside, and Ethan rummaged around in the compartment until he grabbed a shabby duffel bag.

"This one?" he asked. The old man nodded. Ethan slung the duffel bag over one shoulder and, with his free arm, pushed and pulled the man gently until they found the toilet at the back of the bus. The tiny facility was not big enough for two people, so Ethan blocked the door open with his back, tilting forward.

"No one can see you, sir," he whispered. "My back's in the way." He leaned as much as he could and helped the man remove his pants and ancient, soiled underwear and pushed him gently to sit down on the toilet. The smell was awful; the old man had diarrhea, and his skinny legs were covered with it.

Ethan spoke as calmly as he could: "Please wet some paper towels in the sink so I can help you clean up, sir. I can't reach the sink from here."

The old man looked like he was about to cry again. "I'm a retired investor, living on a pension."

Ethan grunted in frustration and tried to push across the man to get to the sink and the paper towels himself. He fell forward onto the old guy and somehow hit his head on the small counter where the sink was embedded. And then he fell into a kind of darkness, his head throbbing with pain and his nose clogged with the smell of bodily waste.

***

Ethan blinked hard; his head felt like tiny imps were hammering his skull from the inside. Somehow, he was back in his seat—the window seat, second row from the front, on the left-hand side of the bus.

He realized that this was wrong, and he wondered what had happened. He squeezed his eyes hard and tried to focus his mind, and finally he started to remember the old man and the toilet and the yellow-garbed "Christian lady" pleading for help. He caught sight of a billboard outside his window:

"Leaving Lodi. Y'all Come Back Now."

What the fuck? He'd seen that billboard before. He'd seen it just prior to the moment the old man had crapped his pants—and before he'd fallen and smashed his skull against the sink counter in the toilet and blacked out.

But that had been in the late morning, just before noon. Now, the sun was dipping much lower in the bright sky outside; it was midafternoon. How was the Greyhound still rolling along, but only just outside of Lodi?

His stomach twisted, emphasizing his confusion. He turned in his seat and spotted the elderly man he had helped earlier, sitting in the back row, staring blankly ahead. The smell was gone. Maybe the same person who'd moved Ethan to his seat had cleaned up the old man and put on his fresh pants.

Ethan scanned the other side of the aisle and caught the eye of the woman in yellow. She gave him a cold stare, like she was mentally asking, *why is that weird white guy staring at me?*

There was nothing in her manner that read gratitude for the help he'd tried to give the old man—the help that she'd pleaded for him to offer.

Ethan dropped his eyes. He stood up and stumbled a bit, lurching toward the old guy. "Sir?" he croaked. "How are you doing? I tried to help you to the toilet, and then I fell and cracked my head. I see you were helped by some-body else—" Ethan stared down at the man's pants. It was the same pair he'd been wearing before, except that they were not soiled now.

It was the *same* pair; he felt it in the pit of his stomach.

The old man turned his blank-looking gaze toward

Ethan and said, "I'm a retired investor, living on a pension."

Ethan face-palmed. The old dude still thought he was a character from *The Godfather, Part II.* Maybe his spare pants were the same color and style as the soiled ones. That was the only explanation he could think of.

He turned across the aisle toward the woman in yellow.

"Ma'am," he said politely. "We spoke earlier. Remember? You wanted me to help that gentleman to the toilet, after he had an accident with his bowels."

The woman eyed him with suspicion, then shook her head firmly. "It's between the brothers, Kay," she said in a frosty voice.

"What?" Ethan asked. "I'm sorry, I didn't understand you, ma'am. Don't you remember me and the old man? The diarrhea attack? I mean, it's pretty hard to forget something like that."

"That's my family, Kay, that's not me," the woman said, still distrustful.

What the fuck? Does everyone here think they are a Godfather character?

Ethan turned to the skinny girl who'd spoken out before about how hard it was to get a Greyhound bus to stop for anything.

"You remember it, don't you?" he asked, his voice rising in desperation. "The old man, the smell, the toilet? Anything?" He gave her a pleading look, hoping for some kind of sympathy, although he wasn't sure he deserved it. Something dreadful was nagging his mind.

The girl scratched her head, regarding him intently. Her lips, pierced with a metal stud, formed the word "yes." But what came out was different. What came out was, "I know it was you, Fredo. You broke my heart."

The bus jolted slightly as it hit a pothole, and a fresh wave of pain surged through Ethan's skull. He pressed his hand to his forehead. He began to panic.

Something is wrong here, he thought. *Very wrong. Horribly, impossibly, hideously wrong. These people aren't real. They're demons, they're devils—or something like that. Denizens of hell.*

Suddenly he heard Johnny Featherweight's voice, talking to him from last night: "Some people see actual demons when they take ayahuasca. It's a very unpredictable drug."

Apparently it hadn't worn off yet, as he'd thought when he boarded the Greyhound that morning. Apparently, it came back.

That was it. Demons. He had to get away from the bus, anyway, anyhow.

He stumbled to the driver's cabin, where a jolly-looking Latino man sat at the wheel, humming along to a country song on the radio.

"Hey! Stop the bus," Ethan demanded. "Something is weird here. I don't feel good. Something bad is gonna happen to me, I can feel it. I took some weird shit last night, shouldn't have done it, but now—"

The driver stopped humming, but barely glanced at him. "We're stoppin' soon, bro. Very soon."

Thank God. The man is actually talking to me. Maybe I'll get some answers.

Ethan grabbed the driver's shoulder lightly, his pulse thundering. "Why are we stopping, sir?"

The driver turned to him with a big smile. "Stopping? . . .It's the smart thing to do. Tessio was always smarter."

Ethan felt cold all over. He had no idea what to do. Maybe he should slump down into his seat, drag his jacket over his head, and hope that the demons would stop tormenting him somehow?

He looked back at all the passengers, scanning their

faces. They met his glance with stone-faced stares. This wasn't real. This couldn't be real.

The bus chugged on, the faded, double-lane blacktop stretching ahead, endlessly, through field after field of corn, tomatoes, and alfalfa. Ethan backed into his seat, gripping the seat in front of him. What now?

Something hopeful pushed its way into the forefront of his reasoning.

The toilet. He would lock himself in it until the bus either stopped or reached Los Angeles—or until it was safe to sit down again in his seat, when the demonic, Godfather-quoting passengers would be gone, as the ayahuasca finally wore off.

He hoped.

Trembling and fearful, Ethan pushed himself up and stumbled toward the back of the bus. He flung the bathroom door open and stared at the cramped, dimly lit space. The toilet gleamed dully under the fluorescent light. There was no sign of the old man's soiled pants and underwear, which he'd helped remove.

He closed the door of the tiny cubicle, locked it, and sat on the toilet. He found a way to turn off the fluorescent light and waited in the dark. And waited some more, anxiety bursting out of his innards like the xenomorph in *Alien*.

Finally, he felt the bus lurch to a stop. *Thank God.* Maybe he could make a run for it just dash toward the doors as fast as he could and push them open before ol' country music smiley-man could stop him. He wouldn't even grab his duffel bag. He figured he'd find a way to hitchhike home, maybe cage some money and borrow a phone from some sympathetic stranger for a call to Johnny. Johnny owed him, big time. That fucking drug. He knew it was bad news. And Johnny was supposed to be his best bud. The shitbag.

Suddenly, he heard new noises from his perch on the

toilet—it sounded like more passengers were boarding the bus. And they were loud and big, stomping in heavy-treaded boots down the aisle.

He wondered who the hell they were. And *where* the hell they were. Probably long past Lodi. The hitch back home to Sacramento would be a long one, assuming he was able to get off the bus.

Then he heard the screams. Terrible, terrifying screams. "No, don't, I can't think—I don't know!" *More screams.* And pounding against the windows, as if the screaming people were trying to get away.

Ethan put his hands to his ears and tried to block out the sound. But it still came through, loud and clear, and pools of sweat dripped off his face and into his lap, and his hands were trembling as he pushed them as hard as he could against his ears.

Someone was screaming his name. "Ethan! Don't—I can't think of anything right now. No, no, no!"

What the fuck? Who knew his name? He hadn't told anyone, not even the old man he had intimately undressed. Something was after him. He was right.

The stomping heavy boots—they were treading to the back rows, coming closer—closer to the toilet. Ethan shrank against the sink, trying to make himself smaller.

"I'm a retired investor, living on a pension," Ethan heard the old man he'd helped croak out loudly in terrified tones.

"Good job," answered a harsh, metallic voice. "You get to live."

A woman screamed. "It's between the brothers, Kay!" she stammered loudly, panicking. Listening from the toilet, Ethan recognized the voice of the woman in yellow. He put a hand to his mouth to keep from screaming himself.

"Very good again," barked another voice, cold and steely. "You also get to live."

"Leave the gun, take the cannoli!" yelled another passenger.

And another: "Can you get me off for old time's sake, Tom?"

And another: "Never go against the family again."

And chillingly, "I don't know, I can't think of anything. Don't—" More horrified screams. The sound of something thrusting, something thudding, again and again. "Oh, please God, no, no, no . . ."

Then, silence. A deadly, chilling silence.

And heavy boots stomping, stomping, to the door of the toilet, finding his hiding place. A heavy rap on the door.

"Ethan Avery? Are you there, Ethan Avery?"

Ethan's blood pounded in his temples. He heard it rushing in his ears. He pulled his knees up to his chest, his arms wrapped tightly around them. He held his breath.

They know my name. They know my name! Demons!

Heavy boots thudded against the locked door, again and again. Ethan lost control of his bowels. If he had been less frightened, he would have appreciated the irony of the embarrassing, uncomfortable moment. Somewhere, a faded, demonic voice crackled. But all he could really concentrate on were the heavy boots pounding against the door of the toilet.

Crack! The flimsy door and its cheap lock gave way.

In the doorway stood a tall figure with impossibly broad shoulders, wearing some kind of black armor that covered its face. Menacing dark goggles covered the eyes.

Behind that figure appeared to be two more black-clad heads, looking over the first one's shoulder.

"Ethan Avery," rang out a harsh voice, "we have just one question for you. I think you know what it is."

Ethan nodded, his lips quivering. His head was clearing. Something was coming into focus, he realized with growing dread. Through his mind flashed the memory of that last poker game, after he took the ayahuasca.

They were playing "Godfather Poker," which he and Johnny had invented. You had to recite a line of dialogue from either *The Godfather* or *The Godfather, Part II* before each round of play. (Quotes from the terrible *The Godfather, Part III* were disqualified.) It had to be a fresh line, too; no repeaters. And it had to be a recognizable line— nothing like "Pass the salt-shaker, Sonny." If you couldn't think of one, you forfeited that round. Most of the bros on their dorm floor were big fans of the two classic films, so they thought it would be a fun game.

Until Ethan took the ayahuasca. With a sickening thud in his gut, he remembered what happened then. His friends turned into demons. At least that's what he thought. Johnny was the biggest demon of them all, a scarlet face with tongues of fire blazing out of his mouth.

He'd grabbed the large buck knife he always wore under his shirt and pulled it out. He'd kept demanding that the demons continue to recite lines from the two films. If they couldn't, he slashed repeatedly, with a rare, white-hot fury. He was a big young man. He easily carried out his tasks, even with four-to-one odds.

"I can't think of anything," Johnny had whispered pathetically, too scared to be able to think, when Ethan had cornered him, the blood of the first three victims dripping from his knife. And Ethan had said, "Forfeited, Demon," and killed him.

I killed Johnny Featherweight. I killed my best friend. And then I left my knife sticking straight out of his chest like the pointer on a sundial.

Ethan brought himself back to the present. Staring at the black-garbed figure looming over him as he sat on the toilet in jeans full of his own waste, Ethan felt his head clear even more. He realized dimly that the figure before him was wearing a SWAT uniform. They were policemen, not demons.

He searched his mind frantically, nevertheless. *Leave the gun, take the cannoli? No, it's been done. Never go against the family again? Done. That's my family, Kay . . .Done.*

Ethan held up his hands in front of his face, as if to ward off a blow.

"I can't think of anything," he whispered to the men in black.

Salvation (In the Eyes of the True Lord)
by
David Bartlett

Barry Horgan drove alone on the Nebraska interstate. Hypnotized by the highway and lost in a haze of rumination, he was *en route* to a late-night rendez-vous with an accommodating old friend he hadn't seen in a year. He could use the company.

Small hometown. University of Nebraska. Business Management. Social. Well-liked. A few close friends. That was Barry. Earl Anderson, with whom he was meeting to-night, was one of those close friends.

Barry graduated college two years ago and had been buckling beneath the weight of expectation ever since. That gnawing feeling that he should be doing more.

Why wasn't he doing more?

Until last year, these anxieties hadn't consumed Barry the way they did now. Until last year, there had been Han-nah. She had been the counterbalance he needed.

Barry picked up his cell phone from the passenger seat of his green Jeep Grand Cherokee and scrolled through his contacts. He dialed Earl's number. Barry's heart sank lower as each unacknowledged ring passed.

"Hi, you've reached Earl. You got my voicemail. Please leave a message and when I can, I'll get back to you."

Earl was the kind of man who put the "when I can" before the "I'll get back to you." Clear boundaries, no bull-shit. He liked that about Earl. Pleasant. But sharp.

Barry didn't bother leaving a message. He knew Earl was dependable. He didn't know why he felt so uneasy. So scared of being abandoned by someone who'd never do that to him. Probably.

He cranked up the radio volume to capacity to drown out his racing thoughts. He'd settled on an old country sta-tion some miles back. And it was "old" country for sure; his grandfather's country music.

As what would be the last song that he'd hear that night faded, the radio crackled violently and the signal was overwhelmed by a static on-rush. Barry huffed in frustra-tion.

"*Salvation!*" bellowed a voice from deep within the radio's fuzz. "You fall to your knees and you beg for it. You *plead* and you say, 'oh please, False Gods on High, please save me!' But the false gods and their heathen prophets who do not demand *realization,* children, and who do not demand adherence to the true path, they can offer you *nothing* in your time of need. They are false idols who *mock* your desperation, watching as it drives you to madness, laughing as you sink deeper into yourself until you are devoid of any self at all. And so, I say this: Let The *True* Lord into your life, for without *him,* you shall fester within these illusions—these *fantasies*!—of your own making. Repent! Repent and be saved, children!"

"Fuckin' garbage," Barry mumbled as he reached to change the station and escape this unwelcome interloper. However, as he scanned the dial, he found the same ex-hausting screed coming through static on every channel.

"The choice is yours, children! Find the glory of The True Lord or live hollow! Without the True Lord, we are but empty vessels shuffling, lost and alone, blind and deaf, down a road that stretches ahead endlessly into an oblivion of our own making. But you can be *saved*, children! You can bask in His one truth above all! And you can *illuminate* your life with the clarity of His light! Yes, I speak the purest of truths when I tell you that you can shine for eternity, illuminated by the most holy glory of the True Lord!"

At the conclusion of the preacher's bizarre sermon, the static on the radio surged to a furious, discordant climax. Barry winced. Then, just as the noise crescendoed to a dizzying staccato apex, a deafening *POP* burst forth fiercely from the Jeep's speakers like a firecracker detonating at close-range, just beyond the fuzz.

Barry leapt slightly in his seat, startled, and the Jeep swerved tightly to the right and then to the left. As he regained control of the car, everything fell into near-silence, with now only a low hum detectable beneath soft white noise.

Frustrated and frazzled in equal measure, Barry shut off the radio and drove in silence, corn stalks looming stoically on either side of the road like twin midnight phalanxes observing his lonely passage.

He thought about the preacher. He thought of the grim irony in having heard this man on the radio tonight preaching that he could be saved. After all, he'd spent most of the ride wondering if he was worth the air it took to keep him alive.

As he saw it, in what world was he worth saving when it was Hannah who could never be saved?

***

Barry saw a dilapidated billboard advertising The Weary Traveler's Diner, where he was to meet Earl, five miles ahead, just off the next exit. Time enough to again pick apart what could have happened that night between leaving home to grab pizza and when he returned.

He'd kissed Hannah, hopped in the Cherokee, and drove down the street to pick up the pizza. When he pulled back up fifteen minutes later to their rental, nothing had seemed out of the ordinary. He'd carried the pizza in, expecting to see her on the couch queuing up a movie. She chose the movies. He never really cared what they watched.

She wasn't on the couch.

"Hannah?"

He'd heard the bathtub running down the hall.

"Hannah? Come on now, I'm hungry." He remembered not being annoyed exactly, but certainly confused.

He saw the light was on in the bathroom, the door ajar. He remembered opening it all the way.

That was his last clear memory of that night.

Through the fog that clouded what he could remember, and shrouded what he could not, all that stood out with any clarity was that the bathwater was mixed with blood.

***

The ensuing year had been a blur—a hazy fugue state of muddled memories and indistinct actions. Barry pulled into the parking lot of the Weary Traveler, damming back the tears that always wanted to come, but seemed happy enough to never actually show up.

He hadn't been to this place since college, and actually hadn't seen Earl since Hannah's death. He couldn't begin to imagine how he'd thank Earl for meeting him so late. Earl wasn't there yet, though, and there were no other cars in the lot.

Barry's phone rang, jarring him back into the moment. He grabbed it, glancing at the caller ID. The screen was blank. No "Unknown Caller" or "Private Number" designation. Just blank.

"Hello?"

"Earl isn't going to be there," said an unknown voice.

"Who is this?"

"Leave the diner. Drive until the road forks. Just a few miles. Take the fork to the right," said the mystery man. He sounded hoarse. "Drive a little further, and at the next fork you see, take the path as far right as you can go."

"Sir, I didn't ask for directions, I asked you who you are."

"Answers lie ahead, child."

"What the hell is that supposed to mean?" His frustration was mounting.

There was no response. He looked down at his phone. The call had ended.

Barry was pissed. He was not going anywhere. No, he would simply sit in the lot and wait for Earl. And he would show. Earl was his very close friend—maybe his closest friend. Why would he listen to some anonymous lunatic over the promise of his closest friend?

He looked through both his windshield and the plate-glass front window of the Weary Traveler. Double layers of glass smudged the late-night tableau of the diner with an uncanny grime; the interior lighting was a jaundiced shade of yellow. There were no patrons and just one exhausted-seeming server behind the front counter, staring down at her phone.

Barry waited. He waited thirty more minutes. Nobody else pulled into the lot.

He started up the Cherokee and drove.

Barry drove those few miles until the road forked. He took the fork to the right as advised.

There were no streetlights. He turned on his high beams. The road was narrow and unpaved. He rattled along, feeling every bump, wondering why he'd never clocked this fork and road before. He'd been out this way enough times.

In truth, upon leaving the diner, any sense of familiarity he felt concerning his surroundings had evaporated. The world had shifted. His reality felt warped in a way he couldn't pin down.

As he drove deeper into his new unreality, small, run-down houses stood intermittently spaced on either side of him. They looked exhausted, standing sentry before asymmetrical, unkempt rows of corn, bent and crooked. Alive, but weary— the diametric opposite of the majestic, proud rows he'd driven past earlier.

Dim, orange light emanated from a few of the homes. It looked like candlelight. These, however, were the exceptions. Most were dark--a stifling, melancholy darkness. If anyone had ever been happy here, it was long enough ago that these houses could no longer remember any of their names.

That thought sat with him.

Barry came upon the second fork. It was a Y-shape, each branch roughly equidistant, barely wide enough for his Jeep. Curiously, at an almost 45-degree angle from the right prong, there was another road obscured partially by matted tangles of sagging corn stalks that led directly into the fields. This, it would seem, was the road he was meant to take, according to the voice on the phone. He began to drive. "Began" being the operative word. Because as soon as he turned onto the hidden road, his Jeep stalled.

"God *damn* it!"

He turned his key, but the engine didn't even sputter. The battery was completely dead. His only choice was to walk. He got out of his car, went around to his trunk, opened the hatch, and pulled out a tire iron. The weight of it in his hand helped to mitigate the fear that was rapidly seeping in and intermingling with his bone-deep despondence. He knew this was a psychological placebo effect, but at this moment, it was the best he could do.

He placed his cell phone in his jeans pocket, took a passing glance at the nearly-full moon above, and trekked forward.

***

Barry was surprised to find that the road was paved. There was even a rectangular, crooked sign on the roadside mounted upon a rusty metal pole. The original print had long since faded away, but something else was painted in its place in jagged, red capital letters:

"THE ROAD TO DAMNATION IS PAVED IN DE-NIAL."

Barry spit forth a joyless laugh and continued onward, kicking jagged pieces of loose pavement as he went. He made note of just how much darker this road was compared to the one before. Entering the cornfield, he felt enveloped in the same despairing blackness that smothered the abandoned houses.

The moon was gone. Dark above. Dark around. Dark within. He couldn't see the cornfields anymore, but he could hear wind rushing through the stalks. The night otherwise felt still. Nothing made sense.

The bleakness of his situation momentarily consumed him. This felt like a one-way trip.

Barry's phone started to ring. He was amazed he had any service at all. He wasn't far from the diner, or from civilization in general, but he felt like he was in another plane of existence.

Pondering this, he heard footsteps coming from further along the road. In the darkness, he couldn't pinpoint their location. His phone still ringing, he stopped walking, and he listened. He was unsure if the footsteps were ahead of him or behind him. He pulled his phone from his pocket and the same blank screen as before lit up what infinitesimal portion of the night that it could.

The footsteps picked up in intensity.

Barry's heart pounded. His grip intensified as he clutched the tire iron in his left hand. He answered the phone with his right.

"What?"

"Salvation is still within reach. The True Lord offers redemption even to those furthest from his embrace. It is their choice whether they choose to accept it. Oh yes. It is their choice."

Piecing together who exactly, inexplicably, he was speaking with, Barry responded.

"Yeah, I heard you on radio earlier saying that same bullshit, you son of a bitch."

The Preacher had already hung up before Barry finished speaking.

The footsteps seemed closer now, echoing from all directions at once. The darkness itself felt even more malevolent than before, swirling aggressively about him in endless swarms of ebony waves. He bellowed into the hostile void. It should have been cathartic.

And yet.

The footsteps, he finally determined, were in fact coming from behind him. They approached at a deliberate pace. They did not sound like his own footsteps though, trodden by work boots. These footsteps made a *CLOP-CLOP* sound he more closely associated with the hooves of a horse or a goat.

The gait sounded bipedal.

He ran in a blind panic further into the blackness. Despite being in a full sprint, and despite the methodical stride of the thing behind him, it seemed to be gaining ground. *CLOP.*

CLOP.

Just as the thing chasing him seemed to get within striking distance, all noise suddenly ceased. The footsteps were gone. The mysterious wind rustling the sickly corn- stalks was gone. He was in a vacuum.

He dropped to his knees, then to his hands and knees, the tire iron softly clanking at his side.

"If this…if this is about Hannah," he rasped to no one in particular, "I am so sorry. I would have helped. I know I could have…"

His voice fell from a rasp to a whisper. It fell to almost nothing at all.

Barry finally cried.

***

He had no idea how long he cried. And once he found the will to continue onward, he had no idea how much fur- ther he walked. He could hear the wind again. The tire iron swinging in his left hand, he moved with purpose. Deter- mination. He felt as though he was walking on air. He felt completely disassociated from reality itself, whatever "re- ality" meant anymore.

He no longer heard footsteps. Not his own and not those of his unseen companion.

Barry's phone rang again. He answered.

"What. Do. You. Want?"

"For you to be saved, child."

"I'm a man. Do not call me '*child*' again, you weird freak."

"We are *all* The True Lord's children."

"Cool. Original. You're very profound."

"Now, now," said the Preacher, "sarcasm is the last line of defense for the coward."

"If you say so, chief."

"We've bantered enough. You and I have matters to attend to. So please…do enter the church."

"What? What church?"

"Look up, then look ahead."

Barry raised his head and felt his eyes widen. A massive, wooden church stood before him. The doors were huge, two halves of a gargantuan archway. At once, a surge of red-orange light lit up the night from within the building. It radiated out from an oversized, stained-glass window that sat centered above the entryway.

The light illuminated the image on the window. It was that of a man nailed to a cross—not Jesus, but rather some other, unknown-to-Barry martyr. The painted man looked forlornly down upon him. Blood, depicted in red glass, dripped from his wounds into a river etched beneath. Blood mixed with water.

The warm radiance from within the church shone bright enough that Barry unconsciously averted his eyes and looked back down at the road. With his world now illuminated in amber, Barry quickly realized the impossible: There was no longer a road beneath his feet.

Barry stood outside space and time. Above, below, and on the edge of nothing.

He compartmentalized his terror and his awe before either or both could consume him and started forward. He took a beat to further compose himself, then ascended the front steps of the church and went inside.

***

He entered the vestibule, which was closed off from the main house of worship by a second set of doors. Barry spoke to The Preacher, who had remained silent on the line for some time while Barry processed all that was happening to him.

"Where am I?"

"You are in The House of the True Lord."

"That's not what I mean. What is any of this?"

"Come in, please, come in child."

"No."

"Your only hope for salvation is to enter The House of The True Lord. Only then can you achieve proper realization. Only then may he grant you salvation if he so chooses."

"Realization? *Salvation*? Answer me straight: Why am I here?"

"Because, child," said The Preacher, his calm voice a far cry from its earlier bombast. "You must understand who you are before you can even begin to hope for redemption."

"I know who I am."

"Are you sure?"

The Preacher hung up.

Barry opened the doors, left the vestibule, and entered the church.

The whole building was a dazzling, candlelit arena of the Lord. The True Lord, apparently. It overwhelmed him. There were hundreds of candles in sconces and candelabras of varying sizes. And yet, the corners of the church were enveloped in darkness. A darkness Barry implicitly understood to be the same as what was outside. It was a darkness that infected the light and then suffocated it in the same bleak hopelessness from which it grew and in which it thrived.

Countless rows of pews extended before him, and a red, carpeted center aisle led to a massive, elevated sanctuary with a broad, cherrywood pulpit. As he proceeded toward the pulpit, he noticed the pews were intermittently filled with kneeling, white-robed figures, their heads bowed, faces enshrouded by hoods. These figures materialized out of the ether as he approached each row. Not there, then suddenly there. He tried to chalk it up to a trick of the candlelight, but even the most logical part of his brain wouldn't buy that.

He tentatively approached the pulpit. Sitting upon it was a small, golden chalice. The chalice rested upon a white tablecloth. It was filled with a dark red liquid.

"The Blood of the True Lord, child," The Preacher boomed from somewhere above him. He turned and saw a majestic, curved balcony at the back of the church. He could make out the outline of a massive organ. It was the only area of the building the candlelight didn't touch at all.

A figure blacker than the blackness stepped forth from the rear of the balcony. It seemed to float weightlessly up to the lip of the guardrail, and then similarly floated downward with a controlled ease to the ground. It landed softly on the red carpet and began to approach the pulpit, its features clarifying into those of a man. The Preacher.

The Preacher wore a black blazer over a black button-up shirt. A black hat, its wide brim pulled low, obscured his forehead and brow. His eyes were hidden behind delicate, round black sunglasses, and his pants, socks and shoes were all as black as the corners of the church.

"Who...who are you? How did you do that?"

"Who am I? I am merely the humble emissary of the True Lord. All else can be explained by one thing: I believe in His majesty."

"Yeah, okay, I've had about enough of this." Barry raised the tire iron threateningly. At that, The Preacher halted his approach. He stood his ground in the middle of the aisle, and Barry stood his at the base of the sanctuary.

"Do you accept His offer? Do you accept your chance to be saved?"

"Do I have a choice?"

"Of course you have a choice. You can *choose* to

continue drowning. Or you can choose to embrace the truth and rise up from this sea of delusion. You can join the Flock of the True Lord and worship gloriously in his embrace."

"No. I won't be joining you, or whoever is out there in those pews…I won't be joining anyone or anything. I'm not buying whatever bullshit you're selling."

"I am not 'selling' anything. I freely offer you only His salvation. Why can you not see this?"

"Because you're a goddamn liar, that's why. You lied about Earl to get me out here to do whatever the hell *this* is, and like an idiot, I listened. I should've just waited for Earl like I damn well planned to. But no, I let you get into my *fucking* head."

"Oh child," sighed The Preacher piteously. "Earl Anderson is dead."

Barry's vision went white. He felt dizzy.

"What did you…what did you say?"

He felt something wet trickle lightly onto his hand. What started as a slow drip became a steady flow. He looked up and saw that the tire iron he held was bleeding profusely from the socket that capped the "L" bend.

"What did you do to me? Did you drug me? What the hell is happening to my…my tire iron?"

"Oh, that is not your tire iron, 'Barry.'"

The Preacher put a funny, almost sardonic emphasis on his name.

"While it certainly became your tool of sorts, it truly belongs to Earl Anderson. As does the Jeep. As did Hannah."

"You keep her name out of your mouth."

"Fine. That is fair. For now, then, let us discuss Earl Anderson."

"If it means I get some goddamn answers, then sure, discuss away."

"Earl Anderson," began The Preacher, "what do we *know* about Earl Anderson? Well, we know he graduated from the University of Nebraska with a degree in business management. We know he graduated two years ago, yet he couldn't find a steady job in his field."

"Stop."

Ignoring him, The Preacher continued.

"Earl had a girlfriend. We both know her name, don't we 'Barry?' She made life worth living for Earl during such unstable times. Is this perhaps sounding familiar?"

"I said *stop*."

"Oh, that I could," said The Preacher with a mirthless chuckle. He continued.

"Now, as I understand it, Earl Anderson told you all of this yesterday evening at the…oh, I think it is called the Weary Traveler? Is that right?"

"Stop lying. *Stop lying!*" Everything else he wanted to scream at this ghastly perversion of a good man was gagged by the simmering apoplexy within him that was approaching its boiling point.

How dare he? How *dare* he?

"Stay calm child," soothed The Preacher, before continuing further.

"You were hitchhiking, and that's where you ended up this time. At that diner. You and Earl struck up a conversation while you ate and as his shift was ending. You were doing exactly as you have always done, except now you are calling yourself Barry Horgan. Tell me—do you even remember your name?"

The Preacher stopped a beat so that The Man Calling Himself Barry could answer, but he remained silent. The Preacher went on.

"So anonymous, my child. You fade into the world unseen, except when you feel the quaintly human need to, well, feel *human* …when you feel the need to remember what it means to feel anything at all.

"Sadness feels so *good* when you've spent so long feeling nothing. It feels human to cry over lost love, even if it was never yours to lose. It's hard to cry, of course. Feeling something with such profundity, it seems so foreign, doesn't it? But when you can…my *goodness*! The euphoria of sorrow in the face of emptiness! Indeed, sorrow feels like joy when you have only ever known cruelty. And you learned young that cruelty was the only thing that the world had for you. So, you forgot *you*. And now, when you cry, it feels like you are crying for something lost, something—*someone*—more true and pure than you could ever know."

"What are you *talking* about?" whimpered The Man Calling Himself Barry.

"Listen to me child, listen and…be…*SAVED*!"

Upon this mighty declaration from The Preacher, the candles in the room intensified in a singular, propulsive rush. At the same time, the robed figures in the pews rose to their feet in silent unison. And when The Man Calling Himself Barry glanced up toward the balcony, he caught a brief glimpse of something massive and inhuman pacing in the darkness beyond the surging firelight. But once the candles returned to their baseline luminescence, the apparition—whatever it was—vanished.

"Earl agreed to bring you to a bus terminal connecting to Lincoln. But he pulled off a particularly desolate exit when you said you felt sick. As you left the car, you handed him your phone. He entered his own number in case you needed help later. He was a kind man. He pitied you. While he did this, you went around the back, to the trunk. You said you had medicine in your bag. But you had seen the tire iron. . ."

"No…"

"Yes. Oh yes. And your body is strong, child. Resilient.

It needed to be in order to survive what you survived. Heavy paternal fist after heavy paternal fist. At any rate, Earl Anderson is now food for crows in a cornfield."

The Man Calling Himself Barry reacted viscerally to this last revelation. He receded inward, hunching and crouching into a standing approximation of the fetal position. The Preacher did not stop.

"As you looked through his wallet and learned his address from his license, the idea of having Hannah…*a* Hannah…in your life rapidly became a soothing balm. The very thought filled the emptiness in a way it had not been filled since…well…since the last time you did this.

"Of course, she was horrified when you came into her home while she was at her most vulnerable. And her reaction, well, it horrified you too. And so now you cannot remember anything but her blood mixed with bathwater.

"You must *face* what you did, child. And what you did, you did with such brutality. Such savagery. The weapon you clutch so dearly for him. Her own bathroom walls for her."

"No."

"This is the truth. This is who you are."

"*No!*"

"*Yes!* You have been doing this for so long. Over and over. Look at yourself. You are not a young man two years out of college. Far from it. You repeat this cycle, imprisoned within your own delusion, in need—so desperately in *need*—of that which The True Lord wishes to offer: Salvation.

"Child, He has such pity for you. He sees the clay from which you were shaped. Rejected. Treated as nothing more than, at best, a mule for a man who kept you hidden away from the world purely to punish you for the crime of your very existence. It is no wonder you do not know who you are. You were never anyone to begin with. Do you not remember what he said to you as your mother lay, dying, beneath his boot for *her* crime of not being able to rise again after those final blows? Do you not remember how he said you no longer had a name as far as he was concerned? Do you remember the sound of that boot against her skull? Or did it all fade away as you helped him bury her?"

From a raw, indefinable place deep within himself—a formless void populated solely by an unclassifiable, feral emotion that, before now, had lashed about desperately with no understanding of how to express itself, something awoke within The Man Calling Himself Barry. It was alive, angry, confused, and above all, deeply hurt, like a dog desperate for the love of an owner who only knows how to hit. Subsumed for so long by the same voracious blackness that greedily devoured the church's corners, it was an emotion beyond pain.

The desperate howl that burst forth from The Man Calling Himself Barry did so with such force that it seemed to throw him outside of his body. The world spun like a tornado amidst the dizzying, overwhelming onrush of this ur-emotion from which all of his anguish, known to him or otherwise, originated.

Suddenly, and with unexpected rapidity, he felt as though he was sucked back into himself with a tight, tangible *POP*. Regaining his bearings, his psychic defenses back in place, he spoke definitively.

"My name is Barry Horgan. I have been out of college for two years. I loved Hannah. I would never hurt her."

"Oh child, you don't even know Hannah's last name–because Earl Anderson never told it to you."

As The Preacher said this, his voice rising in intensity as the sentence progressed from declaration to proclamation, the church trembled. From the balcony, The Man Calling Himself Barry heard the footsteps from the darkness outside. They paced furiously, their rapid, bipedal *CLOP-CLOP* accompanied by a low, moist snarling.

"Let me be very clear, child. Barry Horgan was the man you murdered before Earl Anderson. And Earl Anderson was eventually who you would believe yourself to be."

"Let's say all of this is true," rasped Barry softly, "how can I be 'saved?'"

He added his own lightly-inflected twist to the word "saved."

"Drink from the chalice. Drink the blood of The True Lord, and you *will* be saved. You will become one of the flock. The Flock of the Redeemed. Souls of a…similar ilk…to you and I."

The Man Calling Himself Barry looked at the chalice, looked up at The Preacher, and made one final clear and unambiguous statement before the ability to make clear and unambiguous statements was lost to him forever:

"I. Am. Barry Horgan."

He raised the tire iron and swung at the chalice, blood splashing outward onto the aisle carpet. Red on red. The airborne chalice clanked into the seatback of a first-row pew and fell to the ground.

The Preacher spoke with palpable resignation.

"Oh dear. Oh, my poor, lost child. All could have been forgiven."

The Preacher closed the distance between himself and The Man Calling Himself Barry with baffling speed, arms outstretched and legs straight and unmoving as he glided forward, toes pointed down, his feet hovering slightly off the ground.

At that moment, The Man Calling Himself Barry heard—felt, really—a roar reverberate throughout the church. It was a roar that existed both before and beyond the boundaries of that which mankind erroneously believed to be All Of Existence. It cleaved The Man Calling

Himself Barry's psyche in two. All that had been previously banished to the darkest of all darknesses within him came gushing forth like a geyser at the heart of his newly-formed psychic canyon.

The Preacher smiled wryly, then spoke.

"You have chosen damnation child. Here it is."

The Man Calling Himself Barry vaguely perceived the horned, hulking figure looming at the back of the church aisle, but it was gauzy and out-of-focus. His vision flickered and shimmered. His ears rang and all sounds drifted further away until he felt like he was underwater. He smelled sulfur.

He had two final moments of clarity before all was lost to the formless horror of the wretched un-death that awaited. In that first moment, far from the outer reaches of sanity, where what was once forgotten was forgotten no longer, where the roar of The True Lord echoed for infinite eternities, he remembered his father's only name for him.

That. The Man Calling Himself Barry was That. Deep within, where the gnashing, wounded thing inside him dwelled, it was all he'd ever known himself to be.

***

In the second moment, He Remembered. He Remembered. Jonathan. He Remembered.

Jonathan wept for his mother. He finally knew the person he was crying for.

***

The Preacher grabbed him by his shoulders and pulled him close. Looking him in the eye from behind his sunglasses, he spoke a final time.

"The road to damnation is paved in denial."

The Preacher removed his sunglasses and Jonathan found himself looking into the eyes of fire. He found himself looking into the eyes of brimstone.

Yellow Car
By
SJ Townend

Our souls are entwined. He's the fuel in my tank, the other side of my coin, the jagged-edged piece that completes the puzzle of me. Despite a couple of flaws—the two haircuts going on at the same time, and his overzealous insistence on playing the game—he's the love of my life.

I change gears and nod my head to the electric strum of Hendrix's opening to *All Along the Watchtower* as we cruise down the seemingly infinite stretch of coastal A-road. To my right, the waves dance, making a churned-up mirror of the sea under the endless embrace of an azure midday sky. And on my left, my lover sits.

As he slaps the dashboard in time to the music, with his other hand, all dirty-nailed, he digs pink crescents into my flesh through the gaps in my fishnet tights. I adore him. I'd do anything for him. Together, we drive, and I hope we will always drive; our hearts fused by Cupid's arrow.

Jimi's epic solo kicks in. My paramour plays air guitar, his flailing left elbow causing me to shift over in my seat. There is only so much room upfront in a one-liter hatch-back. I let him have the lion's share. He cranks the stereo up before biting me playfully on the curve of my neck. Giggling, I accelerate. We're flying on the wings of a dove.

The sporadically placed billboard and gas station land-scape blurs into a frantic slideshow of cream and blues and greens. I love him. I love him. I love him. This man is my entire world.

As Hendrix's riff peters out and the radio presenter begins to chat breeze, my beau says, "I appreciate the way you understand my needs," his eyes searching the road once more. He re-immerses himself in our game, locks in like a shark cutting through water. And his nails are again on my thigh, in the diamond-taut meat of my thigh, willing hyphens of blood to the surface. Ocean air carrying top notes of pennies muddles with the faux-pine air freshener perfume, then muddles with the scent of our sex and sweat. "And I also appreciate, my beauty, your desire to help me fulfill them." My heart revs.

"My pleasure," I reply. "I'll help you fulfill your needs with everything I have. With my heart, my soul, with each bone in my body." I roll my window all the way down. The rush of hot air lifts beads of sweat from my arm.

There is no greater reward than making my man happy.

We met last week in a bar.

"Yellow car," he shouts for the fourth time. A Nissan the shade of rich saffron glides past in the other direction, and he punches me on the arm, hard enough to knot blood beneath my skin, but not enough to make me cry. Instead, I wince. Just like I did when we first met, when he accidentally shoved me and his pint spilled all down my blouse.

***

I'd clearly been in his way as I'd been darting between sticky tables collecting spent glasses three hours into my shift. "Sorry," I'd said. Then my lips, I'm sure on reflection, must have contorted into a queer shape caught all tug of war between a polite smile and an awkward frown, but his body language had shown no sign of recognition or receipt of my apology. His eyes hadn't so much as drifted from the screen to connect with mine. Perhaps he hadn't heard me above the ruckus of the punters and the distorted volume of the jukebox? Like the handful of others in the joint except me, he'd been fixated on the live-stream prize fight on the widescreen across the other side of the bar. I'd shouted again, "Sorry. So sorry. My fault."

"Yeah," he'd said, his attention still held by the match. One of the boxers, slick with testosterone and perspiration, had stumbled back into the ropes. "You weren't looking where you were going. Clumsy. *That* was a great blow though." He'd nodded at the screen. "A fucking God-move of a right hook."

"As long as you're okay," I'd said.

"Fuck, yes!" He'd shouted. The taller boxer had gone in for a second swipe. I'd sucked air in through my teeth as blood had jettisoned across the screen. Then my love had looked at me properly for the first time, the blue of his eyes reeling me in, a twist of a grin on his lips. "You didn't like that did you?"

"If I'm honest, no. Boxing, violence—Not really my bag."

And that's when my darling had pointed out that he and I were probably very different, but that our variances didn't matter. Because opposites attract.

"Two types of people in the world when it comes to boxing," he'd said after snaking his arm around my waist and pulling me close enough so that I could smell which specific brand of ale he'd been swigging. "Two ways in which people are wired—some people feel the glory, the euphoria. They take ownership of the strike. Others cower and absorb the distress."

And then he'd let me buy him a drink to replace the one that had gotten spilt.

And when the match was over, and I'd finished my shift, he'd asked me for a lift.

We've been driving ever since, pulling over in motels to sleep and fuck, grabbing snacks and fuel at petrol stations when the tank needs filling up. And now, we head towards the nearest city, where he's insistent the game will peak.

He's the man of my dreams, I swear. My lips bay for his. I've never been more smitten.

***

The yellow Nissan long behind us, I glance at him and push out a smile as pain smarts across my upper arm. I see that glint in his ice-blue eyes, a glint followed by a widening of his pupils. So wide. So black. For a split-second, there's no trace of blue at all. Just black ice. He snorts, rolls down his window, and spits into the road. God, I love this man. He's strong and raw. I become a delicate orchid in his arms. *Petite* he calls me, *mon petit pois*.

"Good one," I reply through gritted teeth. My hands grip the stirring wheel a little harder

"Four nil," he says.

"Could you punch my thigh next time?" My work blouse, the tight red scoop neck shirt still tacky with beer and now also sex and sweat, won't hide the marks today's game will leave.

"Sure," he says, "sure." But who am I kidding? I'm not going back to work. Not any time soon. Not now I've found him, my *raison d'être*. We'll just keep on driving, me and him, together, for as long as fate will allow. "Or how about we get someone else involved? Spice things up a little."

"Someone else?" My heart sinks but he winks at me with those ice-blue eyes and my heart shifts back up into my chest, fluttering there a little faster.

"Yeah, someone else. Anyone. So, I can strike a little harder. You'll still feel it though, won't you, my sweetness, if you watch me do it to someone else, if you witness the smash of my fist on another person's limbs? You'll still feel the impact on your skin as if my fist had landed where intended? And I'll still feel the glory of the smack of my knuckles on flesh and bone."

"I'm not sure." I don't want to share him—can't imagine anything worse. "What exactly do you mean?"

"We just get someone else involved. A hitchhiker, a vagrant, a barfly. Someone game. You're in? I know you're in. Tell me you're in, mon petit pois." Another grin. Another flash of teeth. This man gives me the tingles.

"Okay," I say and bite my lower lip. "I guess we can try it out. I'd do anything to make you happy."

"I know," he says.

"I know you know."

He plants a firm kiss on my cheek. Then returns his focus to the road.

A stream of indifferent traffic fires past, the road busied on our approach of the outskirts of the city. Black car. Grey car. White van. In my rear-view mirror before switching lanes, I spot the yellow Volkswagen on my tail before he does, but I let him call it first. Where is the joy in beating someone anyway, in watching bliss slip, hot butter from a knife, from their face?

"Yellow car," he shouts and squeezes the flesh of my upper arm like a toddler yet to learn their own grip strength, and then he follows this up with a hard punch sure to leave a black nimbus cloud which will eventually fade to yellow. The edge of his sovereign ring tears my skin. Fuck, that hurt.

"Good one," I say. "You're excellent at this. The best." I resist the temptation to rub my arm and instead channel the pain into my solar plexus where a Katherine wheel now sparks and spins. "If it'll make you happy, I'll do it. Let's get someone else involved."

It doesn't take long for our first nibble. "Stop here," he yells, so I pull up in the lay-by. He pokes his head out of his window and yells out to a vagabond, while waving a twenty in the air. "Oi." The old man drops the handful of trash he'd been sifting through and toe-shuffles closer. My love leaves the car and slaps his target on the back. I don't catch their brief exchange over the sound of Freddy Mercury's tinny-speakered rasping tones, but with grins on both their faces, my love ushers his new friend towards the car and they clamber into the back.

"Drive, game on," my love gleefully hollers. So, we cruise, the three of us, around the edge of the city, the evening sun, a burning coin repeating like God's eyes over countless skyscraper windows.

Our new guest sways to his own lost beat as my man primes his fists in preparation for more fun. The men share swigs of something potent concealed in a brown paper bag as I weave through traffic. We creep, never progressing past third gear, past hotels and boutique shops I'll never be able to afford. And this continues until my love calls it once again.

"Yellow car," he shouts, as a yellow van pulls out from a junction. He drives his fist at speed into our life-weathered guest's left arm.

The old man yelps out and beer or something warmer sprays onto the back of my neck

"You fucker," our guest says. He cackles and rubs where my love's fist had landed. "That was fucking hard."

"Five nil," my love shouts. "Five fucking nil. Look, darling, mon petit pois, look." And then my love laughs too, whooping in time with the old man's guffaws, in time with Eddie Vedder's husky voice which is blasting out in surround sound. My love's blue-black eyes catch mine as I twist round to see the damage and both pleasure and guilt ripple down my spine.

And something like torture throbs in my own left arm, a sensation akin to the pain I'd felt when my father had pushed me down the stairs many years ago. I'd landed awkwardly, how improper of me, fracturing my scapula. "Stupid girl," my dad had said, "you must learn to *break* your fall with your hands."

My lover glows as he goes in for another swipe of our hysterical third wheel. Each swing he lands I feel as if it hits me. "Do you feel it?" My love asks between blows. "Do you? Tell me you feel it, my little sweet pea?"

As I slip out of lane, a car honks, drawing my focus back to the wheel. "Yes," I shout. "Yes. Yes."

As my darling, my heart, lashes out repeatedly, the old man's tone descends from mad laughter to droll wails. The power of love. I feel some of my love's glory and all of the old man's agony, although my love has not landed a punch directly on me. My arm burns, throbs. Has a bone in fact shattered? Has an old childhood wound opened up? Has my scapula been cracked back apart?

"Stop, please, I beg you. Mercy," the old man pleads.

"Stop," I yell, remembering the rules. "Please, sweetness. One punch is enough. One punch for a yellow car."

My love does stop and the old man's cries peter out. "Thank you, madam," he says.

"Whatever happened there?" I ask and reach around to stroke my lover on his knee, an effort I am confident will calm him down.

"That was a van, my doll, my lady," my love responds, an air of agitation in his voice. "Five hits for a van."

"Okay," I say. I adjust my headrest which has been knocked out of place. "Seems fair. I think you've had your five."

"Let me out. You've had your money's worth," the old man cries. I pull off the main road onto a side road and stop. He stumbles out of the car.

"Fresh meat," my love shouts as I pull away. And then he shouts louder, "Fresh meat, next round," at the top of his lungs, and in this moment, I know for sure that I love him, and that he loves me.

I know he would never hurt me like he hurt the old man, even though my own arm is screaming out for ice. That's why he asked me to introduce a third person into our romantic love affair, because he has needs, but we all need something, don't we? And none of us are perfect, we all have an inner child wound to heal, potential daddy issues, and he tells me he loves me again, once the tramp is nothing but a blip in the shared past of our rear-view mirror. We're making memories together, stories to share with the grandkids. I already see our unborn children's faces in my love's ice-blue eyes.

My love clambers between the front seats, resuming his position next to me. We drive on, eking our way deeper into the dark core of the city, his reddened hand in my lap. We slide past rundown shops and dive bars with flickering neon signs.

"Yellow car," I say, my voice barely audible over the music, and I tap him ever so politely on his thigh. He growls. I hate how disappointed he is that I spotted the sunny Fiesta first. "Five one," my brain prompts me to say, but the words never make it out of my mouth. Instead, I find myself apologizing and suggesting that the car hadn't even really been yellow at all. "Just chartreuse green," I say, "not yellow, my mistake, just chartreuse." The shade of rotten apples.

"Yeah," my love says, "that one doesn't count. Pull over, turn off down that street. Take me to where the hookers roam."

"Really," I say? "A woman? You want to bring another woman into our world?"

"Doesn't have to be a woman," he says, "could be anyone. As long as they're willing to take a punch."

I shrug and try to reassure myself that this isn't sexual, that his sweet, sweet head will not be turned, as I indicate right.

We drive slowly through the red-light district until a paper-thin woman wearing more make-up than clothes strolls up to our car.

"Get in," my love says, reaching for his wallet, and she eyeballs me, and then my love's raw knuckles and the splatter of blood on the rear seats. I see the excited expectation on my love's face. Oh, how I want to make him happy. But something doesn't sit right in my gut. She's frail. He'd shatter her surely, with just one hit.

As she peers into our car, my love waves a fifty at her. She ogles us both and then shakes her head. "Nah," she says. She tosses the butt of the cigarette she'd been smoking into a drain and then begins to back away. "Nah. No thanks."

"It's okay," I say, and put my car into first ready to pull off. "We'll find someone else."

"But she's perfect." A string of drool shimmers on my love's stubbled chin as he speaks. "She's the same size as you, maybe a tad smaller, and her skin will bruise up a treat."

And my mind plays tricks on me, scattering jealous seeds, perhaps he is the sort to have a roving eye. Maybe he *would* prefer hurting her to hurting me. And the thought of losing him hurts more than any physical injury he could ever inflict on anyone. "But we've got to have her consent," I say. "We have to adhere to the rules."

I mouth goodbye and pull away and he sulks.

"You stupid cow," he shouts again and again and punches the dashboard until it cracks. Until I cry. And I can't deny it, the confusion of my emotions feels both euphoric and hellish at the same time. "We could have persuaded her. We could have offered her more money." And then, in a rapid turn of events as I turn the radio up, he retracts his statements, and declares once more his undying love for me, tells me I'm the only pearl in a world of rotten oysters, the ice in his rum on a hot day. Then, once we're both laughing and nodding to Led Zeppelin, he says, "I'm sure we'll find someone else, my beautiful princess," and he flashes me his best grin and pinches the flesh of my cheek.

"Yeah," I say. "Let's keep driving. Let's keep these four wheels turning." I must keep that sharp smile on his face, must bear witness to the ways his eyes roll like dice when he gets what he wants, the way they flit from blue to black ice, just for a second.

We cruise around for hours in search of someone else to play the game, but we have no joy and we see no yellow cars and before we know it, dusk becomes night–and all cars look grey as slate–and night becomes dawn and we've long since left the city. My eyelids are growing heavy. It feels like we're the only car on the road; the only couple in love in the world.

"Can we find somewhere to kip," I say. "I'm not thinking straight." I'm not driving straight.

"Pussy," he says. "Just because you're losing."

"Yeah, you're right." I correct myself and pull my big girl socks up. "Game on," I say. "I'm sure we'll find someone soon. Let's head to the other side of the city."

***

The sun rises. "A kid." He points at a teen as we drive past a notoriously shitty school. "Loose kids, feral kids. They'll do anything for cash."

I try to withhold a gasp. Did I hear my love correctly or is tiredness stealing my senses? "A kid?"

"Yeah."

I speed straight through the zebra crossing a few hundred yards from the community college where a cluster of schoolgirls in hitched-up kilts and hundred denier tights are waiting patiently to cross.

"No, not a kid." I gulp. "Someone will notice. Their teachers will notice when they don't turn up for registration. And the law. The police, they'll be on our tail and I'd hate to get in trouble. Hate to spend time apart from you." My love grunts and pummels the cushioning on the inside of his door.

"Come on hon, my little sweet pea. I want to play," he sulks. "Take me somewhere better."

Out of the corner of my eye, I check. The gaggle of children make their way across the road, then through the gates of their place of study.

"There's a gym up the road. Let's catch someone taking a morning workout, someone with no place they're hurrying to," I say.

"Yeah. Keep driving. Speed up." My love scratches at the glove-box like an animal caught in a trap. The sensation of claws drags up my legs followed by the appearance of a staff of red lines, snagging my tights, and a jonesing swells in my heart. I can't bear it when my love is not pleased, when I can't provide what it is he craves. He wants to play the yellow car game. He just wants to enjoy the game.

I take a sharp left down a familiar road and pull up outside of Just Move gymnasium, a twenty-four-hour unmanned facility. There, we spot our next competitor: a red-faced, sweaty chap wearing a black top and shorts, with a kit bag hoisted over his shoulder. The gymbod makes his way out of the glass doors. "Him," my love shouts. I love it when my man is all pumped up. "Him, that puny little shrimp."

And before I have a chance to put the car in park, he's grappling at the door handle, he's opening the door, he's climbing out and heading to the unsuspecting fellow. New guy laughs and tilts his head as the early morning sun makes sparkles on his sculpted shoulders. At least he's the same build as my love, I think–a fair match.

The gymbod nods and follows my love back to our car, where my love passes him a rolled fifty.

"This is Mark," my love says and shimmies in after our guest into the back seats. "Says he'll play if we can drop him off three blocks up."

"Sure," I say. "Hi, Mark." The three of us pull away smiling.

"It's a bit of a fucking state in here," Mark says, flexing his muscles. Then he stretches his arms above his head, says "game on, then," before pressing his nose up to his window.

"Yellow car," my love shouts. We've been driving for less than a minute. "Yellow BUS." A school bus, packed with small faces pressed up like merry dolls against its many panes of glass. And my love plants seven thick punches on Mark's bare right arm, one bang after another.

As wet, crimson lacerations split open on our guest's arm, I shriek and squirm as the pain from the wounds my lover inflicts on Mark travel up mirror neurons in my own upper body.

"Shit. Fuck. You're fucking stronger than you look," Mark yells as he defends himself with raised palms, like a boxer backing into the corner. "But fair play, you got me good, mate."

And when my love is done, his eyes bulging with hedonistic pleasure, Mark casually reaches into his gym bag, pulls out sparring mittens and protein bars, and lifts out a towel which he uses to mop blood from his body.

"Did you feel it, darling? Each brutal wallop? My loves sidles forwards in his seat and kisses me from behind on the neck.

"I'm so proud of you, baby," I say. "That win really hurt. I felt it all so badly, in the marrow of my bones." Bruises bloom like warm roses along my own upper arm. "In fact, it hurts a little too much to keep on driving now, to reach and change the gear, but don't worry, I'll push forwards, onwards. I know how much fun you're having." As I turn left, the flesh on my arm bursts open and blood trickles like sap down my skin.

"I love you, boo," my lover says.

"I love you too," I echo.

"What the actual fuck?" Mark eyes the damage to my arm which almost matches his.

"Here," Mark says and passes me the red rag his own towel has become, "you should try and stem the bleeding. Let me out. Now. I'll walk the last part. I don't want any part in this sick fucking show. No more games for me." He tries to pass the fifty back to my love but my love pushes it back in his face.

I take the third exit off a roundabout and Mark shifts over as far as he can into his side of the car, his corner of the ring, with a look of concern on his face.

"Don't be silly," my love says. "We made a deal. She'll drive you all the way. And we've a game to finish. There's time for another round." My love reaches across and smooshes Mark's face against Mark's window. Mark's face, squashed there, looks like a doll put back in its too-tight box, and my love stares out of his opposing side, stares out at his prey like a shark.

I can't speak for Mark, but we're both looking in the same direction and I'm pretty sure by the wet, yelping sound he makes that he spots it also, the string of yellow taxis parked up at the cab stand. A golden jackpot. But I won't call it. I won't shout yellow car. I save it for my darling, my heart. I want him to call this gift first.

But my love is looking the wrong way. I want to turn around and nudge him, give him the advantage, but I can't. Because we all know it's wrong to cheat and defeats the whole point of having rules. To inform my love of the throng of stationary taxis would make a mockery of our game.

As I glance in my rear-view mirror at the pair of them sitting behind me, I catch Mark's eyes, all wide and un-blinking. And I don't know why he's not calling it, shout-ing out yellow car. He shakes his head slightly while mouthing the word no, and then he raises his index finger slowly to his lips. There are six taxis, all of them yellow as yolk, waiting for commuters to flood out of the train station.

I tap loudly on the crest of my steering wheel and de-celerate significantly to give my love a chance to spot the hoard, but he doesn't.

Mark shouts instead. He shouts, "Red car. RED CAR," as a sour-cherry Mazda cuts me off, where I'd been creep-ing along like a snail.

"*Red* car?" I ask. "*Red* car?"

My love repeats my words and turns, a scowl across his brow, to face Mark, but Mark is unplugging his seatbelt and launching the pad of his hard, open palm at my man, and at the same time, with his other hand, Mark is flipping the door handle on my love's side and trying to push him out of the car.

My love, clearly shocked by the switch-up in game play, no longer has the upper hand as Mark shifts his shoulders sideways, ramming his bodyweight into my love. "Red car?" I ask again, unsure what to do, hoping for clarification. My love tumbles out into the road.

I scream but keep my foot on the accelerator because there's a juggernaut right up my arse, honking and screeching on its brakes, and you can't just stop in a dual carriageway; one must follow the rules of the road. "What the fuck?" I yell. I crane my neck. My love spins like Sonic the Hedgehog along tarmac, and smacks into the median strip. "What the actual fuck?"

"New game," Mark says. "Red car." He reaches across and slams the passenger door closed and then clambers into the front next to me. "Red car means you get to push the loser out of a moving vehicle."

"Christ," I reply, my love now a cracked pile some yards behind us; still moving, limbs twitching—I guess he's going to be okay.

"And fuck me, that felt good," Mark yells and he whoops and nudges me for a high five to which I reciprocate—it's the rules isn't it, it's improper to leave someone hanging. And as his hand smacks against mine, I feel nothing. No pain in my upper arm. No wild torture in my shoulder. No burn as his palm slaps into mine. And I feel nothing when, in my rear-view mirror, I see the spasming body slumped against concrete come to a complete standstill. Nothing. Nada. Zilch. No joy. But also, a complete absence of pain.

With the back of his hand, Mark wipes sweat from his face, then dries his hands on his shorts.

And then I feel it, the glory, as I look across at Mark. "Game on?" I ask and stare into his eyes. They glint like precious emeralds. How they sparkle, then flit to obsidian black, before settling back to glorious green. His whole face shines with some sort of post-orgasmic euphoria. I think I love him. I know I do. Mark is the love of my life, my heart, my muse, the creator of new games. I spy our unborn children as they appear in the green apples of his eyes. I list their first names under my breath.

"Sure," Mark says and then cocks his head back and laughs. And I know by the way he laughs, the way he squeezes my leg until the flesh turns white then pink, that he feels the same way too.

Click. I panic and slam on the central locking, because if Mark wins, he'll have to push me out—I only ever play by the rules. And if Mark wins, and I go spinning, then who would be left driving the car? But I fret as I crank up the radio, as he plants a sweet kiss on my cheek, because I know I could never bear to let my lover lose.

New game, I think, red car, and I clutch the steering wheel and take check of my speedometer, to ensure I adhere to the speed limit of the dual carriageway. Fifty, fifty-five, sixty.

I glance across to the right, to the intersection ahead, my attention snatched by the Doppler shift wail of an encroaching siren: the battle cry of a summoned fire engine; a very much probably red truck. The traffic lights flick from apple green to amber. "Hold tight, my love," I shout and Mark screams as I crimp my eyes shut and press down on the accelerator. With the love of my life by my side, I can make it. I know I can. Before the lights turn red, I can make it across the intersection before the fire truck comes hurtling through, before either of us has to call it.

Horsemen
by
Mason Gallaway

The night was coming on like a smooth drunk. The kind of drunk reached by sips and slow savoring. Sitting in his truck, in the deepening shadows beside the liquor store, Jordy took in the evening, as he did the wine from the brown bag in his lap. Nice and easy, appreciating it.

His girlfriend's accusations no longer rang so loudly in his ears. Drunk, broke loser, she had called him. Like his daddy. Worse, like *her* daddy. Jordy was hell-bound and hopeless in Sadie's eyes, it seemed. So, he'd get nice and tanked and then crawl in bed next to her and let her get a good whiff of him. Wonder how much he drank, where he drank it, and whom he drank it with. He knew it was petty, but he didn't care.

Jordy sipped, slow-blinking at the store's side wall, splashed with graffiti, most of it terrible. Fuckers, Jordy thought. His sister owned a McDonald's the next town over, and it was the petty shit like this that took the biggest toll on business owners.

Only now there was a fresh piece of artwork gracing the brick canvas. A creepy, triangular symbol drawn with black paint.

Before he could really study the strange rune, movement flashed in the corner of Jordy's eye. He turned and found a grinning face in his passenger side window. If Jordy hadn't been warmed with wine, he might have jumped out of his skin.

It was only Tim, who lived in a small trailer next to a bigger trailer that had too many leaks. Oddly, sadly, one of the coolest people Jordy knew in this town. Jordy rolled down the window.

"What do you want, T?"

"At it again, huh?" Tim grinned.

"When we don't fight is when I worry."

Tim's eye twinkled at the brown bag in Jordy's lap. Jordy sighed and handed it over, following it with an old coffee cup from his console before Tim could get his lips on the bottle.

"Shit," Tim said, bottle almost to his mouth. "I brush my teeth every damn night." He took the cup, shook out the last drops of coffee, and filled it with wine.

Jordy turned back to the graffiti, the new symbol in particular. It was like an *A* but with no line connecting the sides. A rebel asshole of an *A* that no English word had room for. One side was longer than the other, as though it was reaching down to snatch something.

"Good-looking guy like you," Tim said, sipping, "any woman he wants. Nothing's stopping you—"

Tim dropped his words, noticing Jordy staring at the graffiti.

"*There* it is," Tim said, as if he were facing an old adversary.

"What? You know who drew that?"

Tim shrugged. "Sorta." He laughed. "Fucking kids probably. Got nothing to do. Trying to scare folks."

"Scare?" Jordy straightened out of the slouch he'd been lulled into by the wine. The change in position felt like sacrilege in the growing dark and euphoria. "With shitty graffiti?"

Tim swallowed a gulp, hard, shaking his head.

"I don't know what the hell that is. But it ain't just graffiti. My sister told me about it." Tim raised a grimy, leathery forefinger and traced the shape of the rune on the wall.

"She was here the other night, around closing. Getting herself some of that coconut shit she likes, and some dude walked up…"

He swirled the cup, watching the wine spin like blood in a centrifuge. Then he raised the cup to his lips and drained it. He motioned for the bottle. Jordy grunted and handed it over, knowing the story wasn't going to come cheap. Tim took the cup and filled it.

"…He was standing in the shadows right around here. Dressed in all leather. A biker, but not one of the big, mean ones."

"Crotch-rocket?"

"Yeah, guess so. She said he looked futuristic, whatever the fuck that means. Anyway, he steps out of the shadows, between here and the trash, stops right in front of her. His helmet on, with the visor up, but his face all shadow. All he said was something about ascending and consuming the consumers or some shit."

Tim poked his syllables into the air with his finger.

"Anyway, the guy drew that weird ass symbol with his hand in the air. Like he was chopping it up."

"What'd she do?"

"Nothing. She just hightailed it to her car."

"Jesus."

Tim shook his head. "Doubt he's from around here. But watch your ass just the same."

"I'll be alright," Jordy said, settling back into his cozy slump. "What are you getting into tonight anyway?"

"On my way to see a guy about work."

"Now?" Jordy asked.

Tim drained his cup again, nodded, and tilted his head back with valiance. "Damn straight. No rest for the wise, my friend."

Jordy smiled and winked. "What guy?"

Tim tipped his head toward the field behind the liquor store. The field gave way to a sprawling, well-groomed yard that rose up to a picturesque farmhouse. Owned by an oil tycoon. Eddy Gentle. A man who supposedly lived up to his name. Magnanimous but mysterious. In this hell-hole town, yet somehow not of it. The kind of guy who could probably live anywhere but chose to carve out his own little heaven within small town hell.

Looking up at that place always gave Jordy conflicted feelings of envy, and hope. Jordy eyed Tim skeptically.

"No shit? Gentle?"

Tim nodded proudly. "He's been giving me repair work."

Jordy shrugged and held up his wine bottle in tribute.

Tim tipped the bill of his cap. "Thanks for the swig. I'll see you around."

He pushed himself from the car and walked away. As he passed the graffiti, he swatted at it as if it had spat a taunt, then disappeared around the back of the building.

Jordy settled again and his seat seemed to swell around him. He knew he should go home and handle his problems like an adult, but the soft blanket of falling night felt too good. He pulled it up to his chin and sailed to sleep.

***

But Jordy's sleep wasn't deep, and it wasn't calm. He floated in a half-awake state that projected the night's happenings with a cool, distant, shimmery awareness.

Large diesel trucks became tanks storming the parking lot. Vagrants and junkies were imps and faeries dancing on light and shadow. Sweeping headlights were searchlights trying to expose Jordy's dreams and fears.

And then came the rumble of horses. Roaring metal horses, carrying knights armored with leather and jeans and swinging chains. They whooped and laughed and cheered as they parked their steel beasts and went into the store. They did the same when they came back out, raising their boxes and brown bags like the heads of slain dragons.

In sleep, Jordy envied and admired the road warriors. That power and toughness and freedom. Blowing through shit towns like this one. Loud, and lit, and free. Sampling only the best, and leaving the rest to rot.

Then a new sound burned through his dream. A lean, mean whine like ripping chainsaws. New lights overtook the lot, searing the bikers in hard silhouette.

****

Jordy awoke in a bed of prickly grass. He sat up and looked around him. Somehow, he'd ended up in the field behind the liquor store. Behind him, above him, the Gentle house sat, dark and quiet. But in front of him, the liquor store was on fire.

Jordy shook the grog from his head and blinked, expecting the hellish image before him to dissolve. But it was real. He got up and ran back to the parking lot. The fire hadn't broken though the side where his truck sat. But the store's interior was engulfed with flames that burst through the front windows.

There was no gawking crowd, but there was an overturned Harley. Next to that lay the remains of a biker who was missing not only his helmet but also his head. Jordy stared in shock at the meaty ring of the neck, still trickling blood into the pool that surrounded it.

Dizzy and nauseated, Jordy looked away, but his eyes landed on another body. This one, not headless but throatless. Another lay in a heap; a torso topped with arms and legs like a broken toy set aside for a Saturday repair. More bikes overturned. One near the entrance, now lapped by flames.

Nothing of the hellish scene would settle in Jordy's mind. The blood was too red, the fire too bright, and the heat waves almost pushed him over. Jordy turned and hurried back to his vehicle, thinking of his phone and getting far, far from here.

And then he saw it. On the driver's side door of his beater. That distorted *A*. Bolder, redder, drawn carefully. He hesitated before opening his door, as if the long end of that symbol might strike him like a venomous snake. But Jordy forced himself to get in. Once inside, he grabbed his phone and began dialing. Then he heard the sirens. Someone had already called 911.

But Jordy didn't want to wait around for them. He fired up his truck and burned out of the parking lot and onto the dark stretch of highway. As he sped away, the blazing liquor store receding, he glanced at the house on the hill, wondering about Tim. Had he gotten the job? Had he seen the fire, or whatever led to it? Was he even alive?

What the fuck had happened?

Jordy wanted to just keep driving, but he knew his next stop should be home. He didn't really like Sadie, and she didn't really like him. But they'd been together a long time. And the mark on his door made him fear that whoever hit the other bikers and the store might target him next. Might target Sadie. The thought of some gang of slick bikers burning Sadie up or ripping her apart made him sick.

He wished he could just head out of town. He could see how his sister's restaurant was doing. She'd probably be working tonight. Keeping the place staffed on weekends was a bitch, and she was always filling in. But she loved running the place and serving the best goddamn quarter pounders possible.

But despite everything, he wanted to see Sadie's pudgy, furrowed, pouty face. The face he would never, ever smack (though she had smacked him more than once) was now a face that he just might kiss if she was OK.

The dark highway was barren around him, despite the sirens screaming in the distance. But several times, he heard faint shrieks and whines, the buzz of crotch-rocket motors spitting mischief and malice.

***

The apartment was empty. It looked like Sadie had just been there, going about her post-fight business. The lights were on; the reality show paused mid bitch-out. Ratty blanket thrown aside, pooling on the brown carpet. Snack, Jordy thought. Sadie had gone out for a bite, probably to Crystal Palace. She'd be back soon. He hoped. He could wait on the couch to deliver his near-death story to her as she munched on her sliders, looking at him like he was crazy.

But she was out there, somewhere. And *they* were out there. Whoever they were. The *new* horsemen. Leaner, meaner bikers, of some complex, nastier evolution.

Jordy left the apartment and headed to the fast-food joint.

The restless flames that flickered and danced in the distance did not come as much of a surprise. Police and fire trucks gathered around a building that was not Crystal Palace but some other fast-food joint. As he passed, two police cars pulled out, speeding away in the opposite direction.

The wrath of the freak bikers hadn't yet touched the

Crystal Palace, several lots down. Despite the growing chaos all around, the drive-through line ringed the building.

Jordy felt relief, followed by a flash of resentment. Maybe the patrons hadn't noticed the developing chaos, but Jordy also knew how badly these people wanted their sliders. Nothing short of hellfire would stop them. He reminded himself he shouldn't judge; he too had been that bored, that hungry, that stoned.

He slowed his car and pulled into the parking lot, scanning for Sadie's car. It wasn't in line. Maybe she was on her way home. Jordy drove around, with an unshakable feeling of being a fugitive. Someone running, someone waiting to be caught. When he got around to the other side of the building, he saw the *A* slashed across the side of the restaurant. Every detail of it matched what had been etched in Jordy's mind, and painted on his truck. He slammed the accelerator to the floor and screeched out of the parking lot.

He drove with one hand on the wheel, the other on his phone. *Now* he was going to call the cops to report what he'd witnessed, the markings, that Crystal Palace could be next.

But wait. *Shit.* Sadie's car. It was in the parking lot of the fast-food place on fire down the street, feasted upon by flames.

He knew he should go to see what had happened. But he sped up again, letting the image of his girlfriend's burning car slide from view. He cursed himself; a decent guy would have stopped to inquire, to make sure.

But Jordy knew that Sadie was gone. And eventually he'd get the calls and the confirmations. Now, he just wanted to run. From the flames, the markings, the hungry, and the dead. He wanted to run from the night, the night that had come on so softly and seductively only to claw at his throat.

And the night wasn't through with him. His rearview brightened with beams. It could have been anyone, someone rushing home with fresh burgers and juicy stories of the night's terrors. But Jordy remembered the marking on the side of his door.

The light behind him grew brighter. The whine grew louder, like gargantuan hornets. He expected the light to fragment into several lights, the swarm spreading out to attack from all sides. But the light began to shrink; the terrifying whine began to fade. No leather clad bikers overtook him, their lifeless visors reflecting mechanical, faceless aggression.

Jordy glanced back up at the mirror. The lights were gone. Only darkness was behind him. But the whine returned, now growing even louder. Shadows rose in his rearview. He tapped on his brake lights, revealing sleek, black figures on bikes. Their headlights had been switched off.

The bikes seemed to float in the darkness, as though their wheels weren't touching the road. There were four of them. They grew closer; two remained at Jordy's tail while the other two flanked his truck, riding abreast with the driver and passenger windows. Jordy pressed down on the gas pedal, but he couldn't gain any distance. The bikers matched his moves.

He looked at them, throwing frantic glances side to side, to the rearview. They all just stared ahead, their faces, hidden behind their black visors, appearing sightless. But Jordy knew they saw him. They wanted him, every flabby, saturated pound of him.

These horsemen, or demons, or whatever the fuck, were cleaning things up. Trimming things down. *Consuming those who consume*. Jordy had wanted something like this to happen, more so to others than himself, but if he was honest with himself, he had wished destruction and annihilation upon this town and almost everyone in it. And now it was happening. In a sick way, it almost felt right.

He caught a flash of light in his rearview that gave way to a small flickering ribbon. One of the bikers held a small blueish flame before him. He saw another bright flash, a small explosion of orange and yellow. A breath of fire. Shrinking down again to a flipping blue flame.

Blow torches? No. Flame throwers of some kind.

The two small whipping flames behind him rose up in unison, almost level with Jordy's petrified gaze. The blue flames bloomed to searing orange-yellow clouds. The dark riders disappeared behind the wall of flames engulfing his truck bed. The cab flooded with heat. Jordy tried to accelerate, to let the slipstream pull the flames behind them, but the flames held steady.

Desperate, Jordy slammed on his brakes. Not hard enough to send him fishtailing, but enough to bring him from eighty down to forty-five. Enough for the dark horsemen to slam right into his tailgate.

But just as he hit the brakes and the tires shrieked, the flames fell away, along with the two bikers, fanning out just in time, missing the impact. The smoothness of their evasion was infuriating. These bikers, whoever they were, were much too practiced, too slick. Their efficiency and purity terrified him.

Even though these freaks were assailing him, trying to burn him alive, flay him, he found himself most afraid of what they represented. What he wanted to be, but worse, the *extreme* of what he wanted to be. Fast, efficient, thin, dexterous. Aggressive. Facing his would-be murderers, Jordy felt as much envy and admiration as he did terror.

The two rear bikers had fallen further back, but the front two were still saddling him. Jordy spotted a gleaming flash—blades, machetes. The streetlights kissed their lethal edges.

Jordy threw his truck into the biker to his right. The biker drifted outward toward the shoulder, avoiding the attack. Mocking it. Jordy tried again, but steered too hard to the right, and the truck began to swerve. As Jordy struggled to right the vehicle, the bikers began striking his truck. The repeated blows struck sparks from his truck body, the hubcaps. They were trying to blow out his tires.

Something exploded under Jordy and the truck began to wobble and swing from side to side. He tried to keep the vehicle steady, but the more he tried, the more chaotically the truck behaved, the wheel trying to spring from his hands like a snared animal.

The world spun and rocked in his vision. Jordy was no longer driving but flying to strange, terrible places. Then his truck slammed into something, and Jordy leaned with the rest of the truck for two unending seconds. Would he land on tires and ass or roof and neck? He didn't know. But the world righted itself, and the truck fell back onto its tires, slinging Jordy side to side.

There was no time to gather himself. Jordy saw the dark figures surrounding the truck. He could get out and run, but they'd either hack him to pieces or burn him alive. If he tried to outrun them, they'd simply hop on their rockets and blaze down on him.

Jordy remained put, poised and ready. To do what, he had not a clue. One thing he could do was to get a good look at these fuckers. Who they were, what they were. He turned to the one at his window. Standing maybe three feet away, glossed by the nearby streetlight. All black. Large, orbital helmet, the visor a black mirror. Slim leather jacket, collar upturned and hiding flesh, meeting even slimmer leather pants.

The figure was well under six feet, slender. This was a person. A small person, little more than half Jordy's size. While his mind had unconsciously pegged these devils as men, adult men, Jordy could no longer be sure.

The figure's gloved hand suddenly rose, almost as if to wave or to signal troops to attack. But the hand and fingers went to the neck, grabbing something there. And Jordy spied a lock of white hair creeping out from under the helmet and collar. The fingers quickly tucked it under the collar, out of sight.

"Who the fuck—" Jordy could say no more.

The figure backed up. Jordy looked at the others, who also backed up as if to meld with the night. Then the flame throwers appeared again, flame-tipped phalluses rising. And before he could swear the most desperate swear of his life, his entire world became a bright, hot hell.

Jordy cowered, shrinking into himself to escape the blaze. But the shield of the car and the window provided a moment of reprieve—small, pitiful, but long enough for him to look up. To see the wall, the storm, fire crawling and writhing and dancing over his windows, filling the cab with an unearthly light, an unnatural heat.

The glass would break any moment; the fire would rush inward and lick the flesh from Jordy's bones. Or the windows would hold, but the fumes of his tank would meet the flames, sending Jordy to oblivion. Or none of that would happen. His cab would simply become an oven on broil.

Yes, that would be it, or probably a symphony of all three of those scenarios. But the heat was already starting. It rolled over him, caressed him. Pressed him. Strangled him.

Then there was a pop of sound. Probably his window giving way to the hungry flames. But the flames on his right suddenly disappeared. And there was no sign of the figure with the white hair. Three more pops in the night, louder this time. The fierce flames all extinguished, along with much of the heat.

Jordy sat, afraid to move. All the figures were gone, except one, who was hunched and stumbling. Unable to stand the heat in the cab any longer, Jordy reached for the handle. It seared his hand, and he screamed. He pulled off his tee shirt and wrapped his palm. The moisture of his sweat sizzled against the handle. The door unlatched, and he kicked it open.

Jordy hopped from the truck and crept around it. His assailants' abandoned bikes idled a few yards away. Their bodies slumped in various positions around the truck. The one who'd been nearest Jordy lay with hands behind his or her back, leaking dark liquid onto the asphalt.

In the middle of the street, the last one standing turned to face Jordy, swaying to some silent music, having dropped the flame thrower to the road. Leathered hands rose to the visor and opened it. Then the biker leaned over, and blood spilled forth.

The biker collapsed.

Jordy heard Tim's voice out of the darkness.

"Holy shit, man, are you okay?"

Jordy turned and saw Tim trotting toward him, deer rifle in hand. Tactical gear draped his body; he wore it like a fine skin. Somehow Tim seemed younger, too, like the Tim he was before the alcohol, prostitutes, and crack. Jordy, stunned, opened his arms, and Tim embraced him.

Tim looked at Jordy "Are you *sure* you're OK, man?" Jordy nodded. Then Jordy noticed the others with Tim. Seven or eight of them. Different ages. All dressed like Tim. Carrying automatic rifles, riot guns, and pistols. They trotted out of the shadows that cradled the street. A glorious night army of misfits. One was a woman not much older than Jordy, like Sadie, but with brighter, fiercer eyes. Another was a gaunt man of about seventy.

They all convened around Tim and Jordy. The fierce-looking girl asked tersely, "How many?" Jordy tried his best to answer, to keep it together, but he could not speak. At least not yet.

Tim turned and waved to someone else, outside the group that surrounded him. Jordy turned, and the others parted. Walking toward them was a tall, burly, sterling-haired man in an amalgamation of hunting and tactical gear. He had a large pistol at his hip and an assault rifle hanging from his neck. His hand rested on the rifle's hand-guard as if calming a wild animal.

Jordy knew this man. Eddy Gentle. Gentle approached the group, his step steady, his onyx eyes firm and inquisitive. He looked at the shirtless and sweating Jordy.

"You burned?" he asked.

Jordy shook his head.

"You fucked up? In the head? You okay?"

Jordy shook his head again. Then nodded. Eddie chuckled, showing some relief. Then Eddy reached behind himself and pulled something from either his belt or back pocket.

It was a gun. A semi-auto pistol, a Beretta. Still tense, Jordy half expected Gentle to raise the gun and finish what the dark riders had started, but instead he flipped it and pointed the handle at Jordy.

"Can you shoot? Speak this time."

"Yeah. Yes," Jordy said. And then he reached out to take the gun. But Gentle withdrew the gun before Jordy's fingers could grasp the metal.

"You sure you want to help us stop these fuckers? They hit sooner than we expected. Cops will take too damn long to figure all this out before more die."

"What the fuck is going on?" Jordy asked.

"Long story, but I'll give it to you straight. We've got a cult of elitist, religious, health-crazed freaks who have started a movement. Started with that goddamn dieting church outside of town. The Ascension. Know it? I think something started there and now it's way out of hand. May go deeper than we even know. But now some radicals are tearing up any establishment they think pushes indulgence, obesity, addiction. Fast food joints, liquor stores, sex shops. Killing anyone associated in the process. We're gonna take 'em down."

That's when Jordy remembered. His sister's restaurant.

"Oh shit," he said.

"What?" Eddy pulled the pistol back further.

"My sister. She owns a fast-food place in Springton. I think it's the closest one. Oh fuck," Jordy said, feeling the weight of his words. First Sadie, now his sister.

Gentle extended the gun again. "You ready?"

Jordy nodded, fear leaving him, resolution taking its place. He felt a part of him had burned away in the flamethrower blaze. The sweat of that fire still lingered on him, not cooling. Though the feeling scared him, he liked it.

Jordy took the gun.

Together they all walked back to the idling trucks down the road.

Jordy had nothing better to do anyway.

The Hitchhiker
by
Damon Nomad

Carl slammed on the brakes and the car swerved to a stop on the side of the road. His heart raced with a sense of nervous alertness. The headlights illuminated Mile Marker 167 on Highway 33. He hadn't fallen asleep, but he had gone into a kind of trance. He panicked after realizing he was driving without conscious awareness.

The digital clock above the radio displayed the time to be 11:36 p.m.—so, he was about thirty minutes outside of town. He took in a deep breath and exhaled slowly as the reason for his late-night road trip came back to him. It started just as he got off the second shift at the factory, when a stranger called out his name in the parking lot. The process server slammed papers into his chest and snorted, "You've been served."

The restraining order for his ex-girlfriend, Donna, sent him into a fit of rage. He remembered jumping into his car and driving over to her apartment. He pounded on the door and shouted but there was no response and no sign of anyone inside. People were peeping out their windows and someone shouted at him, 'You better leave or I'm gonna call the cops.'

It was a man's voice, but not coming from Donna's

place. He kicked the door and backed away, fuming mad. That was the last thing he could remember, until moments ago here on the road.

He muttered to himself, "I needed to cool off." *I must've headed for the cabin.*

His grandfather built the cabin in the forest near a state park decades ago; a six-hour trip west out of town. It passed on to him when his father died. His dad drank himself to death and his mother had left them when Carl was five. He knew the baggage of his childhood probably explained why he was short-tempered and prone to outbursts. Even though he didn't like to admit that he had a problem.

He tapped his fingers on the steering wheel as he thought about what he should do. It was late on a Friday, he was already on his way, and a weekend at the cabin would help calm him down. He glanced in his mirrors; there was no traffic in sight. No lights of any sort for that matter. Highway 33 was an old two-lane state highway that meandered through the cornfields and forests of rural backcountry. A small town or village every thirty to fifty miles apart. He put the car into gear and eased back onto the highway.

Carl slowed down and took the gravel exit for the old service station. It was nearly two a.m. and he was down to a quarter tank and this was one of the few twenty-four-hour spots on this stretch of road. He noticed someone in the shadows near the corner of the building as he finished filling the gas tank. Seemed a bit peculiar—it was a cool autumn evening and there were no other cars. No reason to be standing outside in the middle of nowhere. He moved the car to a spot near a streetlight on the parking lot's edge.

"Can you give me a ride?" Carl was startled by the request as he headed inside. The voice came from the dark figure still in the shadows. A rugged, raspy voice of someone a bit older than he was.

Carl stammered, "Uhh . . .well. Which way are you headed?"

"West," came the one-word response. Carl could see that the man was wearing well-worn blue jeans and a dark jacket with a hood, but his face was in the shadows.

"Sorry, I'm headed east." He opened the door and headed into the service station; not quite sure why he lied or what it was that made him wary of the guy.

Carl bought a large coffee and two stale donuts inside. There were two tables and stools near the front window. He sat down. He could use the caffeine, and he hoped the character looking for a ride would disappear.

Carl crept out the front door of the service station after he finished his food; he was relieved there was no sign of the would-be hitchhiker. He headed straight for his car. Then, he heard footsteps behind him and glanced back, seeing a figure near a dumpster just a few feet away. There was something shiny and metallic in the man's hand. *He's got a knife.*

Carl shouted as he spun around and backed away, "What do you want?"

"What?" The man waved something in the air. "Just cleaning the grease out of the fryer."

Carl realized it was the attendant from the service station. He was carrying a pan in one hand and a metal spatula in the other. Carl shrugged. "Sorry, didn't mean to bark out like that." He turned away, embarrassed, and headed for the car.

He jumped in and sped down the long gravel entrance road. He glanced in the rearview mirror before pulling out onto Highway 33. He gasped at the sight of a silhouette of someone standing on the edge of the entrance road maybe ten feet behind his car. It wasn't the attendant; it had to be the guy who wanted a ride. Suddenly, the man marched towards the car.

Carl looked both ways along the highway, saw it was clear, and mashed down the accelerator. He came to a safe cruising speed and turned on the radio as a distraction. He wanted to put Donna and this hitchhiker out of his mind.

Nearly two hours later, Carl struggled to stay awake and he knew that an old rest stop with vending machines was just up ahead. He eased down the slip road that led back into a secluded bit of forest. The old one-story rest-stop building came into view, with some playground equipment and picnic tables surrounding it. Dim lighting spilled out of the front doorway and only a few outside lights were working.

***

All he heard was the rustling of the few leaves still clinging to the trees and crickets chirping as he opened the car door. He grabbed the empty backpack from the trunk to carry some sodas and snacks from the vending machines. He heard footsteps in the gravel behind him as he got close to the doorway. He spun around and backed up against the wall under an exterior light. He listened as he scanned the darkness, but there were no sounds of anyone moving. He figured he kicked up some gravel as he walked and that's the sound he heard.

He backpedaled through the doorway keeping his focus outside, just to be sure. He shivered with a creepy sense that someone was watching him. *Nobody here but me;* he silently assured himself.

He made a quick trip to a urinal in the men's room, rinsed his hands with cold water from the tap, and splashed some on his face. He rubbed his hands dry with some paper towels as he headed back into the main room. He was pleasantly surprised to find that the change machine and vending machines were in working order. He changed a five-dollar bill into quarters, dropped some coins into the slots, and tossed two high-caffeine sodas and two candy bars into the backpack.

He heard the sound of crunching leaves as he exited. Someone moving in the woods next to the building. He froze and looked around the parking lot; his car was still the only one here. His heart raced in response to the sound of quick-moving footsteps. He bolted toward the car and fell to the ground as he glanced over his shoulder, tripping on something.

He sat up and saw who was running through the woods . . .a fat raccoon scurrying away from a trash bin near the corner of the building.

Carl got up, brushed himself off, and tossed the backpack over his right shoulder. He chuckled, "Killer raccoon."

"You said you were headed east." Carl gasped as he turned toward the voice.

He saw the form of someone sitting on the top of one of the picnic tables, maybe thirty feet from where Carl was standing. The voice sounded like the man from the service station but that wasn't possible. *How could he have gotten here? Is he following me?*

Carl wanted to make a run for his car, but figured the guy could probably cut him off. "Who are you? What do you want?" he demanded, as he slowly crept towards the car.

"You don't remember me?" The man went quiet for a few moments. "It'll come back to you. When it does, you'll realize what I want." The man stood up and for just a moment his face was slightly illuminated by some light. A heavily lined face with a scruffy beard that seemed strangely familiar for an instant. But it wasn't someone Carl knew.

Carl made a break for it and was thankful he hadn't

locked the car. He jumped inside and turned the key in the ignition. The car sputtered but it didn't start. He glanced at the picnic table and it was empty. He looked in the rearview mirror and saw the man walking towards the car.He turned the key, but again it sputtered.

"Come on," he shouted to himself.

He looked in the rearview mirror again, but the man wasn't there. A fist tapped on the driver's side window and the man shouted out, "Remember me now." He bent down and his face came into view as he hissed through crooked, yellow teeth, "Take a good look."

Carl turned the key and the car came to life. He floored the accelerator and the car swerved as it threw gravel into the air.

***

Hours later, Carl sipped a cup of fresh coffee in a booth at the old diner where he had eaten a few times over the years. It was only forty miles from the cabin and his last stop. He already topped off the gas tank and parked in the side parking lot.

The sun would be painting the sky a rosy-red soon and peak above the horizon not long before he got to the cabin. He took another bite of his pancake stack as he thought about the service station and rest stop. Carl needed to figure out who this hitchhiking stalker was and what he wanted. *He said I knew him.*

The waitress dropped off the bill and refilled his coffee cup. "Take your time, darlin'."

He looked around. There were a handful of other people in the place; all seemingly dressed in hunting gear. It was that time of year. His thoughts returned to the guy chasing after him. Carl was sure he had never met him but the face seemed familiar, someone he had seen recently.

He closed his eyes for a moment and a brief image of the man's face came back to him, it seemed like blood was coming out of his nose. Carl concentrated, but he couldn't remember where it was or anything else. He opened his eyes and sighed with frustration; he'd had a few fits of rage where he had memory lapses over the years. His last clear memory occurred at Donna's apartment just after someone shouted at him. A man's voice not long after he was served with the restraining order.

He had treated Donna badly and he regretted the night he slapped her about two months back. His temper got the best of him when she said she was leaving him. Donna was a nurse and Carl found out later she was dating a doctor. Then Carl started making harassing phone calls and sitting in his car outside of her apartment or the hospital.

He sighed. *You should've just left her alone.* He remembered the high school principal telling him that his temper would be the end of him when he got suspended for fighting. He took a slow sip of coffee and mumbled, "She doesn't have money to pay a lawyer." But her doctor boyfriend would and maybe he paid someone to keep an eye on Carl after the papers were served on him.

Carl muttered aloud, "He paid the guy to make sure I didn't bother Donna." She was probably at her boyfriend's place now, but Carl didn't know where the doctor lived.

Carl figured the guy followed him to Donna's apartment after he got served. Probably the one who shouted he was going to call the cops. Carl tapped his fingers on the tabletop. *Maybe I spotted him and we had a confrontation— the guy was a bit older but pretty big.* Carl thought he probably punched him and bloodied his nose and it became personal. *He decided to come after me for some payback. Followed me as I drove out of town and kept his car hidden at the service station.*

The guy probably played like a hitchhiker so he could

get the drop on Carl if he let his guard down. *He kept following me and took another shot at the rest stop. The guy is a persistent S.O.B.*

Carl sipped his coffee as he mulled it over. *I don't need her or any more hassles.* He left the guy in the dust at the rest stop and Carl figured the man was surely on his way back to town. No way he would follow him this far over a bloody nose.

He picked up the bill; *seven dollars and twenty-three cents.* He put a ten-dollar bill on top and headed for the men's room. Then he spotted someone in a booth in the back corner. He couldn't see the face, but he was wearing the same jacket and hood as the hitchhiker. Carl sat down at the serving bar, trying to get a better look.

The waitress put a hand on his arm, "Thanks for the tip, sweetie. Did you want something else?"

Carl nodded, "A takeaway cup of coffee for the road. I'm gonna hit the men's room." He headed again toward the restroom and tried to get a better look at the man. He still couldn't see the guy's face.

"Here you go." She put the cup on the counter just moments after Carl sat back down on the stool.

Carl nodded toward the corner, "Do you remember if that guy came in after me? I think I passed him on the way here and he started flashing his lights at me. Maybe thought I cut him off or something." He paused. "I'm not looking for trouble."

"Fred Taylor? He's a local. I don't think he would be hassling you."

Carl turned and looked. "That's not him. My mistake." *Where did he go?* He looked around but didn't see a sign of the hitchhiker in the diner.

Carl picked up the coffee and slipped out the side door. He crept over to the corner of the building. There was no one moving around outside and nobody sitting in any of the cars. *Just my imagination?* He got into his car and put the coffee into the cup holder.

He slowly drove a short distance down the access road, pulled over to the side, and put the gear selector in park. He turned in his seat and watched the door of the diner for a few minutes. No one came out and no cars were following him. He sighed with satisfaction as he put the car into gear and headed for the highway.

Carl exhaled loudly as he drove down the highway. *Time to forget Donna and her new boyfriend.* He felt two powerful hands around his throat and he heard the voice again," You remember me yet?"

Carl saw the man's face in the rearview mirror. The guy must've sneaked into the car when Carl went to the toilet. Carl gasped for air and started to black out. He could sense that the car had gone off the side of the road and was in a tailspin.

He felt the hands let go and he smashed the brake pedal to the floor and put the gear shift into park. He turned off the engine, grabbed the keys, and jumped out the driver's side door. He could scamper down the road a short distance and wait for the dude to cool off. That seemed better than a full-out punching contest.

He spotted an old rusty tire iron on the ground as he ran along the side of the road. He stopped, bent down, and picked it up. This would keep the guy at bay. As he stood up, he saw a car heading down the highway in the opposite direction. A police car of some type. He ran into the road and flagged it down.

The car stopped and a sheriff's deputy gestured at Carl as his window came down. "What's wrong?"

Carl turned and pointed at his car on the opposite side of the road about fifteen yards away. "Somebody tried to kill me; they were hiding in the back seat."

The deputy parked his car on the opposite side of the

road and got out. "Follow me." He called something in on the radio and put his hand on his gun but it stayed in the holster.

The sun was starting to come up as the deputy used his flashlight while he moved around Carl's car. "There's no one here."

Carl pointed at the car and said, "He was in the backseat." Carl could see he wasn't there now. "He's been following me all night, ever since I left the city. I thought he was just trying to scare me over a personal beef. I'm telling you, he tried to choke me to death."

The deputy moved to the front of Carl's car, shined the flashlight around the area, and turned to look at Carl. "No sign of anyone."

Carl waved at the forest. "He must've run into the woods. I'm guessing his car is parked at the diner just down the road."

Carl followed as the deputy walked to the edge of the forest and spoke into his radio for a few moments. He moved back closer to Carl and held out his mobile phone to show a photo. "You recognize this man?"

Carl shouted, "That's him. That's the guy who tried to kill me."

The deputy pointed his flashlight at the front of Carl's car. "Looks like you hit something and that looks like blood."

Carl shuffled a few steps closer to the car, "I didn't hit anything." He stared at the damage to the right front of his car and the splash of red. *Where did that come from?*

The deputy put his hand on his gun but didn't pull it from the holster. "This man, the one you said was trying to kill you. He's dead in the morgue back in the city. Killed by a hit-and-run driver late last night. His body was found between Mile Marker 166 and 167 on Highway 33. Best guess is that he was hitchhiking on the westbound side of the highway."

The image of the man's face in the headlights just before Carl's car hit him flashed into his mind. Carl remembered getting out of the car and looking at him lying on the side of the road, blood running out of his nose. He didn't remember checking whether the man was alive and he didn't remember driving away. The next thing he remembered was hitting the brakes and stopping on the side of the road at Mile Marker 167.

"He's not dead. He's been following me and he tried to kill me!"

Carl heard the hitchhiker's voice from the forest. "I'm gonna use his gun to kill you." Carl saw him peeking out of the woods just behind the deputy.

Carl moved toward the deputy and waved the tire iron at the hitchhiker. "You heard him. There he is! Shoot him."

The deputy drew his gun. "I didn't hear anything." He pointed the gun at Carl. "Stay back. Calm down."

Carl screamed as he ran at the deputy. "Shoot him."

Moments later, Carl lay on the ground and he heard the deputy yelling into his radio. "Shots fired. Shots fired. Suspect down."

Carl felt his life slipping away, as he struggled to open his eyes. The hitchhiker was hovering over him. "I knew you'd remember me."

Brutal
by
Eldon Litchfield

S har shifted through the dried weeds and trash in the field beside the parking lot. They had been looking for Mom for thirty minutes now. It wasn't looking good.

She could be anywhere. Dad wasn't clever in his methods, but it didn't matter. He could drop her off any-where. No one looks at trash.

Shar didn't worry about any curious onlookers. It was a Wednesday, a slow night for attractions, including at the Rootin'-Tootin' Kansas Ghost Town, family fun for all. It was 4 p.m. The parking lot was almost empty.

The last time they were here, August was only three. He'd cried, thinking the reenacted gunfight was real and that people were actually dying. Mom told him they were just pretending. Dad called him a wussy.

Family fun for all.

"Found her," Nicole shouted.

They gathered around their sister. It was a clear plastic garbage bag behind a clump of dried weeds. Up close, one could easily tell it contained a human leg.

Shar tossed the car keys to Nicole, then put on a pair of garden gloves. "Go open the trunk."

Nicole and August ran to the car. Shar gently picked up the bag. It was a piece of meat, but she handled it like it was porcelain.

"Don't worry Momma, we'll find you."

***

Shar turned up the radio. It was Korn, perfect for drowning out intruding thoughts, or making them worse. She shifted the car into drive.

"We need to get ice soon," said Nicole. "What we got is melted."

"I'm hungry," said August.

Shar felt the emptiness in her own belly. "Yeah, let's stop somewhere."

"Can't we just get it at the window?"

Shar sighed. August didn't like dining inside fast-food places. Bad experience once with a perverted patron in the restroom.

"We can't go through the drive-thru, too many questions about why a 15-year-old is driving a car, people would notice. We'll order inside and eat in the car." She looked at her siblings. August was huddled in the space between the front and back seat clutching a stuffed dragon. What was its name? Glittervox. Nicole crouched in the passenger seat staring at her cell phone.

"I'm so tired," said Nicole.

It had been a while since they had a decent night's sleep. Maybe they could risk spending the night in a motel room. Clean bed, clean towels, something close to normal. A night in a real bed sounded wonderful. Shar needed rest. And they needed ice. They were closing in on Dad. He wasn't getting away. But getting a room was risky.

"Keep a lookout for anyplace affordable," Shar said. "Walking distance to a restaurant would be great."

"There," Nicole pointed.

Blue Crown Inn, and next door to a Roast Beef Round-Up and a Chow Clown, plus a small grocery store.

She parked the car a few spaces down from the entrance. Best if the manager didn't get a good view of the car's occupants. She reached into the center console for their cash. They were down to eight hundred and forty-three dollars. "I'll be back."

She exited the car.

Shar walked inside. The manager hastily put out a cigarette and sprayed air freshener. By the time Shar got to the counter, everything smelled of smoky Fresh Linen.

According to the dull bronze and black nametag, the woman's name was Hazel.

Shar went to script.

"How much for one adult and three kids?"

Hazel looked outside. "Where's your…"

"Mom's exhausted. Been driving for nine hours. I offered to come in. She finally decided to leave her boyfriend." Shar gave Hazel her puppy eyes. Not too much, not too little.

Hazel's expression changed as the middle-aged woman shifted into Help Mode. Shar guessed her story wasn't the first of its kind, and wouldn't be the last, for a motel clerk. She felt slightly ashamed, but it was close to the truth. They weren't fleeing but following, not hiding but hunting.

"It'll be eighty for the night, hon."

Shar gave Hazel the money and signed the guest register. Hazel handed her a key card. Shar stopped before leaving. "Oh, where's the ice machine?"

***

Shar returned to the car, taking note of any security

cameras and their blind spots. Once inside the room, they chowed down on Chow Clown. August quickly went to sleep afterwards. Nicole watched the TV. Shar held up a crystal on a thread over a map of the United States. The point was leaning to someplace in Nevada.

Where had they gone to, there? The Goldwell Open Air Museum, as creepy as anything with its wraith-like sculptures. And they stayed at the Clown Motel, which was built next to a closed cemetery.

Dad could go to either one.

It was time to break out the kit.

"Going to be in the bathroom. Don't disturb."

Nicole's eyes didn't leave the TV, but she nodded. August snored.

Shar stopped in front of the bathroom mirror. She was starting to hate mirrors, because they slammed reality into her face. They were all reflected in the glass, Nicole's dull profile staring into the TV, August's feet in dirty socks standing outside the covers on the bed, and herself. She was skinny, pale and tired. She thought her short hair looked like it had gone through a tornado.

Enough with distractions. Time for work.

Shar dragged a chair from the table in front of the room to the bathroom. Then, balancing on tiptoes, she removed the smoke detector from the ceiling. She placed it on the sink counter and removed the batteries. She placed a worn duffle bag on the toilet, then closed the door. She pushed the chair against the door, took out a compass from the kit, found East, and placed a red cloth square on the chair seat, thankful East wasn't where the toilet was. With the lid down it made a convenient table, but it always made the ritual seem awkward.

She placed orange and black candles on the ends, followed by a concave glass of six inches in diameter set on plastic holders between the candles. She checked to make sure it was just in front of the line of candles so no direct light would hit the inner surface. The outside part of the glass was spray-painted black. The interior part looked like black ice. After turning off the light, she took out the small vial of dried blood. Dad's blood. She sat on the edge of the bathtub and took out a book.

She read from the book, although she now knew the words by heart. Shar called upon Andromalius, a great and mighty Earl and Demon of Justice and Revenge.

Staring into the mirror, time lost meaning. She continued the words. Andromalius appeared in the mirror; his head was smooth, a high collar surrounding his neck, his expression sardonic. A large snake coiled around his left arm. The reptile's head swayed slowly. Shar ignored the snake and focused on Andromalius' face.

Andromalius grinned and nodded.

"Oh spirit, I command you (Shar refused to say "thee" as it was written in Mom's book, it seemed overly dramatic) to reveal the location of (Shar always paused, hating to say the name) Herbert Valdez."

Andromalius held out his hand. Shar took the vial of Dad's blood and scraped out a few flakes onto the mirror. There wasn't much left. This was all a gamble. The spirit took the sample into the mirror world and smelled it.

The spirit licked its lips and told Shar where Dad was headed. It wasn't words, or even telepathy really, but information placed into her mind.

Shar came out of the bathroom. Nicole was still watching TV. August was still snoring. She glanced at the clock. The ritual felt like it was only a few minutes, but an hour had passed.

"We're going back to the clown motel," she said.

"I hated that place," replied Nicole.

"So did I," said Shar.

***

The trunk was filled with fresh ice. All the water from melted ice had drained out through the hole Shar had drilled through the trunk bottom. All of Mom was there except for two pieces: her head and her heart. Nicole checked the map app; the estimated drive time to Tonopah was eighteen hours.

They loaded the car. Shar studied her siblings. They were tired but she thought they still had enough energy to finish the job. Off to the clown motel.

Shar's body grew numb after a few hours driving, but her mind was focused on the objective. She turned up the radio and found a fuzzy station playing '80s hits. The DJ sounded like an idiot. August reread his comic books, then drew dinosaurs on the memo paper taken from the motel. He knew all their scientific names and could tell you their geologic time, Triassic, Jurassic, or Cretaceous. Mom always put his drawings up on the fridge with magnets. Shar wondered if any drawings had survived the fire. Nicole focused on her phone, occasionally warning Shar of a speed trap ahead. *Thank you, Google maps,* Shar thought. Lunch was packs of cheese crackers and sodas from the cooler.

An hour outside Denver, they stopped for a bathroom, August complaining he was about to explode.

The rest stop looked like someone's idea of a joke. The structure was a simple wall and roof building with working sinks and a toilet housing placed over a hole in the ground. All waste fell into a pit of excrement. Shar looked at the hole in horror. There were a few aged vending machines in a shelter beside the building. There was just one word to describe it: nasty.

Shar exited the restroom and went to a spot behind the building, just to have a few moments alone. What lay opposite the highway was wilderness, at least to her eye.

Patches of foliage stood out against bare patches of earth. It was as if someone couldn't decide what the landscape should look like. Stark contrasts between harsh and soft, and yet together they looked pretty. Mom knew a lot about plants and trees, and would teach them their names. Shar couldn't remember any of what she taught them; she just thought it was awesome that Mom knew so much.

A man in a sport coat and jeans walked up to her. He had on a faded tee shirt that had CANNIBAL CORPSE on it. Shar turned to face him.

"Hey there, little lady," he said. The man was maybe in his 40s. Hair in a buzz cut. He had a little bit of a beard. Not heavy-set, but not trim. But Shar recognized what he was, he was a monster.

"Walked by your car. Noticed things. Just you and two younger siblings, right? I'm right. I know, I watched. Running away from home? That's okay, life can be a shit show. Got to do what you need to do. You are a very pretty little lady, you know that? Your jeans and that rough tank top just…just really enhances your…attributes. All flat-chested. Oh God, you almost look like a boy. Your brother and sister I'm not interested in, but you. Oh you, you got my system pumping. You help me out, I don't report you to the police as runaways. Maybe I'll even give you a few bucks to help you out. Everyone gets what they need, eh? Let's be a good girl."

The man advanced.

Shar reached behind her. She was wearing Dad's flannel shirt wrapped around her waist. It had been grabbed on the fly. She hated it, but it was practical and the best for concealing things since it was oversized, like the tire iron stuffed into the back of her pants from Dad's little workshop. Shar carried it whenever they stopped somewhere. Ever since August's incident at the fast-food restroom.

The man laughed when Shar pulled the tire iron out,

then his expression changed when he fell to the ground after Nicole kicked behind his left knee.

Shar hadn't noticed her younger sister sneaking up on the man, or August behind her. The man cussed. "You little whore, I'll…"

"Get him," Shar said.

August was ready with a rock. Nicole whaled in with a hammer she carried with her. Shar joined in with her tire iron. They kept raining down blows on the man like a heavy summer rain. At first it was like hitting a mattress, something solid with a little give. Then it was like hitting a soft pillow. Then it became moist, meaty, squishy. There were no screams. The man shriveled, ceased moving. Ceased breathing. They kept going. When they stopped, Shar didn't feel tired but stronger.

August fell on his butt, leaned back and gasped. Nicole stepped away and bent over, hands on her knees, taking in deep breaths. Shar stepped back, looking yet not looking at the prone figure before them. The tire iron was wet, slick, sticky.

"Boy, ya did a number on him."

The trio turned to see an old man in a worn buttoned shirt and sweatpants. Shar noticed he had plastic bags filled with clothes. His matted hair and unkempt beard, all pointed out that the man was homeless. Share motioned her brother and sister to back away from the stranger, unsure what was going to happen.

"I'm Trevor," he said. The man approached the body. He rolled it over, ignoring the blood, and took out the man's wallet. Trevor then plucked out the paper bills and rifled the pockets for loose change, then he dropped the wallet into a nearby garbage bin.

He walked toward the vending machines, waving at Shar. "Looked like he had it comin'. God bless."

Exhaling, Shar turned to her little brother and sister.

August had drops of blood on his forehead. Nicole's knuckles were scratched. Both looked like they had gone through a disaster. The tire iron felt warm in Shar's hands. She used it to point to the dead man, the perv who tried to blackmail her, rape her. She looked at her kin.

"This is what we need to be when we get to Dad, got it?" she said. "No hesitation. Straight to the point. Just lay into him. Go, go, go. Don't stop. Do. Not. Stop. For what he did to Mom. For what he did to us. We need to get this done. The world isn't a nice place. We need to be brutal."

Nicole and August were silent, motionless, but there was psychic communication, a family bond that worked in a silent agreement. When they caught up to their stepfather, their focus would be bringing him down.

They looked at her. Shar looked at them. Their resolve became psychic iron. All three said one word, their mantra.

"Brutal."

They continued to Tonopah.

***

Shar viewed the mile markers as a slow countdown to their next stop. Nicole was asleep with her head tilted back and mouth open, the ever-present phone resting in her open hands. She looked like someone experiencing a religious moment. August was drawing again, making dinosaur noises as he consulted one of his books. She noticed that his skills were improving. Maybe he would grow up to be an artist.

She reflected on her speech at the rest stop. The world wasn't always brutal, she thought. There were good times, great times, but other people forced themselves in and ruined things. She remembered the times before Dad, when it was just her, Nicole, and Mom waiting for August to be born. It was simple, or seemed so. They didn't need anyone.

But Mom thought they did. Even the wise make bad decisions, Shar thought.

A sign said it was ten miles to Tonopah.

***

Shar didn't understand the appeal. Why clowns?

No clown was safe or sane. White face of death with a blood red grin. Eyes way too bright and wide. Slapstick humor was just laughing at pain.

They got lodging easily enough. The clerk didn't question her getting a room. She was surprised they were able to get one for under a hundred. It was labeled Standard, and simply contained three clown prints, one of which was a sad clown that looked sleepy and angry or just drugged. Shar had seen similar expressions on Dad's face. Too often.

August settled in quickly for a nap. Nicole watched the TV and scrolled on her phone.

There was a brochure in the room for "haunted Tonopah," so tourists could learn about the Lady in Red and "Devil" Davis and his pranks. There were other pamphlets for a museum and a tour of a brewing company and a list of delivery places. She didn't bother asking the others, she was in the mood for pasta and placed an online order, marking the delivery time as ASAP. The chicken Alfredo, and everything else, cost forty bucks. Including room, gas, and other expenses, they were now down to five hundred and seventy-one dollars.

Shar would have preferred staying somewhere else, but the hotel had a reputation for being prone to paranormal activity. If so, that would prove helpful if she had to do another ritual. And the Tonopah Cemetery was next door. The perfect holiday. If you were Stephen King, Shar thought.

Shar didn't bother organizing her sister and brother to

help her search; she had a gut feeling that Dad was getting sloppy. After dinner, she walked to the cemetery and looked around. The graves were neat and orderly, all rectangles outlined with small rocks, crowned with simple headstones. The ground had a gritty dryness that crunched softly under her footsteps. She spotted a large rock outside the cemetery that seemed out of place. A thin brown snake with yellow stripes on each side wove its way toward it. Shar recognized it as a whip snake. Was it the same serpent that was on Andromalius's arm? Shar couldn't remember.

Looking around to make sure she wasn't being watched, Shar rolled the rock over and found a hole, filled with a paper grocery bag. Inside was Mom's head. Her left eye was open, mouth closed. The skin looked like bread dough left in the fridge for too long. Shar knew. Mom used to bake.

The snake was nowhere to be seen.

Ignoring the smell, snuffing out all thought of what she was carrying, focusing on finishing the task, she placed the bag gently in the car trunk.

Mom was mostly there. The only thing missing was her heart.

***

Shar performed the Ritual of Andromalius again that night. It used the last of Dad's blood.

The spirit appeared. It understood that this was Endgame and directly answered Shar's question.

The next stop, their last stop, was Las Vegas. Where Dad blew their remaining savings. Mom's savings.

Shar remembered at that time August needed new pants because he'd worn an embarrassing hole through his only pair. Dad said he would buy him twenty pairs of pants after he won big, which didn't happen.

They had gone to a lot of places back then, it had been a wild week, but Shar guessed Dad was where the heart was. It was the last piece. He would be someplace less crowded, secluded, not busy. He would go to the Valley of Fire, where he gave his greatest performance. That's where he convinced Mom that he was on the up-and-up. Before he started selling drugs. Before he started sampling the products. Before he discovered bath salts, before the paranoia, the late-night conversations directed to empty areas on the wall, defecating on the front lawn, threats to kill himself, kill all of them, before the night of the thunderstorm, eating Nicole's hamster alive in front of her. Before killing Mom.

Nicole had looked everything up online. It would cost them fifteen dollars for their car, since they were not residents of Nevada, to enter the park. They could pay in the visitor's center and avoid the risk of going through a drive-through. They would go in at 11 a.m., when it was busy and hopefully able to be unnoticed in the crowd. Peak hours went down after 3 p.m.

When they were here years ago, Dad had spent all his time on the phone. Always yelling. Always blaming someone for his mistakes. Always asking "give me another day" and saying, "Everything will be okay."

Mom took them to look at the petroglyphs made over three thousand years ago by what someone had labeled the Basket Maker Culture. Shar guessed they were good at making baskets. Her mind was boggled that there were people there thousands of years earlier just living life, eating meals, laughing, telling stories, just being human. Everything simple, basic. Did any family, back then, have a psychodad, like theirs? Anyone there addicted to drugs? Any creeps? Any murderers?

No streaming. No internet. No concerns about any faceless entity's opinions. Just each other and the world.

The park was forty thousand acres, a lot of space, Shar thought. She guessed when they confronted Dad, it would be far away from witnesses, which was both bad and good. She wanted a direct confrontation, but if things went south, it would be great if someone with a cell phone was available. But this was a private family matter.

It was Vegas. What happened there, stayed there.

Shar was determined to win.

***

Shar wondered how someplace so dry and barren, with its clear layered lines of stone and earth, would remind her of water. She read somewhere that the desert used to be an ocean. It made sense in her head, from listening to August explaining to Mom about how the earth went through changes over millions of years. She could picture the sediment adding layers over the centuries, each one distinctive in its color and chemistry.

Dad was here, somewhere. Waiting amidst all the beauty.

August asked, "What do we do?"

"We drive around until we find him," Shar answered.

There were the White Domes Trail and the Windstone Arch, but Shar knew that Dad wouldn't go to someplace populated. It would be someplace desolate, sterile. But the roads were limited.

She felt Andromalius's influence in her head, pushing her to a certain area. She drove to where the impulses directed her. The telepathic thoughts were intrusive, and she felt herself fighting them, it was uncomfortable having such things slip into one's mind unbidden. It made her feel helpless. That's when everything exploded into a storm of glass shards.

Adrenaline kicked in right after the impact. Time

slowed down. Her mind analyzed every detail. Dad's car hit her side. She was surprised that he was still driving the neighbor's 1979 Impala. Glass from the driver's side window and the windshield burst in a shower of cutting pieces. Nicole's eyes jerked away from her phone, bewildered terror on her face. Her phone remained clutched in her hand, the screen displaying some bubble shooter game. August's mouth started forming a scream, his face contorted into a wretched expression of fear. The dash clock said it was 3:38. One uneaten cracker from a pack flew into the air. Their car was shoved several feet away, but the Impala kept coming and slammed into the car again, pushing it even further from the road. Shar saw Dad's face through the other car's windshield, wide-eyed and sweaty, insane.

Had he been waiting in ambush, or out hunting for them? Or was it just dumb luck? Why here, why now? Shar wondered.

She watched her father try to put his car in reverse, maybe to gain ground for another charge, but it stalled out, gray smoke spewing from under the collapsed hood.

Shar reached back and grabbed her pack, which held her weapons. "Everyone out! Spread out!" She saw Nicole push against the door, screaming and crying. It wasn't opening. She saw August reaching for Glittervox and noticed that his thumb was bent at the wrong angle. There was blood on his cheek. His eyes were wide in shock. Mom was still in the trunk. It was hopeless. They hadn't even started, and everything had already fallen apart.

It was all up to her now.

He was not going to defeat them.

Gripping her bag in her teeth, Shar pushed herself out through the broken window. She felt the glass carve marks into her skin. She landed headfirst on the rocky ground. Stood up, ignoring the pain. Shar scanned the environment. They were surrounded by large rocks, far away from the road. No passers-by could see them. Shar was okay with that, this was a private matter. It just needed to end.

Her Dad stumbled out of the Impala. A thousand observations flew into her mind; the scars on his forearms, the spittle covering his chin, the stained white tee-shirt, no pants but wearing Mom's underwear, a pair of cheap flip-flops on his feet, one non-functioning eye staring upward, sweat-covered face, wide open mouth, the large knife in his right hand. The wonders of methamphetamine. Shar was surprised he hadn't overdosed by now.

"Knew you were following me," he bellowed. "I could feel it. Should have put you out of my misery a long time ago. Kids are nothing but grief. Parasites. They suck you dry. Your mother went on and on about you all, like you were more important than anything. What about what I needed? You ticks think about me? You're nothing, less than shit."

The knife was something bought out of an overpriced fantasy catalog, decorated with snakes and cheap glass gems, but still sharp, still deadly. Swaying in her Dad's hand, it reflected the sunlight like a blinking spotlight.

It was just him, and her. Shar turned to check on Nicole and August. The car was empty. Shar grabbed her tire iron.

"What have you been up to, Charles, or Charlene?" her father asked.

"Don't call me that," she replied.

Herbert Valdez licked his knife. Blood gushed from his tongue.

"We could have gotten out of our money troubles if your Mom agreed to rent you out a few times a night. Nicky and August would have brought in some money, but I think you would have brought in enough dough to last us a while. You just should have pulled your own weight. Food ain't free. Your Mom didn't see how the world worked. It's brutal out there. You…AH!"

Herbert screamed as August drove the point of a flat-head screwdriver into his right knee. Nicole followed through on his left side, shrieking, armed with two claw hammers, pounding each down on Dad's arm and leg. They had rushed in from the sides. Like ninjas, Shar thought, on the attack.

He fell to his knees; his knife went up. Shar moved in.

She focused the tire iron on Dad's face. Each blow was powered by memory; insults to Mom and them, lies, arguments, all mixed in her mind, becoming the lyrics to the song of Hell. She swung, and hit, a solid thud as her tire iron met flesh. Again, and again. Shar didn't feel any exertion, everything was a flood of rage and desperation. She realized she was shrieking. Nicole howled. August was screaming and crying. The rock walls swallowed the sound.

Shar wasn't aware how long it took, but Herbert Valdez, stepfather to three, murderer and drug addict, was dead. His corpse was now a fleshy bag of pulped and punctured meat. Shar looked up. It was starting to get dark.

August fell back and curled into a ball. Nicole turned away, dropping the hammers, and stared out into the desert.

Shar staggered to the Impala. She wondered how long it would take for the vultures to find his body, and if the birds would be affected by the drugs in his system, becoming anxious and paranoid scavengers flying around a state park.

In the passenger seat lay a Ziplock sandwich bag. Inside was a heart. Shar grabbed it and held it tight to her chest. She beat down the tears wanting to pour out. There was work to do. She went to their car.

She retrieved the car keys and opened the trunk. All the parts of Mom were there, now. Shar took out the book from her backpack and reviewed the notes.

She would need to perform the ritual to summon

Atranrbiabil, a demon associated with fire that could reverse the effects of decay. After that, she would need to do the ritual of Frastiel, who had the power of Life and Death. It would be a long night. She knew the adrenaline would wear off in an hour.

"Guys, I need your help for the last part. Almost done. We can do this."

Nicole and August responded.

***

The next morning.

"Mom, we're out in the desert and we don't have a working car."

Shar's mother smiled softly at her. Shar felt a soft touch in her mind, and knew her mother's thoughts. *Don't worry. I will wait by the road until a car comes by. That will be our new car.*

"And Mom, we haven't eaten since noon yesterday. We're kinda hungry."

We will find food. After I get the car.

Mom didn't look exactly like she had, but she exhibited power that wasn't there before.

Was Mom something new? Something else, now that she was returned to them from the dead?

Shar didn't care. Mom was back. Everything would be okay.

Mom hugged them all in an exceptionally long embrace. It felt weird, but good. Mom felt strong.

It was time to go home.

The Women's Room
by
Blake Kourik

It was half-past nine a.m. and edging toward their take-off time when Peter and Becca came to the women's restrooms.

"Okay, just hurry, honey, we don't have—"

"—I know, Peter, but I have to go before we board, or I won't be able to hold it till they click off the—" Becca grasped for the word, shaking her hand. The strap of the diaper bag dug into her shoulder.

"Fasten seatbelt sign. Okay, but, Becca, hurry. Boarding's already—"

Becca stared at him, and her eyes flared. "I know," she said and handed him the bulging bag.

He let go of his luggage and took it in his free hand, his other clutching the palm of their firstborn, Dylan. In his blue jean overalls and bright orange Astros shirt, his jaw hung open and his head rotated back and forth, taking in the sheer volume of the airport.

In the rows of seating, dozens of passengers awaited their flights to destinations all over the country. Middle-aged commuters munched overpriced snacks. Strung-out businessmen drank stale, burnt coffee. Old women in Bermuda shorts jabbered to restless grandchildren. Young men cradled overstuffed duffel bags. Parents buried their noses in magazines, while their children climbed over the seating. Everywhere people moved, stood, or sat.

Pete's eyes darted down the seemingly never-ending hall, to the gates in the E section. To his right, the sign above the closest alcove read E3. That meant their gate was somewhere down near the end–a connecting flight from Salt Lake City to Tampa, Gate E23.

"I'll hurry," Becca said. Her gaze pierced into him, and he felt as small as his son, holding his hand. As lost as Dylan would be, here, without an adult. She turned, crossed to the bathroom doors, and disappeared inside.

Great, Pete thought. *That's all I need, on top of everything else. Becca mad again.* There wasn't much time, though. They needed to go.

Memories of weekends with his father at the YMCA, rose in his mind, learning to swim by being thrown into the deep end of the pool.

"Sink or swim, Petey," his father would say, watching him flounder.

"Sink or swim," he muttered. A deep sigh hitched from his chest.

Dylan looked up at him. "Big, daddy!" he said, eyebrows lifted. His miniature fist wrapped around the handle of his Thomas the Train suitcase.

"Yeah, pretty big, huh?" He smiled down, mirroring his son.

"Go home?" Dylan asked.

"Pretty soon, buddy. Pretty soon."

Pete's eyes searched the airport, helplessly sliding from person to person. Gate to gate, he took it all in. He hoped they'd make it to their flight. He'd already checked before they left the hotel for any other connecting flight, in case they missed this one.

Tomorrow morning, he had a meeting with his new

boss, and if they didn't make this flight, there wouldn't be another in time. By this evening, he and his family needed to be in Florida, not stuck in Houston. He couldn't afford any more slip-ups. After all the shit at work, this was his last chance.

That'd been his son's favorite word recently—*shit*—a gift he brought home from one of John Park Elementary's fifth graders, Eli Travis. On one of the days when he picked Dylan up from the preschool at John Park, he'd run about forty-five minutes late, and during that time, Eli amused himself in the carline by feeding Dylan an M&M every time he said the word.

The first time his son repeated it, Pete was surprised into laughter, and that only encouraged him, but Becca didn't find it funny. It took weeks to get him to stop saying it.

But *shit* was what it all felt like, when the last deal fell through. It was the biggest one that year and up until the last moment, a sure bet. It should've been his, despite the risk.

His boss, Graham Colley, tried to warn him against it. "If you can make it happen, you'll get VP, but if this goes belly up, it won't be good, Pete."

Everything went perfectly, until a week before closing. Before the end of the quarter, Pete took the executive board of Salaman Industries out to dinner. They ate, drank, discussed logistics, and by the end of the night signed the letter of intent.

Then, five days before the final paperwork, Pete got the voicemail saying they had decided to go with another company. ELO-Solutions beat them out with a $50 million lower price. A $128 million deal disappeared. When news reached upper management, Colley took him outside.

"There's a position in the Tampa sales department. Head of microchip distribution. Nearly the same thing you're doing now."

They sat on a park bench outside the building, beneath blooming magnolia trees. Pete had been silent, unable to think.

"It's a little bit of a pay cut, but it's not a demotion. It's security. I'd be able to get your moving expenses covered. It's not ideal, but I wanted to give you the option at least, so you'd have one," Graham said, sipping slowly from his coffee. "They're going to let you go if you stay. All I can offer you is Florida. There, you'd be under separate management, but here, you're still under Plowman and the gun."

Plowman had been the problem from the very beginning. His boss's boss, one of them at least, and an SOB if Pete ever met one. Plowman knew as much about what he oversaw as a monkey knew about mechanics, but that didn't stop him from acting like he ran the world from his office. Everyone knew it, but they never contradicted him, not when he held over 20 percent of the company. He was right under the owner, Gary Welch, so he had the most swinging power. Old man Welch never lifted a finger against him.

So, here Pete was, waiting for his wife in the terminal, hoping to make it in time, because thought he had the Florida job—the job Colley assured was secure, and that he'd be fine, and not to worry—if he lost that position, his life would fall apart. Every piece would spiderweb and shatter.

They were already in debt for the house in Utah. The new house in Tampa shot a gaping hole in their credit. The company wouldn't pay their moving costs for another two months. They sold both their cars. They still had eighteen months on their student loans. Becca wasn't working, so she could stay home with Dylan. They were hemorrhaging money and they needed this job.

Dylan's hand started to sweat in his own, slicking his

palm.

"Wanna go," he said, letting go of his suitcase to pick at the seat of his overalls.

"Me, too, buddy," Pete muttered and checked his watch. 9:33 a.m. Their flight to Tampa was already boarding. Christ, their flight left at 9:45. They'd already shown up half an hour late. Security nabbed them on the way in, and she should've been out by now. So, where was she? Even with the time it took to find a stall, cover the toilet seat with a nest of toilet paper—like she always did—and perch atop it before finishing , it shouldn't have taken but a few minutes. She'd been in for almost five.

Maybe there was a line, he thought, and, considering the sheer number of people here, that wouldn't be so far-fetched.

But she knew. She knew she should've—

Held it? Like all the car trips he and his siblings took as kids, because their father only made the stops he planned to, no more, no less, and if you had to go, that sounded like your own damn fault.

No. This was different. They were already late, and this wasn't about a trip, or how long it took to get there. This was getting there on time because things depended on it—their livelihood depended on it—and Becca didn't understand that.

Pete checked his watch again and saw the hand tick from 9:33 to 9:34. In the background, layers of voices babbled to one another, mixing, confusing.

The biggest thing was, in the end, he'd grown to hate a part of her. The absent sense. The part of her that felt like she was constantly, partially, somewhere else. Not with him and her son. He loved Becca, but he'd grown to resent the tiredness every time he talked to her, like she was tired of him, tired of them, bored, not wanting to follow through with the family they'd started together.

Although he was the only one working, when it came to trying, he felt he was alone in putting his best foot forward. In raising their son, around the house, doing chores, dishes, laundry, getting Dylan to read—he felt like he did it all, and they both had their shortcomings, but Pete felt like he was raising Dylan on his own.

Dylan still hadn't been potty trained, even though Pete had sat with him in the bathroom for hours on the weekends, trying to get him to go in the pot, so what the hell was she doing while he was gone and she was at home? The kid was nearing two-and-a-half now, and he felt that his son should've started showing signs of at least being trained, but so far, nothing. His son started talking when he was only one but now, at two-and-a-half, he still wore diapers.

During his lunch breaks and the in-between hours of going to work and taking care of what he needed to do at home, he'd gone through all the parenting books, articles, fact sheets, and online blogs. He'd tried to take it all in.

It depends. When your child is ready. When they're comfortable. It all varies.

All the literature boiled down to variables. There were no definite answers, only probabilities, and ranges. Nothing solid or set in stone. Nothing wham-bam-thank-you-ma'am.

Sink or swim, Petey.

Pete lowered the diaper bag to the ground and rubbed his shoulder. He watched the doors of the women's room and anticipated the face of his wife, her hand, her gray slacks, her brown loafers to swing through the frame every time it opened. Yet, none who came and went were her.

A rail-thin woman yanked open the door and skirted inside. Another short woman who looked twelve but couldn't've been younger than thirty, stamped out from the lavatory, adjusting her backpack while typing furiously on her cell phone. Two older women, laughing riotously, wad-dled over from Pancho's Bar and Grill behind him and en-tered the restroom together. One opened the door for the other, missing the handle, and grabbed it again to more whooping laughter from them both.

Every time the door opened, he tried to look inside, to see if she was standing before the mirrors, washing her hands, but the layout of the bathroom only provided out-siders with a view of the wall that formed a horizontal hall, before opening on the room.

When was the last time you even slept together? The thought popped into his head, driving into his gut like a sucker punch. He didn't know. He didn't know, and it didn't matter, because that wasn't what constituted mar-riage, but it couldn't have been that long ago…

When was the last time you kissed? And he didn't know that, either. Clinical pecks had passed between them, more recently. He could remember those…

But really kissed. You don't know, do you? And he didn't.

The women's room door swung open, and the pneu-matic door closer hissed, easing it shut again. Another woman emerged with a face he didn't recognize.

"Daddy, wanna see mommy." Dylan's voice shattered his focus, drawing his gaze.

"I know, buddy. Mommy'll be here shortly, okay?" he tried.

"Okay," his son said, but his brow lowered on his fore-head, scrunching his face.

What's she doing when she's alone then, Pete? If she's not raising Dylan, then how's she spending her time?

Pete tried to slap these thoughts away, but the more he tried to push them down, the more they surfaced, one at a time, like bloated corpses from opaque waters.

"You never really know what you're thinkin' till

you're thinkin.'" His father's voice played in his ears like a broken cassette tape. The almighty sage, the great drinker who gave up his marriage for his never-ending affair with Popov vodka.

Sink or swim.

"Never trust a bitch." Memories of sitting in the living room, watching *ChiPs* with his father flickered over his eyes. Afraid to move because his father wanted to watch the TV together.

"Only alcoholics drink alone, Petey. That's why I always drink with you." He'd laugh at every punchline from the endless stream of shows they watched, until he'd pass out in his leather armchair, with a white Russian cocktail curdling on the nearest end table.

His father, who had worked nine-to-five at a cushy office job, drank all night and every weekend that he had his son over, and then guzzled a pot of coffee every morning before going to work. Even his eyes never betrayed his habits. Nothing that a little saline solution to both peepers couldn't take care of. His mother knew but never could pry it from her son. Not the way he looked up to him, despite it all. Not the way he wanted to—

You're swimmin' now, Petey. Givin' em hell, right where they deserve it. You trusted a bitch, and that's where you slipped up, but, hey, so did I, so who am I to talk?

Laughter swirled his ears as his father guffawed in his thoughts and the two older women emerged from the lavatory again, continuing the conversation they held when they went in.

What was she doing in there? Was she okay? Pete looked down to check his watch again, when another announcement came over the intercom from Gate E9 declaring that the final checks were underway, and the captain would order the doors of the aircraft closed in five minutes. The announcement repeated that this was the final boarding call for Emily and Nick Applegate. The small analog face on Pete's Rolex ticked from 9:34 to 9:35, and beads of sweat dripped down his neck.

"Wanna see Mommy," Dylan whined and tugged at his father's hand. He pointed at the door to the women's room. "Wanna see Mommy, Daddy."

"I know, Dylan. But she's almost done. She'll be out shortly."

Pete reached for his phone to call her when he felt the small bulge in his back pocket. Becca's phone that she'd asked him to hold for her after they passed through security.

"Just grab it for me, Peter, and hold onto it for me, for now," she spat, trying to shove everything back into Dylan's suitcase that the TSA had flipped inside out. All on account of a Capri-Sun juice pouch that their son had packed underneath his clothes.

"You can't take this aboard, sir. This is over the federally regulated ounce size."

"I understand. Our son must've packed it when we were—"

"Nor can you have this," she said, removing a pack of gummy bears. "I'm going to have to ask you and your family to step aside."

They'd spent an extra ten minutes waiting for one of the officers to flip Dylan's bag inside out, then each of their own and Becca had repacked Dylan's case, while Pete repacked his and Becca's and put his and his son's shoes back on, and refilled his pockets.

"Shit," he moaned under his breath. In the surrounding noise, the word came out minute, almost crying, and he felt like crying because he didn't know anymore. He didn't know what his wife was doing, he didn't know if she was okay, or if something had happened, and the clock ticked by as 9:36 turned to 9:37 and—

"Ma'am. Ma'am, excuse me," he spoke out as the

women's room door opened again and a young lady wearing wire-rimmed glasses and an orange sweater that made her look like Velma from *Scooby-Doo*, bustled out, fumbling with her clutch.

"Oh?" she said. Her face tilted up. She let her purse drop to her side.

"I'm sorry to bother you, ma'am, but did you by any chance happen to see a woman inside the restroom with a gray suit jacket on, and, and, uh… medium length, blonde hair, no glasses… she's my wife, and she's been in there for a while and we have to catch our flight, but I'm not sure if she's okay or not and…"

Halfway through his spiel, the young lady shook her head back and forth, a large, almost caricature frown working over her expression. "I'm sorry, but I… I didn't pay too much attention when I was in there. I'm already running late myself, so…I'm sorry," she said and went back to digging in her clutch. She beelined down the long, narrow runway terminal of carpet, seats, and passengers.

What was Becca doing in there? She didn't act like she was sick when they got here, so what was holding her up? Did she fall and hit her head? Did she have an accident? A stroke? A seizure? Nothing had changed in the women coming and going out of the restroom. If something had happened, somebody would've seen, would've said something, would've come out and gotten someone, but that hadn't happened, so what was happening, where was she, and what could he do?

What can you do, Petey? You're right about that—you finally got the right questioning down. What has *she been doing? What* has *she been doing in that big house of yours while you've been gone? Who's been keeping her company while your kid is at pre-K, or off on playdates, while you've been gone, working? Where has* that *part of her been?*

Pete caught another woman going into the restroom

and asked her to check for his wife when she went in, and with wide eyes, the woman agreed, worried. *Sure, I'll take a look for you.*

Where was she? Where was she for him? For Dylan? For them? Why, at every single turn, did it always seem like *he* was the bad guy? Why was she mad, when he was constantly putting his neck out for her, for Dylan, for *them*? For what they built together? Why did he always feel like he was to blame? Why did the sheets smell fresh from the laundry when everything else piled up around the house? Why did their room smell better than it normally did, more of her perfume, when he came home? Why did she never seem there for him—for *them*—even when she and he were in the same room? And could he blame her? Could he even blame her when he was never there for her? Could he be mad at her for giving them everything they ever could've wanted, year after year, never asking for anything in return, but doing it all, breaking his back, making tough decisions, risking his skin every day for *her*, for *them*?

"Wanna see Mommy." Dylan tugged at his hand again, and Pete ripped away from watching the doors of the women's room to glare down at him.

"Not now, Dylan," he hissed. "Mommy'll be out shortly." He pushed the words between clenched teeth, and Dylan began to cry.

He struggled to free his hand from his father's grasp. *"Owww, Daddy. Hurting me,"* he cried. Pete let go and his son yanked his small red hand back and held it close to his chest, covering it with his other.

Biting tears welled in both of Pete's eyes as he stared down at his son.

"I… I'm sorry Dylan," he croaked. "Come here, buddy." He squatted down to his son's level, reaching out, when Dylan bolted for the women's room door. "Dylan, no!" he shouted, and a dozen heads turned toward him, as he grappled all of his family's luggage together and started across the hall.

Another woman opened the door from inside, and, as she stepped out, Dylan slipped in. Pete caught only a flash of his son's blue jean overalls and bright orange Astros tee before he disappeared.

Panic reeled up and down his spine like bolts of electricity. All of his muscles tightened like wire, ready to snap. His teeth clenched in his jaw, and both of his hands held death grips on the handles of their luggage. Over the intercoms, now, he heard the calm voice relay:

"This is the final boarding call for passengers Peter, Rebecca, and Dylan French, booked on flight 372E to Tampa. Please proceed to gate E23 immediately. The final checks are underway, and the captain will order the doors of the aircraft to close in five minutes. I repeat…"

Sink or swim, Petey.

God, what happened to them? From being twenty-four, young, and recently married? Married and in love. Married and happy. These thoughts whispered like lost radio stations among roaring static. The noises of the terminals, of the restaurants, the sights, smells, sounds barraged him. The must of carpet, the rich, fatty smells of food, bitter coffee, bright flashing lights of phones and laptops, televisions, conversations, buzzing LED lights, the voices on the intercom telling all to look out for strange packages, to contact airline personnel for all suspicious behavior, and women, men, people, coming and going.

Sink or swim, Petey. Never trust a bitch.

It's not a demotion. It's security.

You have to go in and see. It's now or never. Sink or swim. Why don't you pull back the curtain and see what's behind there? It's not ideal, but I wanted to give you the option at least, so you'd have one.

Pete let go of their luggage and set it aside, against the

wall by the water fountains, and started toward the women's room, when the door swung open and a woman and her child hustled out, hand in hand. They collided, and a breath of relief puffed from Pete as he looked up to see Becca's face.

"Excuse me, sir," she spat, and the smile beginning to form on Pete's face flew away as his wife began to circle around him.

"Becca," he said, looking down at his son, holding his mother's hand. She continued trying to get around him, but he held his hands up. "Honey. We've got to go. What took you so long? Is Dylan alright? They called our names over the intercom already, and—"

"Sir, I think you've mistaken me for another woman," his wife said, pushing to get around him, with Dylan holding her hand, looking up with suspicious eyes. On his small stature, Dylan's bright blue overalls and his orange Astros shirt stood out like punctuation marks against the gray of the terminal.

"Becca." He grabbed her by both arms and looked into her eyes. "What are you doing?"

The woman yanked free of his grip. "*Sir, let go of me!*" she cried.

Faces in the crowds turned to look at the couple and the little boy who held the woman's hand. Dylan shook by her side, his upturned face twisting in on itself, reddening. He began to cry.

Pete looked down at his son. "Dylan. Dylan, what's the matter, buddy? What's—"

"Get away from my son!" the woman yelled. "Somebody—" she began to shout, looking around, her head on swivel. "Security, please, help me! I don't know this man and he's trying to take my son!"

"Becca. Becca, what are you talking about?"

Pete's breath whistled in and out of his lips. Two

uniformed men rushed from one end of the terminal toward him and his wife, talking into walkie-talkies.

"I don't know you!"

"Dylan," he squatted down, trying again. "It's me, buddy. Dylan?"

His vision doubled, then trebled as the little boy wailed, shrinking away to clutch at his mother.

"Sir," the two men addressed him, separating him from his son, stepping between Pete and the woman and her child. "What's going on?"

"He's trying to take my son!" Becca screeched, now crying herself. "I don't know this man, and he's trying to take my baby!"

"That's my son. That's my son and my wife…" he stammered as one of the two airline security officers helped him back to standing. The other stood guarding his wife and child.

"I've never seen that man before in my life!" Becca squealed, and the other officer talked to her in low tones, trying to calm her.

"Can you come with me, sir?" the security officer asked, grabbing his forearm with a thick, muscular hand.

"No, I can't. That's my wife and my boy. I don't know why she's doing this. That's my son!"

The security officer held him back as he tried to step forward.

"Get off of me!" Pete said and lunged forward. He thrust himself back, away from the man's grip, then threw his hand in his pocket. "Check her wallet. Look at mine," he said and opened it up to show his ID. The officer took it and scrutinized the name and picture. He turned to the other officer and the woman with her child.

"Ma'am," the other officer asked. "Would you mind if we saw your ID?"

The woman's eyes glistened under the lights of the

bathroom alcove, and her son stood behind her, hiding, grabbing handfuls of her suit pants. She shook her head, as if trying to clear her mind, closed her eyes, and reached into her purse. Wordlessly, she withdrew a tan leather wallet and removed her driver's license.

The woman handed it to the officer. He looked at the name and picture, then handed it to his partner.

Pete stood silently as the officer held the two IDs and glanced back and forth between them. He looked up and handed the other officer the ID again.

"We're sorry for the scare, ma'am," he said to the woman, then turned back to face Pete. "Sir, if you'll come with me."

The man grabbed him by the shoulder and began leading him back the way he and his family had come from, toward Security.

"No," Pete's lips felt numb, thick. "No. That's Becca French. Rebecca French. Becca!" he yelled, as the other officer led her away from him, escorting her and her son to their separate flight. "That's my son, Dylan. Dylan!"

"Sir…" The officer's massive fingers dug into Pete's shoulders. "You'll have to come back with me to our office. I understand that you're upset, but–"

"But *bullshit*—let go of me!" He yanked free and ran toward the woman.

"Sir!" The officer ran after him, and his partner turned around as Pete collided with him. The woman scooped her son up, staggered backward, and fell. Her purse spilled out before her. Pete stooped to the ground searching for her driver's license. Among spilled ChapStick, tampons, bags of animal crackers, and a cellphone that Pete had never seen before, he snatched the woman's wallet and tore it open. In the first card slot, he yanked free the ID and glared at the photograph of his wife, her name beside it.

Carolyn Gaines.

The officer who'd been guarding the woman and child grabbed Pete underneath both of his armpits and lifted him off the ground, knocking the air out of his chest.

"Stay here with her," the officer said to the one who'd been guarding Pete, and then began forcing handcuffs onto his wrists. "We're gonna go for a little walk, *pal*."

An audience had gathered on both sides of the terminal aisle. Hundreds of faces, neutral paint swatches, looked at the scene.

Pete felt himself being dragged back toward the security checkpoint and heard his son crying behind him. His wife, too.

Carolyn Gaines.

That's my wife. That's my wife.

The officer pushed him forward, with his arms behind his back. People, men, women gawked and stared at him as he was escorted away from his family.

Carolyn Gaines.

That's my wife. That's my wife, looped in his head. *That's my wife,* and tears streamed down his face. The lights in the terminal burned, glaring down, hot, white, unfeeling. *That's my wife, that's not Carolyn Gaines. She's not Carolyn Gaines. God, please, that's Becca French.*

The officer led him down the corridor, and the woman and her son watched them disappear.

Eventually, the audience dissipated, as the show concluded. The woman and her son boarded their flight, and the other officer grabbed the man's luggage, before returning to the office. Nothing out of the ordinary was found in any of the suitcases. Only clothes for one tucked away into each of the bags. Several dry-cleaned suits, shirts, undergarments, shoes, and belts, divided between the four. Two Samsonite hard cases, a two-tone diaper bag, and a Thomas the Train rolling suitcase.

ÓRDEN
by
Jay T. Levy

"Slow down, Bailey." Hurston glared at the needle hovering at eighty-five. "You want to get us pulled over? That's the last thing we need!"

"Sorry, Hurston." Bailey put his hands immediately at ten and two on the steering wheel. His smile flattened and his voice dropped.

Hurston saw the big guy frown in the dashboard's pale orange light. "It's Hurst, remember." He patted Bailey's arm. "Just, slow down, will you? We need to play it cool until we get to Mexico."

The two men drove in silence as the sun dropped below the horizon and shrouded the landscape in shadow. In the darkness, the window became a tinted black mirror and Hurston's reflection suddenly stared him down, like a bully ready to fight.

"What do you want?" He grumbled under his breath.

"What'd ya say, Hurst?"

"Huh?" He was so focused on his reflection that Hurston didn't pay attention to Bailey's image next to his own in the tinted black window. "Nothing, Bail. I'm just thinking." Hurston sighed at his own image. He was a bulbous troll of a man, with a shaved scalp, crow's feet, and fatty skin hanging limply under his chin.

"Ya know what they say," Bailey said. "Thinking belongs in the head."

Sitting next to Bailey was like sitting next to a bear. His weightlifter arms seemed chiseled from rock and his jaw line would've made Thor envious. But Bailey was far from perfect. He carried a spare tire heavily around his waist and his brain didn't seem to fire on all cylinders. Something about him was off. Gullible. Naive. That was Bailey, Hurston's former cellmate and perfect partner-in-crime.

"Good thing there're no streetlights," Bailey smiled. The dash tinted his teeth sienna yellow and shadowed his mouth from underneath, making him look bizarre and unnatural to Hurston.

"I suppose, my friend."

There was nothing in front of them except the dark and empty highway.

***

"Pull over."

"What," Bailey said, "ya gotta tinkle?"

"Tinkle? I swear, Bail, you talk like you're in kindergarten." Hurston shook his head and pointed a thumb over his shoulder. "We gotta dump him, stupid."

"Don't call me that."

"Alright, alright," Hurston backed off from an argument. "Regardless, partner, I ain't going to Mexico with a guard in the trunk."

Bailey nodded, pulled the car off onto the shoulder, and slowed to a stop. "Kill the lights, too." Hurston got out and looked up and down the desolate highway. "Yeah, this spot'll do."

Bailey got out and approached the trunk.

"Take him over there, Bail." Hurston pointed to a cluster of brush and cacti. "But first, let's change out of these awful uniforms. I told you that detour to the locker room would pay off."

"Yeah, ya did."

"Quickly, now." Hurston changed into a green mesh t-shirt and black sweatpants with 'security' down the side in yellow. "Damn, it's chilly out here tonight."

"Cold as death," Bailey replied, tossing the empty gym bags in the trunk. He also changed into the same style of clothes, but unfortunately his shirt was a bit small. The bottom of his gut hung out and over the waistline of the sweatpants, and each time he tried to tuck it in, his flab oozed back out over that line.

Escaping its prison of clouds, the moon sent waves of light over the dark road.

Bailey lifted the body from the trunk and threw it over his shoulder like a rolled carpet.

"Those arms of yours." Hurston grabbed the shovels and jumpsuits. "Like, unreal strong."

"Why'd ya have to kill him?" Bailey asked as they walked. "We coulda got out on our own."

"We had no choice." Hurston forced a calm he didn't feel. "It's not like I wanted to. But, he saw us. Had to think quick, you know?"

"Yeah, I know."

"Besides, you really think he wasn't going to say anything to anyone?" Hurston went on. "This asshole would've turned us in immediately. Remember that time he almost busted your collar bone?"

Bailey nodded. "I do."

Hurston looked at the body slung over Bailey's shoulder and sneered. "We all hated you, McMullen. I'm glad you're dead."

Bailey dropped the corpse and the head twisted at the

sliced throat. Thickened blood splattered across Bailey's boots. He turned, took a few steps, and fell to his knees, vomiting.

Hurston laughed.

"I swear, Bail, how'd you ever kill a guy? You can't even handle a dead one."

"I never meant to. . . It just happened. He hit me. I hit him back, and only once." Bailey made a sound like a sob. "I didn't know… I didn't know he couldn't take it." He wiped his mouth and stood up. "I'm going back to the car."

"Oh, no you don't!" Hurston handed Bailey a shovel and nodded to the ground. "Let's get some dirt on him, at least. Then, cover that puke."

Bailey nodded, took the shovel, and sighed.

"Hurst?" Bailey asked, throwing his first shovelful to the side.

"Yeah, buddy?"

"If you're so smart, why didn't ya plan for it?" He looked Hurston right in the eyes. "It didn't really need t' happen, ya know? It don't matter what McMullen would'a told them. They're gonna know we ain't there at first check anyway, right?"

"Just dig, for Christ's sake."

In the middle of nowhere in the desert, they buried a guard who was in the wrong place at the wrong time. Bailey wanted to say a few words for the deceased, but Hurston threw up his hands in disgust and returned to the car. He gave Bailey three minutes, and then he was going to leave. Bailey took less than two.

***

Leaving the gravesite behind, the two men drove in silence for miles.

Bailey finally broke the quiet. "I'm hungry."

"Of course you are," Hurston said. "You're always hungry. Not to mention you threw up back there."

"Yeah, well. A guy's gotta eat, right?" Bailey pressed innocently. "Ya think they're going to find it? The puke, I mean."

"Probably." Hurston shrugged. "I'm sure they'll find McMullen—eventually—and they'll search the area. They'll find your puke, but who cares? You'll be in Mexico."

"Yeah, I guess," Bailey whispered, then added more loudly, "boy, my stomach is a-rumbling."

"Oh, for Christ's..." Hurston shook his head. "The next town, we'll stop, quickly. We should stay on the road."

"Yeah? Oh, boy! I'd love a burger right now. Or, a chicken sandwich. Or fish! A fish sandwich. That'd be. . ."

"Your priorities, I swear," Hurston said. "But I'd be lying if I said a burger doesn't sound good right now, especially after all that tasteless prison food. We'll hit a drive-thru and gas up while we're at it, okay?"

"Yes, sir."

They headed south on Highway 70 for a few more miles until they hit Lordsburg.

"Lords," Bailey mocked in a deadpan tone, then laughed. "Oh Lord, it's Lordsburg."

"Bail," Hurston rolled his eyes. "Give it a rest, will you?"

"Sorry, Hurst."

"What's so funny about Lordsburg, anyway?" Hurston pinched the bridge of his nose.

"Lordsburg? I don't know," Bailey said. "It's just like. . . it's like Lords Town, right? Maybe it's a sign, ya know?"

"A sign? Like from God?"

"Yeah," Bailey shrugged. "Why not? We break out together and stop for a meal in a town named after the Lord.

That's no co-in-ki-dink. Don't ya believe in a higher power?"

"No," Hurston said aggressively. "And, you shouldn't either. It's all a bunch of touchy-feely nonsense."

Bailey nodded and the two remained silent, even while gassing up. Using the cash from McMullen's wallet, Hurston went in to pay, donning a baseball cap to better hide his eyes. It wasn't until they reached the McDonald's that one of them spoke again.

"Thank the Lord," Bailey said enthusiastically. "See, Hurst, this one has that twenty-four-hour-a-day sign. That's great!"

"Yeah, bud, how fortuitous," Hurston sneered.

"It was just meant to be, partner."

Hurston looked at Bailey and tried to gauge whether he was being genuine or a smartass.

Being fifth in the drive-thru line, they had plenty of time to look at the Greyhound bus station that shared a parking lot with the fast-food joint.

"Oh, will you look at that one," Hurston moved in his seat to get a better look. "I like her."

"The one in the sweats and the UCLA hoodie?"

"Yeah," Hurston licked his lips. "I don't normally go for college girls. Little more experienced than I'd like. Still, I'd buy her a… Happy Meal." He watched as a middle-aged couple—her parents, he assumed—gave her a long hug. The mother wiped away tears, as the father squeezed her shoulder. Clearly, this was a farewell.

"It was girls like her, wasn't it?" Bailey asked.

"You're damn right," Hurston blew her a kiss. "She's my type—blonde and pretty. I bet she's got a cute ass under those baggy sweatpants, too."

Bailey hesitated a moment. "And. . . they all wanted it? Yer special love and attention?" His words were slow, like a recording with no feeling.

"That's right." Hurston grinned. "They may not have at first, but none of them complained after I was finished with 'em."

"Especially the dead ones," Bailey's eyes glowed somber in the orange dash light.

"Look, Bail." Hurston sat back in his seat. "Why ask if you know you won't like the answer?"

"I don't know."

The girl grabbed a duffle bag and climbed to safety aboard the bus. The car in front of them pulled forward. Finally, their turn.

"Be cool," Hurston said, as they approached the ordering screen. "Do not draw attention."

"I know."

***

With their greasy paper bags in hand, the escapees continued south.

"Remember to hit Rt. 9 towards Puerto Palomas." Hurston handed Bailey his burger and the big guy bounced in his seat. "We still have a ways to go, so don't forget."

"Do ya think we'll pass by Roswell?" Bailey grinned before unwrapping the burger with his teeth.

"Roswell?" Hurston snorted and rolled his eyes. "No, we're not. It's just more nonsense."

"Okay." Bailey devoured his food with haste. Hurston followed suit.

"Oh, yeeeeah." Hurston shoved the last of his double-quarter pounder into his mouth and licked his fingers. "That was a good call, buddy."

"I like burgers a lot," Bailey said, as he wiped his mouth on the back of his sleeve. "'Specially as a last meal."

"As a... what?" Hurston paused with greasy fingers

against his lips.

"Ya, know—last meal as Americans." Bailey grinned the sienna smile once again and Hurston shivered. "We're 'bout to be Mexi Cans!"

They both laughed. Only, Hurston didn't feel the humor. He'd never doubted the big guy, until now. Did Bailey want to get rid of him before reaching Mexico? No, it couldn't be true. But, stranger things…

Hurston looked at the wide-open space of the starlit New Mexico desert and thought about the knife in his pocket. Then, his eyes shifted to Bailey's reflection. Maybe Bailey should end up out there by the end of the night, just like McMullen. It'd be so easy to kill the oaf and leave his body for the buzzards.

Hurston laughed softly.

"What's funny, Hurst? Ya laughing at me?" On the wheel, Bailey's hands tensed, his knuckles whitened.

"No, buddy, I wasn't laughing at you," Hurston reassured, through a false smile. "I was thinking of the good times we're going to have in Mexico—the girls, the booze. Most importantly, no cops looking for us. In Mexico, they won't give a damn who we are! So, relax, Bail."

Having headed south, the pair found themselves on a narrow, backwater road hemmed in by darkness.

"Jesus," Hurston exclaimed. "We've been on this road for an hour. Ain't nothing in sight."

The car's headlights were their only light. There were no streetlights. Eventually, the crossroad signals all blinked yellow, becoming fewer and eventually stopping altogether.

Suddenly, the sound of teeth clattering rattled Hurston. He turned and found Bailey with three fingers in his mouth. A bitten nail flew out and landed in the cup holder.

"Knock that off." Huston demanded. "Why you biting your nails, anyway?"

"I'm scared."

"Of what?" Hurston asked.

"The cop behind us."

"What?" Hurston tried to see in the mirror on his side. "How long's he been there?"

"A minute or so…" Bailey gnawed at another nail.

"Shit! We don't need this."

"He's coming to get us." Bailey sounded terrified. "He's going to pull us over. He knows ya made me steal this car."

"Shut up, Bailey," Hurston scolded. "You're liable to lose control and jerk the wheel. If his red and blues ain't on now, don't give him a reason to put them on. Just stay calm."

"But, this is it," Bailey's voice pitched with fear. "It's back to prison."

Hurston pulled his knife and jabbed it against Bailey's side. "You will calm… the hell… down," he demanded, with the blade against Bailey's ribs, "or I will kill you. No one will stand in my way to Mexico. Not you, and certainly not some patrol pig, you got that? Be cool. We can do this."

The cop followed them for a while longer as Hurston gnashed his teeth, waiting for the light-bar to flash. If this cop pulled them over, everything would get complicated.

The cop began attempting a pass.

"Don't look at him, Bail." Hurston jabbed the knife. "I don't want to kill a cop tonight." At least Bailey was currently alive to help move the body, if needed.

The cop lingered for a moment, but eventually sped up, completed the pass and disappeared into the night.

"There." Hurston folded the knife and put it back in his pocket. "That was downright terrifying. But, we did it."

Bailey drove in silence. Eventually, Hurston had to say something.

"You ok, pal?"

"Were ya really going to kill me?" Bailey asked, fast and angry.

"No, buddy," Hurston said with a smile, patting the big guy on the arm. "I just provided additional motivation. Sometimes we work best under pressure. Trust me, we're seeing the Mexican sunrise together."

He'd made up his mind; Bailey had to go.

***

"Where are we?" Hurston growled. He cupped his hands around his eyes and peered through the passenger window. "Sure would help if they put some goddamn signs on the road."

"Yeah. It's spooky."

Hurston looked at Bailey's reflection and shook his head. Distantly, a sign came into view. It shone emerald in their headlights, eventually revealing a name.

ÓRDEN, 10 MILES.

"Oar-den," Hurston said. "I bet that's Spanish."

"It is," Bailey whispered. "Means Order."

"Well, I'll be," Hurston turned, glaring at his partner. "You speak Spanish, do you? Strange… that never came up before?"

"No," said Bailey in a cold tone, "but I would've told ya, had ya asked. And, it's 'Or-Then,' so y'know. Ya roll the R and D into a TH sound."

"Whatever, Bail." Hurston rolled his eyes and shifted for more comfort in the seat. "Huh, there's a town called Order out here. Strange."

"Why?" Bailey gave Hurston a quick, sideways glance.

Hurston shrugged and looked out the window.

"I don't know," he said. "It just gives me the willies, you know?"

"No, I don't." Bailey said. "But, maybe ya fear law and order so much that the name alone is making ya paranoid? Maybe ya see Order as some kind of higher power?" Bailey nodded, his face changing dramatically with each shifting shadow.

Hurston growled in agitation. "When did you become a shrink?"

Bailey shrugged. Another sign passed.

ÓRDEN, 8 MILES.

They drove further in silence. Hurston thought about the knife in his pocket and slitting McMullen's throat. It'd be a shame to lose Bailey, but he'd only slow Hurston down. Dead weight was the last thing he needed.

Expansive nothingness surrounded them and Hurston swore the darkness had thickened. Even the stars had dimmed and faded. Rolling down the window, Hurston held out a hand.

"What'cha doing?" Bailey asked.

"It looks so thick outside," Hurston said. "Strange. Why so dark?"

"I don't know, partner."

ÓRDEN, 6 MILES.

Hurston checked the side view mirror again for the twentieth time. Something about the creeping darkness made him wary.

Then a dot of light appeared. Hurston quickly spun between the seats.

"Do you see that, Bail?" he said. "That spot in the sky behind us?"

"Kinda..."

"What the hell is that?" Hurston asked. "What does it

look like to you, bud?" Hurston squinted against the darkness, but the taillights cast their red glow over his vision. "It's moving, can't you see it? Up and down."

Bailey shrugged. "I gotta keep my eyes on the road. Ya sure it's moving?"

"Positive. What do you think it is? A plane?"

"I don't know, partner," Bailey said. "But our focus is the road, right?"

Hurston sat back, folded his arms, and picked at his teeth. "Yeah, sure."

ÓRDEN, 3 MILES.

"Maybe we've been seeing by the dash too long." Hurston nervously adjusted the rear-view away from Bailey. "Look at it, moving…"

"Have ya ever seen anything like it before?" Bailey asked.

"No." Hurston frowned.

The light continued to move rhythmically—side to side, up and down. "Never seen nothing like this. The glow… I think it's getting closer, too. It's kinda frightening, don't you think?"

"It'll be okay." Bailey patted Hurston on the shoulder.

"Yeah, you're right." Hurston looked forward again. "It's just a little light. We'll laugh about this in Mexico." Hurston forced a weak chuckle and then regretted it.

"Unless…" Bailey continued. "Unless that cop who passed us called it in and they're sending a helicopter to get us."

Hurston pulled his knife and held it to Bailey's throat.

ÓRDEN, 1 MILE

"Why the hell would you say something like that?" Hurston roared. "Not a good joke, partner! I should kill you here and now."

Hurston's eye twitched at Bailey's silence. He really didn't know what to do. It sickened him—Bailey's level of calm. Where was the nail-biter panicking at the cop about to whisk him back to prison?

"Hurston, this sure is a strange predicament we find ourselves in," Bailey said. He turned both the dash and headlights off, which left the car in total darkness. Hurston jumped back against the door.

Bailey hadn't moved, but Hurston felt his knife pull on flesh when he jumped. Hesitating, Hurston turned on the dome light.

Bailey smiled back; his throat clearly sliced.

There was no blood, just flesh, hanging like a wet paper towel. As Hurston watched, the flesh moved on its own and fused back together, leaving no visible seam.

"What the…?" Hurston paled and dropped the knife.

In a flash, the distant light moved directly above the car and pulsated with dazzling colors. The landscape lit up with vibrancy, only to quickly fade once again.

The car stopped and Hurston felt the shocks relax as Bailey got out. The strobing light ceased and left everything dark. Hurston didn't move until his vision returned.

The first thing he saw was the sign.

ÓRDEN, NEXT LEFT

***

"What's going on, Bailey!" Hurston climbed out of the car and rubbed his eyes. His vision was returning, although a bit blurry

"I don't understand what ya mean."

"The hell you don't!" Hurston bellowed and retrieved his knife. "I saw your neck. You ain't natural! What on Earth are you?"

Bailey rested his elbows on the car roof as the light returned from above.

While bright, it wasn't as blinding as before. This time it formed a two-hundred-foot circle around them. They, and the car, were in its center and completely lit from above.

"Not natural?" Bailey said. "That's a might bit harsh. Just cause I ain't like ya, don't mean I ain't natural."

Hurston looked up through photo-bleached eyes at the source. The pinnacle was like the sun—white and hot. He partially made out a round shape behind the light and noticed a space missing between him and the surrounding stars.

Swallowing hard, Hurston recognized the saucer shape from above. His eyes dropped to Bailey.

"Figured it out, did ya?" Bailey smirked.

"You ain't human."

"We," Bailey pointed up. "We ain't human, and what a relief… for me anyway. Humans have such issues."

"What's going on?" Hurston's outstretched knife quivered as he took several steps backwards.

"I don't know if ya can handle it, partner," Bailey walked around the car and leaned on the passenger side fender. "Since ya don't believe in anythin', no higher power, nothin'. But, if ya promise not to run off, I'll tell ya." He smiled, showing off his neck without a scar.

"Alright," Hurston shuddered, but his voice was strong. "I'm not going anywhere."

"Good," Bailey nodded. "Ya see, when we created humans…."

"You created us?" Hurston interrupted.

"Yeah," Bailey said. "I mean, not me specifically, but we did, yeah. A few hundred millennia ago… a millennia is a hundred thousand years, if ya needed it. . ."

"I know how long a millennia is." Hurston yelled.

Bailey held up a hand and nodded. "Okay. Well, in the distant past, we planted the seed of y'all's evolution. We made ya in our image."

Hurston's eyes widened. Sweat beaded on his brow.

"We monkeyed with your DNA. Oh, ya know the story, Hurst." Bailey cleared his throat dramatically. "The ol' God made man in his likeness thing. Let 'em have dominion over the fish of the sea, the fowl of the air, and the creatures of the Earth. Or did ya never go to Sunday school?"

"You mean…" Hurston whispered.

"Yup," Bailey said. "We're God… in this context, at least." Bailey stood with his chest out rooster-like, proud and confident.

"Y'all's purpose was to exist and experiment, consume and populate." Bailey shrugged. "In other words, we wanted to watch. Would ya squander resources? Would ya travel to space? How would ya'll Earthlings turn out?"

Bailey paused and shook his head. "In development, certain concepts were bound to happen—violence, for example, be it for warfare or personal protection. Our race isn't immune either. However, violence against one's own species is still subject to judgment on an individual level, and not against y'all's entire species. We ain't lookin to wipe y'all out like in the great flood of antiquity; we got too much invested in ya." Bailey took a deep breath. "But that's where I come in, partner. Ya see, my kind, we're everywhere. It's a most fascinatin' duty, being a keeper of humanity. And, while I do mean all of mankind, my current assignment is yerself specifically, Hurston."

"What… what you gonna do, Bailey?" Hurston shivered in the desert heat.

"I've met many guys like ya over the years." Bailey pushed off the fender and took a few steps. "I always keep hoping ya'll stop preying on each other in such vicious ways. But, ya don't. Y'all just get worse and worse."

Bailey pointed a finger at Hurston. "Ya add nothing to

society, nor have any value to the human race. Ya've only taken from your fellow species and gave nothing back. Ya had another chance, even after murderin' McMullen, but the bus station clinched it." Bailey paused and looked up to the light for a moment before meeting Hurston's gaze again. "I'm going to remove ya."

Bailey held up his hand and instantly, a little metallic object no bigger than a snub-nose .38 materialized between his fingers. Hurston recognized Bailey's off-the-cuff stance of a shooter ready to fire.

"No," Hurston pleaded, urine running down his leg. He dropped the knife and fell to his knees. "We're friends, right? Buddy, tell me this is a joke."

Bailey took three steps closer, but didn't say a word.

"We were heading to Mexico." Hurston's voice was shaky and hoarse. "Just drop me off as you head out into the cosmos, yeah?"

"Ain't no point," Bailey said. "Yer future's been forecasted. Yer pattern of behavior will continue. Removing ya will help others, especially young women, to survive. It's just how it's gotta be."

"How can you judge me?" Hurston shot to his feet, taking a step forward and pointing to Bailey's chest. Anger and the fear of death energized his words. "You killed too, Bailey. You're not so high and mighty. You got blood on your hands. What gives you the right?"

"Ah, hell," Bailey shrugged. "That stuff's a bunch of hooey. I made it up. I'm just actin'." He smiled and his mouth widened. Dozens of teeth flashed in a smile far exceeding human capability.

"As fer what gives me the right," Bailey stroked his chin. "I suppose by y'alls standards, nothin', but as your creators, we're responsible for the entirety of human actions. We police affairs in our ways."

"No!" Hurston's heart hammered; his mind raced.

Nothing made sense. He panicked, turning to run, terrified. But, directly behind him was the sign stopping him dead in his tracks.

ÓRDEN, NEXT LEFT

"Órden," Huston whispered.

"Order," Bailey said, "our mission, our cause."

Hurston turned around to face his partner-in-crime. Tears welled, his hands at his sides. Bailey pulled the trigger and a watermelon sized bolt of white light emerged from the tiny, metallic device. It slammed into Hurston's chest and knocked him to the ground. He was paralyzed, except his eyes.

Bailey approached, leaned in close, and tipped an imaginary hat as the light from above intensified.

"As part of the punishment, we give those ya silenced a chance to speak out. Ya have no choice but to listen." Bailey casually patted Hurston on the arm. "Death'll follow soon after. Good-bye, partner."

A stream of multicolored light engulfed Bailey and the big guy's body disintegrated into a swarm of glittering motes. What had been Bailey shimmered, glowed, and was sucked up into the light above as if by a vacuum.

The light continued to pulsate and swirl, mesh and transform. Colors lit up against themselves in strange patterns. New pigments and possibilities emerged that defied Hurston's reason. His mind was putty against the hypnotic light.

Dozens of girls' faces flashed before his eyes, or perhaps inside his mind, he couldn't be sure. They stared at him in digital clarity. He'd hurt every one of them. Many were dead. The faces moved and contorted with sadness and anger. Their luminescent cries enveloped their killer, filling him with heat—a human, emotional intensity—so strong that he experienced their suffering revisited upon himself a hundredfold.

With a flash, the light from above ended, but the screams remained, pounding like hooves. More of the nighttime sky filled Hurston's view as the ship overhead moved up and away—the last thing he saw before slipping into the cold nothingness of oblivion.

Closed In
by
Eliza Hyde

Lucy was only a thief out of desperation. Of course, she felt guilty, but she also needed to be gone, far away from this miserable little town and its sad, sorry inhabitants. It no longer held any comfort or solace for her. It was time to run away. Forget all that came before, and find a new place to call home.

Theft was a small price to pay for a new beginning.

Her entire body was screaming with exhaustion by the time she'd reached the train station, her sides pinching with stitch from all the running and hiding she'd been doing for the past hour. Passers-by looked at her with distaste as they mingled in the waiting area in their fancy coats and expensive dresses, turning their noses up at this bruised and disheveled young woman. Ordinarily, Lucy would have snapped at them: a well-aimed insult to topple them from their judgmental perches, but not today. Not now. Escaping was her priority, before *they* caught up with her.

She fumbled through her pockets, bloodied hands shaking as she felt for her bank card or some change; anything to pay for a ticket. Time was running out, and she wondered if, in her desperation to escape, she'd left her card behind. A small sigh of relief escaped her lips when her fingers touched plastic, but panic soon set in again when she noticed long queues to buy tickets. The self-service machines were out of order, and there wasn't enough time to wait in line before *they* found her. It was logical, thinking that she'd head to the train station, because she couldn't drive. Time was of the essence.

That was when she saw the ticket on the floor. An orange smudge right by the gnarly boots of a scruffy man. His back was turned to her, his long greasy hair trailing down a moth-eaten brown coat. The ticket must have been his, accidentally dropped when he was yanking a tissue out of his pocket, perhaps. The departure time stamped in bold on it read **13:36**—just four minutes from now. Absently, she wondered why he wasn't outside waiting for the train, but the thought trickled away as instinct kicked in. She reached down and snatched the ticket from the ground before heading toward the platform, blood pounding in her ears. She didn't care where the train was going; she just needed to be on it.

Just as Lucy exited into the cool afternoon air, she heard shouting. Glancing over her shoulder, she saw it was the man she'd stolen the ticket from. His eyes were sharp blue, even more piercing as they leered from a grubby, stubbled face, and they were fixed on her.

"Thief!" he yelled, pointing an arthritic finger in her direction, "Your journey will be your *just* reward!" Somehow, he sounded less angry and more gleeful, in a frenzied way.

People started to turn and look in the direction he was pointing.

Panicking, Lucy turned away and raced onto the platform, just as the train arrived. Her heart was exploding as she sprinted towards it, expecting the gross man to tackle her before she could clamber aboard. Whether he was in pursuit or not, she never found out, for the doors of the train squealed open and she was soon inside. She moved away from the doors and sighed with relief once they'd closed. *Time to find a seat.*

It was a much different train to what she'd been expecting. Instead of seat rows and a smattering of tables, there were cabins. It reminded her of something from an Agatha Christie novel, only less posh. The walls and floor were grubby, with random bottles and empty crisp packets littering the floor.

She glanced at the ticket and saw there was no carriage number on it. In fact, there was nothing at all besides the departure time—there wasn't even a destination listed. She moved to the nearest cabin and opened the door slowly, peering into the room. There was a sullen man in a corner by the window in drab clothes. He was staring directly ahead at the wall opposite, but at her intrusion he slowly turned to face her. She gasped despite herself at the utterly haunted look in his eyes. He looked vacant, as if he'd lost everything. . . or done something terrible.

"I-I am so sorry for disturbing you!" Lucy said, and swiftly closed the door.

There was a juddering as the train finally began to move, and Lucy stumbled forward, noticing a steward heading down the corridor towards her. At least, she assumed the woman was a steward. She didn't wear a name badge, but she wore the smart skirt and blouse that stewards usually wore; a pretty woman with neat blonde hair tied into a bun. Her smile was strange though—a little bit too wide, like a crocodile's. "Are you okay, dear?" she asked in a crisp, high voice. Lucy nodded and then quickly shook her head.

"I'm not sure which carriage is mine. I'm hoping I'm on the right train?" she asked, flashing her ticket at the steward.

Somehow the steward's smile grew wider still,

revealing perfectly white teeth. Her bright green eyes flashed. A hand of carefully manicured nails tapped the ticket gently, and then she motioned for Lucy to follow her.

"I can assure you, you're on the correct train," she said, "We have a space for you."

They reached a cabin further down the corridor, and the steward opened the door.

"Here you are, my love," she said, and Lucy entered the room.

"Thank you. One last question – how long will this journey be?"

"Oh," the steward replied, giggling just slightly. "You'll know when it's over."

The girl nodded and sat on the seat provided, the steward closing the door. It wasn't a large cabin, much smaller than the one she'd poked her head in before. Like the rest of the train, it was dingy, with dirty steel walls and floors, covered in smudges and handprints. The room was lit by a bulb because– strangely– there was no window. *That bloke's cabin had a window,* she thought, and then shuddered at the awful look he'd had in his eyes.

The lack of a window made the room seem even smaller than it was, and Lucy found herself hoping that the journey wouldn't be too long. Small spaces unnerved her, ever since her brother had locked her inside her dad's biggest suitcase. She had been a mere five years old at the time; her brother six years her senior and three times as strong . She could still remember the all-consuming darkness, the tightness of her arms and legs pressed so close to her body, unable to move. The stale air, slowly suffocating her. The merciless, muffled sound of her brother laughing, roaring in delight as she screamed and begged. She felt like she'd been buried alive, abandoned to an infinite black void. Her grandmother had died not long before, and young Lucy couldn't help but liken the suitcase to the coffin her gran was buried in. In her hysteria, she'd imagined her gran in that wooden box, 0crying out in that croaky voice of hers for somebody to set her free. The nightmares from that day had plagued Lucy for years, and marked the beginning of a hateful relationship with her brother, one which had grown more abusive as the years went on.

She thought of him now, lying in the hospital bed, fighting for his life. She tried to find some remorse inside herself, some sympathy for him, but as she stroked the bruises on her face, she felt nothing. All the pain he'd caused her, both physically and mentally; the friendships he'd destroyed, the career she'd lost. . . that man had ruined her life. Everything she had was now in this room. Her torn jeans and battered trainers, her dog-eared denim jacket and bank card. Nothing else, not even a phone. That was the way it had to be.

She rested her head against the wall and closed her eyes, slowly steadying her breath after the chaos of the day. She thought of the man she'd stolen the ticket from, and silently thanked him for allowing her this escape. He'd said some weird stuff to her, but then again he looked like an odd kinda guy.

The light bulb flickered momentarily, the fizz of the electricity bringing her back from her thoughts, and she opened her eyes. There was some commotion going on outside of her cabin. She could hear the sound of a woman in distress, and the eerily calm tones of the steward trying to placate her.

"Please let me off here, I'm on the wrong train! Let me off at the next stop, I shouldn't be here!" The woman sounded distraught, every word a hoarse cry accompanied by uncontrollable sobbing.

"I can assure you, you are absolutely on the correct train," the steward replied calmly, and Lucy just knew she was smiling that inhuman way as she spoke. "And the train driver agrees with me. Let's get you back to your cabin, shall we?"

"No. . . *No* !" was the woman's tormented reply.

Lucy felt bad for her. She evidently needed to be somewhere else – why wasn't the steward helping her? Wasn't that her job? The girl rose to her feet, considering to offer help. Yet, she didn't want to bring any unwanted attention to herself. Not now. Reluctantly, she sat back down, and listened to the fading sobs of the woman as she was obviously led away.

It was then she noticed something odd, as unnerving as anything else that had happened today. Somehow, her cabin seemed smaller. As if the walls had nudged themselves in a little. The ceiling seemed lower too. She stood up again and raised her hand. Her fingers only just grazed the ceiling. Had it been that low before? *Probably a trick of the flickering light bulb*, she thought. She sat down and rested her head on the wall beside her, where a window ought to have been.

Lucy managed to drift off to sleep eventually, half-dreams of angry faces and accusatory text messages floating around her mind. Her thoughts eventually settled on her brother, an adult in his hospital gown, standing over her and laughing; laughing as he had all those years ago when he'd locked her in the suitcase for sadistic pleasure. His face began to dissolve as he laughed, reshaping into someone else. A dirty, unshaven face with a broken nose, half-covered by strands of greasy hair, from which shone a pair of piercing blue eyes. The man from the station, her victim and her salvation.

"Your journey will be your just reward!" he yelled, as blood began to ooze from his eyes. Somewhere in the background, she could still hear her brother laughing. . .

Lucy jolted awake, shaking off that last vile image.

She imagined she'd probably be having some pretty twisted dreams for the foreseeable future. Part of the territory. *Get used to it, girl.*

The train started to judder a little under her feet, and for a second she thought it was slowing down, but then it seemed to gain traction again. The train's horn suddenly roared out of nowhere, a surprisingly deafening sound in her little steel cube, like the cry of a dying whale, and then all was quiet again.

Forgetting the unpleasant dream, Lucy began considering what she'd do when she arrived at her mystery destination. Find a homeless shelter for starters, somewhere to eat and sleep. Keep a low profile, keep tabs from afar on her brother. *If he does die,* she pondered, *at least I'll be able to say it was self-defense. And if not, I doubt he'll come looking for me. None of them will. Once they realize I've gone, they'll forget about me. I hope. . .*

It hit her just how excited she was to start again. A scary new world was waiting for her, but one where, eventually, she'd no longer be looking over her shoulder, or fighting against life-destroying lies and physical abuse. At twenty-seven, there were still so many possibilities for her.

The seat was starting to feel uncomfortable, so Lucy stood up, relishing the cracking of her back as she stretched, her arms spread out wide. She felt something tickling the top of her head, and when she glanced up, she realized her hair was grazing the ceiling. Glancing left, she saw that the light bulb dangled much lower than before, just a few feet above the floor.

Swallowing, she closed her eyes for a second, opened them again and looked up. The ceiling was still there, as low as it had been seconds before, her nose inches away from it.

"Shit," she said, and dodging the bulb, she raced to her cabin door.

She tried to yank it open, but it didn't budge. She pushed and pulled to no avail, and then she began to hammer her fist on the cold metal.

"HELLO?" she yelled, unable to control the rising fear in her voice, "CAN SOMEONE, ANYONE HEAR ME?"

There was complete silence from the other side of the door. She tried again, calling out and battering with all her might.

Sweat began to trickle down her forehead, and she leant over, clutching her chest. "This can't be happening," she said softly to herself, as tears began to flow. Her heart was pounding as the horrific realization gripped her. She was trapped; trapped in a room that seemed to be getting smaller. No, not *seemed* to be. It *was* getting smaller.

Taking a deep breath, she straightened up and tried the door again. It still didn't open. Nobody came, nobody could hear her. Or if they could, they were ignoring her. She started to kick it, but it didn't move.

She threw herself against it and that's when she cried fully, the floodgates of her composure smashed through in a tsunami of anger, grief, and fear. And through tear-stained eyes, she saw in horror that the wall at the opposite side of the room had moved even closer. The seat had vanished completely, no trace that it had ever been there. She was in a box. Just her and the light bulb, which was now trailing lazily on the ground.

Suddenly, she heard muffled screams from other cabins. Cries of horror, despair, disbelief. She vaguely heard one man begging something to let go of him, while a woman (the one from earlier?) was howling in terror about her eyes.

Horrible things were happening to everyone, and Lucy realized that each person was being subjected to a different kind of. . . of what? Punishment?

She thought back to the man at the station, the man

she'd stolen from.

"The journey will be your just reward!"

Reward for what? Stealing from him? Attacking her brother? Abandoning her family? Did he know what would happen to her? Had she somehow rescued him from this awful fate?

Corner shadows were lengthening now as the walls edged in before her eyes, and so did the ceiling. It was starting to press down on her head and she sank to the floor, gaping in horror as the walls all slid silently towards her.

And then the bulb went out with a *crack*.

Darkness came, and she curled up into a ball, the horror of what was happening a dreadful secret in the unforgiving blackness. She wrapped her arms around her legs and hugged them close. Her tears were constant streams down her face, her entire body shaking. The door handle cracked off then and dropped onto her head as the ceiling crept further down, pushing it off. Of course, the door didn't open afterward.

She tried to kick out her legs, hoping against hope that she'd touch nothing, but the wall gave her no room to stretch. Her arms were the same, unable to push outwards, her elbows touching metal. She pressed her head into her knees, the screams of those around her filling her head.

It was harder to breath now, and Lucy imagined herself in that suitcase again – a young girl, paralyzed with terror. Unable to move. Trapped in a coffin of someone else's making.

The walls on all sides were now touching her, and the ceiling pressed down on her head as it sat in her lap. She was in agony from the position, her curled back hunched against the door, muscles straining. She couldn't lift her head at all.

And that's when she realized the true horror of her situation. The walls and ceiling had stopped moving now.

Everything was still, aside from her sobbing, and the heavy thumping of her heart. The train no longer seemed to be moving, and the wailing from the other cabins had died away.

She physically couldn't move, her body completely pressed up against the soulless steel walls of the cabin. Absently she wondered where the bulb and the seat had vanished to, her mind soaring off into new hysteria.

Was it worth it all? Standing up to her brother after everything he'd done, or should she have carried on with her miserable existence? Was this worse or better than what she'd run away from? Did she deserve this?

Lucy wanted to wake up, find herself pulled out of a nightmare by someone who loved her. But she knew that in this awful moment, this dreadful, confined, agonizing moment, she was as awake as she had ever been before in her life.

Every joint protested in agony, her clothes soaked with sweat and tears. The terror that had swept over her was paralyzing, and now Lucy was too breathless to even scream.

Somehow, she knew that the walls wouldn't move again, and the door behind her would never open.

This cube of darkness was her last home, the final destination of her escape.

As Lucy sat with arms tight around her legs, her head pressed into her knees by an unyielding steel ceiling, she knew that she would never see the light again.

Route 58
by
Michael Penncavage

"Are all of the doors locked?" asked Kate.

"Yes," replied Roger

"How about the rear ones?" She glanced over behind her seat. The shadows made it too dark to be certain.

"They all lock at the same time."

"You're certain?"

"Yes!"

"Close the window."

"It's hot out."

"Turn on the air conditioning then."

Roger grunted and slid up the window. The sunroof remained open.

"*Why* did we have to go *this* way?" asked Kate as she looked nervously out the car window. "Where are we?"

"You've never been on Route 58?"

Kate ran her fingers through her hair. "I don't know, Roger. I put the address in the Maps App and just follow it. I could care less what road I'm on."

"It runs through most of the state."

Kate unlocked and then re-locked her door nervously. "Well, I guess it's not a part of the state I want to be associated with."

Roger sighed. "Well, you shouldn't have agreed to such a bad location for us to meet Sam and Laura."

"It's been almost half a year since we last saw them. What was I supposed to do?"

"Pick something more central. The restaurant was only a twenty-minute drive for them," grumbled Roger. "And Sam had the nerve to complain about us being late tonight. There's a *reason* why I wanted to go this way."

"And what is that? To see how long it would take for us to get car-jacked?" Kate looked out the window. Condemned buildings flanked them on either side of the street. Some of the houses, though abandoned, still looked like they were inhabited. "Are you *sure* this is the best way?"

He shot a glance at her. "Will you please relax!"

"Keep your eye on the road!" she said. "You might hit someone. Jesus! That's all we need right now!"

Roger sighed and tried to remain calm.

They paused at a red light. An Oldsmobile Cutlass slowly approached them from the rear. Its windows were down and they could hear the heavy *thump, thump, thump* of bass coming from within.

One of the Oldsmobile's doors opened. A man stepped halfway out.

"Maurice!"

A bar, *Rocco's* splashed across the façade, was at the corner. A crowd was loitering by the entrance. A teenager, who didn't look old enough to be served in Rocco's, took notice and yelled back:

"Leroy! What the fuck you want?"

"Close the window," hissed Kate as she slunk down into her seat.

"The windows are closed," answered Roger, tapping the driver's side.

"The sunroof! Close the sunroof!"

"I'm not closing the sunroof."

"You got any shit for me?" yelled Leroy.

"Fuck you!" hollered Maurice. "You're not getting nothing from me! Not until you pay me!"

"I don't owe you shit!"

Maurice became incensed. "You calling me a liar? Why don't you come over here and say that to my face!" Collective laughter rose from the crowd.

Kate watched the traffic light with intensity, waiting for it to turn. "Go! Go! Go! It's green! It's green!"

Roger pressed hard on the gas and they sped through the intersection. It wasn't until he was a block away that he stole a glance into the rear-view mirror.

Leroy had hopped back into the Oldsmobile. His tires squealed in protest as he made a hard left and disappeared from view.

"There. All better now," he said.

Kate wiped the sweat off her brow. "Driving a Mercedes in this town—we are just begging to get shot!"

They passed by a laundromat, a dry-cleaner and three fast food restaurants. All the stores' lights were off, their metal security grates drawn down. Graffiti was everywhere.

A gas station was on the right. Like the stores, it was closed.

"When was the last time you filled the tank?" Kate sputtered out suddenly, in a new panic. "Do we have enough gas?"

"Yes," Roger answered, glancing down at the gauge. "Two-thirds of a tank." He looked at her and smirked. "Gee, I don't think we have enough gas to get home. The car only gets twenty-six miles to the gallon. Better put your walking shoes on."

"Shut up," snapped Kate as she punched him in the arm. "That's not funny."

The wind began to pick up. Newspapers, paper cups

and soda cans whirled past the car's headlights. The boarded-up buildings they passed seemed endless.

Kate glanced down one of the side streets. Another group of people had congregated in the middle of the road. More loud music was playing, but she couldn't tell from where. "Shouldn't there be a noise ordinance?"

A man suddenly appeared next to the passenger side of the car. Kate threw her hands up and screamed.

A spray bottle came into view and the windshield was suddenly doused. Before Roger could tell him to stop, the man, using a rag, began to wipe at the liquid. Either what he sprayed wasn't cleaner or the rag he used wasn't clean, but the windshield quickly turned opaque with grime.

Roger turned the wipers on and the jets shot out cleaner. The man started cursing at them, yelling for his dollar.

The light switched green and Roger pressed the accelerator. Squeegee Man threw his bottle, but Roger had widened the gap too much for the car to be struck.

"Until we get out of this town, I forbid you to stop at any more traffic lights!" shouted Kate.

"Oh really? What should my excuse be after the police pull us over?"

"Police?" repeated Kate, "What police? I haven't seen one patrol car since we entered this town! If we do get pulled over, I'm going to ask them why the fuck they aren't arresting the drug dealers back there on the corner!"

The succession of storefronts ended, replaced by more dilapidated houses. Kate cringed each time they neared a traffic light.

Roger continued driving until the houses gave way to a park.

The park wasn't lit, and the large, gnarled oak trees that leaned from both sides of the road made it look just as ominous as the houses they had just passed.

"Where are we going *now*?" asked Kate, who was beside herself. "Is it your mission to get us killed before the night is over?"

"Relax. Foregate Park isn't that big. We'll be through it in a few minutes."

"Roger, it's *late*," insisted Kate. "It feels like we are driving to Timbuktu!"

Roger turned the high beams. "The park acts like a dividing line."

"For what?"

"Have you ever heard the expression, *it's different on the other side of the tracks*?"

At that moment, the car emerged from the other side of the park. A grin crossed Roger's face. "See? That didn't take so long?"

Kate looked out the window. Her eyes widened in surprise.

Doctored lawns, glistening in the moonlit sky, replaced the crabgrass-infested yards they had passed just moments ago. Professionally manicured shrubs lined the driveways, while recessed lighting lit the walks.

Ornate metal light posts flanked the avenue, making it easy to tell if anyone was out jogging or just attempting to cross.

Kate pressed a button and her window glided down. "Will you look at that house!" she said with awe in her voice. "Are we still on the same road?"

"Yep. Route 58." Roger slowed the car and they both gazed upon the three-floor stucco mini-mansion to their right.

The lawn and garden's automatic sprinklers were on and they could smell the pungent fragrance of flowers in the misty night air. "I wonder how many rooms it has?" she asked.

"Unless they're the Brady Bunch, more than they

could ever need," replied Roger.

Roger drove slowly for several more blocks before turning to Kate. "See? Now wasn't this worth the slight detour?"

"You could have told me this was where you were going!"

"I wanted to surprise you," he slowed the car even further so they could get a good look at another house. "Earlier in the week I was leafing through one of those homes-for-sale booklets. This town had several listed. A few were within our price range. I figured it would be easiest to drive this way after dinner with Sam and Laura."

Kate looked at him excitedly. "It's *so* nice! I wonder if there is a town center? I bet they have a good school system! *Low crime!* We should set up an appointment with the local realtor." She pointed to a nearby side street. "Turn there. I want to see some more houses before we leave."

"But, *it's late*," Roger said, mimicking her.

"Be quiet," Kate answered, smirking.

Roger made a slow turn into the drive. It was narrower than the avenue was, so he kept a close eye on the road.

They passed a colonial on their right. An in-ground swimming pool was illuminated on the side of the house. Steam drifted up from the surface. "Heated," said Kate.

Further down they passed a larger colonial. The outside lights were extinguished and they couldn't see much except that it was *big*.

The drive wound lazily to the right. Roger, who had been looking through Kate's window, stopped short, causing the wheels to squeak on the freshly paved tarmac.

A garage door was less than ten feet in front of them.

"Shit!" he said. "The road ends in someone's driveway."

"You think they would have made it clearer that this was a private drive," said Kate.

Roger turned his head as he put the car into reverse. He began to turn the car around in the narrow space.

No sooner had he started than the house's floodlights turned on, illuminating the driveway and the entire front of the house as if it were daylight.

"Looks like we woke someone up," remarked Roger.

A man who looked like he was in his mid-30s came striding out of the house, dressed in a black terry robe, as if he had just taken a shower.

Roger slid his window down. "Sorry about that," he called out. The man continued walking towards them. "I didn't realize this was a private drive."

"Turn off those damn brights," the man barked. "Who are you? Why are you in my driveway?"

Roger flipped the high beams off. "Again, I *am* sorry. I didn't mean to disturb you this late at night. I hope you weren't asleep." He didn't care for the man's tone and continued backing up the car. In his nervousness, Roger tapped the gas pedal a little too hard and the car lurched back. The bumper struck one of the shrubs lining the driveway.

The man walked up to the driver's window. His heavy cologne made Roger's nose itch. "What in the hell do you think you're doing!" he yelled again. The man was deeply tanned, as if he had just returned from a vacation. Which made the white powder above his upper lip stand out clearly. There was more powder all over his robe.

"We…just took a wrong a turn…" stammered Kate.

"Look what you did to my goddamn hedge! Do you have any idea how much my fucking landscaping cost? More than either of you make in a month!" Agitated, he began pacing back and forth, waving his arms in the air. *It's the coke*, Roger thought.

"I only tapped it," Roger answered, his voice even. *Careful*, he thought. *This guy's right on the edge.*

Roger's calm tone tipped him over it. The man's voice

rose to a scream, and he began pounding his fist on the hood. "Asshole! Asshole! Asshole!" With each *asshole*, another blow to the car.

Roger backed the car away slowly, out of the driveway and onto the private drive leading back to Route 58. He shifted the car into drive.

The man suddenly stepped out in front of the Mercedes. Roger slammed on the brakes and just missed hitting him. "Get the hell out of the way!" He flicked the high beams back on and laid on the horn.

Wild-eyed, the man stared at them. His jaw was clenched.

Suddenly, one of his hands came up into view. He was holding a gun. A .45.

Kate screamed as the windshield burst inwards. Roger jerked and spasmed like a badly controlled puppet beside her.

The man fired until the magazine was empty, smoke drifting upwards until it was swirled away into the suburban evening.

Somewhere nearby, a dog began barking. Lights began turning on in the surrounding homes.

The man stood in front of the Mercedes for a moment, breathing heavily. Beads of perspiration ran down his brow and nose, mixing with the cocaine to form a milky-white liquid.

Licking his upper lip, he shoved the gun in the robe's pocket and began walking back to the house.

Inside the car, Kate leaned against the door, watching a red blotch spread out across her dress. *It's so big*, she thought disjointedly. *It's going to be ruined...*

Roger was slumped over the steering wheel. He wasn't moving.

In the distance Kate heard the wail of approaching sirens.

The last thought that ran through her head as she slipped away into the erasing darkness was a question.
How could this possibly have happened?
It seemed like such a nice neighborhood.

End of the Road
by
Andrew Adams

Something else has gone wrong. It's not just the look in her eyes. It's the way my wife is picking at the skin around her fingernails and drawing blood. Anxiety awakened. Jenna steps into the path of a sun-stained Jeep and the asshole behind the wheel slams the brakes hard enough to screech. He gives her the finger but she doesn't notice. Just crosses the parking lot and finds me at pump number six.

She whispers: "There's something you need to see."

Her eyes are wet.

I'm on edge in an instant.

Things have been rough lately, the fights more frequent since an unexpected surgery demolished our savings, and now the word *divorce* hangs heavy in the air. An ever-present threat. This road trip was meant to bring us together. Inspired by a journey to the Grand Canyon with my father, just before I started middle school. When it was so hot that my shoes stuck on the asphalt. We watched the sunrise from Mather Point, rode donkeys down Bright Angel trail, camped by the river. He taught me how to read stars. I thought that if I could show Jenna and the kids even a fraction of that joy, then maybe. . .Just maybe. . .We'd have a shot.

But here she is, looking miserable, her entire demeanor at odds with the punk rock tee, the manicure, and the hair recently dyed glam-rock red. Vacation mode. Dressed up like the girl she was when we met, just two good kids from two bad bands hooking up in a broken-down tour van.

The brightest person I know, now dimmed by something terrible.

"Let me handle the kids," I say.

Royal and Izzy are in the back of the Subaru, dressed like cowboys and developing new ways to make each other cry. Why we thought a road trip might go smoothly with a five and an eight-year-old in tow, I'll never know. Every day's been a disaster since we left San Diego. First we blew the back tire in Gila Bend and nearly skidded under an eighteen-wheeler. The Wild West shows in Tombstone were fun until an outlaw with a blank-loaded gun made Izzy cry and she peed herself in public. Then Jenna's aunt in Phoenix got her days mixed up and we had no place to stay. Now Royal is rubbing old candy wrappers into Izzy's hair, she's wailing, and I'm forced to use four magic words and a twenty-dollar bill to make it go away. "Who wants ice cream?!"

"Me me me!"

There's a wooden shack on the far side of the parking lot, specializing in pies we can't afford and soft-serve we can. I tell Royal to take care of his sister and they run off, spurs jingling. It's me and Jenna again.

"What's wrong?"

"Just. . .come."

I follow her across the lot. The desert heat is thick and oppressive even in April, with no shade in sight except for the thin lines drawn by saguaros. Inside of the country store is a cheery exercise in nostalgia. Among the homemade jellies, the jerkies and the framed pictures of John Wayne and totem poles of Native chieftains, stands a small crowd of shoppers, but nobody's shopping. They're all standing at check-out, staring up at a television perched behind the leather-skinned lady who runs the counter, but even she's turned away and drinking whiskey from her own supply.

"What the hell happened?" I ask.

No one speaks.

Then the image on the television ripples before my eyes like an optical illusion. It's a wide shot of a familiar suburban neighborhood, lined with tiny houses and quaint green yards. But a rainbow-colored shimmer distorts the view, and lines that *should* be straight—the walls, the curbs, the people in the street—warble and dance. Unsteady. It would be beautiful, almost psychedelic, if it wasn't followed immediately by a column of fire, appearing out of nowhere with the force of a nuclear bomb. One bright flash.

The image glitches, freezes, and stops.

Then begins again. A perpetual loop.

Death on instant replay.

"I don't understand."

The TV reporters offer a deluge of nonsense and bad interpretations as the image repeats again and again. A peaceful suburb. A rainbow shimmer. The column of fire. Suburb. Shimmer. Fire. Suburb. Shimmer. Fire. My ears grow hot as I finally catch words: *no survivors.*

I say it again. "I don't understand."

Jenna takes my hand.

"Honey, that was our *house.*"

***

There's no more information to glean. Nothing useful,

at least. The anchors are stalling for time until another clip comes in. Which could be a while, given that the studio lost touch with any and all staff within a hundred miles of "The Incident." The Incident that took place right over the Dulaneys' new rose garden. Already its own kind of catastrophe.

Our house is gone. Our kitchen cabinets are gone. The dinosaur figurines that made Royal's floor a minefield for bare feet, the ballet shoes we just bought for Izzy. The wedding album. The tax returns. The birth certificates. My side of the bed, and everything else for a hundred miles. The size of my world. My Mom and Dad in Encinitas. Gone. The taco shop that I opened in Oceanside. Gone. My childhood best bud, Carlos, who cooked in the back. My sister, Marissa. Jenna's family. Our friends. Our exes. All gone.

We call everyone, but it goes straight to voicemail. As if the phones don't exist. Everybody we know. . .Just a dial tone.

There's a moment where Jenna screams and drops to the floor. Strangers ignore us. After a while, the cashier comes over to offer some whiskey, then just leaves the bottle.

"What do we tell the kids?" Jenna finally asks.

I'm silent, spinning options. Nothing makes sense. We can't go *back*. We can't call anyone. And we've got nothing to do if we cancel our trip except argue and stress and end a marriage. So, the only plan I can imagine. . .is to keep the kids happy.

"We tell them nothing," I say.

***

When we return to Royal and Izzy, they're enthralled by a reptile on the sidewalk. "That's a yellow-backed spiny lizard," says Royal. "They're *cool*. They hunt by sitting and waiting for prey to come within striking distance." Royal has never necessarily shown a deep level of engagement with math or reading or human kindness, but his knowledge of scaly shit is almost encyclopedic.

They're both covered in chocolate ice cream, which drips down their fingers and forearms. Izzy offers me some, and it turns out that knowing the world might end actually makes ice cream *even sweeter.* Jenna's distracted, maybe shell-shocked, so I kneel down with the kids and I smile wide and I tell them: "I have an idea. You know we were going to rent a cabin in Flagstaff tonight, right?" The kids nod. "Well, turns out it's *snowing* up there. And everything's closed."

"How?" asks Izzy. "It's so *hot.*"

"I know. But Flagstaff is up in the mountains, and they get tons of snow. So, *I* was thinking… We go *straight* to the Grand Canyon. Today." I'm worried there might not be another chance. "Whaddya think?"

The kids are quiet. Sensing something off.

"Can't we do both?" asks Royal.

Jenna starts to answer but then a shadow passes above us, a split-second glimpse of something dark in the sky. A fighter jet, loaded with missiles. Behind it comes the boom. Sound thunders around us like gunshots straight to the heart. Dust swirls and paper flies and the lizard bolts, then two *more* military aircraft pass and two more blasts of sound stick us to the ground.

My heart races.

They are gone.

Three flying weapons, disappearing from sight. Flying west, toward San Diego.

Royal is ecstatic. Izzy is crying. Jenna barely notices.

"We're going to the canyon," I say.

* * *

We arrive at an unmanned security checkpoint four hours later. I'm afraid that one of the world's seven natural wonders won't be enough to enthrall two hard-to-please children, so I've elected to drive through Hualapai land to the Grand Canyon Skywalk. A horseshoe-shaped glass bridge that extends seventy feet out above the Colorado River, with a four-thousand-foot drop down below. A guaranteed hit.

Jenna loses cell service on the way up, except for a moment near Prescott. That's where we hit the intersection. Grand Canyon West to the left, Flagstaff to the right. I was tempted to abort the plan, to find our reservation info and peel off to the cabin, up into those distant mountains where the kids could go sledding while Jenna and I glued ourselves to the news, but it seems better to shield the kids for as long as I can, to avoid any difficult conversations until I have at least one answer. Which is why the canyon won.

But the Skywalk's main lot is eerily empty when we arrive.

A literal tumbleweed blows in front of the car.

We enter the main tent, with its welcome desks and gift shop. There's no one at the front desk, nowhere to pay for our tickets, and no bus to take us down to the bridge.

Jenna gives me a nudge. "Wi-fi." It's her first word in hours. So, I tell the kids to kill some time among the souvenirs, and as soon as they're gone Jenna and I pull out our phones to figure out what the hell's going on.

"How are you doing?" I ask.

"How do you *think?*"

"The kids seem happy."

She's quiet.

I start scanning social media while Jenna goes to news sites. In the hours since The Incident, new videos have leaked online. First there are the images of flaming debris that I assume are the remains of our suburb. Then come photos of Christ the Redeemer shattered on the streets of Rio de Janeiro. The Taj Mahal on fire, with a mysterious rainbow shimmer mirrored in its reflecting pool. Video in Texas of a news helicopter sailing through the sky, only to burst apart as it makes contact with something unseen. Fighter jets, maybe the ones we saw, launch missiles fruitlessly before they are destroyed by flames.

"It's happening all over the world," she says. "Look."

She angles her phone toward me.

There, on the front page of *The New York Times,* are words I can barely comprehend: *interstellar invasion.*

And with it, a video. Sensitive content.

It's shaky cell footage of a flaming neighborhood, dotted with fallen trees and flipped cars and debris that used to be homes. A pink and orange shimmer undulates in the sky. There's a panicked man in a suit running barefoot down the street, until… Debris moves. Its colorings shift. And for one unmistakable moment, two *eyes* appear in the air. Conical, scaly, red. There's a flash of silver, a maw opens, fangs grow from nothing, and a long fleshy tongue lashes out. Wraps around the man. He's sucked away and then, somehow, it's all gone. Where the anomaly just occurred, the world is discolored. Shimmering. I hear tinny digital screams and the video ends.

"Mom?" It's Izzy.

Jenna jams the phone in her pocket.

Before I can even process what the hell I just witnessed, our adorable little girl is wandering over to tell us: "The canyon is closed." There are tears in her eyes.

Royal comes up behind her. "There's nobody here."

Jenna seems devastated. "Oh, honey."

I pretend like nothing is wrong and I say: "That means no one can stop us."

***

I speed along the canyon rim, the words '*interstellar invasion*' knocking around in my head. My adrenaline is coursing for too many reasons. There are no other cars on the road. We've driven past multiple empty checkpoints. But the kids are going "ooh" and "ahh" in the background, marveling at the red cliffs and clawing over each other for better vantage points.

At least they're happy. For now.

But when we finally arrive at the huge adobe building called the Skywalk Center, with all its empty bus lanes, we discover the doors are locked.

"Don't worry," says Jenna. Then whispers, just to me: "Distract the kids."

She has a determined glint in her eyes and I listen, playing hide-and-seek while she pulls out a credit card and tries to pick the lock. It reminds me of falling in love on that shitty punk tour where breaking-and-entering wasn't uncommon. I feel young. My heart pounds. Conjuring up all those early days in love makes it easy to remember the rest of the good about Jenna. Her indomitable spirit, her big opinions, her talent at the mic. The way she chases excitement, letting it lead her. I feel my mood changing. A love rekindling. Despite everything that's changed in our lives, maybe more good remains than I realized.

Jenna finally calls us over, motioning proudly to the open door.

I kiss her on the cheek and she beams.

The day is turning, I feel it.

Though the inside is quiet and empty.

"Are we supposed to be here?" asks Izzy.

"Daddy got special permissions," says Jenna. "C'mon."

That's the spirit. Together. A team.

We crawl under retractable belt barriers, pass personal lockers for stashing phones, until we reach the door to the glass bridge. I grip the handle. And I push. A warm gust of air hits the kids and they gasp, frozen in their tracks and their eyes going wide.

"Wow."

That's it.

That's the moment of wonder that I have spent all day chasing.

For a single second all their petty little squabbles and fears fade away, and they step through the doors in awe. My own mind clears. The red canyon stretches out for miles all around us, full of high jagged walls topped with white sandstone crowns. The river roars below, carving gorgeous curves into the world, and the setting sun has exploded the limestone walls with vivid color and it's everything I wanted and it's everything I'd hoped to share. The kids are taking their first trepidatious steps out onto the bridge and then they're running and skipping and dancing and Jenna slips her hand into mine, looks at me with those deep dark pools, she's smiling now, she's *happy,* for once today the family is *happy,* and she says: "This was a good idea."

I did it.

For the first time in a long time, I have faith in our future.

We kiss. Her lips are so soft. The smell of her, intoxicating. I pull her waist to my own, my hand slides up her shirt, I'm in heaven. Whatever else is gone, the little joys remain.

Then Izzy screams.

Royal, too.

We break the kiss and we run, we drop to our knees, we try to figure out what's wrong, but they're sobbing too hard to understand, tears and snot run onto red cheeks, then

Izzy swallows tears and wails: *"Why are there… bodies?"*

She's pointing down. Through the glass.

Below us, on the rocks, are the piles of the dead. Dozens of corpses. There are long streaks of crimson splattered onto the walls of the canyon where they bounced off the rocks and more puddles beneath them, blood dripping down toward the river below. A mass suicide. There's a bloody teddy bear in the hands of a child.

No wonder the place was closed.

I feel the joy slipping out of my grasp.

I take Izzy and Royal into an embrace, but they won't calm down.

"Why would they *do* that?" Royal cries.

I look to Jenna. "I'm going to tell them," she says. She pulls out her phone. When she opens it up, that same video has already loaded onto the screen. The man in the fiery streets. The almost invisible creature seeming to swallow him whole. "Listen, sweeties. We didn't want to tell you until the day was over, but… There's bad stuff happening everywhere. No one understands it yet. So. Some people are… scared. That's all. But we don't have to be scared, do we? Because we're *together.*"

The kids go quiet as they watch the screen.

"Are those… aliens?" asks Izzy.

"We should have gone to the cabin," says Royal.

"Well… I thought this might be nice," I say.

"But the cabin is *safe,*" says Royal.

"We don't know that."

"Look." He points to the screen. To the creature that can phase out of sight. "It's like a chameleon. Reptilian. And I bet it's warm-blooded. We'd be safe in the snow."

"It would freeze," adds Izzy.

Oh, fuck.

The kids are right.

Jenna smiles. I give Royal a big kiss on the forehead.

I hug Izzy close. "You're right," I say. "You're totally right." There's a safe space waiting for us up in the mountains. An isolated cabin surrounded by snow, and we've got the key code. I almost feel ill for thinking it, but there's even a chance that the owner is dead. How long could we stay? Maybe, just maybe, things are about to break our way.

"Let's go," I say.

I stand and I turn.

That's when the shadow passes above us, just a split-second glimpse of something dark in the sky. For a moment, I trick myself into thinking the jets are back. But then I see the shimmer. A rainbow gloss moving under the clouds, almost as if the heavens are glitching. Neon lines seem to undulate beneath the red and pink and purple sky. For a split second, I can make out the edge of a ship.

Jenna and I lock eyes.

The four of us take hands.

We see the fire, but we never hear it.

I should have told them sooner.

What Waits
by
R.D. Davidson

You spend enough time in these parts and you start to fade into the landscape. The freedom, the wind, the nothing. It all unifies into a single big sky. You can see what you're made of when it's just you and the frontier. It's never been sunshine and kittens out there either. The wasteland has a way of hardening you. It's got to.

I always kept that hardening front-of-mind when I was out there too long. Didn't want to come home and lack something human. So, when I got back, I would hug my daughters and kiss my wife and get back to good, or at least I'd act like I was good. But what waits in the wasteland doesn't give a goddamn about being human, not any definition I'd have of it anyway. Whatever I met that night thirty years ago… hell, I don't have any definition for that at all.

I was coming back from six weeks of pulling oil out of the dirt. The smell would cling to me for weeks, not to mention the stains on my hands. My wife, Mary, always teased me that I must be crawling around the oil fields on all fours. I had one blackened hand on the wheel and the other ashing my cigarette out the cracked window. What had been a sunny October day darkened into clouds and flurries once the sun set. Yellow dashes rolled on forever in the glow of my headlights.

Out in that void, it's not hard for something out of place to catch your eye. And by something out of place, I mean *anything*. My headlights revealed a black Jeep or SUV on the opposite side of the road. Its lights and engine were off, but I could see the outline of a person leaning against the driver-side door. I told myself it was a hell of a mess for someone to get themselves into out here at this hour, but that I should keep driving. Nobody waiting around out here for any good reason. Goddamned if I didn't slow down though. Mary's always telling me I'm just a teddy bear that acts like a Grizzly. I hate it when she's right.

I rolled my window crank and stuck my head into the dark. "Hell of a mess for someone to get themselves into," I said. The person's face was obscured and I could really only tell they had their arms folded across their chest. Could have been a woman, man, or something else entirely. They didn't react to my comment, and honestly I'm not sure what I expected back. If anyone knew this was a hell of a mess, it was the person leaning on a disabled vehicle on a freezing, empty road.

Small puffs of breath rose from the stranger's mouth.

"You need a ride to town?"

The stranger uncrossed their arms and leaned toward me. Wild locks of hair dangled in the low ambient light. "Yeah. I suppose I could," rasped the reply, and I realized it was a man.

Even with the road dividing us, his smell drifted to my nostrils: a metallic tang mixed with earthy decay. I thought about how my brother battled depression his whole adult life and hygiene was always the first to go. I felt pity as the stranger approached my passenger door, which I pushed open. The stranger hopped in. He locked eyes with me as the dome light faded off. The rest of his face was worn and chapped, but his eyes had an intelligence and cunning I didn't expect. I'd have preferred a dullard, to be honest.

"My name's Shannon." I offered a black hand across the bench seat. He didn't take it.

"Dan," he replied. "I'm Dan."

"Dan. Dan the man."

"Just Dan," he said. His voice dropped flat.

I studied his face lit by the dashboard's glow, his eyes fixed to the road. We drove a few miles in silence. I reached between the door and driver seat where I stashed my hunting knife; I liked to feel the grooves carved into its deer antler handle. If I didn't keep my hands and mind occupied, I'd smoke like a locomotive the whole way home.

"Mind if I put on some music?" I asked.

"Your truck," he said.

I turned my radio knob to find an active station. It was usually dead air, or gospel or preachers or doomsayers I didn't care much care for. Radio robbed snake handlers of their greatest asset: the snakes. All the same, the silence could be worse than apocalyptic claptrap. My luck had run out, however I found nothing but static, and I clicked it off.

We rode on until Dan interjected, "This your wife's truck?"

"What's that?" I turned to him.

"I said is this a woman's truck?" He pointed to a dancing flower dashboard ornament pulsing its leaf arms up and down. Its floral face beamed with rosy cheeks.

I laughed. "Oh, no, my daughters thought my truck seemed grumpy. A little reminder of them when I'm on the road."

Dan nodded and drew his lips into a thin line. He wrapped his dirty mop of hair up into a bun and tied it with some kind of leather strap.

"Where you coming from, Dan?"

Dan sighed. "Left Rawlins this afternoon."

I laughed. "You sure about that?"

He finally turned to face me. "Very."

"Well then your ride must have spun out or something, because you were facing the wrong direction."

"Spun out," Dan replied. "Something like that."

Suddenly, a spark of light shone in the distance. Hard to tell in the dark, but it lay about ten miles out. Shadows of scrub jagged out of the dirt when my headlights passed over them. As the light drew closer, the outline of a squat building formed out of the dust.

"Pull over here." Dan nodded forward at the building. "Got a buddy who can pick me up."

"You sure? It's only another hour or so into town."

"Just pull up here. This will do fine."

Honestly, I was a bit relieved he was leaving early. I know if the roles were flipped, I would be thankful as hell that anyone bothered stopping for me. But Dan wasn't the most hospitable passenger. I had regretted stopping for him as soon as he climbed in, but what was I supposed to say to him? *Never mind, this ain't a taxi.* If a man agrees to do something, he does it. If you don't understand that, I probably don't understand *you.*

Mary and I vacationed up in Jackson Hole when we first got together. She'd bought a fancy camera she wanted to turn loose on the mountains. Snow rolled in mid-morning and every yuppie in their European sedans got buried. We passed one of them stuck on the roadside and I figured it'd be my daily good deed to pull them out. I did so and the cosmic scoreboard incremented in my favor. Problem was, I drove past other yuppies in other ditches and Mary started in on me. "What the hell's the difference between those folks and the one you towed out?" The difference, I explained, was that I didn't realize the first person I helped was only one member of a legion of unprepared dummies.

Mary disagreed, and I spent my vacation towing imported sedans out of holes. Not sure if she got any good pictures.

Red neon letters hung from the front of the dusty structure. I could only read them as I crunched over the gravel of the parking lot. "THE DEN." A shabby truck, not unlike my own, was parked at the side of the building. Otherwise, the lot stood empty.

I put the truck in park. "End of the line, Dan the man."

"You mind waiting here for me?" he asked, looking straight at the building. "Just to make sure I can get my buddy on the line? Not even sure these folks'll let me use their phone neither. A lot of assholes out here, you know?"

"Tell me about it," I smiled.

Dan slid out of the truck and disappeared into the bar, his scraggly hair bouncing with each step. I lit a cigarette and tried the radio again. Nothing. This bar and the other truck in the lot were my only sign the world hadn't ended. And frankly, it wasn't all that reassuring.

The ash on my cigarette lengthened and I checked the digital clock on the dash. Ten, maybe twenty minutes? Didn't have a baseline from when Dan had left. I killed the engine and proceeded inside.

The wooden door swung loosely on its hinges and slammed the wall. I jumped at the sound, then took in my surroundings. Dust and dirt gathered in the corners of the hardwood. Various beer brands' neon lights blared from wood paneling. The bar formed a horseshoe into the middle of the room. Smelled like cigarettes and stale beer. Dan slumped there, sipping a bottle.

"The hell you doing?" I asked him. "I was out there waiting for you."

Dan turned to me with reddened eyes and patted the stool next to him. Dust motes flew off the cracked vinyl.

"Dan, I need to get on the road. I'm tired as hell and don't have time for your bullshit."

Dan patted the seat again.

To this day, I'm not sure why I sat down. Sure as hell didn't want to. I don't really drink much and all I wanted was to lay my head down for the night. I just felt a kind of pull to the seat. Almost had a feeling this whole ordeal wasn't going to end without me sitting there.

Dan kneeled on his stool seat and leaned over the glossy bar. He knocked around liquor bottles in the well on the other side. "What's your poison?"

"Where's the bartender?" I asked.

"Don't worry about that," Dan said. "I know him well. He won't care."

I scanned the room looking for the poor soul. Only other lifeforms were stuffed trophy foxes mounted in action poses around the room. Taxidermist must have been running a sale. "I don't drink much."

"When you do, what do you drink? Not a hard question." Dan's voice took on an edge.

"Something fruity, I guess. Maybe schnapps?"

The bottles stopped clinking and Dan turned his piercing eyes on me. Hate's a good word for the look he wore.

"Bourbon it is." Dan pitched the bottle end-over-end and caught it. He poured into a highball glass until it brimmed. He slapped it on the bar in front of me and it splashed on the wood.

"Your buddy coming for you?" I asked. "I should really get on the road."

"No answer when I called," Dan said vacantly after a pause. "Was just about to try him again." Dan's stool screeched on the wood and he marched past the bar into the swinging double doors of the kitchen. I saw my blurry reflection in the chrome as the door swung to a stop.

I sipped my drink and it tasted like gasoline. I leaned over the bar and dumped it into the sink.

A few minutes passed as I drummed my fingers on the

bar. No sounds came from the kitchen. Ceiling-mounted speakers hissed with static since the jukebox wasn't running.

"A lot of assholes out here is right," I muttered. I turned from the bar to the exit when I heard a loud, metallic clang. The kitchen doors pulsed a bit like a breeze blew behind them.

Don't check on him. He doesn't give a damn about you, you don't have to give one about him.

I sighed and proceeded to the kitchen. I propped the door open with my forearm. "Dan?" I shouted. "You alright, buddy?"

No one answered. A persistent bubbling sound pulsed in the back of the kitchen. Immediately upon entering the room, I saw an old-style rotary phone. Its connection to the wall frayed and severed, I couldn't ascertain when the damage could have occurred. Pursuing the noise again, I followed it past greasy chrome fryers and stovetops. The air bit my nostrils with a smell of old pennies. Steam or smoke rolled from a black kettle on the stove at the kitchen's rear. I waved smoke out of my face and pulled my shirt over my nostrils as I approached the stove to turn it off.

It took a minute to process what I saw. Honestly, I don't really like to recount it, but I started telling this story so I may as well finish it.

Hard to say what body part it was exactly, but a red chunk of meat lay in the center of the pot. Could have been an organ, but it had striations like a bicep or thigh muscle. Blood rolled and popped in the pot surrounding the flesh braising it. Human fingers lay on a cutting board to the side of the stove. A stainless-steel bowl lay overturned on the floor. Stray teeth spread over the tile like a grisly game of marbles. Blood pounded in my ears as I backed away and toppled a rack of oven trays. Something darted past the corner of my eye and proceeded deeper into the kitchen.

I sprinted out the kitchen door and back into the bar.

Glassy, black fox eyes glared at me from every wall. Big-band music warbled from the speakers; I didn't recognize the tune, but the words were clear enough.

Sweetheart, too sweet

Every bite, every bit

Sweet enough to eat

Horns droned as the disk wobbled in the jukebox. Sweat stung my eyes. I barreled at the exit and burst outside. Gravel kicked up behind my feet and cold air burned my lungs as I rushed to my truck. I fumbled the keys into the lock and jumped inside. The engine roared to life and brought the headlights on.

Just at the edge of the light, I could see him crouched. Half dark, half light. His body swayed a bit and the truck's beams caught his eyes. Those red eyes, like a roadside animal stalking in the shadows.

Dan stood and strode fully into the headlights and paused. Smoke from my exhaust swirled around him. His mouth and shirt were ringed in blood. The light reflecting in his eyes deadened his expression, almost like he was bored. He articulated his left palm toward me, and a glint reported from beside his hand. I groped beside my seat for the knife but found nothing. I looked back through the windshield and Dan was gone.

I reversed in an arc and started to pull forward. Out of the dust, I saw a shadow leap into my truck bed. The shocks rebounded as Dan reared up and kicked out my cab's rear window. Flecks of glass coated the back of my neck, and I could hear Dan fishing his arm through the opening behind me. I stomped the gas pedal and sent him tumbling into the dirt. I bounced in the cab as I returned to the highway. The Den's red light faded in the rearview.

Now, life ain't a horror movie. I didn't try to take

matters into my own hands. I didn't drive home and hope that Dan hadn't checked my registration or insurance card in my glovebox—every night a hope and prayer that son of a bitch couldn't find my family. No, I did what any sane person would do, and went to the police station as soon as I got to town.

It's hard to recount a story like that without sounding crazy, especially to police officers. They kept exchanging glances with each other while I was talking. Almost like they knew what I was going to say before I said it. When I finished, they asked me to show them where I had been.

Between the drive from the bar to their station, providing a statement, and returning to the scene of the crime, the sun had crested the horizon. The parking lot was empty and the front door slouched open. Again, this isn't a spooky story for around the campfire; some climax where the blood, viscera, and appendages vanished and my sanity is called into question. No, it was all there. The blood had mostly evaporated, leaving a glaze on burnt cast iron. The fingers had gone gray and the police almost ground a tooth or two into the tile with their boots. Dan's jeep waited on the roadside ahead. The VIN was registered with The Den's owner. She's never been found.

Couple of weeks later, the lab returned results on the human bits from the kitchen. Not a single common print among the eleven fingers. The teeth were all different shapes, sizes, and ages. None of the prints matched the bar's owner either. I still drive that highway every month or two. Violent winds surge from the plains and buffet me from lane to lane. I just grip the wheel and keep my eyes forward. God help whoever waits on the side of the road. My eyes are closed to them.

A Cottage on the Interstate
by
Patrick Wright

The van slid on wet grass until its tail end splashed against the creek bed too, coming to rest at a canted angle, half-in and half-out of filthy water, like a soup ladle with a family in it. After some crying and panic and slobbery bellowing over Dad's unconscious body, Mom, headachey and haggard, got everyone calmed down enough to take stock of the situation.

It looked like Dad was having a heart attack, or maybe some sort of seizure. He wasn't totally out, but he wasn't lucid. His forehead was beaded with sweat, his eyes pinched shut. He moaned in a pathetic way that big men like Dad don't usually take to. Cody, his son, the older child, felt ashamed for him.

The van was out of commission. The water in the engine block had fouled something up and it wouldn't crank again. And who knew if they could even dredge the old girl out of the creek, if it were even able to get going again?

They were in the middle of nowhere. It was a quarter of midnight. No other cars on the road, and the truck Dad had been playing fender-tag with hadn't even slowed down when it saw the van lose control and run off the road. There weren't even taillights on the far end of the Interstate anymore; it was long gone. The driver was probably laughing at them.

Cody took a look around. Luckily, the moon was close enough to full to cast a silver glow on the blacktop. It lightened the dense woods lining both sides of the road to a darkness soft enough to decipher the pine treetops from the black trunks beneath them. There was a median between the northbound and southbound lanes, with its own small patch of trees. *An island*, thought Cody. There were many islands along the Interstate.

Where there were trees, beds of pine needles lay at their feet. Though state landscapers probably came frequently to mow the hills along the roadsides, no one was caring for the woods. No one scooping up the leaves and needles and depositing them in waste bags. They were layered deep, in season after season of old death. Old leaves rotting into sodden earth, the border between them indistinguishable and soft. That meant the island was deserted. Cody liked to think about that, and not about his Dad, who was dying.

Dad's heart attack, or whatever it was, had been brought on by the rage of his battle with the pickup truck. He had been screaming and spitting, and they had all been scared, tossed all over the van by his wild driving. The hatred Dad held for that driver made *Cody* feel sick and nervous, and not just because of the erratic jolting of the van on the uneven blacktop. He could sense the fury Dad funneled into his driving wanted to strike elsewhere, was *directed* elsewhere, and that the driver of the truck meant nothing to him at all. Cody, young as he was, could only sense this incompletely, and it was a yawning horror to him. He wished he was older. It might have all made sense to him if he was.

Mom had been at the end of her rope, even before the crash, dealt the unfair hand of caring for both kids, her husband, and all the travel stressors, which made her volatile and prone to snapping bitterly. Cody and Sidney always got nervous about road trips; they were horrible occasions.

"I don't know where the next exit is," Mom despaired, beleaguered by the siege of noise from Cody and Sidney's sobbing and desperate pleas for comfort, "and I don't know what to do." She stood with her hands on her hips, glaring at the children.

"You *gotta* know what to do!" Sidney, the little one, said.

"Well, I don't! Do *you* know what I should do?" she asked, then turned to Cody. "Do *you*?"

Cody only kept crying and shook his head. He knew better than to respond. Mom, ashamed, turned away and sat, simmering, saying nothing. Then, after a while, she burst out with another angry, declarative, "Well, I don't know what to do."

They sat there in the dark for another half hour before Mom sighed and stood up. "I'll go look for help. There must be an exit coming up soon. I'll walk until I find one, then go get help at a gas station. You," she looked at Cody, "stay here with your sister, and keep Dad comfortable. I'll be back as soon as I can. And if somebody comes before I get back, please, God, flag them down."

She gathered up some supplies for the road and set off. Cody and Sidney, tears drying on their faces, sat close to one another for comfort as they watched the dark splotch of Mom recede down the shoulder of the interstate, away from her children, into the softer sounds of the night; the lull of drowsy insects and the murmur of rasping frogs.

She wasn't gone five minutes before Cody looked over at the deserted island of trees and saw something pale standing there. It was not like Mom's night figure; hers was dark, shifting with footsteps, getting smaller, getting gone.

This was an unmoving thing, and a luminous off-white - some tarnished shade of nudity - and it was facing them, not walking away.

Cody expected it to disappear, but it just hung there, leaning out from a tree, hanging from the trunk by its arm, its legs crossed. It looked like it had stopped mid-spin around the tree, like a dancer rounding a street sign in an old movie he'd once seen. But it was frozen there, just watching them. Its body was thin, but did not look particularly spry.

Cody thought, *a castaway*. He wished again that he was older.

Cody petted his sister's head and told her it was okay, it was okay. Sidney could sense Cody's rising panic, and knew that his clumsy, uncareful patting of her head, matting her hair and trying to mash her skull square with her shoulders, was more to comfort himself than her. He was using her as a doll, and had forgotten she was his sister, though he still habitually muttered her name. Sidney felt very afraid. But she did not see the thing hanging from the tree.

After maybe ten minutes of watching them, it was gone. Simply stepped back into the forest. It did not flit away, did not make fanfare of itself, only stepped away as one might step back into a house after taking a moment to enjoy the morning dew. It did not care if it was seen watching, and it did not care if it was seen departing.

Cody had stopped petting Sidney now, and was holding her head tightly to his chest. She wriggled and he realized he must be pulling her skin and stretching her eyes wide and her scalp taut, and let her go. Dad was moaning, making pathetic dream whispers under his breath that Cody could not make out, talking to people that weren't there. He thought his Dad might be speaking not to people but to angels, and might be bartering for his life.

Cody was afraid of the pale, naked, moon-glowing thing out on the island, but still he said, "I think we should stretch our legs."

They got out of the van and crossed at a shallow point of the creek, onto the blacktop. Sidney looked down the length of the interstate both ways. It was late, and there were still no cars. It stretched out either way, straight and narrow, under shades of dark, cresting the foothills in intervals all the way down until all she could see, gleaming by moonlight, were treetops.

Cody wasn't looking down the road, but toward the island.

Though the figure hadn't struck Cody as agile, it must have been; it had left them a gift on the rim of the road, where the weeds crept onto blacktop. It stood out from the dark, glistening an even purer white than the thing did. It was a small animal skull, just the right size to be palmed and taken away by a child. It was bleached clean and crowned in flowers.

Despite his weariness, Cody was drawn to the macabre beauty of the thing, and approached it with Sidney, hand in hand.

Cody saw that little stems of something floral were pressing from beneath the white teeth of the skull. Upon closer inspection, he thought it might have belonged to a young raccoon, or maybe a cat. He bent to lift it.

Beneath the skull, on the cold, wet asphalt, was a bundle of limp honeysuckles.

Sidney took one, and drank its nectar. Cody almost stopped her, but was too distracted by the creeping dark of the island's woods. The trees towered before the children—they were very old - and Cody searched the pockets of night between their trunks for signs of a skirting paleness.

And as if it knew he was looking its way, the nude

thing slid into view from between two trees, body moving with none of the gravity of footsteps, hovering, and stared at Cody. The thing was dry and cracked, with skin like dead leaves. "Hello," it said, pretending to notice Cody for the first time. It was nude but sexless, human-like, but emaciated like a mummified corpse. Its head was large, shallow-skinned and smiling. Its pallid scalp showed through thin hair like their grandmother's did. The hair ran straight back from the forehead toward the nape of the neck in stiff, dark bristles; one could almost mistake them for pine needles implanted into the scalp in lieu of the real thing. Cody stared. Sidney rose from her honeysuckles, startled, and clung to Cody for comfort. He held her shoulders. "Hello," Cody said back to it.

"I like your clothes," the thing said, its eyes wide from skin stretched too tight across its skull. Its eyes darted with glistening precision to their dress. "I like their colors, and the designs on them. Very pretty. Are you lost?" Its voice was thin, androgynous. Cody could see now that it had breasts, and that they sagged, but still there was an ambiguity to the thing's form. Its lack of visible sex organs made its gender unclear. There was a sense of arid rot about it; the genitals could have easily dropped away, like shriveled autumn leaves slipping from their trees or spoiled apples detaching from their stem to fall to the ground and re-seed the earth.

"No," said Cody, and started patting his sister again.

"Where are your mother and father?"

"My father's asleep in the car."

"I should like to speak with him. Shouldn't any boy and girl of your age be left alone to wander my blacktop? This isn't a place for walking, or for things which like to live like men. Perhaps," it gestured to itself, "you have guessed by now that this is why I have taken up residency. This is my home. It is my paradise."

It gestured to the blotches of shadow that made up the patch of woods. Gentle wind blew through the trees.

"An island," Cody said.

"An island. It's where I keep my cottage. My cottage is heated by a hearth, and I keep it very warm. I have lots to eat, because I live very much alone. May I speak with your father?"

Cody and Sidney said nothing for a moment. Cody clung to Sidney's head like it was all that was left of her. "No," Cody said, "I told you he was sleeping."

The thing's gleaming-wet eyes—the only wet or lively or spry part of its decrepit anatomy—flitted to the van. "I see." It seemed to be calculating, and Cody took a step backward, hauling Sidney along with him. He was too scared to put her behind him. His fingers dug into her shoulders.

"I suspect you are alone. Please don't back away. You are frightened of me, because I don't look like you. Is that any way to treat another? I am clearly an intelligent thing, which means I know that I am observed. I know there is a God who watches me, and that makes me a bashful thing and one prone to embarrassment. So please, don't embarrass me."

It covered itself, angling its knees inward with shame. Sidney felt her cheeks burn.

"We don't mean to embarrass you," said Cody, struggling to speak above a whisper, through hitches in his throat.

"Are you hungry?" the thing asked, its wet eyes suddenly bright and excited. "You could come visit me on my island. It's very warm in my cottage. And then I won't be alone, and neither will you. It's a poor condition, to be alone. And yet, here I am. Alone on my island paradise." It caressed tree bark with a slender, icy finger like one might run a hand along a lover's belly.

"Why do you stay here, if you don't want to be alone?"

"It's a deserted island. You could call me a castaway. I am a stranger to others, because I am the last that I am, and that makes me stranger *than* others. Where, then, is your mother? Haven't you got one?"

"We have a mother," said Sidney finally, and haughtily, like it was obvious.

Lithe wet eyes, twinkling with moonlight, cut toward her. The eyes danced, but not fast; not a jig, but a waltz, more like. Clever, slow eyes. These were eyes that did not panic, which held still whatever object gazed upon until they had observed the item in totality and were ready for it to move again. Cody wished he was older.

"How silly of me, little one." It spoke so softly, and so lyrically, and was so kind. "I have no mother. I have no children. I am the last that I am. I'm an island castaway, and I have no mother." It cast its head down and it sounded like it was *boo-hoo*ing, which is what Dad liked to call it when Sidney cried about Dad yelling at her about her bike tire going flat. He would say, waving a hand, "Oh, stop the boo-hooing."

"Don't cry," Cody said. He was revolted by the putrid, dead thing - because it was *certainly* dead, even if it didn't know as much; nothing with skin that tight which split to show the old, pruned muscle beneath could live, and maybe that's what made it a castaway - but he hated to see such pure, lonely sorrow go uncomforted. It was the same impulse that drove Sidney to cry when they used their paper towels at home; the rolls had little teddy bear families on them, and it hurt her to watch them waste away and die as they soaked up spilled raspberry juice. She liked to save paper towels under the desk in their room.

Cody would never run to hug this thing, or come to trust it, but extending his warmth to something that threatened to grow cold was more compulsion than anything. He was bad at it though, and his words came out stilted. He petted his sister's head like one might scrub bristles on a hairbrush.

"Am I not alone?" asked the thing, its sorrow deep and chasmic. It spoke with the same drowning desperation that their mother took on when feeling overwhelmed with tasks. The tone she used to help them feel like the weight of the world on her back, and their part in it. But it was this thing's emptiness which weighed it down, and it sought the children as its buoys.

It was a horrible thing, but it had a lovely voice, once you got used to it; it was only that its teeth were old, yellow and cracked, that it spoke with such harshness. These were not things it could control. You had to forgive it these things. "No," Cody said with a tone of hope, and finality, and he almost wanted to smile for how well he sold it, how truthful it sounded to its listener, because it smiled too. But then, it was always smiling.

"Then may I have a guest? Or two? If your sister will allow you to join us?" It had turned its attention to Sidney now, hands on its knobby knees, grinning and delicate with putrefaction, but it really wasn't so horrible.

"I will," smiled Sidney.

"I like to cook," said the dry, dead thing. "I will cook for you."

"Our mother will be waiting," warned Sidney.

"I'm sure she will, little one," smiled the dead thing. "But I will have you back in the morning with your belly full from my breakfast. And if it is cold in the morning when the sun hits the dew, you will be warm from the weight of my feeding you. You won't waste away with a mother like me. I am so lonely, you see, and I wish only to know motherhood for one night. One tiny night in a sea of desolate life. It'll be another kind of island paradise, a patch of light in my boundless dark. Won't you be my children, oh, just for the night?"

The dry thing was so excited, and it is hard to disappoint a joyous mother, a hopeful spirit. It was such an innocent excitement it held, and yet its eyes were so wide they showed no joy, and its smile was so tight there clung no life to its glee. But it spoke so well.

Sidney looked at Cody, and he hoped for a desperate plea, a *Please take me home* look, but instead she looked at him hopefully, because she wanted to go, and he knew he could not turn the dead thing down.

"Yes," said Cody, and the dead thing clapped and bounced.

"Oh, yes! Yes, a mother alive. You do me such a kindness in this, my children. My lovely children," it said as it extended its hand, and it was still dancing. Cody took the hand, and Sidney, her palm and fingers much smaller than his, but warmer, slipped in beside him. "You'll bring blood to my skin again! I'll well up and bleed, and it will be a wonderful thing! There will be such color! If only you could see it, but there are no lights in my house!"

It led them, dancing, into the island of trees, into the full dark of the pine canopy, and soon they were dancing too, but quietly so as not to wake their father; it was only the sound of tree branches cracking, and dead leaves rustling, to give their private party away.

Not Much Left
by
D.C. Kugtima

Jose drove the bus across a hellishly monotonous landscape. Utterly flat, trampled bare dirt, treeless, grassless, hot and dusty with the occasional concrete foundation on the side of the highway. Kansas had always been a boring drive, but nothing like this. Carefully keeping pace with the vehicles ahead and behind, he glanced at the speedometer.

Fifty-seven miles an hour. Exactly as fast as the thing that chased them. At least this part of the highway was bare. The loose, drifting soil was a deadly hazard. The snowplow could only do so much.

Jasmine walked up the aisle with a cup in her hand. "Jose?" She said gently, knowing better than to startle a tired driver. He turned, and she offered a chipped coffee mug.

He peered inside to see a few ounces of a thin brown liquid. "Tea?" He didn't like tea, but any taste that wasn't dust was a welcome change.

"Coffee… not much left."

He nodded his thanks, and sipped the cool beverage. *Not much left…* that's what should have been written on the road signs. If all the road signs hadn't already been torn out of the ground and flattened.

She waited quietly while he drank, as quietly as the rest of the passengers, most of whom did nothing but sleep, or stare blankly ahead. Nobody looked back. Nobody.

When he finished the coffee, he handed back the cup. She took it, then, still a bit embarrassed, glanced at the empty detergent jug sitting under his seat. "Do you need to…"

Jose shook his head. There'd been a time, a few months ago, when a woman offering to unzip his pants would have been exciting, arousing. Now…nothing. Jasmine had been pretty enough, before the worry lines, and the dust, and the stink. If Doc's crazy plan worked, maybe, just maybe, he'd… what? Ask her out? Take her to a nonexistent restaurant to eat nonexistent food; maybe they could fuck and breed a little kid to feed the monsters? Jose knew he had to fight this black despair. He was a driver, THE driver, and this responsibility for his passengers was all that kept him going.

He forced a smile. "Thanks for the coffee." He wiped his lips on the dirty sleeve of his uniform.

Jasmine shyly nodded. "You don't have to drive all the time."

"It's my bus. And I only drive…" his brain struggled with the simple math. He was tired.

Her math was better. "…eighteen hours a day. Maybe, you could teach me?"

He was pondering an answer, when Brewster, the kid in the hopped-up Subaru, drove

by and waved for them to stop, then drove up the line, waving and pointing. Jose shook his head, but allowed the bus to drift to a stop. He set the brake and opened the door, leaving the diesel running. Some of the passengers stood up, but he angrily waved them down. "This is not a rest stop!" He was answered by a few groans, maybe some quiet crying. But they listened, because he carried a fully loaded .45, and he'd used it before.

He got up, trying not to cry out as the back spasms hit him. Jasmine looked concerned, and held out a hand to help, but he waved it off. "Keep them in the seats. I've got to find out what's going on." He stretched as he exited the bus, looking forward, to see the mighty snowplow and a few passenger vans pulled over. Behind them, a variety of cars, SUVs and minivans waited, engines running. Their surviving motorcycle scouts warily circled the convoy.

Jose looked at a nearby pickup, raising his hands in a "what the hell?" gesture, when he saw the problem. A dented compact, with a bunch of suitcases tied to the roof rack, slowly drifted next to the bus on bald tires, with a huge cloud of steam hissing out from under the hood. Another radiator hose failure. They'd already lost a number of vehicles to these minor mechanical problems. Even if they'd had spare hoses, the thing was only thirty miles behind them. There was rarely even time to change a tire, and most of the vehicles were riding bald by now. They'd driven over fifty thousand miles in the past two months. If Doc's plan didn't work…

The man driving the compact turned off the engine, it dieseled and chugged for half a minute before giving up the ghost. He staggered out of his car, unshaven, stinking—with piss-stained pants—followed by a wife and young boy.

Jose sighed. "Need a ride?"

"Fuck yeah." The man ran to the roof rack and started untying the suitcases, as his wife pulled the boy from wandering off the tarmac.

Jose shook his head. "Leave them. I'm already overloaded. Food and water only."

The man paused, a look of anger crossing his haggard face, then nodded. "We haven't eaten in a couple of days."

"How much gas?"

"A couple of gallons."

Jose yelled "GAS!" as he guided the family into the bus, "Come on, hurry!"

The man stopped when he looked at the seats, all filled. "There's no. . ." Jose had no time for this. He'd already heard the rumble of a hundred million tons of rampaging biomass approaching at fifty-seven miles an hour.

"Sit in the aisle! Move it!"

Moments later, the bus slowly accelerated away, as teenagers with hoses quickly siphoned the compact dry.

***

Hours later, as the sun set, that enigmatic woman they only referred to as "The Navigator" led them, from her seat up front in the snowplow, to a safe spot—a vast stretch of asphalt that had probably once been a shopping mall's parking lot. Maybe a stadium. Jose surveyed the vast black expanse as he parked the bus. Pavement was safe. All too often, if they landed on soil, some crazed, patchwork nightmare would erupt, to feed or absorb or do whatever it was the monsters did.

Doc, standing nearby, somehow knew exactly what Jose was thinking. "If we're only ever safe on pavement, will we evolve softer feet?"

Jose looked at the skinny young genius, as grey and haggard as the rest of them, and wondered how he could even imagine a future beyond the next few days. "You really think we'll survive long enough to evolve?"

Doc forced a smile. "That's the plan Jose, that's the plan." The plan. Literally the only thing that kept them going. Humanity had been shocked when the things had erupted from that laboratory, rapidly absorbing every living thing in their path. When every last bit of the world's biomass was turning into monsters, and everybody they touched, bit, or stung turned into even more monsters, there was no time to plan. Just time to react—but there were never enough bullets, never enough Molotovs, never enough poison gas or nukes.

If the things could work together, humanity would already be extinct. But the monsters were competitive, battling each other, eating and absorbing each other. And this evolution favored size. The biggest ones always won. Until North America was ruled by dozens of monsters, literal oceans of rapidly transforming flesh; each utterly territorial, utterly hungry, huge beyond imagination.

Doc, some kind of biologist with a good head for math, figured out their great weakness. Calories. They were burning calories at an unbelievable rate. They could have settled down, put roots into the soil and photosynthesized. They'd absorbed all the plants; they had the genes for this—but they liked to live fast. They liked being animals. Maybe the plant forms couldn't compete.

The monsters relentlessly hunted any other life they could find. Those oceans of flesh sprouted myriad legs, tentacles, fins, anything to push millions of tons of predator forward at breakneck speed. And they could be lured, endlessly chasing a tasty convoy, until the alien flesh overheated, or starved, or drowned in metabolic poisons.

Or until the gas ran out.

Gunshots pulled Jose out of his reverie. He ran past his disembarking passengers, drawing his weapon. He found a number of armed women and men, nervously surrounding a wriggling, horse sized thing that was thrashing on the ground. Idiots. "Back the fuck off!"

They nervously turned to him, then stepped away from the creature. The thing was some odd mix of mammal and fungus, with five huge grasshopper legs, a collar of spiky tentacles and a couple of howling human faces rising from its twisted spine. Dark red blood pumped from a dozen bullet holes.

Angie, the tough, elderly snowplow driver, strode forward, raising her much feared shotgun. "Did anyone get touched? Anyone?"

Everyone shook their heads. They all knew to stay the fuck away from the monsters, especially after last week's massacre.

Jose holstered his weapon. Bullets couldn't kill something with cellular growth that fast, and they didn't have enough gasoline to burn it. He crouched around thirty feet away, watching the bullet holes grow over with flesh, scales, and spikes, as the thing struggled to its feet. Jose gazed into its human eyes, hoping it understood him. "Get the fuck outta here or we're going to burn you. . .You understand?"

The thing stood up, even taller as its legs stretched and grew. The human eyes all blinked rapidly–maybe some attempt at communication–and the thing walked away, then sped off in a series of odd leaps.

Angie scowled as she lowered her shotgun. "When they attack, we burn. They need to be scared of us."

Jose shook his head. "It wasn't attacking. Just running from the big one." That was the beauty of Doc's plan. Like a planet clearing it's orbital path, their gargantuan pursuer ate or scared off the endless hordes of monsters they'd otherwise have to face. Right in front of the monster was the safest place you could be.

Jose walked over to join the nightly meeting. He found them monotonous, but he needed to show his face, in case there was a battle over food and fuel. Angie was there, as was the Navigator.

The Night Blades were represented—daring crews who drove off-road to set up elaborate booby traps. Their improvised blades, spikes and pits caused a lot of damage to the monster. Not enough to stop it, not any more than a sandcastle could stop a tide, but they'd taught the big, stupid thing caution. They'd trained it not to run at night. Apparently, it didn't have the genes for night vision.

The pumpers were present as well. Heavily armed crews who used GPS to find the locations of gas stations and then pump fuel from the surviving underground tanks. Mostlycops and soldiers; they took a lot of casualties, as often as not shooting their own infected members.

The final faction was the foragers. They used metal detectors, shovels and rakes to find canned food, speeding far ahead of the convoy to lengthen search times. Their job was the most dangerous; their digging often stirred up subterranean monsters. Lacking fuel for flamethrowers, they were fairly defenseless, and often fled from their dying, transforming comrades.

Jose looked at the stained map spread over the hood of a rusty pickup. There were hundreds of blue circles marked all over the state. But the majority of them were X'd out–

destroyed or used up. Jose sighed. Despair seemed to be the realistic outlook.

Angie was arguing. ". . .three cars today. How many more tomorrow?"

Doc shook his head. "Losing cars isn't a problem. We're more efficient with less cars. And less chance of infiltration." Doc was right about that. Cars that lost their way tended to return with human-looking drivers. If it wasn't for Angie's brutal order–to immediately kill anybody they'd lost touch with–they'd probably all be infected by now.

Jose listened for a bit, then wandered off. More of the same discussion he heard every night. There was less fuel and food available, less people to get the food and fuel, and the monster wasn't dead yet. He walked back to the bus, where Jasmine was waiting.

"Well?" She asked.

Jose shrugged. "Same-ole. Just stick to the plan."

She took his hand and led him to an old futon set in the middle of the road, guarded by fairly well-rested bus passengers. They knew how important Jose was. "The plan?"

Jose sat on the futon. He glanced around, but his guards were considerately out of earshot. "We're bait."

"I know. It's crazy." She knelt and started unlacing his shoes.

"I used to think so. But we're still alive. And everyone else is dead."

Jasmine shook her head. "But the thing isn't dead."

"Not yet. Doc did the math. He says it's got to be getting a lot smaller. It's…" Jose tried to remember the college words. "It's running out of bio-mass. It's turning into carbon monoxide…dioxide…something."

She looked just a bit hopeful. "Are we going to make it?"

Jose wanted to reassure her, but he thought he'd lose her with a lie. "We might."

She nodded solemnly, and pushed him down on the futon. "Sleep. We need you rested." He rested his head on a dirty pillow and closed his eyes. Just a few more weeks. . .a few more weeks.

***

Jose had always looked forward to Missouri River bridge day. The monster always struggled on the steep banks of the river, buying them an additional four hours to stretch their legs and maintain their vehicles. But now, Jose got nervous when he saw a cloud of mist by the bridge.

Seeing brake lights ahead, Jose slammed on the

brakes. The bus skidded to a halt, with a number of passengers crying out as they tumbled into the aisle. Jose blanched at what he saw through the windshield.

The middle of the bridge was gone. Enormous tentacles the size of redwoods were busily constricting around the concrete spans, slowly crumbling away the road surface. Jose turned off the motor and rushed out onto the road.

He pushed through the disbelief to ask a question. "What. . .what happened?" Nothing in the river had ever been large enough to do this.

Doc turned away from the shattered bridge. "Rain. With no vegetation to soak up thewater, the river flooded high enough for one of the behemoths to swim up from the Gulf. It probably ate everything else in the river."

Brewster's WRX skidded to a halt next to Doc, and the young man waved the genius over.

Jose turned to see Angie standing next to her snowplow, directing each of the cars, SUVs and pickups to speed away north or south, overland, running parallel to the riverbank. The dirt bikes were well on their way, but all the street bikes had gathered together, waiting by the bridgehead.

"What are we doing?" asked Jose.

"Scattering, running for it," she answered harshly. "Some of us, anyways."

Jose saw that a few of the bald-tired vehicles had already gotten stuck in the soft, dusty dirt. At least half of the convoy wasn't going to escape, caught in the tangle of dead trees to the north, or the impassable ruins of Kansas City to the south. And that included the bus. It was far too heavy to cross the loosely packed soil. He felt a sudden pang of guilt. His passengers had trusted him. . .

But he'd tried. They'd all tried. He wanted to run back to the bus and grab his passengers, shove them into other, overloaded vehicles. But it was clearly too late.

Anyone who wasn't already well on their way was doomed.

He felt something being pushed into his hands. A box of .45 shells. Jose looked to Angie, then to the rapidly growing shape on the horizon. "What are these going to do?"

She sighed and shook her head. "Don't feed the monster." She looked to the bus, and he understood.

He wanted to end with hope. Some kind of hope. Anything. "Where's The Navigator?"

"I put her in Brewster's car. And Doc. The kid is fast."

Jose nodded. "And what about you?"

Angie gave a bitter grin. "Burning rags in the fuel tanks, I'm going to smash into that bastard at eighty miles an hour." They both knew it wouldn't make any real difference, but Jose appreciated the gesture. The survivors would regroup. And this battle, Leviathan versus Behemoth, might last for weeks, maybe months. It might be enough to end these two creatures.

Jose held out his hand, and they shook. Then he turned and walked back to the bus.

Time to deal with the passengers.

* * *

When it was done, he stood quietly with Jasmine, ignoring the scattered rows of bodies. Nobody had argued, they'd all understood.

They stood side by side, watching the bikers nerve themselves up for the jump. At least two of the crotch rockets had made the sixty-foot jump, though the tentacles had gotten most of the rest. They turned away after the last two bikers died, looking away from the horrific thing that was growing a forest of legs and tentacles as it clawed its way out of the river.

They walked away from the bus, heading back on the road, towards the thing that dominated the horizon. Dominated, but it did not fill. Doc was right. It was smaller, not more than twenty miles wide. Just a hint of a smile crossed Jose's face. He gently squeezed Jasmine's hand. "I wish we'd met a few years ago."

She nodded and wiped a tear from her eye. She looked at the thing, an ocean of flowing meat, studded with millions of screaming human heads, and other, far worse appendages. "Do you think being. . .*absorbed* is like. . .still being alive?"

As he held the pistol to the back of her head, he was glad to know his last bullet would make sure she never got to answer that question.

Though he might.

Passengers
by
Meg Belviso

The girl had been riding with them all day. Daddy didn't know it, because he didn't talk to her or look at her, or kick her out of the car onto the highway.

Ellen tried to ignore the girl. She looked out the window, or at the back of the seat in front of her, or at her bear. Sometimes she couldn't help it, though, and at those times when she did turn her head, she hoped the girl would have disappeared. But she was still there every time, beside her in the back seat, going wherever Ellen's father was taking them.

The girl had brown hair. She wore jeans and a flowy shirt with little flowers of red and yellow thread around the edges, and brown rope bracelets on her wrists. Her fingernails were dirty. Some were broken and smeared with mud and blood. Her left pinky was black and blue and swollen, and it stuck out at a strange angle that Ellen couldn't duplicate with any of her own fingers.

The girl smelled funny, like wet dog and Juicy Fruit gum. The air around her was damp and darker than in the rest of the car, which was bright with sunshine and dry from the air conditioner.

"What's the first thing you want to do when we get to

Disney World?" Daddy asked suddenly. His voice was loud and jolly. "Flying Dumbo? Teacups? Haunted Mansion?"

"I don't know," said Ellen. She wished Daddy wouldn't talk about Disney World in front of the girl. She didn't want her to know where they were going. "Teacups, maybe."

"Every kid should go to Disney World," said Daddy. "I can't believe your mom never did."

Ellen was supposed to see her father every other weekend, but Daddy didn't always come on his scheduled times. Often, he would go for months without seeing Ellen and then loudly reappear, like now, promising big, wonderful surprises. This time they'd gone to Build-a-Bear and a famous ice cream parlor, and a horse race.

It should have been fun, but wasn't, like things always were with Daddy. By Sunday evening Ellen had a stomachache and wanted to go home. That's when Daddy announced the trip to Disney World–a place, he kept reminding her–her mother had never taken her. "Just think how jealous she'll be when you tell her about it," he said.

"It's almost night," Ellen had pointed out. People didn't go to Disney World at night, did they?

"It's far away," her father answered. "We won't get there until tomorrow."

He put two suitcases in the trunk of his big red car, and Ellen climbed into the backseat with her Bear-She-Built, for whom she hadn't yet decided on a name. The girl had not been with them then. The sky was pink and pale blue when they set off, the sun flashing in painful orange bursts through the windshield, and they drove until the sky was blue-black and the highway was two ribbons side by side, white and red.

By the time they pulled into the motel, Ellen was pretty sure she had never been up so late in her entire life.

Daddy bought two packets of cookies from a vending machine for dinner, and a man at a counter gave them a red plastic shape with a key on it for their room. There were two beds, and a green carpet that matched the bedspreads, and a picture of a highway like the one they'd just been on.

"Cookies for dinner, how fun is that?" her father said, tearing open the packet.

"Can I call Mommy?" Ellen asked.

Daddy laid her suitcase on the bed furthest from the door. He was moving around the room the way he did sometimes, like he was scared or angry, or a combination of the two. It made Ellen think of bees, which had scared her ever since she got stung in an orchard.

"Not tonight," he said. "It's too late. We don't want to wake her up. I said we'd call her when we got to Disney World. Brush your teeth. We're getting an early start in the morning. Very early."

Ellen got into bed with her bear, but she didn't sleep. She and Daddy watched TV together, although Daddy switched the channels too fast for Ellen to understand what was going on with any channel. She thought about names for her bear instead. Benny, maybe. Or Clark. Or Mr. Honey, because of the color of his fur. She really just wanted to go home.

Eventually, Daddy got into the other bed and turned out the light. Ellen stared at the motel window, listening to the cars that came by. She imagined sneaking over to the old-fashioned phone on the nightstand and calling Mommy—she knew her cell phone number by heart—but Daddy was still awake. She could hear it in his breathing. She fell asleep imagining she could hear him buzz.

They did not make an early start. It was after eleven in the morning when Daddy paid the man at the counter—a different man this time, who smelled like medicine—and put Ellen's suitcase in the car.

The strange, silent girl was in the backseat, waiting.

"Who's that?" asked Ellen, pointing through the window.

"You, of course," said Daddy. He thought she was pointing at her own reflection.

Ellen thought the girl might be a friend of her father's—he sometimes introduced her to ladies he was friends with—but those ladies usually made a fuss over Ellen. This girl stared straight ahead as if she was impatient to get going, even as Ellen climbed carefully into the seat beside her. She looked angry or mean or lost or scared. Ellen couldn't look at her for long enough to figure out which.

"I'm hungry," Ellen said turning to her father.

"We'll get breakfast on the road," he said. His phone started to ring, but he made it stop.

The new girl's dark eyes flashed in the rearview mirror, but Daddy didn't say anything.

"Can he see you?" Ellen asked, without looking at her.

"Can who see me?" Daddy asked. He sounded annoyed.

"We're going to Disney World," Ellen whispered. She'd hoped that saying it out loud, even softly, would help her feel happy, but it didn't work. She didn't want to go to Disney World. She really just wanted to go home.

They got hamburgers at a drive-thru and Daddy ordered them both large fries. Back on the highway, Ellen pretended to feed one to Albear. That's what she'd named her stuffed toy—like Albert but without the "t"—because he was a bear. She laid one fry on the seat and nudged it over to the girl.

It lay there for a while. Ellen imagined the girl's blue-and-purple pinky inching toward it, sliding it away with one of her chipped-polish nails. But the girl's hand didn't move.

When Ellen risked a peek up at the girl, she saw that

she, too, was staring at the French fry getting cold on the seat. The girl looked very hungry, but not for hamburgers or French fries.

Ellen hugged Albear tight and rested her chin on his head. She squeezed her eyes shut, counted to ten and told herself that when she opened them the girl would be gone, but she wasn't surprised when that didn't work. The sky outside Ellen's window was still bright blue, but the window on the girl's side looked as if dusk had fallen. Not a summer dusk full of fireflies either, but late fall, like November.

Daddy's phone buzzed again. He glanced at it angrily, rejected the call, put the phone down, picked it up again, stared at it, then tossed it onto the seat beside him.

"I wanted to take you to Disney World for your birthday when you were two. Did your mother tell you that?" he said. "She said you were too young, but did she ever take you since? No. She's always got a reason it won't work, and if there isn't a reason she'll make one. She could suck the life out of anything."

"Mommy says things are more fun when you finish everything you have to do first," Ellen mumbled. The clock on the dashboard said it was almost three. Back home the school day would be ending. Ellen would spend two hours at Enrichment until Mommy picked her up after work. She would do homework at the kitchen table while her mother made dinner. Maybe they would have fish sticks.

Daddy picked up his phone again, then he slapped it down hard. He was buzzing again. Instead of walking back and forth, he jerked the car suddenly to the left and sped up to pass the van in front of him. There was another car in front of that one, so he couldn't do it.

"Goddammit!" Daddy said. He hit the brakes hard, and returned to his place behind the van, still swearing.

Ellen hugged Albear with one hand, gripped the

armrest with the other, and hoped she wouldn't throw up.

The girl was examining her broken finger as if seeing it for the first time, trying to push and twist it back to lay straight like the others. Ellen saw that what she had mistaken for rope bracelets were brownish-red scab marks around her wrists. The girl pressed at them experimentally with her good finger.

Ellen took a deep breath because that sometimes helped when she was nauseous. "I have to go to the bathroom," she said.

"Bitch," her father said.

Ellen jumped. She thought the girl beside her might have jumped too, but Daddy wasn't speaking to either of them.

"Bathroom?" Ellen repeated.

"You just went at the restaurant," he said. His voice had lost the jolly tone—it always did eventually. The restaurant was hours ago and Ellen had drunk a Coke since then, but she didn't say that.

"'M'sorry."

"Well, don't whine about it. You just have to hold it until the exit."

An exit came and went, but Daddy didn't stop. Ellen wasn't sure if he'd forgotten or if he was just being mean. The girl was hugging herself and scraping her broken fingernails down her face like she wanted to tear it off.

Ellen leaned over to the girl close enough to almost taste the sweet, moldy smell that wafted off of her and whispered, "Do you have a phone?"

The girl was definitely old enough to be in high school and all high school girls had phones. Ellen knew her mother's cell phone number by heart. She thought she could send her mother a text without her father knowing. Ask her to come and get her. Maybe Mommy would give the girl a ride home too.

The girl didn't look at her. She didn't speak and she didn't produce a phone. Eventually Daddy pulled off the highway and into a gas station. A man who worked there gave them another plastic keychain. This one was green.

"The bathroom's around the building that way," Daddy said, handing it to her. "Hurry up."

Ellen had never opened a door with a key before. It took her a minute to get it to work.

If her mother had been there, she would have said "good job."

The bathroom was small with concrete walls and smelled like old water. Both sink and toilet had rusty spots that looked like the scabs on the girl's thin wrists, and Ellen couldn't get the door to close right. She perched herself on the very edge of the toilet so she could jump up if someone suddenly came in. The sound of pee hitting the water in the bowl made her want to cry, and there wasn't any toilet paper.

"I want to go home," she whispered.

The mirror above the sink was chipped and stained and Ellen was glad it was too high up on the wall for her to see herself in it. The big plastic keychain had an address printed on it: *A.J. Mobile,* it said. *Mifflinburg, Pennsylvania.*

Disney World was in Florida, she knew that. How far away was that from Pennsylvania? She tried to picture the U.S. map that hung on the wall in her class at school. It had a star pasted on New Jersey. Florida stuck out at the bottom.

Daddy said they were going to Disney World, but Daddy sometimes lied.

If she asked the man at the gas station, she wondered, would he call her mother? Or would he tell Daddy on her?

There was a sudden pounding on the door and it flew open. Ellen dropped the key.

"Go on back to the car," said Daddy, grabbing the key

off the floor. "I'll be there in a second." He shut the door behind him and kicked it to make it close.

A lady was filling up her car at the pumps, shushing a little dog barking at her through the window. Ellen imagined running to her, asking her to drive her home. *I live in Mendham, New Jersey*, she imagined herself saying. *My mother works in Morristown. Her cell phone number is. . .*

But she wasn't supposed to talk to strangers, and the woman would ask her how she came to be at the gas station by herself. Her father would come out of the bathroom and call to her.

Ellen cast her eyes up at the woodsy area behind the lot. She could hide behind a tree, maybe, or just run until she found someone to help her, but she didn't know which way to run, or what to say to avoid being brought back to her father. . .

"Get in!" her father shouted, coming out of the bathroom with the key, and then it was too late to do anything.

The girl was waiting. Ellen thought she probably never went to the bathroom. Daddy was angry when he got into the car, probably because Ellen had taken too long to pee. The imaginary buzzing always seemed to get louder when he was mad. Ellen thought the girl might hear it too, because her dark, angry gaze seemed fixed on Daddy's head.

They stopped for dinner at another McDonald's. Ellen got a small Coke this time. They ate together in near silence. Daddy had stopped buzzing at last, and Ellen thought she should have been happy, but she wasn't. Without the buzzing he seemed like a stranger, and strangers meant dangers. She'd learned that in school. He stared out the window at the dark parking lot, eating his fries one by one.

"Did your mother ever tell you about the day you were born?" he asked quietly.

Ellen wasn't sure if it was her or her mother that was being tested with the question.

"No?"

"I took her to the hospital in the morning. She didn't have the baby for hours but I stayed there at the hospital. I was there until four a.m. and I had to work that day."

Ellen wiped her hands on her napkin because French fries were greasy, her mother always said.

"So, finally, a nurse brought you out and she put you in my arms. She said, 'This is your daddy.' Because Daddys are important—the most important person in a little girl's life. You don't know that because your mother took you away. She thinks kids only need their mother. Mothers are important—every kid needs their mother to take care of them and all that. But your father, your father provides, your father protects you. Looking down at you in my arms that day—you were so small, I couldn't believe it—I wanted—I vowed to protect you. . ." His voice broke off almost as if he was about to cry. He shook his head and rubbed his hand over his face. "It all went to shit. It's all shit."

Ellen looked at a booth nearby, where a lady and a little girl were chatting, each dipping their French fries into the same little dish of ketchup. She imagined the girl out in the car, waiting for them to get back on the road, and Albear on the seat beside her.

"I have to pee," she said.

Daddy walked with her to the restrooms. They were nicer here than at the gas station, with normal stalls that closed. There was nobody else inside, no ladies or older girls who might let her use their phone, if she gave them her mother's number, which she knew by heart. She sat on the toilet long after she'd finished peeing.

What if she stayed in here forever? Daddy couldn't come into the ladies' room, could he? She imagined him standing there like a dummy, knocking on the door. Good, she thought. He was a dummy and a butt hole and a. . . what had she heard Mommy call him once? —a loser. Ellen was supposed to be back home by now. There was a schedule. She didn't want to go to Disney World. She hadn't wanted to spend the weekend with him.

Next time, she would lock herself in her room and refuse to go. Mommy would let her stay home, especially when she told her how Daddy gave her cookies for dinner and didn't tell her to brush her teeth and said "shit."

There was a knock at the door and Daddy said, "Hurry up!" He was angry again, she could tell, but he wasn't yelling because somebody might hear. He couldn't come in, though, because this was the girl's room. He couldn't come in. He couldn't come in. He couldn't. . . Daddy came in. Ellen saw his shoes under the stall door. They were brown with laces, one of which was coming loose. "What the hell are you doing?" he demanded, kicking the stall door lightly with one of them.

"I'm coming."

Daddy didn't tell her to wash her hands. He just led her out of the restaurant and back to the car.

"I want to go home," Ellen said, but she didn't expect him to answer.

Hours later, they were back on some highway. All the roads looked the same. White headlights coming toward them, red taillights in front of them. It was late at night, later than the time they'd stopped at the motel, but Daddy was still driving.

The girl hadn't moved. She still stared ahead, sitting up straight, as if expecting something to come into view any second. Ellen wasn't afraid of the strange girl anymore. She almost thought she could understand her now. She wanted to get home, just like Ellen did, and she'd ride in whatever car might get her there.

Ellen was going to get home too. She had a plan. She'd worked it out with Albear. She was going to tell Daddy she had to pee again. Eventually, Daddy would pull off at a gas station or a restaurant or even a motel. When they got there, Ellen would go up to the first lady she saw. She would tell her she was in trouble and to call her Mommy. She wouldn't be scared, she wouldn't be shy. If necessary, she would even tell the lady that Daddy was A Stranger. Then everyone would have to call her mother, whose phone number Ellen knew by heart.

She practiced what she would say to the lady over and over, whispering it into Albear's ear. "My name is Ellen and I live in New Jersey. I am lost. My mother expected me home two days ago. Please call my mother and tell her where I am. I need help. Please help."

She practiced her speech over and over, picturing the lady she might say it too. She saw the lady look surprised, then concerned. She would put her arm on Ellen's shoulder and take out her cell phone. She wouldn't let Daddy stop her. She'd say, "This young lady asked for my help and I'm going to help her."

Ellen took a deep breath. "I have to go to the bathroom," she said.

Daddy looked at her in the rearview mirror as if he'd forgotten she was there. He had been quiet for a long time. More quiet than Ellen ever remembered him being. Almost like it was him who wasn't there at all.

He said, "We'll stop soon."

Daddy kept driving. Ellen dozed in the back seat, lulled by the car engine. She woke up when she felt the car turn to the right off an exit and coast to a stop. Ellen glanced over at the girl, who for the first time was looking in her direction. She could almost hear the girl telling her to go now and she did. She opened up the door while Daddy was still taking off his seatbelt.

But when she got outside, there was no gas station, no restaurant, no motel. Just a lot of tall grass. Worst of all, there were no people, except the ones whizzing by on the highway behind them.

"Where's the bathroom?" she said.

"You can go in the grass," her father said. His voice sounded as if it was coming from far away across the field. "I'll go with you."

She would find no nice ladies in the dark grass. Had Daddy heard her whispering to Albear? What if he never took her to a real bathroom again?

"Here's good," her father said, in that same faraway voice.

Ellen did have to pee, and she did it quickly. She considered running away, disappearing into the weeds, just running until she found a nice lady with a phone. But that wouldn't work. She would be like a Hansel and Gretel lost in a woods without any breadcrumbs to follow and no witch with a gingerbread phone that she could use.

"We can't go to Disney World," her father said suddenly right behind her.

Ellen buttoned her pants. "That's okay," she said. "Let's just go home."

"You should have gotten to go to Disney World," he said. Something in his voice made it clear that this was her fault and Ellen almost apologized, as if it were somehow up to her whether she went to Disney World or not, or whether she went anywhere at all.

"Please take me home," she repeated.

He didn't seem to hear her. In fact, he seemed to be listening to something far away, gazing out over the tall, ugly grass and black sky.

When he moved, it was so fast that Ellen didn't see him coming. She was just suddenly in the grass, with Daddy's face above her. He was still looking away at the sky or the highway. His hands around her neck were hot and dry, his hard thumbs pressing on her throat. Ellen kicked and thrashed and tried to draw a breath to scream, but there was no breath. It was like somebody shut her throat up tight. Her blood rushed violently inside her skull. Violet and yellow spots exploded in the dark before her eyes. Daddy's face turned into a mass of sparkling things.

But then, over his shoulder, Ellen saw somebody else. Someone with long brown hair and a white flowy shirt.

The girl from the car was here. She was looking down at Ellen, as if for the first time, she could actually see Ellen.

I want to go home! Ellen thought. *Take me home! Take me home! Shit! Shit! Shit! I want to go home!* But the girl was already fading away, as everything grew dim, then dark, then fully black.

***

The sun beat brightly down on the asphalt in the parking lot outside the motel. Different cars that all belonged to different people. The black truck belonged to a man with tattoos who smoked a lot. Ellen didn't much want to ride with him. The white car belonged to a couple with white hair and matching jackets. They seemed nice, but they were going to Florida. Ellen didn't like Florida, though she didn't remember why. She chose a dark red minivan with a crate for a dog and a sticker on the back that said Alhern Elementary School.

She just slipped into the very back seat of the minivan. Soon the lady who owned it came out of the motel with a little white dog, two little girls and a boy. Ellen liked riding in cars with kids, especially when those cars didn't come with a father.

It took a while for the family to settle into their car. Nobody noticed Ellen in the far back seat. Not the boy riding shotgun, or the two girls in the back. Not the mother, even when she adjusted the rearview mirror; not even the rearview mirror itself. Only the dog whined and barked at the blank space on the seat where Ellen was.

"What's the matter with Louis?" one of the girls asked.

"I don't know," said the mother. "Maybe he sees a ghost."

Finally, she started the car. Ellen kept her eyes on the road ahead of her. She had been traveling a long time. Months, maybe, or even years. But there were lots of cars on the highway, going lots of places. Sooner or later, someone would take her home.

Give the Mountain Death
by
Sean Seebach

Whenever I am with nature, walking amongst the trees and their shadows, do I feel a true sense of belonging. But in the morning after I set up camp on the eastern side of the mountain, both nature, and my affection for it, deceived me.

Behind pluming breath, my eyes opened. I anticipated the aroma of coffee, yet the air remained pure and silent. Planting my face against my bed roll's soft outer shell, I hid from the icy air seeping through my pup tent. My bladder throbbed, but I was warm, and I was not yet ready to replace one comfort with another.

Douglass and I had been travelling for roughly seven days, following our guide, Samuel, and we were determined to reach the summit. Funny thing about getting sober: you exchange one longing for another. I used to occupy my time nursing bottles inside dimly lit taverns, exchanging pleasantries and stories with my fellow sots. So, after thirty days of drying out, Douglass suggested a trip to celebrate. Douglass didn't know the real reason why I was celebrating, though. Those thirty days may've been the best days of my life, for reasons that went far beyond sobriety alone. Just the same, I figured I'd look for a permanent job when we returned, after finding the parts of me I'd lost to alcohol.

I thought about the blurry days, all the time I had wasted exaggerating my life story from town to town, stopping only long enough to take the next drink, the next job forking hay and shoveling manure. Farm work paid well, and it was the only work available for a guy like me, one who had spent his entire life building distorted relationships instead of honing a craft. I was at peace with that on the mountain, until the throbbing in my bladder turned to pain and melted away my recollections.

I was unused to sleeping on the ground, and my body felt it. To melt the chill from my bones, I blew into my hands and wiggled my fingers while my joints continued to creak and pop.

Outside, the firs and pines flanking me pillared toward the night sky. The camp was a floor, in a boreal cathedral. The beauty of it all forced me to gasp at the starlight. Still, I felt for the Bowie knife strapped to my calf. Nature is violent, without prejudice. It's easy to let your guard down out here. Nature can deceive you that way. Show itself to you fully, but lie to you at the same time.

I approached a thatch of bunchgrass and opened my fly, feeling as though I had stepped into a hushed vacuum. The notion that the thin air had this affect wasn't lost on me. The surrounding quiet demanded I glance over my shoulder. Not even an ember of last night's fire so much as glowed, a complete change from the roaring blaze of only a few hours earlier.

I finished, shimmied my shoulders, and listened for Samuel, when an odd thing occurred to me. He had snored loudly each night, yet this morning all was quiet around me. Stranger still, my watch read 9:19 a.m., and the sun hadn't yet crowned above the horizon of the neighboring valley.

My hand searched my parka until my fingers curled around a compass, only to fumble and drop it as I pulled it from my pocket. A branch snapped, breaking my focus. Such a laborious thing to do, removing a metal object in a cold this deep. Still listening, I bent over and retrieved the compass. The cold metal casing stuck to the pads of my already numb fingers despite the brief time I had been out there.

I set the compass on my palm and faced east. Scratching the thick growth under my chin, my lips parted. The needle faced west for a moment, before mockingly settling due south.

South? How could that be? Samuel had been leading us north. Of course, we may have deviated a few degrees west, but we never ventured far enough to face south. South should've been behind us, or under us, however you perceived it.

I flicked the face of the compass. The needle remained on S, with drunken stubbornness. Soon I felt a peculiar static in the air, as if before a light rainfall. It gave me a sense of claustrophobia, a sudden urge to navigate away from the trees and into the openness of the valley across from our camp. My mind had felt as though it was filled with helium the instant I approached Samuel's tent, and began brushing my knuckles against it to rouse him awake without startling him.

Nothing stirred within the tent. I abandoned the idea of waking him quietly. "Samuel! You must see this at once!"

Gathering myself, I inhaled slowly, deeply, until the spinning sensation ceased, until my eyes orientated on unmoving ground. My breath plumed Samuel's name again.

My gaze diverted to Douglass's tent. Yelling Samuel's name should have earned a peek from him at the very least.

Disregarding manners, I unzipped Samuel's tent. His

clothes sat in a pile atop his bedroll, next to his pack and our provisions. According to Douglass, Samuel grew up on this mountain. He was homeschooled, later becoming a lumberjack in the small town of Geja, a quarter mile from the mountain's base. I thought maybe Samuel had gone to the creek for a wash. But why at this hour, in this cold? If he knew the sun hadn't properly risen, why hadn't *he* awakened us? It only seemed proper, him being the guide of this expedition and all.

My gaze fixed on his clothes, disheveled as if something had urged him out of there in a hurry. I glanced at the clothesline I had strung up the day before, where all our towels were still hanging.

I recalled the woman at the station seven days prior, admonishing us to stay together, as if she didn't trust Samuel to lead us. She had a hostile look in her eyes, like we were intruding on her privacy. Samuel assured us not to worry, that we were well equipped and suspicion ran deep among the mountain folk.

Now I thought maybe she'd been hiding something, because I'd seen that look before.

***

My father sometimes stared at me with a faraway look, as if on the brink of announcing either something completely profound or utterly dumb. Even though he never ended up saying a word when that glazed, blank stare was on him, my mother would say that this was the liquor talking.

I never knew what she meant, until I began sneaking nips from his bottle, labeled RYE in generic print, and escaping into the woods behind the tarpaper shack we called home. It was here that nature protected me and it was here that I grew a faraway look of my own, gazing at the trees, and sometimes wildlife, not sensing my presence. I could either kill these creatures or allow them to fend for themselves, I imagined my look saying. It never dawned on me, until much later, that perhaps my father had the same thoughts about me.

My father never raised a fist at his only child, only gave me that look, questioning the legitimacy of our relation. That drunken look haunted me, and made me question not only myself but my manhood as well. Could I ever measure up to my father's standards as a day laborer, of being the alpha among my peers?

Long after those questions had been answered, I still had my doubts, even after the inevitable beast inside of him showed its face on a warm Fall morning.

The leaves had reached their full beauty. The entire forest was ablaze in oranges and reds and yellows. I remember my mother, with her back to me in her rocking chair, knitting a new quilt for my cot, due to a growth spurt that had me ducking through doorways over the summer.

Even the shadows in the corner of our home couldn't hide the fresh bruises on her arms, the swelling on her high, tender cheek angled in modesty. She focused on the needles and spoke while facing the wall. "Go outside and help your father, Ren."

My jaw tightened upon noticing a familiar bottle on the kitchen table, where one of the chairs had somehow earned a busted leg. It leaned crookedly against the chair next to it, in a sloppy attempt to disguise the damage. Arithmetic was never my strong suit, but I added things up pretty quickly that day.

Outside, I shielded my face from the sun sluicing through the branches and leaves, and found my father working under his truck. He responded to the sounds of my footfalls against the gravel by ordering me to fetch him a wrench from his toolkit.

In the time it took me to go inside and pack a small bag, I'd already dropped both jacks and watched until my father's legs stopped twitching.

Later, the constable would hike up his pants, hook his thumbs through the belt loops, and declare the tire jacks malfunctioning as cause of death. That sounded good to my seventeen-year-old mind, at least. My mother would be left alone, but in peace, with a paid off shack in the middle of nowhere to complement her newly widowed life.

Rye had been good to me, until it hadn't. I kept seeing Dad peering at me from the dark corners of whatever barn I happened to find work in. Even when I made good with one farmer's daughter, first kissing her against a horse stall, then again when we were naked together on a blanket, that face, with its faraway look, it never left me.

Scared me right into celibacy.

Time passed, and I eventually found work at a diner washing dishes. I graduated to fry cook soon enough, after watching the owner work the spatula whenever my dishes were caught up. Not only did my paycheck benefit, but I could also now afford to keep the strong stuff hidden below the breakfast bar, splashing it into a Styrofoam cup that sometimes also held coffee.

It was at that diner where I met Douglass, and he's responsible for this retelling. I must pass this down, lest, like my father, I also become the haunter.

***

"Douglass. . ." His name crept from my mouth in a hiss. I didn't want to startle my friend. He scared easily, jumped at the slightest of sounds, which is why it had taken us the better part of a week just to climb a quarter of the mountain. No sense in either of our hearts beating harder than they needed to.

I approached his tent and dropped to a knee. "Douglass. . ."

My hand motioned to the tent's zipper when my watch began ticking loudly. The second and minute hands began spinning backward in confusion. I crinkled my brow; the sudden whirring in my pocket arrested my attention. It was the compass, its needle lurching east before also wheeling with uncertainty. With a thousand volts of panic spiraling through my chest, I ripped open Douglass's tent.

His mouth was unnaturally stretched, in a shape I could not recognize. Arthritic fingers curled around a small portrait of his family. No need to check for a pulse. His chest cavity had been snapped open, and the organs were missing. My buttocks met the vinyl of the tent floor. Warm sweat beaded across my face. The most fascinating part of the scene was the lack of a struggle. His pack and belongings were neatly stowed away in the corner, as if something had marched right in there for his soul, with utmost efficiency, and left without disturbing anything else.

After crawling a short distance away, I rose and stumbled, an action I was far too familiar with, and slammed into a pine with low branches. Hot pain jolted down my shoulder. I slumped against the trunk as if it were a sober friend there for comfort.

"Samuel!" I cupped a hand around a corner of my mouth, words echoing back to me like they had come from no one of importance. "Samuel!"

Saliva filled my mouth at the thought of a comforting drink. I closed my eyes, chest heaving, trying hard to execute what I had learned from sitting in on thirty meetings in just as many days, breaking down the walls of my weakness, reconstructing a foundation of strength. But the memory of Douglass's remains was ever present, somewhere near the phantom sound of ice tinkling in a highball.

I bit my lower lip until I tasted blood, until I

remembered how far I had come. My drinking may have shaved years from my life, but I wanted to find out how many more I had remaining.

Eventually, I spilled inside Samuel's tent.

I ripped through the duffle bag, tossed aside the pot and skillet, tongs and other utensils, and found a chrome flashlight. I flicked it on, bathing the tent in an orange glow. The tent walls threatened to smother me through my labored breathing, much like this mountain had planned to, choking me into submission. But seeing the happy faces of Douglass and his family, shared with me at our campfire for the duration of our trip, struck me with an ache I could never describe, partly because I could never be that man in the picture.

Shaking the map open, I spread it out, nailing it underneath the flashlight beam. A series of red marks that weren't there a day ago ran across the map and ended a quarter mile from our camp. The dashes led to a triangle, encircled also in red. Three lines stemmed from the outside of it all, perhaps signifying a neck and two arms. Next to that, the mark of infinity.

＊

I must've hiked for an hour, and still no sun. No matter how far I travelled, I wound up back at our camp, the valley across from it never leaving my sight. The feeling that there was something unseen resting just above my eyes grew prominent, constant; a tingling sensation, followed by a slight and uneasy pressure. A third eye threatening to bloom.

I chewed on my knuckle, rubbing a thumbnail against my forefinger, apprehensive about following the markings on the map since the mountain wouldn't allow me passage otherwise. To prepare, I gathered granola and jerky, arced the flashlight beam toward the valley across the mountain's edge, then above, wondering how far the light would carry. Darkness swallowed it somewhere below the treetops.

I breathed slow and deep, not allowing the strangeness of the mountain to drown me in madness as I recited a small prayer outside Douglass's tent. May he find peace in whatever lay beyond.

Only one way to go, it seemed, and I followed that way at last.

The beam lit the curved path up along the mountainside. The valley ran behind me now, out of sight. Indeed, north was the only direction I could travel. Perhaps the only way out was in.

I stopped to quench my thirst, removing my pack and resting my limbs. Nothing sang or moved within the forest, my boot heels disturbing the foliage the only sound. I played the light across the trees, wondering what I would say to Douglass's family if I ever left this godforsaken place. And it was then my mind began conjuring up stories about what had happened and why it was me on their front stoop and not Douglass cradling them in his arms. Certainly, they would inquire about his body, but I doubted anyone would ever find our camp.

And there was my father, lurking in the shadows again. His arms crossed disapprovingly across a plain white tee.

I gasped a little, forced my thoughts away from him, back to what I would tell Douglass's family. A bear had attacked us, among other lies, when I noticed a section of bark had been removed from a nearby tree. A perfect circle was shaved down to the core, and may have represented my own face for what was to come. Three grooves were stuck in orbit around the sphere, etched so deep sap had oozed from the engravings.

I flared my nostrils at the vibrant stink of pine, and a bottle's throw away stood my father again, clean shaven with his hair slicked back, chest cavity exposed and crushed, holding one of the tire jacks I had used in retaliation as if it were an axe.

He shouldn't have been there.

I hurried up the trail, until all life from my body seemed to leave me. Burning daggers twisted through my chest. I bent over, glanced around: the symbols were on every surrounding tree.

The pack slid off my shoulder and hooked around the flashlight, around my white knuckles clutching it. I had stopped seeing visions of my dead father after getting sober. This wasn't part of the deal. I was not supposed to see him anymore, and somehow this was worse than seeing my friend completely opened up.

The sounds of a snapping fire drew me to a clearing. There, a blaze leapt from the inside of an oil drum. Long flames lapped at the air, emitting black smoke which huddled in conference before dissipating, breaking free above something unseen. I shuddered and yanked my poncho hood tight over my head. I briefly wondered: if I could go back, would I find myself in another continual loop urging me forward, with my father hot on my trail?

Behind the oil drum loomed a mammoth tree oddly shaped like a church. Branches formed an A framed steeple, leaves wove together to resemble a great bell. Amorphous shapes danced along the trunk, like nothing I had ever seen.

I side-stepped, craned my neck for a better angle, trying to penetrate the optical illusion and find reality, when I observed an entrance bored inside the trunk. I could see that it opened upon a room. Fluorescent light spilled over folding tables and chairs. The comforting aroma of brewed coffee urged me forward. As I stepped inside, my ears popped and my head became airy. It felt as though I had drunk from nightfall all the way to dawn, and maintained that buzz well into the afternoon. Drinking yourself sober, is what we called it, though there was nothing clear-headed about it.

Upon entering, a primordial stench reached my nose. The stink of raw meat and wet bones combined with an earthy aroma, wringing my guts. I had smelled that odor before, whenever my father had dressed deer in our shed when I was a child.

I covered my nose with the crook of my arm. On the wall of this other place was a bear head in full roar. A skinned mountain lion served as a crude rug at Samuel's feet. He was facing the wall, as my mother had been the last time I saw her. Samuel and I were not alone, either. Sitting on one of the folding chairs, leaning forward with his face in his hands, was my father.

Stripped of clothes and hunched over, Samuel turned and faced me. His lips smeared into a smile. Soft red matter bulged through his fingers and dangled underneath his hand. Chunks of the fleshy mass protruded from his teeth. I didn't even notice the brick outline on the wall until he spoke.

"Renny, welcome home," Samuel said. "I knew you would find me."

"The mountain. My fa-fa-father."

Samuel's eyes bulged. "Yes! Purely window dressing for the occasion. The father who haunts you is long dead, but your fear of him lives on, and on. But the mountain will protect you, if you let Her. I've known Her all my life, better than any friend or lover, or parent for that matter. The mountain. . ." his gaze drifted, threatened to match a gaze I was all too familiar with, then back to me ". . .it breathes. Can you feel it?"

Possibly I had. Maybe the sensation haunting me between my eyes was what he referred to. Even more disturbing was the way my father began to disintegrate like almost every memory I've ever had of him. His flesh sloughed to the gleaming tile floor until there was nothing left but a skeleton leaning to the side, jaw open like some October prop in a general store.

Samuel cleared his throat, and gestured toward the coffee and donuts that were the staples of every AA meeting I had ever been to. They could not be real. "This has been quite the journey, yes? And you have already overcome great obstacles in your life."

He took a chunk from the bleeding organ in his hand and chewed. The aorta was unmistakable. After swallowing hard, he sighed.

"We both can agree Douglass was not built for this experience. I knew it the moment he requested we bring you along. Douglass was a fragile man, frightened by death. But *you*, Renny, *you* are different. I saw your confidence the moment we began."

Samuel frowned. "I'm not proud of what I have done, but the mountain must receive death in order to give life."

"We are already alive, Samuel! How could you. . .to our friend? And this. . ." I spread out my arms uselessly. "What is happening?"

The malevolence in Samuel's chuckle sent a cold ripple across my skin. "Our only friend is the mountain." Then, as if to part way for something immense, he stepped aside and lifted a lantern I hadn't realized he'd been holding with his free hand. "Motion yourself this way."

But the walls began shaking. A stark light burst from the brick outlined on the wall. A shattering wail burst into my hearing, my mind. I lost all composure, covering my ears. Invisible probes pierced my ear drums and rattled my skull. The terrible pain in my head squeezed my eyes shut.

When the noise at last faded to a bearable level, I opened them.

Samuel stood in front of me. Blood stained his shrunken phallus, peppered his thatch of pubic hair with tiny pink bubbles. I raised my focus and met his eyes as I reached for my Bowie knife. With an outstretched arm, Samuel turned.

Bloody handprints covered the bricks where the wall had opened.

"Come through the door with me, Renny." Then he gestured to the pile of bones that either was—or was not—my father. "Don't allow your mind to play foolish games with you. Your real life lies beyond the threshold."

I could not look away, compelled by the lanternlight. My terror quieted to a murmur. My shoulders relaxed and my breathing calmed. The light washed away all concerns. I felt like I could live in what lay on the other side of that door forever.

"Follow me through, Renny, and become extraordinary."

My legs began moving, lifting me up. Comfort enclosed me, as though I lay in bed after a hot shower with two days of holiday ahead. I did not want the feeling to ever leave me.

"Don't allow Douglass's fate to dissuade you." His lips brushed against my ear lobe as he spoke. "He gave his life for you, Renny. Accept his gift."

Samuel's words dripped with cunning, sparking the memory of the first time I met Douglass, down at the church building's basement (this basement?), at my first AA meeting. Lots of nodding, an exchange of smiles in an understanding of each other, but most of all, a mutual recognition of who we were. The family photo, destined to rot with Douglass's remains, flashed into my mind. Adrenaline surged down my arm, and without even realizing it, I plunged the knife into Samuel's neck. All the way to the hilt.

I caught him by the underarms as his eyes, wide as saucers, stared intently into my own. His fingers grazed the handle as choking gasps escaped his throat. Whatever force was enchanting me had broken away.

Spittle flew from my mouth with the urgency of my words. "What happens when the mountain receives death?"

Samuel gurgled, his bare feet thrumming against the wooden floor while I hoisted and sped him forward, using his bulk as a barrier between me, and whatever lay beyond the once-hidden door. An angry wind raged beyond the threshold. I lunged forward, Samuel in front of me, and released him.

I leaped at the flashing, unnaturally lit EXIT sign, watched the façade I had entered dissolve. The illusion of the church was gone. The tree was now just another tree.

Parts of the mountain exploded in flames. Smoke rose high above the forest, no longer concentrating at tree level. I scrambled down the trail, shedding the poncho, running toward the base of the mountain, away from the fire, chucking the useless compass into the blaze.

Sometime later the sun rose. Day had finally broken. I remained whole, on the outside at least. No one masters alcoholism, only each passing day life brings you.

＊＊＊

After visiting Douglass's wife, I fell back on an old crutch. The welt on my cheek, considerably smaller now that a week had passed, reminded me that a sober mind wasn't always an honest one. I told Margarie what had happened, expressing my sorrow for not finding her husband before the fires. He had wandered off alone, I said, and by the time the flames had spread, there was nothing Samuel or I could do. We had split up and searched for him, but the heat and smoke had separated us.

"It's best to consider him as passed on," I said.

Even though the newspapers confirmed I was the sole survivor, I would've struck me too.

Sometimes, when the wind is right, ash covers my trailer like a hearty snowfall and that blinding light visits me. Douglass's face creeps through the brightness. Inside the O shape of his mouth resides Samuel's own grin, sinister and bloodied, jolting me upright on my cot in a cold sweat.

I want to scream on those nights but before the sound leaves my throat, my senses return to me, inside my trailer, here in the small mountain town of Geja. I have gotten used to its people. Together we behold a great and ancient secret.

After assuming the role of mountain guide, I've come to enjoy hiking amongst Her beauty, away from the scarred line of earth now concealed with briars and venomous plants. Yet at times She beckons me, sends a prickle that massages the flesh between my eyes, reminds me of doorways throughout Her that cannot be seen upon first glance.

Though I may one day succumb to Her, I no longer see visions of my father. I at least owe Her that.

And the whiskey here is good.

Comanche Country
by
Todd Mitternacht

The Comanche muttered to himself in Spanish as we crested the hill to gaze down across the prairie to Plum Creek, where Moseley reckoned Montague Briscoe made off with his loot. Beneath a black silk stovepipe hat with an owl feather jammed in its band, the Comanche's seamed face wore a perpetual frown.

"Well, *compadre*, what did the man say?" Moseley turned to Zavala, who hid under the shade of his big sombrero—his smiling teeth like rows of hominy corn beneath his brushy mustache.

Zavala jutted his chin down to the hollow below us. "He says there is much danger here. This is cursed land. We have to go around."

"Bullshit," Chapman spoke up, scoffing at them and spitting a brown stream of chaw down to the earth.

Covered in black wiry hair from his toes up to his Stetson, Chapman wore an unkempt beard that started high on his cheekbones like a troglodyte's. He rode an Appaloosa roan with black spots, damn near seventeen hands high. To be honest, I didn't like him much, but Moseley said he was the best gun for hire this side of the Sabine. And I didn't doubt him.

Chuckling, Moseley grinned and his perfect teeth sparkled in the sun. He had the cleanest teeth I ever saw in these parts, a sign of civility and most of all, money, which is something that Absalom Moseley had plenty of. He had even more before Briscoe made off with the Iturbide reals from the first Mexican Empire. How he came into possession of them, I figure I won't ever know.

Especially now.

"What, pray tell, is the curse over this land?" Moseley asked. "It seems like everywhere I turn is cursed land and Indian burial grounds. Sounds like a lot of fear mongering."

Wolf Prince stared at Moseley as if he could understand him. Supposedly, the Comanche only knew his own tongue and Spanish, which is why we hired Zavala, the translator. But I had a sneaking suspicion that Wolf Prince could *comprende* as much as he wanted to.

"It's an old creek bed," Zavala explained. "Years ago, a creek joined what is now Plum Creek and the Mayhard. The Comanche say it's a *matadero*. How you say in English?"

"An abattoir?" Moseley asked, an eyebrow cocked high.

Chapman grunted. "Ain't none of you seen the inside of an abattoir, slaughterhouse, or killing floor. Bunch of panty-waist lily-livers." He spit on the ground.

Moseley seemed bemused by the big fellow's boorish behavior, not having mixed company with such a man of action. Instead, he'd been a man of high society, such as it was out here on the frontier. "But what would make this desolate place an abattoir?"

"*Jack shit*," Chapman scoffed.

Zavala ignored him. "You don't know about the Plum Creek lights?"

Wolf Prince glanced briefly at the Tejano—a flash of

the eyes that betrayed something held secret from us. Zavala held up his palm to the Comanche and nodded. "The Comanche say ghost lights pass through this cursed land in the night," he said. "Not all nights, *pero* when the orientation of the sun and the moon are correct, white lights pass through here. And during the day, they pass unseen. Either way, they can kill you if you cross their path."

A shiver ran down my back. "I seen 'em," I admitted.

"Aha!" Moseley said, both eyebrows raised now. The pursuit seemed for the moment a distraction as the lore of the land diverted him. "Let us hear, my good man. I love a good tale."

"Oh, yessirree," I said. "Me and my little brother was out here hunting deer, I reckon I must have been—what—nineteen? A lot younger than I am now. My pa had a ranch just this side of Bastrop and we heard the tales from the Comanche, when they weren't trying to kill us."

Wolf Prince sneered at me. I'd been right that he understood every word I said.

Ignoring him, I continued. "We got stuck out here for the night, me and Mort. We weren't too keen on running into our Comanche friends out in the open, so we pitched camp in the lowest land we could find, which was down in that general. . ."

"Quit your jabbering," Chapman blurted, cutting me off. He pointed out into the wilderness before us. "I see him. Dead ahead about a half mile out. On horseback and leaving a dust trail."

Chapman turned to Wolf Prince, glaring, then over to Moseley. "How much you paying these two idjits? I thought Comanche could see over them hills and this one can't even track your boy, Briscoe." He spit on the ground.

"That's my business." Moseley said, tight-lipped.

"I ain't got time for this," Chapman snarled. "Keep up with me or catch up later." With a swift poke with his spurs, he goaded his roan hard and it lurched forward with a cry and raced down the slope.

"Sonofabitch," I muttered, watching him gallop down to the old creek bed—the hard dirt, packed and dry like the ancient *El Camino Real* trail up from Mexico.

"Gentlemen," Moseley said. "I vote we catch up later like he suggested." He smiled at us. "We might avoid some gunplay and other unfortunate spectacles that follow Mr. Chapman." He pulled a spyglass from his pack and extended it. It was damned near a telescope and as fat around as a beer bottle. More like something you'd see on the high seas rather than the high prairie.

Reaching into my coat pocket, I pulled out my own scope, embarrassed by it. Just a rinky-dink little tube the size of a pen, but it was better than nothing. Zavala and Wolf Prince looked with derision as I raised it to my eye, as if they were too good for technology.

"Holy shit!" Moseley exclaimed, his voice exploding loud enough to make me jump in the saddle and make Sally nicker.

"What happened?" I asked, lifting my eye from the scope.

Moseley replied, "Something picked them up and tossed them across the clearing. Damnedest thing I ever saw."

Chapman had interrupted my tale. If he had taken a moment to listen, maybe he wouldn't have gone charging down there without a fear in the world. But that would have required something other than rocks in his head. What Moseley saw was something I had seen, decades before.

I wasn't ready to see it again, but I had an inkling I would, and soon.

"Where's Chapman?" I asked, but just then I spotted him.

Chapman's horse was a shadow in the dust cloud.

Surefooted, the steed tore through the landscape and rock-eted to that flat place the Tejano said was cursed—an abat-toir there in the silent sprawl of land. Something like light-ning flashed, though not a cloud dotted the sky. A huge gust rose and carried the dust away in an instant.

Suddenly, Chapman and his roan careened up off the ground, each tumbling like dolls. An equine scream ripped through the air and sent a shudder down my spine. The roan's legs pumped, trying to find purchase as it tumbled, but only found air. After a hundred feet or so, it landed neck first with a sickening pop. As for Chapman, he cartwheeled head over heels like a thrown axe. Through my cheap scope, it looked like the sheer velocity of the spin tore the man to shreds.

It was as if they had been struck by a steam engine flying through the open plains at full speed, if not faster. Yet there was not even a passing shadow nor any sound except for their cries and their bodies breaking on the rocks.

"Damn," Moseley said. "We're going to have to go down there and check on them. Are y'all confident you can pick out a path so we don't meet the same fate?"

That was a question for Zavala and the Comanche, but the only answer was a crow laughing at us from some-where in the trees. I pulled my eye from the glass to look at them.

But they were already gone.

***

Moseley and I picked our way down the slope to where Briscoe and Chapman lay. I kept looking behind us. I didn't like those two vanishing without a word.

"Did the sight of blood scare them off?" Moseley asked.

"Naw," I replied. "Don't think that ever bothered those

gentlemen. My gut tells me they're up in the ridge behind us, watching what happens next."

Moseley nodded. "What's that going to be?"

Pulling Sally to a stop, I surveyed the surroundings. Live oaks dotted the flowing prairie slope, filled in between with cedar elm and pecan, closing tighter as we descended.

Turning to Moseley, I shrugged, finally answering his question. "I reckon they're just waiting for us to reach the same fate as your boys, so they can come pick off your silver. It's worth a hell of a lot more than what you owe them for this job."

"Very astute," Moseley whispered, looking up at the trees on either side of us. "Can we get around this?"

I nodded. "There's a way to get past it. If only Chapman had listened for a moment—not that his ears ever worked good anyway." I cocked my head forward. "We'll have to stop before we get too close and wait until dark."

Raising his eyebrow, Moseley asked, "Whatever for?"

"So, we can see them coming. You heard Zavala. They ain't visible in the daylight. At night, we'll be able to cross to the other side unscathed."

"And are you sure of that?" Moseley inquired.

"Like I was saying, I've seen them before. If you want your silver, we'll have to hunker down until dark, then make our move."

"Ah, yes," Moseley replied, grinning now. "There was a tale you were about to tell. Let's hear it as we ride."

***

I told Moseley my tale, starting over again when me and Mort had pitched camp somewhere near this stretch of creek bed. It was about '59 and the deer were in their autumn rut. A dumb buck come out into the hollow, bowing up and grunting at us. It got real quiet, then the woods lit up like a lightning storm. Ball lightning, they say. With it came a sudden wind, and *pow*! That white light zipped by, sending the buck cartwheeling down the creek bed.

Well, that dummy Mort, he jumped up and ran at it, trying to get a look. And I went after him. When we got to the middle of the creek, I saw twin sets of red lights, like eyes, demonic and twinkling, in the distance. They floated in the blackness until they vanished around the curve.

Suddenly, another white light came blasting through. Blinding beams, like lightning suspended in time, pinned us down with horror. These were a new set of demon eyes, white like limelight, driving forth a cacophonous roar and howling wind. Some creature of massive girth—the size of a locomotive—hurtled through the black, leaving the stench of electricity.

We ran and hid in the trees, trembling in the darkness. We never slept a wink that night, waiting for those demon eyes to return.

***

Mosely and me covered the distance at a slow pace, killing time. There was no way I was going to chance crossing that creek bed without using the night to help give away those demonic Plum Creek lights. The sun crawled below the horizon and the sky deepened to indigo as darkness fell. A gibbous moon rose, broken as an old, lost pearl button, and peeked through the trees at us as if spying on us.

"What do you think they are?" Moseley asked, lighting his pipe as his gelding sauntered alongside me and Sally.

"Demons with red eyes and bodies like Leviathan escaped from Sheol." I quoted Scripture: '*And his tail drew the third part of the stars of heaven, and did cast them to the earth'*." I glanced at Moseley, who stared at the ground, but cocked one eyebrow in that particular way he does. It didn't take a genius to realize this man with immense riches wasn't a believer.

He lifted his gaze at me. "And what about your brother, Mort? What happened to him?"

I nodded. "Mort caught a Minié ball at Antietam back in '62. It shattered his thigh bone, and he died of gangrene after the sawbones had their way with him. He and I were in the 5th Texas Infantry. His bones are buried somewhere in Maryland. To his dying day, he was convinced whatever happened that night, we weren't even in our world."

I trailed off, thinking about those horrid days of ashes and rot. I was supposed to keep him out of danger. My maw and paw never forgave me.

"What did he mean by that?" Moseley asked with one hand on his pipe.

"Mort noticed when we arrived in their dominion, the sky was overcast, when it was clear before. The weather hadn't shifted—we had. Or that's what Mort thought. He might be right, but if so, then for a brief moment, we were in Hell."

"Was there fire and brimstone?" Moseley questioned, but I thought he was picking at me.

A voice full of defeat called out from the shadows. "Over here, boys. You got me fair and square."

Moseley answered, his voice filling the hollow where the creek bed ran. "That you, Briscoe?"

"Yep," he said. He lit a match, revealing his location with a flash that faded to flame in a puff of smoke. "Leg's broke," he said. "Can't stand up. Horse is clobbered dead. And your boy's even worse off."

Moseley continued to approach, but I caught him.

"Hold up. Let me check it out first," I said, sliding out

from the saddle.

Moseley nodded and halted his horse. "Is Chapman dead?"

"Goddarnit, you went and hired *him* to track me?" Briscoe whined.

Leading old Sally by the reins, I approached the creek bed on foot. I didn't rightly know what I was looking for, except for the white lightning or red lights bearing down on me. It looked safe so I waved Moseley forward.

Moseley and I crossed the dry creek bed without incident.

"I thought you'd take that as a complement," Moseley said. "The famous bounty hunter himself, coming after *you*."

"I reckon so," Briscoe said. "But he ain't doing much good now, other than drawin' flies. You boys gonna finish me off? If you hired Chapman, you must mean business."

"That depends," Moseley said, sucking on his pipe, thick smoke coiling out from the bowl in the still air. "You still got my silver? That's all I really want." His words were flat in the silence.

Briscoe nodded at the dead horse at his side. "In the saddle bags. You ain't gonna leave me here, are ya?"

"Oh please," Moseley replied, looking up as lightning flickered behind us. "We are civilized men. We can settle our differences and live another day."

"Oh thank—"

A shot rang out. Briscoe's head exploded.

Turning toward the source of the gunshot, I saw Zavala standing on the edge of that cursed creek bed, rifle at his shoulder. The flickering white light illuminated him and windswept trees beyond. He had not been there before, not until this demonic scintillation began.

I drew a bead and fired, smoke erupting from my rifle, whipped by the wind. I thought I saw Zavala crumple before the darkness swallowed him. Gunsmoke burned my eyes and nose.

"Did you see Wolf Prince?" I could barely hear Moseley's voice over the ringing in my ears.

"No," I replied, watching the flickering light cascade southward to the curve in the creek bed, taking the whirlwind with it.

"Help me with this," Moseley demanded.

One cricket in the grass started its trill, then was joined by hundreds of others hidden in the night, as if the twilight orchestra had been counted in by its maestro. But I could scarcely tell the difference between the buzzing in the night and the one in my ears.

After I sauntered over to Moseley, he heaved a bag from the horse carcass and thrust it into my hands. Catching it, I stumbled back. It must have weighed thirty pounds.

"There are three more," Moseley said, panic carved on his face—eyes wide and teeth gritted. "Load these before the other one shows up."

The fear on his face was pathetic, but also, it was the first time I had seen that particular emotion sculpted there. The privilege of having lived so long and not having his senses deadened to the point of grim nonchalance seemed like another luxury he possessed. If I had a mirror, I'm sure my own expression was as flat and lifeless as a corpse. I'd seen too much to be surprised anymore.

I looked at Sally—two sacks of silver would max her out. Now I knew why we had caught up with Briscoe so quickly—his ride must have been sweating foam with a hundred and twenty pounds of silver plus another two hundred pounds of Briscoe himself.

"Go!" Moseley demanded as he drew out another bag.

My old bones were lucky to carry just one sack without dragging it. I made my way over to Sally and hoisted it up to the saddlebag. She nickered as the saddle hung lopsided. "I'll even you out in a bit," I said as I turned back.

Once again, a hush fell and a flickering white light came crackling down from the creek's north end, casting Moseley in silhouette as he burrowed in the dark for the saddlebags. Another shape caught my eye. A shadow crouched low like a—well, like a wolf, creeping up on its prey and clenching daggers in both fists.

As I hollered, he turned to me. But just as Moseley lifted his gaze, Wolf Prince pounced across the remaining distance.

My rifle was worthless. I hadn't reloaded. So, I drew my Colt .45. The round I fired was off-target, but it caused the Comanche to hop and roll, giving Moseley time to draw.

Wolf Prince was quicker and he slashed out with his blades—two Arkansas toothpicks glinting in the diseased moonlight.

Moseley cried out. His revolver tumbled to the ground. He clutched his cut gun hand and writhed in pain, leaving himself wide open.

Clambering through the brush, I fired again to distract the Comanche. It was too dark and too far to get a clean shot. Instead of slicing Moseley again, he threw a knife at me. Those things weren't made for throwing and as good as a man could get with them in combat wasn't good enough when blood was on the line. The knife skittered through the bushes—bouncing off branches instead.

Wolf Prince's tactic was the same as mine—a diversion. With his free hand, he socked Moseley in the jaw, knocking him back on his ass. With the remaining knife clenched in his teeth, Wolf Prince hoisted two bags from the ground and made for the creek bed.

Firing again, I stumbled through the bushes trying to get closer, but that round went wild as well, and I thought if I kept blasting, I might hit Moseley.

Moseley lurched out into the hollow after Wolf Prince.

All this time, that demonic light was passing us with a tremendous whoosh of wind. Wolf Prince's silhouette stood in contrast to the flickering as if he was caught in the glare of lightning. He trudged forward with a sack of silver in each hand, the sixty-some-odd pounds slowing him down as he staggered along the light's edge, close enough for the wind to knock the feathered hat from his head.

With less fear than sense now, Moseley barreled after him, catching up as they entered the light as it thrummed by. He hadn't stopped to retrieve his revolver from where it lay in the dirt, so there weren't no telling what his plan was.

I pursued, but just before I reached them, the light flickered out, as if whatever demonic creature it was had completed its passage through this curve in the creek. The wind died as well, and for just a moment, I caught red eyes in the distance vanishing around the curve.

Wolf Prince and Moseley were gone.

***

Standing there for a moment, I observed the night. The crickets started up again like an orchestra warming up to a tone before a symphony. The gibbous moon shone whiter now like a bleached bone.

Zavala was still where I had laid him out.

"*Agua, por favor*," he said.

Knowing enough Spanish to comply, I lowered my canteen. "Where'd I get ya?" I asked, placing the canteen to his lips. He was on his belly and propped up on his elbows. His rifle was well out of reach, but I kicked it further away for good measure.

"*Estomago*," he replied before pursing his lips to catch the water.

Gut shot. He'd be here dying for a while. Leaving a

man gut shot was not something I wanted to carry on my conscience, any more than I wanted to give him a coup de grâce. It made my own guts roil.

"What is that?" I nodded out to the hollow.

Zavala struggled to smile. "Wolf Prince says that light is a crack between worlds."

"Between worlds?" I asked. "You mean between this world and *Hell*?"

Wincing, Zavala shook his head. "No different than the *Hell* we're in."

"Then what is it?" I demanded.

Zavala chuckled, gazing at me leering over him in the dark. "See for yourself, *pendajo*."

"But where does it go?" I asked.

"*Nowhere*," Zavala said. "It's here, but not here, *comprende*? At least, that's what Wolf Prince says." He motioned for the canteen again, so I obliged, watching the water running from the blood-caked corners of his mouth.

"How does he know that?" I asked.

"Because," Zavala said when he finished drinking. "That is where Wolf Prince is *from*. He laughed some more, until the pain made him bite down on his amusement.

***

Having half a mind to let Zavala die there, his fate determined by my own cowardice, I left him and faced the dry creek bed alone. Standing vigilant, I wiped the blood off my canteen's mouth and took a swig, cringing at the copper taste. It was only a matter of time before another crackle of light would come through. I just didn't want to get caught off guard.

Turns out it was hours.

Waiting there so long, listening to the crickets sing, I started thinking about Sharpsburg, Maryland on

September 17th, 1862, with the Texas Fifth Infantry. Right there alongside my brother, Mort—that dumb kid, bright-eyed and excited to see some action. Time to live like Davy Crockett and Jim Bowie. Except, they didn't live. I was scared, not enough to be cowardly about it, but Mort was ready to climb a wall of bullets to get to those Yanks. I didn't have much to say about it, except it was duty. Our sacred duty to lay down our lives to die for the rich—like Absalom Moseley—we should have thanked them for the opportunity on our way out of Texas—how rude of us to forget. But we're just rubes and hayseeds—common folk with dirt under our fingernails, doing our duty to go down into the meat grinder so the fat cats could dine on the sausage of our suffering.

If I could change one thing in my life, I'd keep Mort's dumb ass from volunteering. Save Maw the grief and save Paw the ire he had for me for letting Mort get killed. Instead of being hacked to death by the sawbones, he might have lived to settle down and raise a family of his own, and I would have nieces and nephews. They might have been as dumb as him, but at least he'd have lived life. It might not be as pampered and powdered as Moseley's, but even a life of labor is better than no life at all.

That milk was spilt twenty-five years ago. Maw and Paw are dead now. I reckon I ain't too far behind. Sometimes at night you start thinking about your own mortality, whether it's on a cornfield in Maryland or an unnamed creek bed in Texas.

Saving Mort is at the top of the list of things I would have done different with my miserable life. Granted, that list is a mile long, but it's the first thing on it.

The third hour caught me dozing, my head dropping just as the crickets drew to a silence. Opening my eyes, I felt the wind on my face—carrying that metallic stench that smelled like a thunderstorm.

From around the bend, the white light came, crackling and flickering like silent lightning in the distance. Getting to my feet, I held my old Kentucky—loaded now—across my chest and walked to the edge where I had seen Moseley and Wolf Prince vanish. As the luminescence lit the hollow, I could see them running as if not a second had passed since their silhouettes had last flashed across my eyes.

Keeping to the edge, I followed, making sure not to cross the path and end up like Chapman or Briscoe or their horses for that matter. The closer I got, the light flickered less and stayed constant—twin spotlights of blinding demon eyes approached us.

Wolf Prince looked back—knife still in his teeth—ponderous bags of silver hanging from each arm. The immediate monstrosity—a mechanism rather than a beast—the size of two locomotives stacked one atop the other—passed us with a roar. The wind from its wake was like a typhoon, the shockwave turning my body, almost sucking me into its drag. As the thing pulled away into the darkness, red lights on its rear stared back like the demon eyes I had seen decades before.

"Come back here, you!" Moseley cried out. He staggered after Wolf Prince, who clambered across the deadly path.

That's when the Comanche turned, dropped one bag and pulled the knife from his teeth.

"Hold it right there, amigo," I yelled out, drawing a bead on Wolf Prince.

He froze, furrowing his brow as I approached with the rifle. The other bag dropped from his grasp with a jingle. He put the knife away and held up his hands.

Moseley stepped up to him. "That there is my silver. Hand it over."

"That's *not* your silver," Wolf Prince said in perfect English.

"I knew it," I remarked. "He can speak English."

"Goddamn it," Moseley shook his head. "Why'd I have to hire a damned interpreter if you could speak English this whole time?"

Wolf Prince sneered. "We were never going to give you back the silver. Zavala and I were going to split it."

"Once you led us into the trap," I said.

Nodding, Wolf Prince sized me up. "So, you figured it out—the Plum Creek lights. And now, here we are in the middle of them. You assholes ain't in Kansas anymore."

"What in tarnation does that mean?" Moseley asked. "You sure talk funny, even for a Comanche."

Shaking his head, Wolf Prince scoffed. "You fuckers don't know *shit*."

"I know you got my silver, that's good enough for me."

"*That* silver is Mexican, printed in Mexico, stolen from the *Mexica* to fill Spanish coffers. But we are in *Comanche* country now, which means it belongs to *my* people."

"Well," I said, pointing the rifle at him still. "Considering I have the guns, I reckon it belongs to *us*."

Wolf Prince laughed. "You might take the silver, true. But one thing is for sure, you'll never get back home without *my* help."

"Why's that?" Moseley asked.

Smiling, Wolf Prince explained with a raised eyebrow, "Because you might only be ten miles from town, but you are hundreds of years away."

Those words tumbled in my mind for seconds and I could see the clockwork behind Moseley's eyes ticking along. Wolf Prince stared, his eyes expressionless and bouncing back and forth between us as we digested what he just said.

"Did you say '*hundreds of years*'?" Moseley asked.

Wolf Prince's teeth gleamed in the gloom like a Cheshire cat grinning in the darkness. "Look around and what do you see?"

I hadn't noticed it before, but the landscape around us had changed—the native vegetation stripped away so not even the rotting remnants remained. Tufts of weeds sprouted in the dusty rocks and gyrated in the soft breeze. The path where we stood was like a black ribbon that laced through the topography. It was wide enough for four train tracks side by side like a rail yard. Clouds crowded the sky above, lit like dawn on a rainy day and pressing a steamy humidity onto our skin.

"Zavala said you were *from* here," I held the rifle on him still.

Wolf Prince stepped aside and reclaimed the stovepipe hat he had lost in the brief pursuit. "He's only half-right," he said. "I come *through* here from somewhere else." He cocked his chin at the path before us. "This is the central path."

"But why?" Moseley asked.

I was still trying to understand what Wolf Prince was talking about, but Moseley was a man of letters and money, so I assumed he understood something I didn't.

"For that." Wolf Prince kicked one of the silver bags. The bag jingled as it toppled over. "That's worth a lot more to me than you. There's a lot of good it can do instead of sitting in some rich man's safe."

Moseley said, "That's mine and I bought that from a Mexican antique dealer in Piedras Negras. Gave him a damned good price on it, too. More than he deserved."

Wolf Prince replied, "At least I can feed some hungry mouths with this."

While they were arguing about the silver, the gears in my head were catching up. "Wait a minute, if you're not from here, then where are we?"

Shrugging, Wolf Prince turned back to me, focusing on my rifle barrel and lifting an eyebrow.

I noticed that look and lowered the rifle to the ground. I didn't blame him. I didn't take kindly to guns pointed at me either.

"Thank you," Wolf Prince said. He nodded south from where we stood. "Those things must be freighters running down to Mexico. They come back up north also, but I don't know where they go. I've been up and down this road and even out as far as fifty miles, but there ain't no towns or signs of life, except these damn weeds. I don't know what happened here. But I figure whatever those things are, whatever propels them—whether it's magnetic or nuclear—they're wearing ruts in space and time—"

"Excuse me, what—" Moseley interrupted, but Wolf Prince ignored him.

"—like wagon wheels cutting tracks in time instead of rock. Like Roman chariots, English carts, wagon trains, or whatever this is," he continued. "This road cuts through time. I followed the Plum Creek lights here and found your era. And others. I've been up and down it and cross over when the freighters run through."

"But where are you from?" I asked.

"Now why would I tell you that?" he grinned. "I don't want you following me."

An idea came to my head, half-formed, but taking shape as he spoke. "You reckon I could get to 1862 by following this road?"

Moseley scoffed. "Now, why on earth would you want to go back to 1862, even if it was possible?"

"I got my reasons." I squinted.

"Eighteen-sixty-two was horrible." Moseley shook his head, paying no mind to anything but his own opinion. "The damned War Between the States, constant Indian raids—"

"Moseley, you couldn't have been nothing but a toddler back then with a powdered bottom and sucking on your mother's teat," I stated. "Some of us bled and died in those days." All I could think about was that damned fool Mort. Nineteen years old and full of piss and vinegar, signing up at the first chance, and my daddy insisting I go with him to keep him out of trouble.

"Well," Wolf Prince said. "In general, if you go south, you go back. If you go north, then you go forward." He pointed to the north bend. "I'm headed north with your permission, in possession of these two sacks."

I slung the rifle onto my shoulder and looked south. "How far do you reckon *I* should go?"

"Hold on just a minute," Moseley demanded. "You can't just let him make off with that silver."

I nodded. "Well, since I have the only guns here, I reckon *I* make the rules." I put my hand on the Colt .45 in my holster.

Moseley's eyes doubled in size and his mouth gaped. "Strother, I pay you an hourly wage!"

"You got two sacks back there off the trail, which is plenty enough for a miser's hoard," I said, eyeing him up. "You let this man proceed and be on his way."

Moseley's mouth worked up and down, as if he was trying to find words, but couldn't quite put them together.

Wolf Prince pointed. "Just stay a little off the path and you will be safe. You'll have to go about ten miles to get where you want. You might have to confirm where you land a couple of times, but just follow the lights like you did to get here and you'll be fine. Just don't go too far."

"Why's that?" I asked.

"Then you'll *really* be in Comanche country and you'll have some explaining to do," he laughed. He hoisted the bags by their necks and turned north.

"Wait a cotton-pickin' minute, gentlemen," Moseley

said. "I object to this whole-heartedly!"

"You best be ready for the next round of lights, Moseley," I replied. "There are two sacks of your silver out there waiting for you. Zavala ain't dead yet and he might haul them off along with the horses."

"You didn't tell me that." Moseley twisted where he stood, not knowing which way to go.

"Don't move too far up or down the path," Wolf Prince called out, stopping to set the bags down. "You might end up in next month or next year. If they think you're dead back in town, where would your riches be then? You might lose *everything*."

Moseley's eyes bugged out of his skull in frustration and all he could say was "Goddamnit!"

"Good luck," I called out to the Comanche as we parted ways.

"And to you," he replied. "My journey is farther, and my load is heavier and I'll need all the luck I can get."

Nodding, I turned, wondering if his burden was indeed heavier. I just had one person to save, but by the sound of it, he had many. I wished him well as I traveled south to prevent that fateful day in that cursed Maryland cornfield in 1862.

The Banished Road
by
Ricardo D. Rebelo

"We are going to die out here," Celia muttered, fanning her shirt. The sun pressed against the Prius, baking on the road. The phone dock sagged, warping like taffy in the heat. She reminded Tom to re-charge the air conditioner coolant before the trip, but Tom was busy playing videogames and forgot.

"We're not going to die," Tom said, sounding hopeful.

Celia's anger was escalating, and she wondered if Tom could sense it.

It was supposed to be a relaxing day. A two-hour drive west to Brimfield, Massachusetts. Three times a year, they headed up from Fall River to go to the antique Flea Market. Old Yankee folklore bonded Tom and Celia. They had originally met on a Facebook group called Yankee Village.

The air stank of burnt rubber. The road shimmered in the heat, rippling like water. It made everything seem unnatural. Celia could not see it, but sensed that there had been one hell of a car accident up ahead. Black plumes of toxic smoke filled the air in a foreboding way.

Celia and Tom squirmed in their seats, tense and itching to escape. Celia drummed her fingers on the steering wheel. They rolled up the windows to stave off asphyxiation from the unnatural ebony smoke. This made the already hot car insufferable. They were both sweating and twitching, and Celia felt consumed by anxiety and discomfort.

They'd taken the Providence route to avoid an accident on Route 24, skipping their usual path through 495 and the Mass Pike. But instead of clear roads, they hit a jam on Route 146—a narrow, two-lane stretch that felt like the Puritan father, Roger Williams himself, had paved it.

Once a major thoroughfare before the post-WWII highway boom, 146 now looked forgotten. Abandoned buildings lined the road like sun-bleached fossils, overgrown with vines and slowly under nature's reclamation. "What the fuck are we going to do now?"

"I don't know," Tom replied. "Try the Waze GPS app," he added, trying to be helpful.

"It's going to take us through a bunch of fucked-up back roads."

"Yeah, but we will be moving and not breathing burned tire smoke. Besides, it's nice out here. We might see some cool old farms."

Celia was wiping sweat from her head and armpits with a left-over McDonald's napkin and shaking her head.

"Fine. . . shit," she said, and grabbed her phone from the dock.

"Fuck," she snapped, and dropped her phone. Tom took a handkerchief he was using to wipe his own brow and picked it up.

"Hot Potato," he said. Celia shook her head, and Tom went to work to find an alternate route. A few phone taps later, he exclaimed, "I got something."

The driving app showed an alternative route that began with getting off on Elmwood Street and then getting on to Route Twenty.

"Turn left up here," Tom said.

Celia made the turn, "Here comes the back-road bull-shit," she said.

The road narrowed, dipping into a hollow shaded by old oaks. The light seemed to shift—less golden sun; more like a pale, overcast blanket.

Tom leaned forward, squinting. A slab of slate jutted from the roadside, half-swallowed by weeds. "Someone has spray-painted a word across that sign in faded red," he said. "Did you see it?"

"See what?"

Tom hesitated. "It read 'Banished.' And I think it had a pentagram under it. But it's probably nothing," he said. "Just. . . keep going."

The road narrowed until the rough sides rubbed against the tire walls. The dense canopy of trees made the world seem darker. The couple sat in silence, watching the evolution of the road. They had rolled the windows back down and taken deep breaths. The air here was different. It filled their lungs with a cleansing pleasantness, but it also seemed to have an odd quality that clouded their minds.

A wave of frosty air hit, suddenly and sharply. Celia shivered, goosebumps racing up her arms. Then she felt her skin tightening, damp sweat on her chest, freezing into ice. She gasped, pressing her palm against the fabric of her shirt, feeling the ice. Thin, but real. "What's Waze saying?" she asked.

Tom seemed lost in a daydream, but peeked out of it to look at her phone.

"What the fuck?" he said in a crude but gentle tone.

"What," Celia asked.

"The phone died."

"What do you mean, the phone died? It was on the charger the whole time!"

Tom held down the power button and waited for the cell provider's jingle to start and tell him it was starting back up. But it never came.

"What?"

"It's not starting. I don't know what to tell you."

"Try your phone."

Tom reached into the door pocket.

Nothing.

He looked at Celia. The gorge seemingly grew in his throat, his eyes were contracted to pinpoints. Celia felt her heart drop into her stomach and knew without words what the answer was. Instinctively, she turned back to the steering and threw the car in reverse.

A brutal jolt hit as the brake threw them forward, Celia's chest slamming against the wheel as the car screeched to a dead stop. Tom's seatbelt yanked tight, nearly choking him. For a second, neither of them moved.

Then Celia sucked in a breath, pain shooting through her ribs. "What the—what the fuck was that?" Tom's breath hitched. His hands fumbled at the seatbelt, then froze. Slowly, he turned—seemingly not wanting to look, but unable to stop himself. He blinked once. Twice.

The road was gone.

A white pine stood where asphalt had been, thick as a building, its bark smooth and unblemished. No wreckage. No broken branches. Just the silent, impossible truth of it. "Are you OK?" Tom asked.

"This can't be real," said Celia. But there was no crash, no damage—just the sudden, impossible reality of it.

Celia sat staring out the windshield, incredulous. The road or path still lay in front of them. It went on for as long as the eye could see.

"Only one way to go," Tom added.

Celia turned back and slapped the steering wheel in frustration. "Fucking Waze! Fucking back-road bullshit!"

Behind them, something rustled in the branches of the white pine. Tom's head snapped toward the sound. "There seems to be something hulking in the mist," said Tom. "Shadow of a man. Giant and hunched, lumbering back into the gray. C'mon," he added.

Celia took a deep breath; when she exhaled, a plume of vapor came out of her mouth and fogged the windshield. She rubbed a clear patch on it and drove the car forward.

The mist returned to clouding the windshield and this time, when Celia moved to clear it, she realized the moisture was on the outside of the car and not the inside.

A fog had rolled in around them. Gray and indifferent to their plight. Swallowing them in its gullet. Celia drove the Prius so slowly that the gas engine never kicked in and it was running solely on the battery. It felt like they were floating in storm clouds. Occasionally, a tree branch or bush would scrape against the side of the car with a sickening screech. It was unnerving, but there was no other path but forward.

Out of the mist, a figure formed in front of their car like a phantom.

Celia yelled and slammed on the brakes. Both stared out the windshield at the figure. It was an old man. Withered and wizened, he looked like a skeleton covered in Saran Wrap, his yellow teeth the color of dried corn. His hair was a bright, white Brillo pad sticking to the top of his gray pate. The white contrasted with the entire world now surrounding them.

Celia gripped the wheel so hard her knuckles ached. In the hollow pits of the man's skull, two pale blue eyes scanned her.

Everything had gone quiet. Celia could hear the couple's fast and arrhythmic heart beats pounding out a tattoo of terror, as if anticipating something horrible.

The gaunt man walked around the car to the driver's side window. With a knurled switch he tapped the glass. Celia jumped in her seat and kept looking forward in hope that the man would disappear.

"Are you lost?" the man said. His voice came from a place deep inside his chest. A place that sounded like it was covered in moss and decay.

Celia turned her head slowly, by instinct and not will, and looked at the cadaverous man and nodded in affirmation.

"Farm up ahead, they might help you get back on the main road–or get you situated," the phantom corpse continued.

Celia and Tom both nodded in affirmation this time. Everything had become so surreal. *Whatever ride they were on, it wasn't theirs anymore*, thought Celia. And she was sure they both wanted to get off.

Celia lifted her foot off the brake and depressed the gas pedal so slightly that the car floated forward, rather than being propelled.

The phantom disappeared in the rear-view mirror, consumed by the fog as fast as he had materialized from it. They drove on for only a few minutes, but inside the Prius, the time felt like hours.

The fog then became thinner and dissipated, to reveal a colonial-style farmhouse. The cedar shingles had long since turned from the mellow amber of their youth to the gray and black patina of age and wear. Moss hung from the building as if in despair. The fog rolled back in and surrounded them and the house. A woman stepped out onto the rotted porch. The deck could barely hold her weight, though she was slight of build. She wiped her trembling hands on a threadbare towel, smearing streaks of red across the faded fabric.

Celia's heart stopped, and she did not breathe for a few moments. She turned to Tom, who was as white as a dinner plate. His left eye twitched with anxiety and fear. Celia forced herself to breathe as the world around her darkened at the edges of her vision. She didn't want to pass out now and leave herself to whatever those shaking hands were planning.

The old woman walked off the porch toward the car, much in the same floating way the old man had before her. She continued to wipe her hands clean as she stood across from Celia.

"Pardon my hands girl, I just slaughtered a chicken for supper," the old woman said. She had a Yankee accent, which sounded anachronistic.

"Now don't be frightened, I know you're lost, and this place doesn't seem very hospitable, but I assure you we Swamp Yankees are good people."

"Swamp Yankees?" asked Celia.

"That's just a name for us old folk. C'mon out of there. We have a fire inside," the old woman added.

Celia turned back to looking out of the windshield. Her fingers still gripped the steering wheel. The tops of the knuckles were white as moons.

"What do you want to do?" She asked Tom.

"What choices do we have?"

"We could run."

"Run where? Into the clouds?"

Tom looked out of his car window. Shapes were moving in the gray fog. Shapes that were mostly human. Phantoms, surfing dark tides of mist, waiting to crash on them. The phantoms were asymmetrical. Legs and arms were too long and too short. The house was at least some sort of shelter to whatever was waiting for them out here.

Tom opened his door a crack. To Celia, it felt like a seal had been broken; the outside could now come inside. Tom's entire body seemed to shake with the first breeze that invaded the space. Celia stared at him, transfixed, waiting to see what the repercussions of entering this world would be. Other than a chill breeze, nothing happened.

Tom stepped out of the car and stood looking around, the void of gray engulfing him.

Celia took a deep breath. Her chest was so tense that it felt like she was breathing through a cocktail straw. She closed her eyes and grabbed the door handle. Her hands were shaking so hard that it was hard to keep a grip. She leaned against the door for strength and stability and pushed. With the barrier seemingly broken, she fell out into the chalky abyss. Using the door, Celia pushed herself upright.

"There, that wasn't so hard," the old woman said. "Follow me," the woman added and walked up the old rotten stairs. When she was at the door, the old woman turned back to the couple and cracked a sly smile.

"Come now and stop being silly. You must be weak from hunger. We here know how important it is to…eat."

Celia and Tom shook their heads in unison and crept forward to the stairs. With each step they took up, the aged wood beneath their feet groaned in despair. Though technically Celia and Tom were moving upward, something inside them felt like it was descending.

The old woman had already gone inside, leaving them to complete the short yet endless journey. Once Celia broke the threshold, the scent of mold and mildew hit her. As a little girl, her parents would rent a house on the coast of Little Compton, Rhode Island. The entire back of the house hung over the water of the Atlantic. When the tide was low, it smelled like this place: dank and moldy.

The house's interior was lit only with the soft gray diffused light of the outside and the orange yellow flame of a hearth. The ceilings were marbled with water stains that had dried and moistened over decades. The rest of the interior was sparse. Two wooden chairs book-ended the hearth.

"Sit please," the old woman said. Celia shook and

shrugged like she had been stricken by the old woman's words.

Celia and Tom now moved on subconscious rails. To Celia, they had become spectators to their own lives and somehow their souls had become external to their carmate selves.

"I'll be back with something for you to eat," the old woman said.

They were numb.

It was the only way to remain sane.

Every muscle, nerve and fiber of their being was shaking. They could not stop trembling. This was alien to Celia. She prided herself with being in control, but here she was in a world where she had no agency.

At some point, the old woman returned with a large serving tray that held two bowls. She placed them in the hands of Celia and Tom.

"Now there you go, eat up," she said.

"Who are you? What is this place?" Celia asked.

"Yes, you must be disoriented. I'm Millicent Hayes and I have lived here. . . well. . . for a long time, you could say. What year is it?"

"It's 2025," Tom responded.

Millicent Hayes' eyes opened wide. You could see the red capillaries in the strain and her pupils' contracted pinpoints; she sucked her lower lip into her mouth and bit it. She released the lip with a deep exhale.

"It's 2025, you said, two thousand and twenty-five?"

"Yes, what year did you think it was?" Tom asked.

A smile came over her face like a mask. But the corners of the old woman's lips tightened and trembled. They were restraining something.

"No, that's about right. How are your chicken and dumplings?"

Celia had eaten a small piece of dumpling; it tasted off,

but the warmth of it and the gooey texture of the sauce comforted her. It was old Yankee food prepared in an old Yankee way that was comforting.

"What is this place?" Celia pressed after swallowing her dumpling.

"This place, our farm, this is the banished place."

"Banished? Why call it that? Why banished?" asked Celia.

"That's what they called it when they brought us here. They said we were banished, banished for all eternity."

Tom choked on a piece of chicken bone and coughed. When he recovered, he asked, "Who's *they*?"

"The witches," Millicent said, in a matter-of-fact way.

Celia took a turn choking, but it was from shock and not an errant bone.

"What?"

"You felt it. When you came over the barrier, you transferred into our realm, the realm of the banished. The farm of the ghouls."

"I thought your name was Hayes. Who are the Goulds?"

"No, no child, not Gould—ghouls, this farm, this place is where the ghouls live."

Every drop of blood in Celia's body dropped into her stomach, making her dizzy. Her arms and legs no longer felt connected to her body, as if turned off with a switch.

"Oh, you look pale. I must've startled you," Millicent said. "Let me explain. It was 1690. John Moxley—you saw him earlier—had a brutal winter. Failed crops, a dying family. His wife, Mary, was the first to go. He planned to bury her in the orchard, but desperation warped his thinking. He believed her flesh might nourish next season's soil. An offering."

Tom and Celia sat frozen; her disbelief drowned in the surreal environment.

"John had heard the old Algonquin stories—of the Wendigo. A creature born of starvation. Endless hunger. He didn't become one, but the legend inspired him. So, he butchered Mary in the shed he used for deer. Cooked her with pine needles to mask the taste. The kids never questioned it. They ate. They slept."

Millicent stirred a pot on the fire.

"But something changed. When John woke them, their skin was gray. Eyes sunken. He thought they were dead. He carted them to the cemetery. As he passed the graves, hunger overwhelmed him. He found a fresh one, dug it up like a madman, and took a bite."

She paused, watching their faces.

"The meat was warm, tender. Life came back to him. His skin turned pink. He looked down the hole again. Behind him, his children stirred. Alive. He fed them a strip of flesh, like dogs at a table. When they finished, they were restored too. Youthful. Bright-eyed."

Millicent smiled grimly. "That's when he knew. They weren't dead. They were ghouls."

"Zombies?" Tom asked, struggling to talk.

Millicent bristled. "No. Zombies are dead things that walk. Ghouls are the living who feed on the dead."

Celia dropped her bowl. The ancient clay shattered on the hardwood floor.

"Done with your meal, my dear?" Millicent inquired. The old woman stood up and went into the kitchen.

Celia sat frozen, still looking at the spot where Millicent had told the ghoulish tale.

"We're going to die here," she said to Tom, without turning.

"Yup," was all that Tom could muster.

The old woman returned with a mop and bucket. "I bet you're wondering what happened to that family," she said rhetorically. Millicent first picked up the chunks of pottery and laid them in the bucket and then mopped the floor.

"Well, the family looked normal to everyone else in Salem Village and went about their business, but as days passed, they decayed again, and the only solution was to eat more carrion. Do you know what carrion is, girl?" Millicent stopped mopping and looked directly at Celia.

Celia stared right through the old lady, but responded.

"Necrotic flesh," she said.

"If that means dead flesh, it was necrotic indeed, and the only place to get it was the cemetery. After a while, the townsfolk noticed all the upturned earth on the graves. They assumed it was the witches. The witches knew it was not them and wanted to root out whatever dark magic was consuming the carrion. They knew no good could come of it. So, one night when John and his children slept, the witches formed a circle around their farm. They chanted for hours. They chanted for binding and banishment. That was when the fog rolled in. It consumed the house in a wave and just like that. . . we came here."

"We?" Celia asked.

"Yes, we," Millicent responded.

"Who's we?"

"Well, me. . . my father. . . and my brother."

"You?" asked Tom.

"Yes, who did you think?"

"You're the little girl, John's daughter?"

"Of course. How else would I know about this tale? My father has told it to me on many nights while we waited."

"Waited for what?" Celia asked.

"For you, my dear. . .well. . .people like you. . .fools who come down the banished road."

Celia was triggered by Millicent's words. She stood up and grabbed the old woman around the neck. Millicent let out a yelp of pain and choked as her windpipe shrank in

Celia's hands. Celia throttled the old woman back and forth, hoping to hurry on her strangling, but then something clouded up in her eyes. The blood once again receded from Celia's hands, and she weakened.

The old woman laughed.

Celia collapsed to the floor. Tom stood up and came at Millicent and a step before he reached her, he collapsed too.

***

Millicent laughed harder.

"Well, that took a while longer than expected. I must have made the poison less potent today," she said, to the couple lying on the floor.

The door to the kitchen opened to reveal John and his son, Jeremiah. Jeremiah was very fat for a ghoul.

"What took you so long?" John asked.

"Sorry, Father, but they must have not eaten much of that chicken. All the same," Jeremiah added, grabbing Celia under her arms and lifting her up.

"Of course, you take the light one," John said as he picked up Tom and carried him out the front door.

They dragged the bodies across the front yard to a shed they kept especially for gutting and cleaning.

"I don't understand, Father, why don't we just eat them raw?" Jeremiah said.

"Cause it ain't proper. You gotta let the mortis set in if you want the meat tender. You get more out of them that way too. Never know when the next idiots are going to come down that road."

Celia and Tom acquired a generous amount of mud, as they reached the abattoir. The two men thew them atop a table that had a patina of blood and gore that was formed through decades of slaughter.

***

Celia's eyes opened as the night turned from jet black to gray and the cock crowed. She looked at the ceiling, not knowing where she was.

Tom groaned.

"You alive?" Celia asked in disbelief.

"What a fucked-up dream," Tom said.

Celia sat up on the table. She could see the farmhouse through a crack in the door.

"I don't think it was a dream."

"Ok, a nightmare then?"

"If it was, it's not over."

As she finished her statement, the door of the farmhouse opened. John and Jeremiah came tumbling out.

"Oh shit, they're coming," Celia exclaimed.

"Who's they?"

"John and some fat piece of shit."

"Fuck!"

Celia looked around the room for a weapon. There was a cleaver hung on a rusted nail. She grabbed it. Tom found a broken mop handle. Celia looked at Tom and nodded. Flanking the door they waited to set their own trap.

John had opened it first and stepped inside. Jeremiah's girth kept him in the doorway. Tom was the first to strike. He took the jagged tip of the broken handle and jammed it under John's chin and sank it until it hit the roof of the old man's mouth. Blood flowed out of John's lips and down the shaft of the mop handle, turning the gray staff into a crimson spear.

"Father!" Jeremiah cried out.

Celia pivoted and buried the cleaver into the hulking giant's chest. Jeremiah's scream hit a high note as the pain reached its zenith. He took a step back and Celia pushed him down the rest of the way.

"C'mon," she yelled to Tom over her shoulder. The couple took off down the dusty road without looking back.

***

John grabbed the gore-soaked handle impaled on his face and yanked it out.

"Bastards," he screamed through a mouth full of blood. Jeremiah pulled the cleaver out of his chest.

"They hurt me, Pa," he said. "They're gonna get away."

"No, they ain't," John said.

It took a while for John and Jeremiah to reach Celia and Tom. Miraculously, their wounds healed during the slow slog back to the couple.

"There they are, the dogs," John shouted.

Without another word, Jeremiah picked up Tom and slung him over his shoulder like a sack of potatoes. John was not as strong as his son now, and chose to drag Celia by her feet through the forest.

***

The tree stumps and rocks brought Celia back to consciousness. Her eyes opened to a gray sky that went on for eternity. She could feel that someone was pulling her over the uneven road.

"We should just do them now," Jeremiah said. His voice sounded as if it filtered through seaweed.

"No, there is a process to these things, a ceremony," John replied. Celia could hear the two men.

"Ok, get them in the house, we need to make this quick. I can feel the muscles coming off my bones," John said.

Celia heard the ancient door creaking open and the oaf of a son bursting through it ahead of them. Then she was being dragged up the four steps to the house, her head banging on each, the pain shooting down her body.

"Drop them next to the fire, I'll get Millicent, and we can be done with this," John said. Celia felt Tom's body land in a thud next to her.

Celia lay on the floor, feeling the heat of the fire. It made her mind race. She thought of something she read in the Bible as a little girl.

Thou shalt not suffer a witch to live.

Celia then thought of the horror movies she watched on TV when she was a child, the British ones. The towns-people always shouted. . .

Burn the Witch. . .Burn the Witch.

"I see they still look pretty good," Millicent said. It caused Celia to re-focus. She could see the three: father, son, and daughter, out of the corner of her eye. She dared not turn her head to them.

"Do the prayer like old times," John said.

"If I must, Father," Millicent said.

"You must," John countered.

Millicent reached the top of her dress and withdrew a silver pentacle. She held it above her head in an inverted position.

"Mother Gaia, give us your ears," she began.

Celia reached up to grab a log out of the fire.

"Great mother, take this flesh that we sacrifice to you and with it endow us with the force of life."

Celia now had her hand wrapped tight around the un-burnt end of a log. The heat from the burning part seared her fingers, but Celia knew that she needed the fire.

Millicent lowered the pentagram and reached into a pocket in her dress to reveal a knife. The handle, made of deer antlers, had been carved to represent a serpent, and the blade was as black as obsidian and more like slate, from a time when steel had not existed.

"Now, Mother Gaia, drink the blood deep into your stone and transform the flesh into the soil of forever," Millicent said and then held the blade above the couple.

As she brought the ancient blade down, Celia swung with an energy that came from another body and met the blade. The force of the swing thrust Millicent's hand and the blade backward into her chest.

The entire blade was consumed in the fire. It stuck out of Millicent like the wrath of God. She caught fire like crepe paper and was consumed entirely.

Thou shalt not suffer a witch to live, Celia thought again.

"Heretic!" John yelled. He came after Celia and grabbed her by the throat. This time, John did not have enough strength to throttle her. His powers had waned. Celia, still holding the stump, thrust it into the ancient man's gut. It went through with the ease of a knife cutting summer butter. His innards had dried like leaves in late fall and then he too was consumed.

Jeremiah did not have the courage of his father or sister; he turned and lumbered toward the door.

Celia, now in a fury, thrust the flaming log through the back of the oaf like a rat on a skewer.

He was consumed too.

With the trio dispatched, she looked back at Tom who was now coughing on the floor.

"Wake up," she said. Celia took the log now and placed it at the bottom of the ratty curtains setting them ablaze. She put an arm under Tom's shoulder and lifted him to his feet.

"We gotta get out," she said. Tom now coughed himself fully awake and looked at the blaze surrounding him. He straightened himself to head out the door. Celia kept her arm around him. The couple ran across the living room and stumbled through the exit. Once they were about fifty yards from the old farm, they both collapsed.

They lay on their backs for what seemed like an eternity.

Celia felt something burning through her eye lids. It was not fire though, but something else, something familiar. . . sunlight.

She opened her eyes against the bright light to see the farm ablaze. And behind it in the sky, the sun burnt bright.

What truly took her aback was the smoke. Instead of coming *from* the ancient structure, it was going *into* it. The gray world she had been in was being consumed by the flame.

Telaraña
by
D. Winchester

The desert wind spit grit against Jeff's face as he manned the pump at the Fuel and Fly. Sixty dollars ticked past, but compared to his fear that his engine would sputter into silence somewhere deep in the Mojave, the money was meaningless. Getting stuck wouldn't just be inconvenient. It would be fatal.

Tonight, after they finally exhausted their search for someplace that didn't seem to actually exist, he and his friends would make the long drive back to LA, and he wanted to be ready. He had no intention of stopping again after dark; they'd been staying in sketchy desert motels all weekend, and he had no interest in meeting any more crackheads.

While the gas flowed into the tank, he looked around nervously, but aside from a passing car or the line of graffitied boxcars waiting in vain on the rail spur across the street, he and his friends were alone.

They'd pretty much have to be in a place like this. This place consisted of little more than a pair of gas stations, a couple of drive-through joints, and a few aging trailers.

That's pretty sad, but not as sad as how this little adventure is turning out, Jeff thought. He sighed.

As he watched, Jose came out of the gas station with an armload of soda cans, but he could only see frustration in Jose's expression. Ryan, for his part, seemed to be taking their failure in stride, but then all of this had been his idea.

"Come help me look for a ghost town, guys," he'd told them. "It will make for great content!"

Jeff supposed that would have been true, if the town had actually been out here somewhere, but increasingly, it looked like Telaraña didn't exist. Before all of this, he'd never heard of the place, but the internet buzzed with rumors about it. Over the last few nights, he'd spent hours flipping through websites, looking for clues, because no one agreed on its location.

The internet accounts and pictures were pretty consistent. Consistently unhelpful.

They described it as a community partway between Las Vegas and LA that sprang up around a single gas pump and, later, a hotel or two that had been abandoned for decades. Articles described it as an ancient party town for artists and weirdos before Palm Springs had stolen its thunder but never offered real clues about its actual whereabouts.

He looked at the map Ryan held while sitting in the back seat, which showed all of Southern California. The thing had been well-used, and he'd marked nearly every highway between the Los Angeles Mountains and Death Valley with highlighter. Some, in multiple colors, showed just how much driving they'd done in the last forty-eight hours.

Telaraña's name was Spanish for spiderweb, and it came from its location at the intersection of two important highways; the problem was that no one could agree on which two highways those were. They'd been everywhere, and except for a fifty-mile stretch and one more small loop before they turned around, there didn't seem to be any place left for this hypothetical town to hide from them.

He tried leaning in for a closer look at Ryan's map, but the pump tripped off before he could get too close. As he turned to hang up the nozzle, Jose walked up behind him, looked at the price, and let out a low whistle. "Ouch, eighty-nine dollars. Fucking painful."

"Yeah, well, I think that's the last fill-up for the trip, at least," Jeff said, trying not to sound too negative while Ryan could hear them. He already felt bad about the way the weekend had gone and had no desire to rub the failure in and make the drive home more awkward.

"At least. . .nah," Jose sighed. He opened his mouth again but wisely closed it, rolled his eyes, and got in the front passenger seat without another word.

Even without talking, the atmosphere felt contentious enough. The tension only increased when Jose started asking "How about that one? Could that be it?" as they passed every town. No matter how many times someone had asked those questions on this trip, none of these places had been the elusive Telaraña. Every time they drove by someplace that seemed promising, some detail didn't fit.

Jeff had already decided yesterday that the place didn't exist; it had emerged as a patchwork of stolen stories and towns that had been spliced together, like some boomer Neverland. He'd thought about telling Ryan that, but they were almost done with the search, so he didn't feel the need to rain on his friend's parade. A few more miles would take care of that.

It was the only explanation. There'd been no new pictures since the '80s, but no one could say where the town had gone. Ryan was a good dude, when he wasn't chasing half-baked plans for viral fame, but once he'd latched on to this quest weeks ago, he wouldn't let go.

Eventually, they'd set out, but now that they'd put in an honest effort, he and Jose just wanted it to be over. Still, that wasn't going to happen until they drove down every last road, and it took another hour and one heavy sigh from the backseat before Jeff crossed the place off of his list. "Well, guys, I don't think we're gonna find it," he said, failing to hide his disappointment.

By then, the sun was low, and the most distant part of the road before them had been reduced to a flowing black river by heat shimmer. "Thank Christ," Jose whispered.

Ryan pretended he hadn't heard the comment, but Jeff chimed in to change the subject. "Well, we tried and got to hang out. I guess that's all you can ask for." When no one seemed interested in talking, he turned on the radio and looked for a good place to turn around.

He managed to find a gap in traffic, okay, and a wide enough space to flip a U-turn, but once he started heading back toward the 99 that would take them most of the way back to the city, the radio started to cut in and out, replacing the song they wanted with oldies and a Spanish evangelical station at random intervals.

Jeff was less concerned about that, though, than about the way his GPS started bouncing around. He didn't really need it. He knew the way back blindfolded, but as the horizon reddened, he couldn't deny that something felt off.

Then Ryan started complaining about how his signal had died as they entered the next valley. That got Jeff's attention, but not as much as the junkyard they were heading toward. They'd come down this road less than twenty minutes ago, but no matter how many strange places they'd seen on this trip, he would have remembered it if they'd driven through a junkyard.

"Hey guys, what the hell is that place?" he asked. "You remember a junkyard?" Neither of his friends paid attention at first. Jose just leaned back in his seat and stared at the ceiling while Ryan tried to make his phone work. Neither of them looked up until he added, "Wait, it's not a junkyard. It's just a town with a shitload of parked cars."

That got their attention. Suddenly, everyone looked at the postage stamp of a town as he approached. It had maybe two dozen buildings, crowded around a single point where two roads intersected, but there had to be a hundred cars.

Jeff *expected* that nowhere towns would be clogged with junkers. Given the heat, he didn't even find the lack of people strange. The weird part was how nice many of the cars were. Between the baking sun and the scouring windblown sand, the desert ate paint, but somehow, here, that didn't seem to be a problem. Pristine Ford Galaxies sat next to vintage Mustangs and eighties Jags. While not every car was a treasure, there were enough to get his attention.

In fact, he was so focused on the vehicles that he barely noticed Ryan listing off all the relevant landmarks. It wasn't until Ryan pointed out the ruins of a burned-down building with a bizarre sign and said, "Right there. That's The Widow. That bar is half the reason people came here in the '70s, before it burned down."

"Holy fucking shit," Jose shouted. "You actually found it!"

The light was fading fast, making it harder to take in many of the details of the town. At least one of the buildings was occupied; the Hotel Perdido's lights glowed brightly enough to stand out against the gathering gloom.

The three of them paused at the traffic light at the center of town, debating what to do next. Ryan and Jose were divided. "I'm not staying in some freak show overnight, man," Jose warned. "That's just asking for it, *comprende*?"

"But it's too dark to get the footage I need," Ryan insisted. "If we just drive through, then we wasted the whole weekend for nothing."

Jeff could see that Jose was about to agree with that

statement in the rudest way he could think of, so instead, he said, "How about we drive around with our high beams on and see what we see? Then we can decide."

Everyone agreed to that much, but his high beams failed to illuminate enough of the scene for Ryan's camera to capture this place's haunting emptiness. By the time they'd circled around the town, Jeff's idea had obviously been a bust.

At first, he'd been on Ryan's side. He didn't see this place being any crazier than the last hotel they'd stayed at, in Mojave. That place was practically a crack den. This time, the town seemed strange, but the hotel looked half-way decent.

It was the lack of people that bothered him. They should have seen someone by now. Even a single soul would have put his mind at ease.

As if on cue, the motel clerk popped out the front door for a cigarette break. She was a busty brunette with huge movie-star-style sunglasses. Just Jose's type. Jeff could almost see the switch in Jose's head flip from *go* to *stay*.

Jeff wasn't so sure. Not only did her timing seem uncanny, but the shadows of her limbs on the building behind her looked wrong, somehow. Logically, he knew that her shadows skittered because of the dying neon sign on the front of the building, but something about the image creeped him out. He looked uneasily at Jose.

"What?" Jose protested. "A woman like that has to be lonely out here. Maybe she needs someone to help her stay warm on these cold desert nights." Jeff didn't even try to argue. He just looked for a parking place. The three of them grabbed their bags and went inside.

Once there, though, Jeff had a hard time suppressing his laughter. Jose had spent the last minute talking about how hot the receptionist was. Unfortunately, the harsh lights of reception revealed a terrible truth.

She looked ancient. She had to be near sixty, but a lifetime in the desert sun made her look even older than that. Her skin was the consistency of old leather. She'd probably been a beauty once, based on how she dressed and carried herself. Still, it was clear to him that even her industrial-strength bra was decades outdated.

Even more hilariously, she actually flirted with Jose as the three of them signed the old-fashioned guest register. There wasn't a computer in sight. Ryan tried to ask her questions about the town, but other than confirming that they really were in Telaraña, she just kept smiling at Jose, sunglasses still obscuring her eyes. She leaned on the counter. Her cleavage looked like the Grand Canyon. "If you want a private tour, big boy, you just let me know."

Somehow, the three of them kept a straight face until they were outside and around the corner. Then Jeff and Ryan busted up. "Yeah, yeah," Jose sighed, "laugh it up."

"What's the matter?" Ryan asked. "I thought you were going to hit that shit like it was going out of style."

"Man. . ." Jose rubbed his head. "Did you see them titties? They were way past their expiration date. There's not enough Cuervo in the world to drink her pretty."

At least Ryan was happy. "After we get some real footage of this place tomorrow and post it online, all of us are going to be internet legends," he crowed.

"Just as long as it doesn't take too long," Jose smiled darkly. "Don't leave me alone with granny. She might get some ideas."

They laughed again and went to their rooms, which were as comfortable as they were dated. The air conditioner ran all the way to ice-cold if Jeff wanted it, and if it hadn't been for the lack of Wi-Fi and cell service, it would have been the nicest place he'd stayed in for a while.

That night, he dreamt of driving aimlessly and being pursued by a predator he couldn't see. In the morning, though, his only problem was the light of sunrise streaming in to wake him through the thin, patterned curtains.

Jeff got up immediately and got dressed. "The sooner we get that footage, the sooner we can get out of here," he told himself.

He knocked on Ryan's door. After half a minute, he knocked again. He had just enough time to worry that something had happened to his friend when Ryan finally opened the door and rubbed sleep out of his eyes.

"Man, it's early," Ryan complained.

"The early bird gets the footage," Jeff responded. "Now, let's get moving. I got shit to do tonight, and it doesn't involve being here."

Ryan nodded and then closed the door to get dressed. Jeff paced back and forth in the parking lot, puzzling over the strangest feeling that he was forgetting something. It wasn't until the two of them were walking toward his car that it clicked. "Oh shit, we forgot about Jose!"

He turned, but before he could walk back to room 14, he heard something that chilled his blood. "Who?" Ryan asked.

"Jose, you know, our friend?" Jeff asked as he stopped in his tracks. When he didn't see a look of recognition on Ryan's face, he said, "Jose, who gave you a hard time about this trip? Jose, who you almost killed yesterday when he wouldn't shut up?"

"Are you feeling okay?" Ryan asked him, in a concerned tone that made Jeff absolutely certain that his friend was fucking with him now.

"Jose, the guy who wanted to bang the receptionist before he figured out she was old enough to be his grandmother!" Jeff blurted out, shocked he didn't get a reaction. "We all laughed about it on the way to our rooms. . ."

After that, there was nothing left to do but pound on the door of Jose's room, but no matter how long he knocked, their friend didn't come out. Ryan seemed genuinely worried for his sanity.

"Come on," Jeff said, starting to doubt himself. "We're going to get to the bottom of this."

They checked his car first, but Jeff couldn't find any concrete evidence that Jose had ever been in the vehicle. His bag wasn't in the trunk, and his drink was missing from the passenger side.

Next, they went to the reception desk, where the woman they found looked completely different from the one they'd seen last night. It took him several seconds to realize it was the same receptionist.

*Wait, wasn't she. . .*Jeff wondered at how much younger she looked before refocusing on his friend.

"Uhm, do you know if our friend maybe changed rooms last night?" Jeff asked. "He's not in room 14."

"Friend? I don't recall a third guest. Can you describe him?" the receptionist asked.

"He's about this tall, and. . ." Jeff answered, but as he opened his mouth, he could feel the details slipping away. He tried again, but with no more luck than he'd had the first time, so he looked to Ryan, who only shook his head.

He could no longer remember what Jose had looked like, but that didn't change his certainty that the man had existed. "I'm telling you, there was someone else in the car with us," he stated, ignoring the strange looks he was getting from both Ryan and the receptionist.

"I don't think I even *know* a Jose," Ryan said, with a shake of his head.

"Okay, if we've been doing this trip all alone, just the two of us, then why do I remember you being in the back seat half the time?" Jeff countered. "Why wouldn't the two of us just ride together upfront."

"I. . .That's a good question," Ryan agreed, looking less sure for the first time since the start of this conversation.

Finally, feeling less crazy, he turned back to study the woman. Yesterday, he remembered thinking that she looked like a sunbaked grandmother. Somehow, her spider web of wrinkles vanished. She'd gone from her sixties to her thirties overnight.

Jeff's mind would have been screaming "vampire" if she hadn't been sitting by a window in the sun. *What in the hell is going on?* He was tempted to ask her about that, but knew he'd sound crazy, so he focused again on Jose.

"Are you sure you haven't seen anyone?" he asked. "Anyone at all?"

"See for yourself, hon," she said, turning the guest book around so he could read it. "You and your friend here are the last people to show up here in years. It's just you, me, and the tumbleweeds." Jeff studied the book, noticing that the last signatures above his were dated from 2021, and there was no evidence that any lines had been erased.

"Weird," Jeff said, shaking his head as he returned her book. He and Ryan left her, and swept the run-down motel a second time before getting in Jeff's car. He checked the gas gauge as they drove through the town again. Half a tank. Plenty to make it back to Mojave or Four Corners.

"Jose!" he yelled, at random intersections, "Where you at, man, why are you playing games?" Ryan just stared at him from the passenger seat.

All they found were tumbleweeds, wrecks, and ruins. "Maybe we should call the cops," Ryan said finally. "This seems like their deal, not ours."

Jeff fought back the urge to scream and instead asked, "With what fucking signal?" in a strained voice.

Ryan didn't answer. He just pointed at where the road out of town climbed the hill and went toward the highway, just outside the ugly valley they were in.

Jeff sighed, then. "Ryan, respectfully, we just spent all

weekend trying to find this place. I don't believe in magic or aliens, but I feel like if we leave, even to get help, we might never find our way back."

"I get that," his friend agreed, "and I'm not saying we should abandon this Jose guy, whoever he is. I'm just saying that we'd get a better signal up there."

Jeff had a hard time arguing with that, and he made a left turn and headed back out of town. But the hill remained out of reach; as they drove toward it, it seemed further and further away.

For the first twenty minutes, Jeff silently questioned his own sanity. Finally, though, Ryan said what they were both thinking. The hill wasn't getting any closer.

"Was this bullshit in any of the stories you read about this place?" Jeff asked, increasingly tempted to cut across the open desert and stop taking no for an answer. If his car had four-wheel drive, he would have. Ryan shook his head, *no*.

When their endless ribbon of asphalt reached a dirt road, he took that, trying to cut across to one of the other paved roads a few miles away. It was a dusty, bumpy ride, and did them no good at all.

"What is going on?" Jeff demanded, banging on his steering wheel. "I see the hill. *You* see the hill. It's right there. Right fucking there!"

Ryan didn't answer, but the mere fact that his friend was seeing the same crazy shit that he was made Jeff feel better. Not much, though. They'd been driving for over half an hour, but they'd grown no closer to what should have been five minutes away.

Jeff settled his hands grimly on the steering wheel and floored it whenever the road allowed. Ryan rolled down his window. Every so often, he picked up a piece of trash from the car and dropped it outside. He looked over at Jeff. "Leaving a trail where we've been."

"Well, whatever's happening, it's obviously related to how hard it was to get here in the first place," Jeff said. His gas gauge was getting low.

"Is that why there's no one else here, but all those cars?" Ryan asked. "Maybe the only way to escape is to leave your car behind and walk."

"That's a thought," Jeff agreed, shocked that he was considering any of this. "But that doesn't explain the woman, and we can't leave without Jose."

"I'm going to be real, man," Ryan sighed. "I can see how there might be gaps in my memory, but I still don't remember this guy. Neither do you, really."

"Well, if he were here and couldn't remember anyone named Ryan, I'd still be saying the same thing," Jeff shot back, and kept driving.

The car sputtered, then stalled. Jeff looked at the gas gauge. E. "Shit!" Jeff yelled, and slammed his hands on the steering wheel. "Now what?" "We walk," Ryan said. "We'll never get a better chance," he insisted. "We're almost there!"

"What are you *talking* about?" Jeff exploded. "We've barely moved at all. It's as far away as it's always been!"

"If we walk, we can make it!" Ryan urged. "Fuck the roads. We just go straight and—"

"If we start hiking out from here in this heat, we're dead." Jeff countered. "Going back to town for water is dangerous for reasons too insane to contemplate, but less dangerous than that. I say we go back, stay clear of that woman, look for Jose one more time, and then leave at sunset."

"What if she does something to us?" Ryan asked.

"Whatever she does won't be as bad as dying of heat stroke," Jeff said wearily.

"Fine," Ryan answered, "but I'm only going back to get footage and some water. If we don't find this Jose by nightfall, I'm walking out of here with or without you."

Jeff didn't argue with that. Together, they started back toward Telaraña.

They'd been driving for two hours. Telaraña should have been eight hours away on foot. They didn't even have a chance to finish their conversation about how strange it was that there seemed to be only one person left in town before they reached the outskirts. The woman at the motel.

"I'm telling you, she's not what she seems," Jeff insisted. "Last night, she was way older than she looked this morning."

"I'm not worried about her age, man," Ryan said, "I wonder more why she's the only one left in town." *Why should he see what I see?* Jeff reflected. He believes *I'm* the crazy one, not her.

As they walked through town, they paused several times so that Ryan could take some video and Jeff could try to find water. He *really* didn't want to go back to the motel.

But they had to. Even though they'd only been walking for an hour, it was under the desert sun at over a hundred degrees. They took the long way around the motel so the proprietor wouldn't see them from the lobby, and headed for the pool in the rear. Jeff took his phone and wallet out of his pockets, then kicked off his shoes and jumped in, allowing a blissful chill to wash over him. Even after it faded, he allowed himself to float weightless for a few seconds, wondering if he'd gone straight out of his mind.

We drove for almost two hours and burned half a tank of gas, but we walked back in half an hour. Make it make sense!

He couldn't, though. Time and space couldn't fold like a map, or could it? It was an aberration that made the empty town that much scarier. Where had all the people gone? Maybe Ryan was right...why *was* there just one old woman left? What was her deal?

Jeff surfaced, expecting to find Ryan in the pool. Instead, Ryan was talking to *her*. The woman from the motel. He wanted to scream, to warn Ryan away. Cramping, his gut told him in no uncertain terms, that whatever Ryan was talking to, it wasn't just some aging beauty or the last resident of a forgotten town.

Cooled by the water, he could almost see a terrible darkness around her. He tried to call out to Ryan, but the same terror that made him so sure of her wrongness paralyzed him, and no sound escaped his throat. *What the fuck is he thinking?!* Jeff's mind screamed helplessly.

He kept expecting to see the woman start to devour his friend, or drag him back into the motel and do something terrible to him. Instead, she turned and left. Ryan finally noticed him and walked back over to the pool.

Seeing his stricken expression, Ryan said, "Calm down, man. She just asked why we were back so soon. So, I told her about our car trouble, and she went off to get some towels, and—"

"Car troubles?" Jeff exploded as his pent-up terror was unleashed. "Did you tell her about the twilight zone bullshit that made the roads last forever?"

"Look, I know, man, chill. Chill!" Ryan sighed. "What do you want me to say? I got it on video. As soon as we figure out how to get out of here, the whole world will see what we saw, but right now, if she's really involved, you don't want to let on that we know, do you? We just act normal, get the towels, get what we need, and we're gone at sunset. Don't freak out."

Jeff saw his friend's point, but no matter how much Jeff tried to explain his fear, Ryan seemed unperturbed. Jeff stood in the shallow end and Ryan sat on the edge with his legs in the water.

There she was, walking toward them with a stack of

towels in her arms. "All right, here you are, boys," she said, so normally that Jeff wanted to believe he was going crazy.

But he wasn't. Something was terribly wrong. As Ryan hopped up and moved toward her, Jeff tried to grab for him. And missed.

He scrambled up the pool steps to try to stop Ryan, but he was too slow. One second, his friend was taking the white towels from the woman with a thank you and a smile, and the next second, he simply wasn't.

She grabbed Ryan's hand, and he just turned to dust. From ten feet away, Jeff saw his friend's musculature deflate, and his shirt grow frayed and worn, as it aged years in milliseconds.

As he watched, she grew younger and younger as his friend evaporated.

By the time she'd finished, his friend had blown away as dust on the wind. Worse even than watching his friend's disappearance, Jeff found he could no longer remember his name. It was as if she'd reached into his head and made his friend disappear there too.

Jeff stood rooted in place. Something was wrong with the space around him. Something titanic had just missed him. Something was wrong with time. He'd gotten out of the pool seconds before, but his clothing had completely dried.

He stopped moving toward her and looked around for a weapon. Any weapon. "What did you do with. . .with. . ." Jeff demanded, struggling to remember the name of the man he saw disappear. He felt certain he'd known it only a second before.

"Ryan?" she asked with a smile, ignoring the pipe he'd just picked up.t. "Was that his name? I find it so hard to remember once they. . .leave here. I wish it could have lasted longer, but all good things come to an end. . ."

"Liar!" Jeff shouted, backpedaling and taking a half-hearted swing as she approached him. "You killed him!" He knew he should aim for her face. He knew the woman before him wasn't human. Still, even if she was a monster, some part of him rebelled at hitting her. It wasn't until he reached the edge of the fenced-in pool area that he took another swing at her.

This time, he aimed for her skull, but she grabbed the pipe almost casually, and laughed. "I like it rough, but maybe not that rough."

As she spoke, the pipe corroded at her touch, rusting away until it was no more substantial than the nameless man he'd just watched her murder. Jeff dropped his weapon before that terrible corrosion could reach him, and when the thing turned to dust before it hit the ground, he knew he'd made the right decision.

"What *are* you?" he asked.

"Me?" she smiled. "Well, I do love talking about myself, but I'd much rather talk about you, Jeff. You might be my last meal for a long time, and I want to enjoy you…"

His only hope was to distract her enough to make a break for it, so he tried again. "If you won't tell me what you are, will you at least tell me what this place is?"

"Telaraña? It's not just *a* web. It's *my* web," she laughed, spreading her arms widely, as much to point to the world around them as to show off her cleavage, which seemed to be more ample than ever. "Just look around. It's my web, and all roads lead to its center."

Jeff looked around. He'd already looked at this cursed valley for this entire day, but somehow, he hadn't noticed until she pointed it out. It really did look like a web. Highways radiated in all directions, with smaller connecting roads.

It doesn't make sense, he told himself. *A place like this should be easy to find. All roads lead here. . .*

It was a mystery, just like what had happened to the

drivers of all these other cars or the idea that he'd come here with anyone else. "But if this really is a spider web the spider at the center would have to be—"

"Unknowable? Unfathomable?" she purred, taking a step forward with each word. "Well, let me be the first to admit it. I have. . .Substantial appetites."

"Huge. The spider would need to be *huge*," he said. "And it would have to devour hundreds of people."

"Thousands, actually," she said huskily. "As to the size of this hypothetical predator, well, it's just like the web. It's all a matter of perception."

Wasn't she smaller a moment ago? Jeff wondered, trying to understand how that could be possible. But she couldn't have been. Not when he had to look up, craning his neck painfully, to look her in the eyes.

She had a vast and terrible beauty. He looked past her shoulder, and for a second, all he could see was a ten-story black widow. The woman he was talking to wasn't even a woman. She was the merest tip of its giant pedipalp.

He tried to dismiss the vision. *It's just one more false memory,* he told himself, *like the idea that I came here with anyone else.*

He'd been looking for Telaraña alone, for days, and it had obviously gotten to him. All those words came from the rational part of his mind, and they barely brushed his consciousness, given how loudly the rest of his mind was screaming. Pure terror gripped him, freezing him in place.

"It—it's just too hot," he said, staggering back, trying to unsee the clouds that eclipsed the sun as the thing's body towered over him. *Those are telephone poles, telephone poles!* His mind shouted desperately. *Not legs. Not legs.* That became harder after he blinked, and they were in a new position. She was a woman again. Fiercely attractive.

"Well, I like to think so," the woman smiled, preening before him, stroking her own body. "Ryan certainly thought so. . ."

"Ryan?" Jeff said, struggling to remember. Who was Ryan? He stepped back, away from her, coming up against the chain link fence at the edge of the property, "I. . . I don't know who that is, but I'm not interested in whatever this is."

"No? Pity," she pretended to pout, pinning him there with her giant, dark sunglasses. "I suppose we'll do this the hard way, then."

Jeff tried to bring his hands up in a warding-off gesture, but he couldn't. The fence gripped his arm, refusing to let go, as he pulled against it. He tried to break free of that grasp, but he was stuck fast, as if the fence was made of some flexible and powerful adhesive.

"If you don't want to devour me, I think it's well past time I devour you," she said, pushing his arms back against the fence and binding him tighter. She smiled, her mouth beginning to unfold in ways that no human mouth should. As she spoke, she reached up and finally pulled down her sunglasses.

Eight shining black eyes met his. They dispelled whatever illusion he clung to that there was a woman before him. As the illusion that hid her true form fell away, it took the rest of Jeff's sanity.

He struggled against the steel web while the giant ebony spider towered over him. The enormous red hourglass on her massive abdomen filled his vision in those last moments. Her hourglass had only been partially filled, but as her fangs lashed out and filled him with a poison that burned more than the desert sun, he saw the terrible symbol fill up a little more, a little more time for *her*, before the whole world faded to black.

The Last Migration
by
Ann O'Mara Heyward

*W*e made it again, Kate thought, looking out the car window at the land rolling by. Nebraska springs were unpredictable, bringing anything from blizzards to tornadoes. Today, it was cold, relentless rain, with them on I-80 West since they left the Omaha airport headed for Kearney.

They were behind a cattle truck, throwing a spray of rainwater onto their windshield. Sam pulled into the passing lane. Kate looked at the trailer as they drove by. Empty. She was relieved; no load of doomed animals on board. She glanced up at the driver in his cab; he was glaring down at her. She lip-read his mouth shaping the word *bitch*. Shocked, she shifted her eyes to her lap, then over to Sam. He smiled at her, then turned back to the road.

They didn't usually say much to each other on road trips; theirs was companionable silence. She didn't want to spoil Sam's good mood by telling him about the truck driver. She watched the truck recede behind them, relieved as their distance from it grew.

I wonder how that feels every day, she thought. *Carrying animals to the slaughterhouse.*

Kate had never been a good traveler. Leaving home

always brought out her anxiety in full force. At home, she could control her environment. Out in the world, who knew what could happen? In the early days with Sam, this brought out his protectiveness. He reveled in his competence to fix whatever went wrong, to right her world for her.

Ten years in, her anxiety seemed to tire him. She didn't blame him. Her anxiousness was an extra burden overlaid on every trip. She wanted to get better.

So, therapy. Her therapist thought the roots of her anxiety lay, unsurprisingly, in childhood. Movement then meant loss of security, never knowing what was next. Just as she relaxed into tentative hope that *this time, this place* would be permanent, her mother's lips would tighten into a thin line, and the boxes would bloom again like mushrooms after rain in rooms only just grown familiar.

Fewer boxes each time, as they shed possessions that were nonessential and too expensive to move to another place. Grandmother's china and the everyday dishes became just the everyday dishes. The dining room table and chairs and the dinette set became just the dinette set. No sentimental boxes of toys or clothes, outgrown but still cherished.

An endless and purposeless migration, her restless father's never-ending search for *better*, whatever that meant. He was an educated man who never learned to get along with other people, let alone navigate around them, dooming his academic career to assistant professorships that became adjunct professorships that became instructorships. Never tenure track. A nomadic existence.

As his prospects shrank and became less appealing, so did their dwellings. The first house she remembered became a smaller house, then one smaller still and in poorer condition, then a series of apartments. The two-bedroom apartment became a one-bedroom, at which point she was old enough to leave home, and the sagging living room couch she slept on, behind.

For all those years, amid all that kept diminishing around her, she was afraid that if she stayed with them, she'd disappear one day, too.

Dr. Silver said it was remarkable that her anxiety only manifested when she traveled, and it wouldn't have been surprising if she had become a hoarder, instead. Oddly, she was the opposite. She didn't permit herself attachment to possessions. What you didn't care about would not hurt you, if it were taken away.

Her own academic career was flourishing. The consistent, dogged work of research was comforting to her. Ornithology was her specialty. In particular, the migratory behavior of *Grus canadensis*, the Sandhill Crane. Every April, she and Sam traveled to the Platte River Valley in Nebraska to observe nearly a million cranes, stopping to feed and gain strength for the journey ahead to Canada and Alaska.

She appreciated the irony that her life's work was studying birds that never really stopped moving. The first time she had seen hundreds of thousands of them rising from the river at sunrise in a roar of wings and chorus of calling, she had wept.

It was worth everything to get here, she thought then, and reminded herself it still was now. Over time, she took on the arrangements for this annual trip. After all, it was for her work, and she wanted to show Sam she could do it as a functioning adult. Preparing the lecture she'd give at the bird sanctuary. Buying plane tickets, booking a place to stay and a rental car. Packing, including her camera, computer and recording gear. Arranging with their cat sitter, Edie, to take care of Chloe and Jones. Getting to the airport, checking baggage, getting through the anxiousness of security screening, even with TSA-Pre. A layover in

Chicago or Minneapolis, a connecting flight to Omaha or Denver, then driving either west or east to get to Kearney in the middle of the state.

There was so much that *could* go wrong. Before each trip, Kate tried to imagine all of it. Thinking of the possibilities ahead of time, then trying to solve each difficulty in her head. After all, short of a plane crash that *killed* her and Sam, there really was no issue that couldn't be dealt with, she told herself.

She turned on the radio and got the NPR station out of Lincoln. The tail end of one of the Brandenburg concertos. Then the news. Which had not been good over several weeks, and which was not good today. They'd considered not coming this year, out of a vague sense that it might be good to stick closer to home until things settled down again. *Fuck it*, Sam had said. *We can't live our lives jumping every time the dickhead-in-chief waggles his dick at another dickhead.* Which not only made her laugh; it pegged the absurdity of the situation perfectly, Kate thought, as she listened to the reporter's dissection of that day's rising tensions.

"Jesus," Sam said over the news broadcast, "is there anybody who isn't pissed at us?" A rhetorical question, she knew. The answer was probably no. But the real question was whether anyone would do something terrible, something that couldn't be taken back or negotiated away. She had to believe that the answer to that question was no, too.

So thinking, she let the hissing white noise of the tires on the wet highway take her to sleep.

***

She awakened when the car stopped. "We're here," Sam said, and smiled at her again, relieved to have the drive in the rain over with. He had stopped at the hotel entrance, where they could unload the car without getting soaked. She stood up, stiff from the drive, and stretched. They hauled their luggage and her equipment case into the lobby. While Sam parked, she went to the desk to check in.

On the wall-mounted TV behind the desk, CNN was broadcasting live from the Qatar summit, which was not going well. The desk clerk turned from watching and offered her a strained smile. *He looks about eighteen,* she thought. *But he looks worried enough for forty. I feel you, brother.*

"Welcome," he said, "I'm Dustin. How can I help you?"

"Hi," Kate said. "Reservation for O'Connell? Kate and Sam?"

Dustin tapped his computer keys and looked back up at her. "Staying a full week?"

"Yep. We're here for the birds."

Dustin smiled again, shyly. "We get a lot of folks here in spring for the cranes. Fewer this year, though. I guess more people are staying home while this is going on," tipping his head backward at the TV behind him. "Crazy stuff."

"Crazy, for sure," Kate replied, and meant it. The dickhead-in-chief, as Sam liked to refer to him, had threatened to invade Greenland. Denmark and Greenland then moved to expel U.S. forces at Ptuffik Space Base. U.S. forces refused to budge, citing the base's role in missile defense, missile warning, and space surveillance. NATO split into Denmark's supporters, and those not wishing to cross the U.S. Ever opportunistic, Russia seized the dissension within NATO to move troops toward the Finnish border, and at least one nuclear sub into the Baltic Sea, claiming the sub was merely an exercise. Exercise or not, Sweden and Norway ratcheted up their defense forces along with their friends in Finland. Canada was squarely on the side of Denmark, as was the UK.

The Qataris offered to host all parties for diplomacy on neutral territory. *Bet they're regretting that,* Kate thought. Talks had been going nowhere for at least a week, the delegations living high on Qatari hospitality while presenting press conferences to report progress. Progress had been minimal; the press conferences had largely been exchanges of insults, grievances and threats. The Qataris were probably banging their heads against the wall by now.

The eternal question, Kate thought: *Why are you banging your head against the wall?* And the eternal answer, *because it feels so good when you stop.*

"What do you think will happen?" she asked Dustin. "It sounds like they're at a standstill."

He shrugged. "Maybe after they've all had their say two or three more times, they'll go home. My best friend Rich enlisted right after we graduated. I just hope nothing stupid happens."

Kate nodded. "Amen to that."

Dustin handed her two plastic keycards. "Well, have a nice stay, anyway. Let us know if you need anything."

"Thanks, we will." She could see Sam coming from the parking lot, holding his jacket over his head to keep the rain off. They would have an early night, to allow her to be up and get to the sanctuary and give her lecture before the cranes' dawn takeoff tomorrow.

***

She was used to it by now, but the sanctuary looked eerie before dawn, amid the acres of surrounding blackness. In order not to disturb the birds, which were sensitive to white light, the sanctuary parking lot was lit only by red lamps.

On a wet morning like this one, it made the parking lot look like it was drenched in blood.

In the middle of her lecture, her phone vibrated. She ignored it to finish her talk and then answer questions from the audience. Bundled in warm, dark clothing per the sanctuary's instructions, a crowd of about sixty people had come from across the U.S. —and beyond—to witness this event. Anyone who loved the birds enough to come to Nebraska in the spring and pay to sit for two hours in a dark blind by the river certainly deserved her full attention.

Her phone vibrated again, more insistently. Belatedly, she realized the first one had been the quick buzz of a text; this one was a call. She ignored it again, as a few people came up to thank her for the talk.

After the last ones departed, trailing the guides with their red flashlights to the observation blinds through the pre-dawn darkness, she pulled her phone from her pocket.

The first notification was that their flight leaving from Omaha at the end of the week was cancelled. The phone call was from Sam.

Shit, somebody died, she thought. *My mom or dad, or his, or somebody else.* Bracing herself, she listened to his voice mail. Uncharacteristically, Sam's voice was shaky and ragged.

Come back to the hotel as soon as you get this. All the fucking flights have been cancelled. Not just ours. Everybody's. Everywhere. We need to get the hell out of Nebraska as fast as we can.

Shaken, she couldn't make sense of Sam's message. Why would they cancel all the flights? And who were *they*? And, why, if the flights were all stopped, would Sam say they needed to *get out of Nebraska*, versus just saying they needed to get home? The anxiety she'd been stepping on since they left yesterday morning was fighting to come into full and poisonous bloom.

Data, she thought, *I need data.* By which she meant, she needed to know what the fuck was happening. She headed for the sanctuary director's office and knocked on the closed door. She'd known Mitchell since graduate school, when she'd first started coming here and volunteering each spring. He was in his sixties now; he was planning to retire next year, he'd told her.

Mitch opened the door. His eyes were red and swollen. As if he'd been rubbing them, hard, or as if he'd been crying.

"Is anything on the news?" she asked. He told her.

****

She drove as fast as she could back to the hotel. Some of the roads leading to the sanctuary were gravel, with uncertain traction, and she didn't want to slide into a ditch. When she reached two lane black top, she put her foot down. She eased off a little when the speedometer hit eighty.

Her phone buzzed again. She didn't dare look at it, going this fast. She'd be at the hotel in five more minutes, anyway.

She pulled into the closest parking space to their room. Before she got out, she checked her phone again. This time it was a text from Edie.

I'm so sorry. Got 2 get 2 Mom and Dad. Left xtra food, water out. Hope I can come back. B safe.

Kate's stomach dropped to what felt like her knees. Edie bailing on Chloe and Jones, somehow, penetrated the sickening sense of unreality enveloping her, in a way that even Mitch's somber *The shit has hit the fan, my friend,* had not. She pulled the room key from her pocket and opened the door.

Sam stood beside the bed, staring at her bleakly. He had the TV on but the sound off. She went to him. "Thank God you're back," he said, and hugged her. She picked up the remote from where it lay on the bedspread and clicked the sound back on. She didn't really need to, though. The live shots of choked highways, looting, and people running through the streets of cities across America and Europe told her everything; the frantic voices of the correspondents were just meaningless babble, from which the only word that registered was *nuclear*. She muted the TV again, then turned it off.

"What do we do?" she asked him.

"We get in the car and go."

* * *

An hour later, they were on I-80, going east this time, realizing the mistake they had made. They had debated taking 44 North to 30 East; 30 paralleled 1-80 nearly to Grand Island; 34 would take them to Lincoln, where they could pick up 6 toward Omaha. Despite the chaos on the roads on the lobby TV behind the check-in counter, they thought the interstate was the quickest way out.

Kate had remembered seeing some folded maps neatly slotted into the lobby's rack of brochures about tourist attractions. The Archway. Fort Kearny Historical Park. And, of course, the Sandhill Crane migration. For some reason, she wanted the reassurance of a paper map.

"It would make me feel better," she said.

Sam shrugged. "If it makes you feel better, fine."

Dustin was on desk duty, again. Kate told him they were checking out and getting on I-80, heading east. He shook his head and looked more troubled than he already did. "Everybody will go that way," he said, "trying to get away from the missile silos in the western part of the state. It's the only major highway heading east from there. If anybody decides to nuke us, those silos are targets."

Leaving the hotel parking lot, they had decided to

stick with their original plan. But Dustin was right. The traffic was heavier than normal, when they took the ramp onto I-80 from 44, but at least it had been moving. It was only barely moving now, though. Kate opened the map app on her phone, and showed it to Sam. The line that was I-80 on the map was orange, turning to solid red ahead. She scrolled the map with her finger, looking for the end of the bottleneck, and saw the little road accident icon.

"Shit," Sam said, and slammed his hands on the steering wheel in frustration. "Where's the nearest off ramp?"

"We can get off at 10-D, go north to Shelton and pick up 30 there," she said.

Sam edged into the right lane and they crept the next few miles to the exit. They weren't the only ones who had the idea; one pickup peeled off the highway onto the ramp ahead of them. The route was bordered on both sides by fields, waiting to be planted.

They were halfway to Shelton when the engine died, along with the radio. Sam coasted to the side of the road. Kate sat silent, fighting the panic wanting to crawl out of her chest, as Sam looked at the engine, then came back to the driver's seat. He left the hood up, the universal signal to potential passers-by that *we're fucked, thank you very much for asking*. He tried turning the ignition key; not even a click.

"Can you tell what's wrong?" she asked.

"It's like the car's electrical system just died," he said. He was sweating, she noticed, even though the morning outside the car was still chilly. "I hope to hell that car trouble is *all* it is. Let me see your phone a minute."

Kate handed it to him without even looking at it, her eyes on Sam's face. He looked at her phone, then dropped his forehead onto the steering wheel.

"What is it?" Wordlessly, Sam held out her phone screen. Solid black. No icons for apps, nothing. It was dead.

"I charged it up last night," she said, "how can it be dead already?"

"I think it was a fucking EMP," he said. He saw the question on her face. "Electromagnetic pulse. A nuke at a high enough altitude to knock out everything electrical, over a wide area. Too high to create a blast wave, but kiss your phone, your car, your computers, and the whole U.S. fucking power grid goodbye." He paused, his expression grim.

"What about fallout?" she asked.

"If it was high enough up, that's the least of our worries. There's plenty of other stuff to be afraid of. Like no communication, no warning systems. I just hope whoever did this is content with putting us back in the twelfth century."

Kate got her car door open just in time, before what little she had in her stomach from the morning came rushing up in a flood of bile that burned her throat.

***

Kate started to pull her suitcase out of the car, then realized it was pointless. If Sam was right, no friendly Nebraskan in a pickup truck was going to drive by and ask *need help, folks?* Because the pickup trucks were fried, too, unless they were very frigging old. With no electronic ignition.

If they were going to reach shelter, it would have to be on foot.

And if Sam was right, none of her equipment would ever work again. She pulled her laptop from its pocket in her backpack, threw it on the back seat, and stuffed underwear and socks into the space in her pack instead. She pulled on the fleece sweater from her suitcase, then put her jacket on over it.

Déjà vu, she thought. *I'm leaving things behind again.* Only now she no longer cared. Now she only wanted to have something between her and Sam and the immense sky overhead. The sky above the Great Plains had always seemed bigger than it did anywhere else. Now it also seemed menacing, poised to rain down destruction on everyone and everything.

Before she shut the car door for the last time, she spotted the map she'd gotten in the hotel lobby and grabbed it. She wasn't sure how useful it would be, but one thing was true: it did make her feel better.

They began walking north. The fields around them were silent. *Waiting for whatever was coming next*, Kate thought.

Sam was the first to spot the stalled pickup ahead. Like their car, it was pulled to the side of the road.

"Well, it's not just us, then. Maybe they'll know something more," he said.

"I don't see anyone around, though," Kate said. "Maybe they started walking too."

Gradually, the tailgate of the truck, adorned by a Nebraska National Guard bumper sticker, grew nearer. As they approached it both Kate and Sam could see something was obviously wrong. The rear window was shattered and covered in dark blotches of what looked like blood.

"Stay here a minute," Sam said. "I'll see if they need help."

Kate understood what he hadn't said. *They might be beyond help.* She watched him walk to the driver's side door and peer in, then drop to his knees on the road and vomit.

I guess it was his turn, she thought disjointedly, and ran toward him. He waved her away, weakly, but she looked in the driver's window, nonetheless.

Knowing was better than not knowing.

The driver, dressed in his Guard uniform, had shot himself in the head with his service pistol, still clutched in his right hand. The top of his skull lay against what little remained of the shattered rear window. His left arm, with its MP insignia, lay limply in his lap, wallet open in his hand to a photo of a pretty young woman and a little girl, about two. It was spattered with blood, as were the papers on the passenger seat. Amid the blotches, Kate could only clearly make out *Duty Status: Title 10* and *evacuation operation Omaha.*

Sam sat in the middle of the road, his head propped on both hands. He looked up at her, then his shoulders started to shake. At first Kate thought he was crying, then she realized he was shaking with laughter. *Shock,* she thought, and waited until his laughter subsided. Sam wiped his eyes.

"He knew something more, all right. He knew we're dead. We're *all* dead. You and I and everybody else are the walking dead, now, Kate. We just didn't know it. It's just a matter of time, and I don't think we've got much left."

"I thought we didn't need to worry about fallout." She wasn't accusatory, just genuinely puzzled. Not to mention scared shitless by what he was saying.

"Not from the EMP, we don't. But if that guy was on his way to support an evacuation of Omaha under Title 10, it was a presidential order. If he blew his own brains out, when he's got a wife and kid, he knew it was a one-way ticket."

"At least let's get under cover," she pleaded, and tugged at his hand. She wasn't big enough to pull him up, but he got to his feet and shouldered his pack again. "It should be less than a mile to Shelton now." Hand in hand, they began walking.

It began to rain again.

***

Just outside Shelton, they spotted a farmhouse and heard a dog barking. His barks were hoarse, as if he'd been barking for a long time. They looked at each other uncertainly, then started walking up the drive. They mounted the steps to the front porch.

Sam knocked on the front door. "Hello. . .Anybody home?" They listened carefully for sounds of movement, under the continued volley of barks. Nothing stirred. Sam knocked again, harder this time. He turned the knob, and the door swung open. Kate's memory flashed back to *Texas Chainsaw Massacre*, Pam entering the house she *thought* was deserted, only to wind up on a meat hook. *Stop it*, she told herself.

Tentatively, they stepped just inside the door. "Hello!" Sam called again. "Anyone here?" Silence.

"I'll check the kitchen and down here," she said. He nodded and started up the narrow stairs that led off from the living room.

Afterward, she wished she had paused to kiss him one last time.

The kitchen was orderly and clean. She was taking a glass from a cupboard for some water—*surely whoever lived here wouldn't begrudge me that*, she thought—when the shotgun blast roared overhead, and she heard something falling down the stairs. *Thump. Thump. Thump.* The glass slipped from her hand and shattered on the red and white checked linoleum.

Sam. Oh dear God no. She ran to the living room. Sam lay at the bottom of the stairs. His chest, that chest she had rested her head on so many times, blown open, a grotesque red and white and blackened cavity of shredded flesh and bone. Her hands flew to her face; she howled her shock and grief to whoever was overhead, whoever had taken him from her.

The shotgun roared again. This time, the newel post at the bottom of the stairs disintegrated, missing her by inches.

Kate ran for the front door and onto the porch. Her backpack unbalanced her and she half-ran, half-fell down the steps and into the yard. She scrambled to her feet and looked frantically for a place to hide.

The barn. She ran for its open door. Desperate to get out of sight, she spotted the ladder to the hayloft and began climbing.

***

An hour passed. She waited for Sam's killer to come looking for her. She lay on her stomach at the edge of the hayloft, watching the barn floor beneath. Listening to the dog bark.

Another hour later, the adrenaline wore off and she began weeping, trying to stay silent, not wanting to give away her hiding place. At least the dog finally stopped barking.

She watched the weak sunlight coming through the open barn door grow stronger and change its angle across the floor as the afternoon passed. It must have stopped raining. Finally, she crept back from the edge of the loft and sat with her back against the wall. Exhausted, she dozed, until the memory of what happened snapped her awake again.

Should she stay here until whatever happened was all over, or go?

What the fuck does it matter? she thought, despairing. She'd be dead soon, either way. Whoever killed Sam would kill her too, or somebody, somewhere, would give the launch order that would kill everybody.

Moving, versus staying, did matter, she realized. She could stay here and let somebody else decide how and where she died, or she could at least choose something of her end for herself. She pulled the map from her pack and opened it.

***

She waited until nightfall, then climbed down the ladder, feeling carefully for each rung with her foot in the darkness. Whatever lights lit the farmyard last night were gone now, just as dead as their car by the side of the road.

Just as dead as Sam. At that thought, she almost missed a step but caught herself just in time. *I will not die of a broken neck on the fucking floor of this barn.* Finally, she reached the last rung. She slipped out of the door and around the corner of the barn. The yard was dark, and so was her clothing, chosen not to scare the birds at the Sanctuary this morning at dawn.

What a difference a day makes. The cliché brought unbidden, hysterical laughter that wanted to break free. She clapped her hand over her mouth. *Not now, Kate.*

The dog started barking again, sounding utterly exhausted.

Go, get the fuck out of here, she told herself.

Thanks to the map, she knew the way to the Sanctuary from here. She'd walk through the night, first to Gibbon, then turn south on 10-C, then turn left on Elm Island Road. It was about fourteen miles. She should be there by sunrise. Going across fields might be faster, but she had no flashlight, and it was too dark to see her way. Starlight or moonlight would have helped, but the cloud cover had returned.

The first two miles, she kept looking over her shoulder and listening for footsteps, expecting Sam's killer to be behind her, stalking her. Her flight from the farm had seemed too easy. But all that was behind her was the road, just dimly visible.

After what felt like a couple of hours, she thought she

would be getting close to Gibbon, where she would turn south. But her initial pace had slowed, as she put distance between herself and the farmhouse. She'd had no food or water since early morning. She needed to stop and rest. She eased her pack from her shoulders, then sat down on the road.

All she heard was the wind. The one constant in Nebraska.

She badly wanted to lie down with her head on the pack and go to sleep. Instead, she struggled back to her feet. *Keep moving.* In Gibbon, she could find food and water.

***

The cloud cover broke enough to afford some minimal visibility, but Gibbon was still just a dark island in a darker sea. Here and there, she saw the glow of a lantern behind drawn curtains, but she would not approach a house. Not after what had happened. She tried the doors of one business after another. Locked, all of them, their owners either gone, afraid of looting, or both.

Please, she thought, *please.* Unsure who or what she was pleading to.

She rounded a corner and saw the windows of the dollar store, dimly lit but lit nonetheless, by candle flames dancing and flickering in the darkness. She pulled on the door and, comically, nearly fell backwards onto the sidewalk when it opened unexpectedly.

She looked around in wonder. More candles were around the store, giving just enough light to see down each aisle. A plastic tablecloth (*party supplies aisle*, her mind whispered) with writing scrawled on it in marker—*Matt 24:25 take what u need*—was draped over the checkout counter with its useless cash registers, empty drawers left open.

She cried again, this time from relief. Snuffling, wiping her face on the sleeve of her jacket, she found a bottle of water in a defunct cooler near the register, and a box of protein bars down a food aisle. She put down her pack, leaned against the wall, and slid down to the floor. The water tasted so good. So did the food.

But now she had time to think.

The hysterical laughter wanted to bubble up again. Alone in the store, she let it. *Talk about a bad fucking trip*, she thought, as tears of laughter streamed down her face. *Here I was, all worried about flight connections and lost luggage and screwed up reservations. I thought the absolute worst that could happen was a plane crash that killed us both.*

At least we would have died together. That thought stopped her laughter like a slap across the face. Her mind marched insistently into the land of might-have-been. *I wish we'd never left. Sam would still be alive. Instead, he's dead, and I had to leave him behind. We would have been home, with Chloe and Jones. I left them behind, too.*

We could have at least all died together. Full circle.

That thought broke her utterly. She wailed, and clawed at her face, drawing blood, her grief and anger pouring out in screams that echoed faintly down the deserted streets.

***

One more step. Then another. She told herself that for seven more miles.

At last, the Sanctuary. Deserted. Everyone scattered to the four winds, trying to outrun what was coming. Except the birds. Except her.

She sat down quietly on the riverbank, arms clasped around her knees, waiting for the sunrise. Listening to the birds, muttering among themselves, as the sky began to flush faintly in the east.

The sun began to breach the horizon. First an orange glow, then a crimson sliver at the edge of the world. The croaking of the birds, and the rustling of their wings and bodies, reached a crescendo as the sun became a flaming circle.

In the distance, she heard the sirens, wailing. Before the white flash burned out her retinas, she saw hundreds of thousands of cranes, rising from the river, one last time.

Watch Me Go
by
Randall Drum

Quit fuckin' staring at me, Devon.
He couldn't help it, though, and I suppose a part of me appreciated the attention. He has the kind of eyes that look deep into your soul while he waits for you to answer your own question. Green, if you need to know. Always paying close attention to every detail. Hanging on every word, even the ones you didn't say, and the way your body moved. My mom used to say that was called "reading people," and someone with that skill could make a lot of money as a fake psychic. I guess that means she thought there were real ones. Devon was too good for that kind of nonsense and eventually put a "PsyD" after his name. He worked at a facility where kids who the world has given up on are tucked away for safe keeping. You know the place—the one on the side of town you never visited unless you lived there, and then it just seemed like it was too goddamn close to the city. Breakouts weren't common, but they happened.

But now, with the top half of his head lying on the floor, Devon just stared at me. Unblinking, twenty-four by seven. Considering what happened to him, though, I'm not sure I'll make it to seven.

And you.

I look at the hole in the middle of the floor. I'm not sure, but I think it's bigger today.

You. Fuck you!

I don't know if it hears me. Don't know if it understands me. Don't know if it fucking cares. Don't know if it's alive or just a drain. There's been no noise from it since I woke up. I could have been out two minutes or twenty. I don't really think time matters much anymore. Not for me, anyway. I'm sure Devon would've had a different opinion. He was quick to play devil's advocate, even if it was just for the sake of being contrary to get you more riled up.

My hands hurt from banging on the walls. My fingers ache from searching for any seam, any crack, any sign of how we got in this thing and how to get out. I stopped a while ago. Whoever built this thing was good. Machined to such a fine point there's no sign of it being anything other than an unbroken solid surface. The wall bulges behind me, nudging me toward the hole, which slowly expands and contracts, as if it's breathing.

No.

I lean back, pushing as hard as I can.

Not yet, fucko.

***

Two (or three?) days ago, Devon and I were just two riders in the great American countryside. Two pale lanes of weathered desert asphalt stretched out in front of us like a scar across the Sonoran. The cracked shoulders of the road dissolved into scrub and stone, and I remember thinking *here's the blurry, messy line where nature starts to reclaim what it rightfully owns.* It really put some perspective in my mind, when I'd otherwise just focus on how numb my ass was from riding non-stop for the past hour and a half.

Devon joked when we hit the desert that it doesn't give a shit if you live or die. His insights were usually on point, and given his condition, I don't think he was being overly philosophical. And looking at Devon now, I think I know which way the desert is leaning.

I rode ahead of Devon by about fifty yards or so, his Harley growling every now and then as he threatened to overtake me. We used to make those noises with our mouths as kids when we rode around our Rochester neighborhood.

"Watch me go!" Devon would yell and laugh as he stood tall on his pedals. I don't think I ever ripped as much out of life as he did in moments like those. We rode like that for years until we knew every square inch of road and path between all the houses. In time, we discovered the best routes through the woods to the Genesee River where we would take rods and stand on the shore, pretending we knew more about fishing than we really did. During our college years we both shifted to riding motorcycles, which were just as fun and gave us more range. Shortly after graduation, we decided to take every long ride we could afford. We had amazing trips. Even made it to St. Louis once. Careers and families kept us mostly grounded after a while, but we still managed one or two "big rides" each year.

All that changed two years ago when Devon got his diagnosis. He spit words like "tumor" and "inoperable" when he called me, raging at how he wasn't going to live long enough to see his kid graduate from high school, let alone see him learn how to ride a bike, and how Lauren would be on her own. The last call from his doctor came just about a month ago now. The doc said based on his experience, Devon had less than a year (probably not much more than six months) left.

That's when he called me with the idea for one last ride. The last big ride, the longest yet: cross the Midwest, through the heartland, down into the desert, up the Golden Coast, and eventually land in Portland. Said he saw a food truck place up there on TV once during chemo and figured that would be a good place for lunch. Lauren wasn't having any of it, not at first anyway. Jen and I had them over for dinner and after three courses of some French dishes I still can't pronounce (Jen was taking a class) and a couple of bottles of wine, Lauren relented. We hit the road after two weeks of planning and a lot of promises to our wives that we would be just fine.

You sure you want to do this, brother? I wanted to give him another chance to bag out, but there was no talking him out of it. Not that I wanted to, though. A true cross-country ride on my bike? I was in. We both packed light: daily meds, light camping gear in case the motels were shitty (they mostly are), and a few changes of clothes. We figured we'd find laundromats along the way and the bigger gas stations would have showers.

I don't have clothes anymore.

The last shower I had was when that hole opened up wide and something, I mean some*thing*, shredded my dying friend.

I'm hungry.

***

Some kind of art project? Science experiment?

That's what Devon and I settled on when we came across the collection of cubes. Fifty maybe, I don't know, scattered alongside the highway for at least a quarter-mile stretch. Big, glowing cubes. Most were a pure white, but I counted six that pulsed with various shades of red, from pale pink to a deep crimson. We eyeballed them at about sixteen feet per side and at least the same height. They appeared to be completely smooth and, ain't this the fucking kicker, they hovered a few feet above the desert floor and despite the low angle of the evening sun, they didn't cast shadows.

How are they glowing? I couldn't see any sign of power cables or any kind of support.

Check it out. They get brighter the closer you get. Devon bounced back and forth amongst the cubes, being careful not to touch them—because what the fuck—like a human pinball pinging off bumpers in some giant desert dystopia arcade pinball machine.

Whoo! He called out. *Watch me go!*

I remember reaching into my jacket pocket to pull out my phone when a burst of light flashed nearby, bright and quick as could be. It was the kind of flash that if you blinked at the right time, you would've never known it happened.

What was that?

No reply.

Hey, Dev, what was that? I walked to the last cube I saw him near. I couldn't make sense of what I found.

Crumpled on the ground were Devon's clothes. Boots, socks, boxers. Everything. Funny how the first thing that came to mind was the rapture. Devon was a staunch atheist, and I didn't see him as being a likely candidate to be suddenly pulled up to heaven. I called his name several times and even dropped down to look under the cubes; looking for his naked feet and legs to be running around, part of some joke. But there was nothing. I stood up and spun around, but all I could see were the cubes. No road. No desert mountains. No setting sun or twilight stars. My heart thrashed against my ribs, and I couldn't draw a breath into my tightening chest. I've had panic attacks before, and this felt no different. A shimmering white light, shifting its shape with every pulse of my heart, overwhelmed my vision until it was all I could see. Closing my eyes didn't help at all. And then, in an instant, I no longer felt the desert floor under my boots.

***

The tongue slips out of the hole again.

I saw the teeth a little while ago. They clicked and scraped against each other as they pushed up from the darkness beyond the edge. I think that's what woke me up. Whatever they belong to, I think there's more than one. These look smaller than they did last time. The tongue is the same, though. It's like a tentacle you'd see on dimly lit footage from the sea floor on a Saturday morning nature show narrated by some random zoo director or news anchor on a weekend gig. Only, you never get to see what it's attached to.

Notice how the slithering pink protuberance pokes and prods, twists and wraps itself around every object it encounters as it explores the rim of its habitat before daring to slip out from its hiding place. Not much is known about the tongue, if it even is a tongue, but just marvel at how it glides across the surface in search of prey.

And hunt it does. It sopped up the last of Devon's blood hours ago. I pull my feet away from it and the edge of the expanding void. If it gets much bigger, I don't know how I'll avoid it.

There's an occasional spark of light moving in there. Tiny, flickering pinpoints, dancing just on the edge of my awareness. Maybe it's a lack of oxygen—I mean, how much of it can be left in this box—or maybe a trick of the eye, but I *know* I've seen them. Where they come from and where they go I can't tell but there's no lights now. Just the ruddy tongue with its thick saliva and the glistening trail it leaves in its wake. I feel my own tongue, thick and dry in my mouth. I haven't had anything to drink since Devon and I woke up here. Don't know if I should really be too worried about it. I figure the thing on the other side of that hole will dehydrate me before long.

***

"Where are you, babe?" Jen slipped out from underneath the sheets and rolled closer to where I sat on the edge of the bed. She reached up to scratch my back and it sent a shiver down to my feet as I brushed my toes across the nubs of carpet.

As usual, I was lost in my thoughts and could only muster a "hmm" that bordered on disinterest.

"Hey," she stopped scratching. "You okay?"

"Yeah, yeah," I lied. "Totally fine."

There was nothing else I could say. I couldn't tell her what was going on inside my head because I wasn't quite sure myself. I nudged her over and laid down again, still unable to find a comfortable position on my lumpy pillow.

Jen slid closer, wrapped a leg over me, and stroked my face before moving her hand to my waist.

"Well, I don't know where you've gone off to in that head of yours," said, as she climbed on top of me. "But I think I know how to find you."

I held her close as we pushed and pulled, moving against and with each other at the same time. Our arms and legs tangled as we twisted, wrapping ourselves in the sheets.

Still on top of me after we finished, Jen lay her head on my chest. I brushed my fingers through her hair, which she always said was her favorite thing in the world.

"You know something?" I asked. "I'm pretty sure I love you."

Jen shifted, sliding a leg up, her foot tickling my shins.

"I loaAAAHH!" Jen's body stiffened. A sudden

pinprick in my leg made me jump, but Jen's grip tightened around my chest, her nails digging into my back as they had done only minutes before. Then an abrupt explosion of pain, liquid and stinging, setting every nerve in my leg ablaze. I wanted to cry out but could barely breathe. Jen's head twisted, and I could feel her teeth as she dragged them across my chest before lifting her face to mine. What I saw there was not my Jen.

Misshapen. Vile. Her features slid into and around each other. Jen's shriveled eyes and enlarged mouth braided into a shrieking, drooling, perverted mass. She grunted with every convulsion in this violent seizure, and she bounced her head into my chest so hard I thought she might break through. She lifted again. Her hair, now slicked with blood and saliva, fell to the side and I watched as her face wilted, receding inward, deeper and deeper, until it was just a rim of flesh fading into a well of darkness.

I mustered all my strength and breath before pushing Jen off me, screaming into that darkened pit.

***

Searing.

I know the sensation—learned it as a kid working in fast-food restaurants. Stand too close to the fryer and it's only a matter of time until some bad shit happens. I still carry a few spotty reminders on my left arm.

I lurch up and back, hitting my head on the wall as I pull my knees up to my chest. I open my eyes, echoes of the dream still flickering across my retinas, to see the tongue writhing around my ankle as it grips and releases, grips and releases. With every squeeze comes an incandescent shock that bores into my flesh, sending tremors through the muscle and bone. My blood seeps through the gaps as the tongue coils around my foot. A pitiful, anemic scream is all I can muster.

I jerk my foot back the first moment I feel the tongue slacken and push myself as flat against the wall as I can. The tongue sops up the blood I smeared on the floor. It slinks back to the hole and is replaced by something I haven't seen before. There's a breeze, almost a sucking, which pulls the air from the cube toward the growing black maw. My ears pop as the pressure changes.

Large scales, shades of black and green, slide across the other side. I swallow hard and my ears reopen, only to be deluged by the roar of wind. But there's something else in the mix. I can't call it a voice. It doesn't sound *spoken*, but there are rhythmic sounds. Discordant and rotten. Guttural then lilting to high peaks. Notes and harmonies in a music no one has heard before. The scaled thing finally disappears into the nothingness and the song fades just before the teeth return with their incessant chittering.

shut up. shut up. SHUT UP!

My voice is weak, nearing its breaking point, and my body is not far behind. I touch my foot with my trembling hand but the pain is too much. The burn is fading, but the stinging just won't stop. It reminds me of every scrape or cut I ever got as a kid, which had my mother running to the medicine cabinet for the hydrogen peroxide. Looking at it now I see five sets of concentric pinholes corkscrewed around my foot and ankle. I'm surprised the bleeding stopped so quickly. The varicose veins that slink up my ankle and into my leg darken before my eyes with every passing second, and my foot feels like a distended balloon, saturated with whatever poison that thing just put into me.

I'm feeling so heavy, so tired.

Tired of this fight—*is that even what this is?* Exhaustion seeps into me and I drop my arms, letting go of my leg. I can't. I can't go on like this.

Jen.

Her face flashes across my eyes.

What. . .Jen. I can't see you. I can't. . .kee. . .o. . .pen.

***

I think I dreamed about Jen again. I'm not sure. It's been hours, or maybe just minutes, since the tongue bit me. I'm done trying to figure it out.

Hey, Dev. Look at this.

I point at my withering leg, which is now almost entirely black. *Maybe you're the lucky one.*

How long have I been here? So thirsty.

My belly, chest, and other leg are a roadmap now as the poison spreads. My skin is turning gray as every vein and capillary thrust this horror, this *cancer*, forward, inch by inch in its pursuit of consumption. Every beat of my heart propels that malignancy as it prowls and discovers new depths in which to burrow. My body is numbing, which is strangely calming, and I drop in and out of consciousness as I lie on the floor. Every time my body twitches awake I discover I am more emaciated than the last time I opened my eyes, which themselves have changed. I have forfeited all color, with all things nuanced in mottled degrees of gray and black. The radiant white of my prison (or is it coffin) has paled and is no brighter than an overcast day.

Devon's once brilliant eyes reflect my depleted frame. Hell, I'm not sure I can call it a frame anymore. I have atrophied, and my blackened limbs aren't much more than burnt matchsticks. My sunken chest and the wasting organs inside betray a bitter hunger that swells in a craving, which dilates and floods every vessel, if I even have them anymore. I'm left restless while a cold fever overwhelms what's left of me.

I raise my arm and bring my hand closer to my eyes.

Desiccated. I brush my fingers across my face, feeling skin that is cracked, sloughing away even as I touch it. My nose has become a thin ridge barely rising above the surface. My mouth has dilated and my lips have receded, fully exposing every tooth.

That's when I hear the teeth in the hole chattering louder than they have before, fighting for their place around the edge. My voice was stolen along with the rest of me, and I can no longer speak. I can only open and close my mouth, clicking my teeth in retort. I stretch my arms out before me and with every bit of strength I can marshal, I crawl inch by inch toward the widening hole.

The points of light have returned. The closer I get to the edge, my teeth clicking and gnashing in unison with those inside, I can make out an eternal expanse of stars. An aurora, dazzling with colors I can no longer see, ebbs and surges as if it's alive, sparkling before dissipating only to glow brightly again. In the moments of brightness, I can see something coiled around it. Whether it means to contain the light or something else, I don't know. I'm reminded of the first time Devon and I stopped on our journey into the desert to take in its infinite majesty. Simultaneously awed and frightened and in love and, just as now, I had no words to describe what I felt.

Scaled, glistening with ice that shatters and reforms as it snakes itself through the vacillating aurora, the behemoth glides in silence. Closer, I see the creatures whose teeth have hounded me. Decayed, frail, and shrunken, just as I have become. They reach out with their frozen, clawed fingers, beckoning me as I twist and drop my legs over the edge of the hole. It's cold there—wherever *there* is—but I'm not frightened of it now. These are my new brothers in famine. Together we chatter as we share an insatiable appetite. I turn to lower myself into the frozen expanse on the other side of my prison. I can feel my brethren as they guide me to my new home. I pause before I fully immerse myself in my new existence and look to my best friend one last time.

Hey Dev, watch me go.

Travel Companions
by
Nicola Lombardi

Michele was awakened by the screeching of brakes, and as he opened his eyes abruptly, he realized that the train was slowing down.

The station was, by then, nearby. But it wasn't his, yet. He would have to keep that cushioned seat warm for a few more hours before arriving home. Rubbing his eyes, he directed them toward the window to his right as he tried to bring into focus the landscape lazily drifting by, beneath the reddening sun of late afternoon.

He massaged the muscles of his legs. Christ, how dreadfully tired he was! But it was not so much the trip itself that had worn him out. It was the fear, at every station, that someone would board the train and come to settle down in his compartment. Up until that moment, all had gone well for him. The train was almost empty, and he had lodged himself fiercely into the corner of his den, firmly drawing shut the curtain to the side aisle to signal his determination tobe left alone. Enclosed inside, along with five empty seats, that was pure tranquility; that was truly a relaxing trip.

It was not that he had ever had a traumatic experience in the past that made him dread the presence of strangers along with him in his compartment. No, the fact was that he simply felt freer to breathe, to move about, to cough, to blow his nose, to unwrap candies without having to share them, to eat a cheese sandwich without having to worry about the smell or the subsequent need to make use of a toothpick, and things of that sort. All small matters, of course, but for Michele, being able to do them in peaceful solitude, versus under the observation of a stranger, was infinitely preferable. Thus, traveling alone was the *sine qua non* for preserving his internal serenity.

At times he had traveled with people sleeping; then it became a problem to read if the light had been turned off, or to step through a tedious entanglement of outstretched legs to get up and exit. At times, he had to endure, in patient silence, rowdy little kids, loud, chatty women, or persons with obnoxious tics that led to a series of disgusting noises from their mouths. Or worse still, persons eager to engage him in conversations dealing with subjects that invariably meant nothing to him, such as sports, or politics, or even the crops in the regions the train was passing through. And so, whenever he managed to retain personal hegemony within the conquered territory of his compartment, Michele kept his fingers crossed at every station, whispering pointless spells and staring with feral eyes at anyone who was walking through the corridor and glancing inside in search of a place. By so doing, he thought, he would discourage a good percentage of the newly arrived. He himself, he reasoned, would never ever enter a compartment where a guy with such an unwelcoming manner was entrenched. But others obviously did not think as he did, and they came in anyway. In such cases—in actual fact, rather frequently—there was nothing left for him to do but to lower his eyes and hope to doze off (but then, he knew his nerves would often contract slightly, causing an embarrassing twitching in his arms and legs) or else to bury himself in some gothic novel or a horror comic.

With a whistle and a clattering tremor, the train stopped.

Michele considered the squalor of the station, with its grey mesh of tracks infested by raggedy, molting pigeons and hunched figures in blue overalls busy picking up discarded papers and dried chewing gum. Much to his regret, the entry to the train from the station's platform was on the side opposite from his window; and so, for all he knew, a hundred passengers could have climbed aboard, or only one. What mattered was that no one chose his coach, or—if someone did—that they did not choose his compartment. From the moment he had closed the curtains, it became pointless to resort to his practice of scowling and displaying the vaguely antisocial look he had tried out many times before. Still, he did not want to get up and push them back, because of the risk that someone, prowling outside, would notice the five tempting unoccupied seats in his compartment. He had no desire to shoot himself in the foot, metaphorically speaking.

The stop did not last for more than a minute. A good sign.

The stationmaster's whistle resonated like a melody in Michele's ears, and he found himself smiling at his own image faintly reflected in the window glass. Outside, the light was a golden red, and the landscape that now resumed its fitful flow past his gaze took on the tones and contours of the deepening twilight.

But he was not yet completely out of danger. Michele had learned through bitter experience that, from the time the train left the station to the moment he could reasonably breathe a sigh of relief, a full five minutes had to pass. Often, passengers who had just boarded roamed for a while down the aisles, evaluating and identifying the most comfortable spaces, before taking a seat. Michele was still in that suspended state where anything could still happen, and all at once . . .

The compartment door abruptly slid open with a clatter of glass and metal that cut through Michele's sigh of relief like a pair of shears. The compartment curtain, however, allowed him to see only the black shoes and trousers of the intruder.

Dear Lord, let it be the conductor, he thought, biting his lip. *Let it be just the conductor*.

A gnarled hand slipped between the folds of the fabric, and with a decisive tug, the curtain was sent to the side, into its corner.

It wasn't the conductor. Michele's heart skipped a beat. Standing on the threshold of the compartment was a tall man, about fifty, dressed in dark clothing and with an unsettling pair of shaded glasses that reminded him very much of those worn by blind men.

"Are these seats free?" he asked in a coarse voice, without disturbing a single feature on his face. Clearly, he was not blind.

"Yes," replied Michele. He hoped, desperately and absurdly, that the man wanted exactly the opposite. He felt his throat grow dry.

The fellow did not enter right away, but turned his head toward the corridor.

"Come on in," he said calmly. "There's room for everyone."

Room for everyone? My God, how many of them were there? Michele brought his feet back beneath the seat and tried to swallow. With eyes wide open, he sat unmoving as he stared at the quiet but relentless flow of entering men, with whom he would have to spend at least an hour. If, that is, he was fortunate and they got off at the next stop.

The first man, the one with glasses whose lenses were black as pitch, moved next to the window, sitting right across from Michele. A second fellow came in, also dressed in dark hues, but shorter and balder than the first, and with an unpleasant oddity that immediately caught Michele's eye. His lips were turned inward into his mouth, wrapping around gums that obviously lacked any teeth. This one sat down beside Michele, who—as he watched a third with a massive build and a single black glove wedged into his rigid right hand enter—was gripped by a nervous tremor. Was it possible there were no other seats in the entire train? Did they have to come right in there with him? First, one who seemed to have problems with his eyes, then another without teeth, then a third with just one hand. . .and it wasn't over yet.

A fourth individual came in, his face as serious and impassive as all the others. The fact that the left sleeve of his jacket was pinned, empty, to his shoulder, came as no surprise to Michele: by then the situation seemed almost comical. *Ok, are you all here?* he thought, suppressing nervous laughter. There was still an open spot, after all. Another one might as well come in, obviously with some sort of disfigurement—at least then he would have had something truly incredible to tell his friends!

A crutch appeared in the opening that connected the corridor to the compartment, and Michele's wish was granted. A fifth man, with one empty trouser leg rolled upwards and tied with a string beneath his stump of a thigh, settled into the last remaining seat with a dexterity that demonstrated long years of experience. He propped his crutch by his side, and after closing the glass compartment door tightly, he pulled the curtain shut as well. Michele would have liked to interrupt him, to tell him that if he was closing it only because it was closed before, it really wasn't necessary any longer. Instead, he remained silent and motionless, looking out the window without seeing anything else but the chaotic spirals of his own thoughts whirling inside his head. He had acknowledged none of them, just as none of them had greeted him. He thought for a second that he would have preferred continuing his journey on the outside, clinging to one of the train's handgrips, rather than being forced to share his compartment with these men.

And now the final rays of the sun had fused into a dark aura, coloring the houses, trees, and fields that were speeding past with sinister reflections, to become lost in the infinite nothingness that the train was leaving behind.

If he had been alone in the compartment, Michele would have, at that moment, turned on the light, but he did not feel at all like getting up, or asking if he could.

The five strangers sat motionless, without speaking. *This is absurd*, thought Michele. The mute hostility he directed towards them might be callous in view of their unfortunate physical conditions, but the fact remained that these five characters were, in their own quiet way, ruining his trip. This was enough to make them more than a little disagreeable in his eyes. He wondered where they could have come from and where they were going. They resembled each other, vaguely, and were all dressed in dark colors; perhaps they were brothers. But for all five of them, collectively, to be in such a state? Whoever they were, without a doubt, they personified the most singular and disturbing company Michele had ever been among.

He realized that the man sitting across from him was staring at him impassively, and this was disconcerting. Certainly, it was possible he wasn't doing it on purpose, given that underneath those black glasses he might very well have already sunk into a quick catnap; but he conveyed a sense of unease to Michele that was beginning to burn a hole in his stomach. He decided that the situation needed to be faced without letting the presence of those silent characters overwhelm him psychologically. He snatched up the comic book that had slipped between his thigh and the armrest when he had dozed off while reading it about a half hour before.

But he realized at once that the light coming from the outside was now too weak to allow him to make out the graphics and the words. He raised his head, discomfited that he would no longer be able to hide behind the pages. That's when he felt as if a blow had been struck against the inside of his ribs. *Every one of those five characters was staring at him!* It was no longer simple embarrassment that he felt, but actual physical distress: nausea, and dizziness. It seemed impossible for him to be in such a situation, and he would have given anything to escape it. What kind of attitude should he have assumed? Perhaps it would have been convenient to smile, or better yet, say something humorous that could defuse the tortured awkwardness. But the only thing he did, without realizing it, was to sit there with an open mouth, struggling like a fool caught among tentacles of confusion and dread.

After a few seconds, or a few centuries—Michele was not sure which—the man to his left, the one without teeth, spoke to him. Rather, he uttered a series of vocal sounds combined with a frightful sucking in of saliva. Michele, at that point, visualized himself abruptly lowering the window and jumping out with a scream. He barely found enough breath to whisper, "What were you. . .I'm sorry, what were you saying?"

The fellow, continuing to stare into his eyes from the distance of a foot or so, repeated, undeterred, the same incomprehensible sounds and noises. Michele decided at that point that he would get out of there—excusing himself to visit the toilet—with the firm intention of no longer returning to that compartment until the train had brought him to his destination, and then, only to retrieve his suitcase. Yes, of course, he would have done just that, when, all of a sudden. . .the words of the man missing a hand compelled him, at least for the moment, to sit still where he was.

"He said you had some very fine teeth, young man."

"Very fine teeth?" repeated Michele in amazement. And then he noticed that the toothless man, still with his eyes riveted on him, or, better yet, on his mouth, had extracted from an inner pocket of his jacket a small black leather case that could have held a pair of deluxe fountain pens. The man released a small metal tab, and the cover flipped open. Within, rather than two pens, lay an object with an unmistakable quality: a pair of dental pliers.

Michele felt as if his heart were about to shatter. This was surely some kind of joke; it could not be anything else. *Do not panic*, he told himself. *Just don't panic.*

At that point, the one-handed man spoke again.

"And you also have two splendid hands, don't you know?"

Michele made a choking noise that he would have liked to have turned into a kind of laughter.

The fellow with the empty sleeve then joined in. "That's true. And also, two magnificent arms." That being said, he bent over to lift up a black piece of luggage, to which Michele had not paid any attention at all—a briefcase which, placed across the man's knees, sprang open like the jaws of a dragon to reveal its contents: a small carpenter's saw.

In the meantime, the fifth character was repeating, "And sturdy legs! Sturdy legs!" as he rested an elbow on his crutch and leaned over towards Michele.

At that moment, the possibility that this was all some macabre joke dissolved from Michele's mind into thin air, and he read the deadly seriousness of the faces surrounding him.Numb in both body and mind, he tried to rise from his seat, but his muscles, paralyzed by terror, refused to respond.

Then the man sitting across from him, slowly

removing his black glasses, spoke up. "You also have two very beautiful eyes, young man."

Michele looked at him as if hypnotized. The right eye was there. The left one wasn't. The man slipped a hand inside his jacket. When he extracted it, he was gripping a small metal object.

And it was that object, at first sight so harmless, yet absurdly lethal, that finally freedthe stifled shriek from the depths of Michele's lungs. But his cry was drowned out by the deafening whistle of the train, swallowed up by the dark gullet of a tunnel. The night plummeted over Michele as that small object, whose image was now deeply branded into his widening eyes, came closer to his face.

A teaspoon.

Translated by J. Weintraub

Killer Road Trip
by
DW Milton

We were all hanging at the lake, drinking, smoking, you know, keeping cool by being cool, when Brody's thick finger pointed at a crumpled envelope in the corner of the truck bed.

"Hey man, what's that?"

Brody reached for the correspondence addressed to Occupant and removed the stained contents. His heavy brow furrowed and then he shoved the letter into John's face. "You think it's real?"

John usually would have shoved Brody's lineman-like bulk aside, hollering, "Get that crap out of my face!" However, something on that tattered piece of paper must have caught his eye.

He tilted his head to the side and took what Brody offered.

With a strange eagerness, John beckoned to me, "Hey Katie, get a load of this.

I crawled over Jenn and Mike who were making out on Mike's dad's dusty blanket. My foot accidentally (maybe on purpose) kicked Mike in the kidney, which promptly elicited, "Hey! Watch it, bitch!"

"Get a room," I mumbled. My scuffed combat boot

was loaded for a double tap, but I decided against it.

I squeezed in next to John, displacing Heather. She shot me a dirty look, which I ignored.

"What do you know about this?" John flapped the creased correspondence at me. "You seem into this urban legend shit."

I reached for the paper, causing my sleeve to rise above the inside of my wrist, exposing the black lettering of my "Skelter" tattoo.

Before I could shove the cloth back over my skin, Brody noticed it and muttered, "Freak."

Heather's manicured hand pushed my arm roughly aside. "Is someone making a movie?"

She leaned over my shoulder for a better view of the announcement:

Hey there Slashers—Looking for a thrill? Kill as many as you can! And then some more! Pick a pair—your best bud, your little cousin, your best friend's girl. Select a weapon! A mask! Create a signature move. Become one of the best! Only two rules: It must be REAL and captured on film. Send the VHS tape of your kills to PO Box 666 Tucson, AZ 85737 and watch the splatter fly!

"That is some sick serial killer kind of stuff. How lame!" Heather clicked her tongue on her front teeth in disgust.

"Naw, it says slashers, not serial killers." Brody's tongue tripped on the "sh" of slashers.

"That's what I said, moron." Heather whined, "serial killers are slashers. God, everyone knows that."

John shook his beautiful head. "I don't think so, Heather. Serial killers don't always use a knife."

"Actually," I said. I hesitated, not wanting to armchair the starting quarterback. I mean, here I was, the new girl who just moved from the city to this Podunk town, first time invitee to their little soirée. Already different because of my clothes, thick eyeliner and dyed black hair, I was lonely and missed my friends back home, so I accepted John's invitation to hang, to drink and chill in the back of Mike's truck. But I could not let it go. "Slashers aren't real. They are fictional characters like Jason Voorhees or Michael Myers. They do what serial killers do, but just not in real life."

"That doesn't make sense," chided Heather, brushing her feathered bangs from her perfectly framed forehead. "It says right there, it must be *real* and on film. How can it be both?"

"Yeah," slobbered Brody. He elbowed John. "Back in Black Katie doesn't know what she's talking about." He then turned to ogle his crush. "Right, Heather?"

Heather's eyes rolled under her lids, heavily shadowed with baby-blue, and they almost disappeared inside her head.

I handed the ad back to John, my finger lingering at his thumb. Man, did I miss Sid, my boyfriend back in the city.

I frowned, "They probably meant to say *realistic*." Wanting to move the conversation along, I suggested, "We could make a realistic movie with a slasher character like Jason Voorhees and kill each other off."

"Uh, ok," John hesitated as if thinking hard. "But we are not really going to kill each other?" He looked at me. "Right, Katie?"

"Don't be silly," I reassured him. Uncrossing my legs, I began. "We need a backstory and probably a mask and a catchy name based on the backstory. Definitely something that has a Clive Barker's *The Forbidden* feel to it."

"What the hell are you talking about, freak?" Heather knew I had the group's attention and did not like it.

"Like that movie where the kiddies get picked off while the counselors are doing it!"

Brody nudged Mike's butt with his sneaker, snickering; Mike and Jenn had already come up for air, interested.

John snorted. "Yeah, and then they reopen the camp, and all the counselors start dying."

He glanced at Brody with giggle-tears in his eyes. "The sluts get killed first, huh, Jenn?"

"Shut up!" Jenn snapped, which only caused John and Brody to laugh harder, further irritating her.

Jenn rolled away from Mike, rebuttoned her shirt, and sat with her knees up, arms crossed. Her wavy red hair covered her freckled face, but it could not conceal her pouting.

"Nobody does shit like that near here." Brody's massive shoulders shrugged. "The only thing we get is some stupid hunter shootin' some other idiot thinkin' it's a deer."

Heather groaned. That was her uncle last season. He mistook a park ranger for a six-point buck.

Jenn sat up in her corner, "What about The Crystal Palace massacre?"

"What about it?" Mike fluffed his over-styled hair.

"That's where some Satanists were going to sacrifice some girl." Jenn crawled forward.

"Yeah, Jenn, a virgin, but you wouldn't know anything about that since, what? Sixth grade?" Brody taunted, and the boys chimed in.

Jenn's cheeks colored a distinct crimson at the jab. Nevertheless, it was an idea. A great idea for a slasher film.

"Forget the virgin." I rubbed my hands together. "It's the virgin's father or grandmother or eighth grade English teacher who takes revenge on behalf of her sacrifice that's important." I looked at her. "Jenn, you are a genius. We will need to change some things, but I think it's totally doable."

Heather glared at me as if I just shat in her cereal.

Changing the subject, I asked, "Does anyone have a video camera?"

***

The door chimed when Brody shoved his bulk against the glass storefront door. A typical meathead, he let the door slip back, nearly knocking Jenn in the face.

"Hey, asshole!" Jenn rubbed her elbow that had caught the brunt of the glass door instead.

Mike shoved past Jenn, nearly bopping her in the nose, to punch Brody in the shoulder.

"Ladies first, dumbass."

From the back of the group, I smirked at their bad manners and thought today might be more fun than I had hoped.

Ryan Hardaway stood behind the counter of his uncle's rental VHS shop watching us file inside. The air conditioning was dead, so three rotating fans hummed and clicked and buzzed. The end of Madonna's *La Isla Bonita* tinkled through the overhead speakers, creating an awful alternative soundtrack to the horror film *Evil Dead 2,* which was playing on the TV.

"Hey geek," Brody grinned at the thin, angular teen, who shriveled in the oversized jock's presence.

"Welcome to Victor's VHS Vault." Ryan flashed a fake-looking smile. He turned back to the screen with a frown confirming that Ryan and Brody were never on good terms.

Jenn and Mike ignored him and headed over to the new releases section, while Brody loomed over the counter, closer.

John returned the smile. "Hey Ryan? Busy today?"

The empty store, rotating fans, and the Bangles' *Walk Like an Egyptian* answered back.

"Naw, pretty slow. Mr. Peterson stopped by for a return but. . ."

Brody interrupted, "Don't care, chicken shit. We want a video player."

Sick to death of Brody already, I pushed his mass aside and stepped forward, "Hi Ryan, we actually need a camcorder. Does your uncle rent those?"

"Oh hey, Katie, I didn't see you come in." The door closed behind me as Ryan's frown deepened. "Are you with them?"

I shrugged. Ryan and I had a few AP classes together, but I would not call us close. It was obvious that he believed me to be out of place with this bunch, but was sly enough not to say it aloud.

Then he noticed Heather and perked up.

"What did you say you wanted?" His eyes followed her Sasson jeans down the aisle. He wound around, bumping a bony hip hard enough into the counter to rock the display of stacked Sno-Caps, Junior Mints and Raisinettes.

"Hey there, Heather," he smiled, eyes downcast. "Are you looking for something in particular?"

Heather cringed. "I don't know. Whatever the freak in black said."

Ryan turned back to look at me, confused.

"A camcorder," I replied.

***

The ride there was a killer. An hour and a half, cramped in the back of the cab of the truck that belonged to Mike's dad. All five of us, now including Ryan. It was the price we had to pay for the use of the video camera. He would be the cameraman, of course, since we couldn't also cover the deposit. John and Brody followed in Brody's MR2.

Heather did everything she could to ride with John, but Brody's car was a true two-seater and with Brody taking up one and a half of the seats, she was banished to the floorboards of Mike's truck with me and Ryan, while Mike drove and Jenn rode shotgun.

On the way, I filled Ryan in on the plan, showed him the advertisement and outlined the backstory. I was animated, but Ryan ignored most of what I said, preferring to gaze dreamily at Heather. Heather, on the other hand, sulked.

Before switching up the road to The Crystal Palace, we stopped by the secondhand store for costumes and masks. Halloween was months away, but the thrift store had some passed-over coveralls and raincoats hanging on a back rack. Heather and Jenn selected trench coats that looked like they had been through the Cold War and Mike chose an ill-fitting Batman cape from the kid's section.

Like my favorite cinematic serial killer Jason Voorhees, I preferred the swing of a machete, but there were no hockey masks, so I had to settle on a goofy clown mask. John got a kick out of the click from a plastic switchblade he found in a motley crew selection of items. He then grabbed a ski mask for the final effect. Brody loved the rubber axe he found in the housewares aisle, topping it off with a threadbare Scooby-Doo pillowcase with two ripped out wonky eyeholes. And then, there was Ryan. Simple, shy Ryan; the final addition to our act. He too wanted a mask, but since he would remain behind the VHS camera, he settled for a Freddy Kruger-style fedora.

Before we got back on the road, we stopped at the local Mickey-Ds for a bite and raided it for every last ketchup packet they had.

"Are you sure that's enough?" I asked.

Two miles from The Crystal Palace, Brody and John ducked into the Piggly-Wiggly for a few extra ketchup bottles, just in case. We didn't want to run out, especially since it was supposed to look realistic on film.

***

Finally, we arrived. Streetlights should have been on, as it was dusk when Mike and Brody pulled their vehicles into the deserted parking lot, but they weren't. A few of the lot lights hummed with their bulbs flickering. As we piled out, our legs cramped and still asleep from the long ride, I knew exactly what we had forgotten.

"Did anyone grab a flashlight?"

"Aw shit!" Brody groaned. "Wasn't that Jenn's job?"

"On what planet! You were the one lollygagging in the kitchen section," she retorted.

Mike smacked the back of Brody's oversized head. "Leave her out of it. You were the one who was supposed to be looking for candles and shit."

"Uh, hey guys," Ryan turned back to the group after placing the camcorder on his shoulder. "How are we going to get in?"

***

The Crystal Palace sat at the back end of the cruddy parking lot. A former strip joint turned into an adult book and video store, the building had no windows along the front, just a set of heavy fire doors that doubled as a front entry.

"Didn't your mom used to work here, Jenn?" Brody snickered.

Jenn shot him a bird and held Mike's arm a little tighter.

"Doesn't look like the spot for a Satanic church," John claimed, as he grabbed the bags of costumes and fake weapons.

"Well," I considered, "I guess Satanists don't like to

advertise. They like to keep things on the down low."

"Just like you Brody," Ryan muttered under his breath, but Brody missed it.

***

Around the back of the building, we found a shattered window with a loose board. It was obvious that someone else had been here before us, but after the devil-worshipers. Mike had discovered a Maglite flashlight in the glove box of his dad's truck. Standing on Brody's shoulders, John was able to crawl through the window. *Petite* and a varsity cheerleader, Heather passed off the Maglite to John and then shimmied off Brody's shoulders into the derelict edifice.

"Are you good?" Mike called into the hole.

"We are good," John hollered back. "Go back around to the front and we'll open the doors."

Jenn hugged herself tighter, "What if someone is already in there?"

Mike scoffed at Jenn. "No way."

Ryan gulped. "I am not so sure, man. I think someone just drove up."

A set of headlights bounced in the dip at the opposite end of the lot. We all slid behind the corner of the building. An overgrown hedge afforded us some camouflage.

"What if it's the cops? Maybe John and Heather tripped an alarm," Jenn groaned. "We are trespassing and if we get caught, my dad will kill me." She grabbed Mike's arm and pulled him to her.

He shrugged her off. "No, Jenn, it can't be the cops. No way."

The headlights drove straight over to Mike's truck and then stopped.

Mike was right. It wasn't the usual shape of an

officer's patrol sedan. No tell-tale roof lights, either. This vehicle was sleeker, heavier.

"Can you see anyone?" Jenn whispered from behind Mike.

"Shut up, Jenn!" Mike hissed.

Two shadows sat motionless behind the windshield.

Ryan crouched next to Mike. "What do you think, man?"

Before Mike could answer, the engine groaned as the gears shifted into reverse. Tires screeched and the head-lights traced back from where they came at full speed. Just before the ditch, the driver expertly spun the car around and flew out onto the highway.

"What the hell was that all about?" Brody bumped into Jenn, knocking her down

"I have no idea," Mike replied, "but at least it wasn't the cops. Let's do this and then blow this Popsicle stand."

Jenn reached out a hand to her boyfriend, "A little help here." Mike ignored her, stepping out from behind the brush.

I took Jenn's hand but before she shifted her weight, John exploded from out of nowhere.

Still unnerved from the mystery car, Jenn screamed and yanked on my arm. I landed on the ground next to her.

"Gotcha!" John grinned. "Come on slow pokes, Heather's holding open the front door and guess what?"

"What?" Jenn spat, irritated and annoyed.

"We don't need no stinking flashlights. The electricity still works."

***

Although only the emergency floodlights worked, it totally set the mood. As we explored, it was difficult to contain my excitement.

Heather echoed my enthusiasm. "This place is perfect!" she beamed from the open front door. "It has such a creepy vibe! I can almost hear the demonic chanting."

Brody strode by like a pimp.

John laughed at Brody's goofy strut. "Yeah, maybe in another life, big man."

"How can the lights be working?" Jenn's eyes darted around, bewildered. She turned to accuse me: "I thought that the murders happened like a decade ago."

On any other day, I would have agreed with her. It definitely would have been strange; however, I remained non-committal. "Yeah, I don't know."

Ryan shifted the camera on his shoulder. "If we are going to do this, then let's do this, especially before whoever that was decides to come back or sends over the cops."

For the first time, Heather gave Ryan her full attention. "What are you talking about?"

Mike shrugged. "Nothing, man. Some car drove in and out of the parking lot but it wasn't the cops, so who cares."

"Where's the blood?" John was rummaging in the bags from the stores. Finding it, he held up one of the ketchup bottles. "Who wants to be the first victim?"

***

I agreed to be the first person killed. In what appeared to be the main room, we found a few mangled merchandise racks. John had the brilliant idea that I would lie prone on top of the more demented-looking racks with pieces tucked under my arms and between my legs, ketchup blood dripping, as if I was crucified.

"I think that's a little too artsy for a slasher," was my reply.

Finally, we settled on a séance. Inside a cabinet in one of the offices off the back hallway, Heather found a candle and a piece of chalk. With it, I drew a circle inscribed with a pentagram and set the candle in the center.

John donned his ski mask and my machete while I borrowed Heather's coat. I threw it over my shoulders like a cloak, for added effect. As the leader of the communing, I would be the first to be slaughtered with the others taking off in flight. Then, I could help John stage the other's deaths with the ketchup and fake weapons.

Ryan gauged the lighting. It was dim and hard to see via the camera, but the low light intensified the eerie atmosphere.

We gathered at the edge of the circle. Mike, the only smoker of the group, lit the wick with his lighter, and then sat back.

I looked at Ryan for his cue that we were recording. He gave me a thumbs up.

"We are here this evening to contact the spirit of the lost soul sacrificed in The Crystal Palace. Seven years ago, on this very night," I embellished, "your soul was taken by a coven of evil devil worshippers."

Prior to filming, we agreed that John should attack when I exclaimed, *Speak! Speak to us now!*

Ryan walked around the circle before stopping directly behind Heather, who sat across from me. He held still, pressing the button to zoom in on my face. Jenn sat next to Heather. Over Jenn's shoulder, beyond where Ryan stood, I noticed movement, causing me to hesitate before beginning my incantation.

"We gather tonight to hear your story. We want to know the truth. Speak! I command you. Speak to us now!"

Nothing moved.

Heather, who was cross-legged next to Brody, looked around, impatient. She whispered something to Brody who shrugged.

In the candlelight, I saw that Jenn had shut her eyes

tight. Ryan tilted his head away from the viewfinder of the camcorder and looked at me as if to say, "What the hell is he doing?"

Not wanting to break character in case John was working up the suspense, I spoke again. Louder. "Speak! Speak to us now!"

A blood-curdling scream came from somewhere behind me. We all sat stunned.

Then Brody smiled, like he got the joke. Snickering, his shoulders hunched and shook.

Tears rolled down his face. And then finally, he let out a huge snort. Mike smacked his shoulder.

As a poor effort at improvisation, Brody said, "Oh no! Those devil worshippers are killing John! But he's not a virgin either!"

Mike caught the giggle bug next. A huge guffaw escaped his mouth. Tears swam down his face, too, as he bowled into Brody. The two began hugging and wrestling with their mirth so that they almost rolled into the candle, snuffing it out.

Shaking his head, Ryan placed the camera next to him and lay down on the dusty floor, exasperated. "Assholes."

"Hey you guys," Heather whined, "you just totally ruined it." She called back into the darkness, "What are you doing out there, John? We are waiting for you to attack Katie."

"Yeah, dumbass," Brody tittered. His giggles slowing. "Quit playing with yourself and come kill Katie."

Nothing. Only silence from the back of the room followed by a quick movement. The same movement I saw over Jenn's shoulder. A gleam of something metal and sharp caught the weak beam of the emergency lamp. The glare disappeared and reappeared as it crossed the space behind her and stopped.

Brody, not laughing anymore, sat with eyes wide and

mumbled, "What in the world?"

Mike's gaze followed Brody's line of sight.

"Who the hell are you?" Mike asked.

I turned around and looked behind me to see a figure in solid black, carrying a camcorder much like the one Ryan brought. The little red light was on indicating that the camera was filming.

Then Jenn screamed. A silky, black-gloved hand seized her by the hair while the other held the shiny metal of a serrated hunting knife at her neck. Although the face above was covered in a hunter's balaclava and goggles, I recognized the scripted "Helter" tattoo on the inner wrist that matched my "Skelter" one. Slowly, the blade sliced into her skin, releasing the blood. So much beautiful blood.

***

Later that night, when we watched the tape that Sid and my friends (my *real* friends from the city) and I made before sending it to the PO Box in Tucson, I realized that even as realistic as film can be, there is no substitute for the real thing.

And we definitely did not need all that ketchup.

The Last Hitcher
by
Kevin Hollaway

The road shined on.

He had made a guessing-game of his situation, consisting of three questions ranging in difficulty from easy to hard, before he reached the third vehicle: one–number of occupants (two points). Two–the positions the victims ended up in (six points). And three, the items left behind that were usable (ten points). He kept score on a pocket-sized steno pad, with a pencil from the glove box of the old Cadillac he had hitched the last ten miles in.

A nice elderly gentlemen had been driving, and had died so perfectly frozen in place with the cruise control engaged, it was half a mile before the Caddy finally started to drift onto the road's shoulder. The sound of grinding sand in the wheel wells and stray rocks pelting the door had jarred the Hitcher from his nap. He turned to see the driver sinking in his direction like a masterless puppet, and instinctively dodged the body to grab the wheel and shut off the cruise control. The world teetered briefly as he slapped the gear into neutral and glided to a stop.

Once the dust cleared, the Hitcher realized how close he had come to disaster. The next car was about twenty yards ahead of the Caddy at the start of a steady incline, sitting perfectly parked in the lane. Had those old dead hands held onto the wheel for a few seconds longer, it would have been instant and total.

The occurrences were easily explained at first. He'd just picked an old guy whose ticker ticked out at the wrong place, wrong time—bad luck. Everybody has it coming, just grin and move on. He did the most decent thing he could think of by straightening up the body—reclining the seat to make sure it wouldn't fall over again—and left a note under the lapel of the man's plaid sport coat: *Died of natural causes.* He would have made a call, but there wasn't a phone to be found and the Hitcher had left his far behind.

Well. . .that's why you took this jaunt, isn't it? To disconnect, leave with just the bare essentials, drop your worries and go.

He'd thrown on his pack and headed to the next car. Just a young kid in an old VW bug, head resting on top of the wheel, one hand hanging on by two fingers. Sure. . .fell asleep—happens every day. *Poor kid, probably going cross-country to see his folks.*

A careful rock of the kid's shoulder caused the fingers to slip free and fall limp in his lap. The Hitcher swallowed hard as he tried to find a pulse, then things started to slip as the desert dust cleared, revealing more up ahead. He cast a bemused glance back at the car he was in, then back at the VW.

Yep, would've rammed right into you, buddy. Maybe better that way. Immediately he locked the thought away, behind a door along with *why me? am I the only one? how many dead? is it because, no one else hitchhikes? what the hell happened?* and a hundred other questions that the mere attempt to answer meant instant madness.

He'd searched maniacally for another door he could step through to safety, and found it.

A voice sounded in his head, the booming, false voice of a practiced game show host. WELCOME TO OUR SHOW, DRIFTER FROM NOWHERE! YOU KNOW THE RULES, NOW LET'S PLAY!!

So, the game had begun, ending all of his searching for lucid explanations. Something to do, a reason to keep going.

The current score was 48.

Not bad, but he had it easy at first. The cars were randomly spaced, making the silhouettes of their occupants easy to distinguish and count. Barring any kids that were shorter than the seat, questions one and two were no-brainers.

Question three was the only one that provided a real challenge. The best he could make before reaching each vehicle—

coffin...

—was an educated guess based on the headcount and type of car. Old cars–like the Caddy he had been in–deserved little more than a speculation on a weapon or cell phone.

He got the first one off the bat, great way to start the game. It was an old tank of a Buick, sandy brown, sprinkled with rust and a broken taillight. An elderly woman, well past seventy, sat perfectly erect at the wheel, hands still on the old ten-and-two position, pupils magnified through bottle-thick glasses. Searching the car, the Hitcher remembered his uncle joking about how old people died quietly because they earned it. Under the seat was a worn fanny pack containing a small semi-automatic.

Guess Uncle was right, you never knew what hit you, he thought, tucking the pistol in the small of his back and moving on. *Good for you lady, and thanks for packing some heat.*

Next was an SUV near the top of the hill. Three

silhouettes could be made out through the rear window and a pile of luggage stuffed behind the back seat.

Audience. . .very quiet, please.

Married couple taking their kid on a road trip, kid bent forward playing a game, Mom's head turned to the right, Dad's facing down, cell phone, and food—too easy.

Score! All except for the kid; she was watching a movie on the built-in DVD player behind Mom's seat.

BUT DON'T FRET, YOU STILL GET 16 POINTS! TELL HIM WHAT HE'S WON!

He peered in the back seat. The girl was slumped forward like she had fallen asleep during the movie, the muffled soundtrack still feeding her ears through the headphones. Her eyes were closed, maybe she had been napping. The Hitcher thought about his uncle again.

Maybe the young died quietly too.

"I'm wishing. . .I'm wishing. . ."

It was Snow White on the player, she was singing at the wishing well. He quietly shut it off, as if there were still a danger of waking the girl up.

Don't worry, she won't.

The Hitcher jerked his head around and saw the mother's eyes peering at him over the top of the seat. He fell backwards out the door, hitting his head on the frame and collapsing in a fit of dry heaves as his stomach tried to empty what wasn't there.

Food... yes. . .they have food—ten points for food.

He checked his head for blood, gathered himself, and went to the driver's door. The father's chin was down in a low nod, one hand still lazily gripping the bottom of the wheel. The other stretched across the console, resting on his wife's knee. He forced his gaze up to see for sure but her head was turned away, leaning against the window— thank God.

Wouldn't get those points if she wasn't; can't break

your streak.

The Hitcher opened the center console and grabbed the cell phone. It was on with about half the battery left and wouldn't you know, it no signal. He let out a hiss of manic laughter at the thought of making a call and popped the rear hatch.

Sorry sir, all circuits are dead—just like you should be.

A glint from the far side mirror caught his eye as he shut the driver's door. In the reflection was the mother's face leaning against the window in a bizarre distortion like unformed clay. The Hitcher leaned back in with a frown and pulled her upright. Her head lobbed over his direction and his breath froze at the feeling of cold silk when the chin grazed his hand. He started to jerk away, but finished the corpse's balancing act, fairly easy with rigor mortis setting in. Then he thought morbidly that before he got much farther, he wouldn't have to worry about that, as everyone would be frozen in whatever position their final breath left them.

In the back were shopping bags full of food. He downed two granola bars with an energy drink while walking to the edge of the hilltop. The bottom of the far side was not a pretty sight: a cluster of cars riddled the blacktop locked in multiple collisions. The sound of horns floated upward.

At least there's something to listen to, any more of this stale desert wind and I'll go deaf.

Beyond that, the asphalt gradually brightened as the road shined with the glimmer of paint and chrome in the midday sun. A steady stream of cars led to the horizon like they were lined up for the greatest concert on Earth.

God, where were they going? What the hell did I miss? Was I sleeping that long? Would I be dead if I hadn't been?

More questions for the Insanity Door. The Hitcher metaphorically threw another padlock on it, took a deep breath—dreading the guesses he would make for what lie up ahead—wiped the sweat from his forehead, and went back to the SUV. He filled his pack with some bottled water, fresh fruit, chips—then donned his sunglasses, and journeyed on.

OUTSTANDING! NOW GET READY FOR THE NEXT ROUND!

A new game was made by trying to count how many horns were going off, but by the time he reached the bottom of the hill, it had blended into such a bizarre symphony of warning that he gave up and made his usual guess on the first collision he saw.

He got it half right. A four-door Honda with the engine screaming was buried in the driver's side of a red Nissan sports car. The Honda's rear-end hovered inches above the ground, spinning its wheels frantically, while a steady thump-thump-boom from the Nissan trembled up the Hitcher's legs. His teeth clenched when he saw the BABY ON BOARD sticker in the rear window of the Honda, feeling damned for hoping the baby was dead—rational as the thought was. Hard enough to figure out how he was going to stay alive, much less how to feed a helpless infant. *Please,* he thought as the baby seat edged into view through the side window, *please just let it be. . .*

Empty.

He sighed and rested his head on the roof, knowing full well if he kept investing so much in such minor hopes he would be drained dry. Inside, the Insanity Door rattled again, enough to start working the screws loose from the hinges. He steadied it with his hand and continued the game.

A middle-aged professional woman was hanging like a skydiver in a forty-five-degree angle by her seatbelt, her face buried in the deflated air bag, giving the bizarre scene a caricature artist's rendition of a pie-in-the-face. The blue glow of her Bluetooth cycled on and off beneath a tangled weave of brown hair, her right thumb resting on her phone keyboard, caught in text mode. Three letters were on the screen:

W-T-F?

Boy, you said it lady.

Points for question One: Zero. He had guessed two occupants (thank God).

Question Two: Six points. Bingo! Though he didn't guess the airbag, the judges gave it to him anyway.

Question Three: Five points. He guessed she had a phone again, but was only awarded half-credit as phones were no longer considered usable supplies. It was the same model as his, though, so he took the battery.

He smiled at the thought of a possible bonus question: was it the texting that killed her or something else?

NOT EXACTLY WHERE YOU WANT TO BE AT THIS POINT, BUT DON'T GIVE UP! YOU STILL HAVE A CHANCE.

The Hitcher smirked at the idiot sardonic announcer in his head as he killed the engine and jotted down the score when the pencil lead snapped. He cursed and scratched off the wood with his thumbnail to get more, the one he always left a little overgrown.

Friend in high school, what was his name? Yeah, Blake, he always left his thumbnail overgrown, never know when you may need it he said, like to get more lead to keep score on everyone that died around you.

He cackled as the Door to Insanity rattled on its hinges and made his way to the Nissan. As expected, it was much worse.

The thump-thump-boom swelled like an army of giants trying to escape the depths underneath, then he made out a muffled guitar riff coming from inside and realized the car had a very expensive sound system.

On the passenger side, he came face-to-face with the driver, the tempered window wrapped around his mug in a spider-web of a million red multifaceted starbursts, runners of blood following the strands of cracked glass arteries to endless destinations.

No points there. He had guessed the windshield instead of the side window—-should've known better.

UH-OH! YOU'RE SLIPPING. CAREFUL NOW, TIME IS RUNNING OUT!

The Madness Door rattled again, stronger this time, enough to pop a hinge loose. He threw another lock on it as he pulled the car door.

All the coagulating blood had stuck the window to the driver like cellophane. Music blared out as the door swung open. The window settled but refused to let go, dragging the body by the neck. A pair of twisted legs flopped out revealing a pair of thick, boot-style shoes. The Hitcher gave his worn-out running shoes a casual glance, and put his foot next to the driver's. Close enough.

Damn, would've been another ten points if you had guessed the shoes, he thought, holding his breath to keep his food down while he removed the driver's footwear.

Van Halen yelled from the speakers, the song was *Top of the World.*

Yeah, Ma. Finally made it. Top of the big dead heap.

He killed the stereo and opened the glove box. Resting on some loose papers and the insurance card was an iPod with some earbuds coiled next to it. He *had* guessed that the second he heard the music—ten points. A rapid search of the Nissan yielded a pair of sunglasses in the center console. The Hitcher took them and tossed away his pair with the loose hinge he always meant to get fixed.

Loose hinge, better pay attention to those hinges in your head buddy, before that door holding all the questions blows clean off.

A muffled death rattle came from the driver, his body releasing the last of its life in a gurgling hiss. The Hitcher would have searched more thoroughly, but the stench of blood and death was suffocating. He abandoned the scene quickly, knowing full well that wherever he slept that night, it would be filled with details of that macabre scene.

The whole world's going to smell like that before long, how do you plan to breathe then, he thought in a rapid fit, as he felt another hinge on his mental door pop off. He tried to maintain control by adding the new points to his score. The pencil lead snapped as he wrote the total. He frantically started to carve the wood around it but the break was too clean this time.

DON'T GIVE UP, YOU STILL HAVE THE BONUS ROUN—

Oh. . .shut up and go to hell!

Game Over.

The Hitcher tossed the pad and snapped the pencil in two. Memories of his father flooded in. Stories of how he always did that after taking a final exam in school. Pencil didn't deserve any more torture, his dad had said.

Up ahead, beyond another cluster of cars and blaring horns, was an ambulance. Good thing he quit when he did. Trying to use that for points would have disqualified him for cheating, the answers on supplies alone were too obvious.

He opened the back doors of the vehicle. Thankfully, there was no body on the gurney, just the driver and paramedic in front, leaning on the other's shoulder across the seats like star-crossed lovers—never would've guessed that. The Hitcher laughed, filling his pack with painkillers, cold packs, a blanket, bandages, masks, everything he could until it was busting at the seams. Last, he grabbed an oxygen tank.

Rounding the front of the ambulance, the air stuck to

his lungs as a massive cylinder of orange-and-black filled his view: a school bus. He forced an exhale and concentrated on the next breath, not addressing the rampage of thoughts stampeding through his mind as he passed the stretch of erect bodies in the windows. Not guessing if any of the children were alive. Not hoping if any weren't. No worries, they were old enough to get his attention if they needed it.

The last hinge to the Door of Questions started to pop free, but he wouldn't have it. He shut his eyes and set it firmly back in the frame, realizing the bus was the final threshold. Make it past that and he could handle anything.

He focused on the STOP sign jutting out from the side, using the rhythm of the flashing red lights to pull him forward, each blink forcing another lethargic step. Once past, he started to breathe again and thought of the Door of Madness, full of Hows and Whys.

Yes, the questions needed to be answered, but one at a time. That would be the new game.

Approaching the madness in order to prevent madness.

A refreshing surge of confidence and adrenaline hit him. He had enough to survive on, at least for a while, and there were a lot more cars to go through when he needed more.

More for what? Where are you going?

The irony brought a cackle of laughter as he moved among the next few vehicles, casually pulling the drivers off the horns for some peace and quiet. Then there was nothing to hear but the desert wind again, so he put on the iPod for some much better sound.

Dark clouds billowed on the horizon.

The Last Hitcher ventured forth.

A storm was coming.

And the road shined on.

About the Editors

Ann O'Mara Heyward is a horror fiction and nonfiction writer based in Cleveland, Ohio. Ann's fiction has been described as "quiet horror, with a gut punch." She likes to draw on real memories and experiences to inspire her fiction, which often mashes up normality and absurdity with the darker and bleaker sides of human nature and the natural world. Her academic training in mathematics and engineering compels her to impose scientific accuracy even in her strangest stories, and her internet research in support of this goal is horrifying in and of itself. Her stories often feature real places in her hometown of Cleveland, or wherever her frequent travels take her. Which led to the idea for this book, exploring one of Ann's all-time favorite themes in horror film and fiction.

Ann's short story "The Carny" won The Ghost Story's Supernatural Fiction Award (Spring 2023, theghost-story.com/the-carny) and was nominated for a Pushcart Prize. Her fiction has appeared in Solar Press *Horror Vol.1*, *Jane Nightshade's Serial Encounters* (Hellbound Books), *GASPS* curated by Judith Sonnet, *21ˢᵗ Century Ghost Stories Volume II* (Wyrd Harvest Press), *Stories to Take to Your Grave, Mortuary Edition* and *Carnival of Horror* (both, Undertaker Books), *Behind the Shadows II* and *Behind the Shadows III* (Inkd Publishing), *Thuggish Itch: School* (Gypsum Sound Tales), *It's Dark in Their Minds: Horror Anthology Volume 1* (RDG Press), parABnormal Magazine, and been aired multiple times by the NoSleep Podcast. Her fiction will also be published in Undertaker Books' forthcoming *Stories to Take to Your Grave: Tattoo Edition*, and Sliced Up Press' *Saturday Mourning Television*.

Ann is currently also at work on a nonfiction book on horror film, entitled "The Thinking Woman's Guide to Horror Movies." You can bet your ass there's a chapter in there about bad trips. Her debut short story collection will be published in 2026 by Lefthand Path Publishing. Find her on Facebook at www.FaceBook.com/AnnOHeyward, and on Amazon at https://www.amazon.com/stores/Ann-OMara-Heyward/author/B0CXMMJLDZ. Her story "The Carny" is free online at theghoststory.com/the-carny, and her story "Consignment" is free online at https://www.lefthandpathpress.com/newsletter/.Ann is an affiliate member of the HWA.

Jane Nightshade

Jane Nightshade was "that kid" who always wanted to tell spooky stories at sleepovers or campfire gatherings.

She is a former corporate communications manager turned horror and speculative writer. Her fiction has appeared in more than thirty anthologies and magazines, and has been dramatized by NoSleep Podcast and Octoberpod.

She is the author or editor of four published story collections: *The Drowning Game: A Novella of the Supernatural,* independently published in digital form on Amazon; *A Scream Full of Ghosts,* from Dark Ink Publishing; the anthology *Jane Nightshade's Serial Encounters* from Hell-Bound Books; and *Ghosts Never Leave* from Baynam Books Publishing. Her most recent stories published are *Sabina, Sabina,* included in the anthology *Supernatural Parables: Into Darkness* from Dead Birds Publishing (2025), and *Summer of '74* in the *Anthology of Horror* (2024), from HellBound Books Publishing. Her nonfiction writing has been published by several major horror sites, including Horrornews.net.

Jane is hard at work currently on a screenplay based on several stories from *Ghosts Never Leave* and on a non-fiction book called *How to Write a Ghost Story.*

Online, Jane mostly hangs out on Twitter/X at @JaneNightshade, or on Instagram @janenightshade639.

OTHER HELLBOUND BOOKS
www.hellboundbooks.com

Anthology of Pandemic Horror
Two-Dozen Skin-Crawling Tales of Death, Disease and Madness!

With the heady days of COVID-19 well and truly in our rear view mirror, that modern-day plague just an awful memory, we at HellBound Books decided it was high-time to revisit the horror enthusiast's' unfaltering love affair with tales of pandemic terror.

We have here, for your delight, two-dozen horrific short stories of sickness, plagues, sinister microbial outbreaks, killer viruses, demonic infections, the devilpox, cannibals, and, of course, the ultimate in pandemic terror: zombies!

No one is truly ever safe from these dreaded diseases, which affect – and *infect* – young and old alike, good folks from all walks of life, creed, and color, across the centuries – from medieval times to the modern day.

So, pull up a deathbed, don your mask, and enjoy these twenty-four exceptional stories from a bunch of the very best horror authors in the business.

Anthology of Campfire Stories

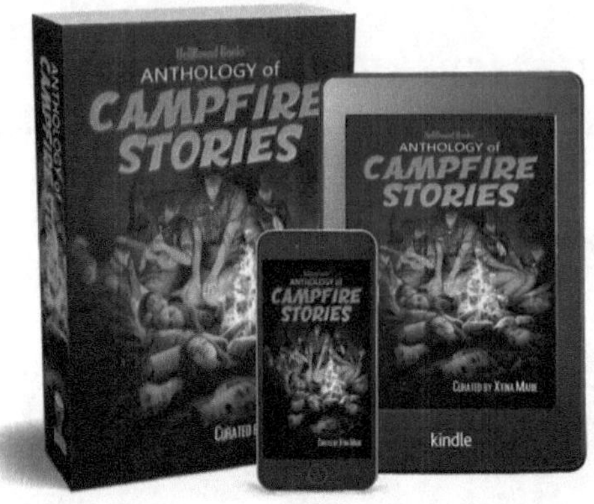

Ever since our ancestors first discovered fire, we have used it to sit around and scare one another silly with creepy tales of ghosts, ghouls, bloodthirsty creatures, maniac killers, and everything in between.

But, what if those stories, related in the dark of night with trembling voices, flashlight held resolutely beneath the chin, are more than just horrifying tales meant to send shivers down the spine and cause a few sleepless nights? What if the snapping of a twig deep in the woods is *actually* a real-life serial killer looking to brutally slaughter his next victim and steal her eyeballs? Or what if the wasp that stung you was no ordinary insect but something far, far more menacing…?

And, how about that very nice stranger you met on earlier on the hiking trail? His odd behavior was merely his fun eccentricities, and definitely nothing nefarious whatsoever.

Right?

Right?

So, why not shuffle your sturdy log an inch or two closer to the warm, flickering comfort of the campfire and chill your blood with 21 strange and dreadful tales that will have you glancing over your shoulder in terror as you make your way to your tent tonight. But never fear, after all… they're just campfire stories.

Anthology of Extreme Horror

If you prefer to take your horror yarns with copious amounts of spilled blood, eviscerated guts, dollops of messy gore, and dark, disturbing themes, then boy howdy, does HellBound Books have a terrifying treat in store for you!

If not, please not this book is definitely *not* for the faint of heart!

With a foreword and brand-spanking-new, never-read-before short story by the grand maestro of extreme horror himself, Matt Shaw, this collection of eighteen stomach-churning tales of terror is guaranteed to have the bile rising and heart thumping with each turn of the page.

So, buckle in, dear reader, and brace yourself for a blood-soaked ride littered with assorted body parts and particularly nasty doers of evil. And, for heaven's sakes, please don't attempt to eat while you're reading this anthology! You have been warned…

Anthology of Splatterpunk Volume II

splat·ter·punk
noun
informal
noun: splatterpunk
Definition: "A literary genre characterized by graphically described scenes of an extremely gory nature."

Welcome once again, fellow gore lovers, to HellBound Books' second foray into the deliciously bloody, innards-strewn world of splatterpunk!

Death, dismemberment, and destruction abound within these pages, as we bring to you nineteen perfectly ghoulish tales of terror that are definitely not to be read while eating!

Go on, we dare you!

You have short tales from: Shannon Blake Skelton, Juan Ozuna, Sarah Moon, Seaton Kay-Smith, S.C. Vincent, S. Michael Wilson, Carson Demmans, Diana Parrilla, Michael Errol Swaim, John Schlimm, P.J. Verfall, Karly Foland, W.L. Lewis, Caleb James K., Brian J. Smith, D.J. Tuskmor, Terry Grimwood, Dave Davis, and Paul Allih.

Anthology of Creature Features

Come on, admit it, we all love a gripping tale of our fellow creatures gone bad. Think *Jaws*, *The Rats*, *The Crabs*, *Pede*, *Them!* – the list is practically endless (hell, they even made a movie about killer bunny rabbits! *Night of the Lepus*, 1972, anyone?).

There's just something so inherently terrifying about the animals we see every day and take for granted are going to stay in their dens, burrows, nests, swamps, and crevices going on a murderous rampage of mayhem and outright slaughter against us poor human beings. Knowing what they are truly capable of has us keeping one wary eye on the critters, that's for sure.

And so, gathered within the pages of this skin-crawling, nerve-jangling anthology, you'll discover a collection of the most horrifying examples of Mother Nature gone psycho we could unearth. We have killer goldfish, a murderous mantis, a hellish giant arachnid, giant lizards, turtles, something altogether indescribable with tentacles, and so much more. Heck, there's even a tale of butterflies we guarantee will chill you to your very soul!

Featuring zoological tales of terror from: *Tim Newton Anderson, R. D. Tyler, Chad Barger, Seaton Kay-Smith, Milan Kovačević, Julien Jayus, Robb White, Serena Daniels, Rose Strickman, Janna Layton, J. Neira*, and the amazing *Cliff McNish*.

The Last Customer

One hot August evening in the small town of Dodge Junction, Wisconsin, Win and Garth Gasper close their family-owned liquor store for the night.

When the demons Sammael and Jezebeth show up in search of Father Leslie Gardner—the priest that many years ago exorcised Sammael—the Gaspers are forced to confront the most terrifying customers they have ever experienced!

Up the hill from the liquor store, Father Gardner senses he is being challenged by the demons. Unable to ignore their foul presence, he makes his way to where the demons have kicked off their destructively sinister plans for the evening.

Now, Garth, Win, Gardner and three unexpected armed robbers must fight their way out of the liquor store where their flesh and souls are being shredded by the denizens of Hell.

Father Gardner must revisit his terrifying past and renew his faith to defeat the nastiest demon he's ever encountered and protect the lives of his neighbors against the last - and by far the worst - customer of the night.

And Then You Die

Following a drunken, hedonistic night out in New Orleans, highly successful businesswoman and sexual deviant, Claire Jepson, accidentally soils herself in her car. The resulting excrement comes to life as a sardonic fecal spirit, and not only dishes out a gruesome death to Claire's unfaithful, gold-digging fiancé, but also thwarts a kidnap/murder plot by her employees. It then introduces Claire to a world of depraved pleasures beyond her imagination.

A year later, the errant spirit has spiraled wildly out of control - its insatiable appetite for perverted sex and human flesh and has destroyed Claire's life. Then, to her horror, Claire discovers the fecal spirit must consume her unborn child to attain immortality; she must return to the seedy underbelly of the Big Easy in a heart-pounding race against time to confront the spirit's creator - a high priest of an ancient, deadly order, who is the only one who can put a stop to the spirit's murderous intentions.

A wicked, fast-paced story laced with tongue-in-cheek, dark humor, which is at the same time incredibly erotic and stomach churning. Most definitely not one to be read whilst eating!

Anthology of Bizarro

Welcome to the wonderfully horrific world of Bizarro - that dark, forbidding corner of the horror genre where absolutely anything goes and one may delve into the farthest recesses of the authors' warped imaginations.
Prepare yourself, dear reader, for a journey into the unknown reaches of terror, from which you can only hope you will return with your sanity intact...
Enjoy 16 outstanding stories from:
Scott McGregor, A.L. King, Garvan Giltinan, Keith Kennedy, Robert Prescott, T.M. Morgan, Lee Rozelle, John W. Leonard, A.L. King, Matthew McKiernan, Aron Beauregard, Ken Goldman, Victor Marrow, Ryan Woods, and Stephen Daultrey

A HellBound Books Publishing LLC Publication

www.hellboundbooks.com

Printed in the United States

www.ingramcontent.com/pod-product-compliance
Lightning Source LLC
Chambersburg PA
CBHW030911300726
48970CB00001B/104